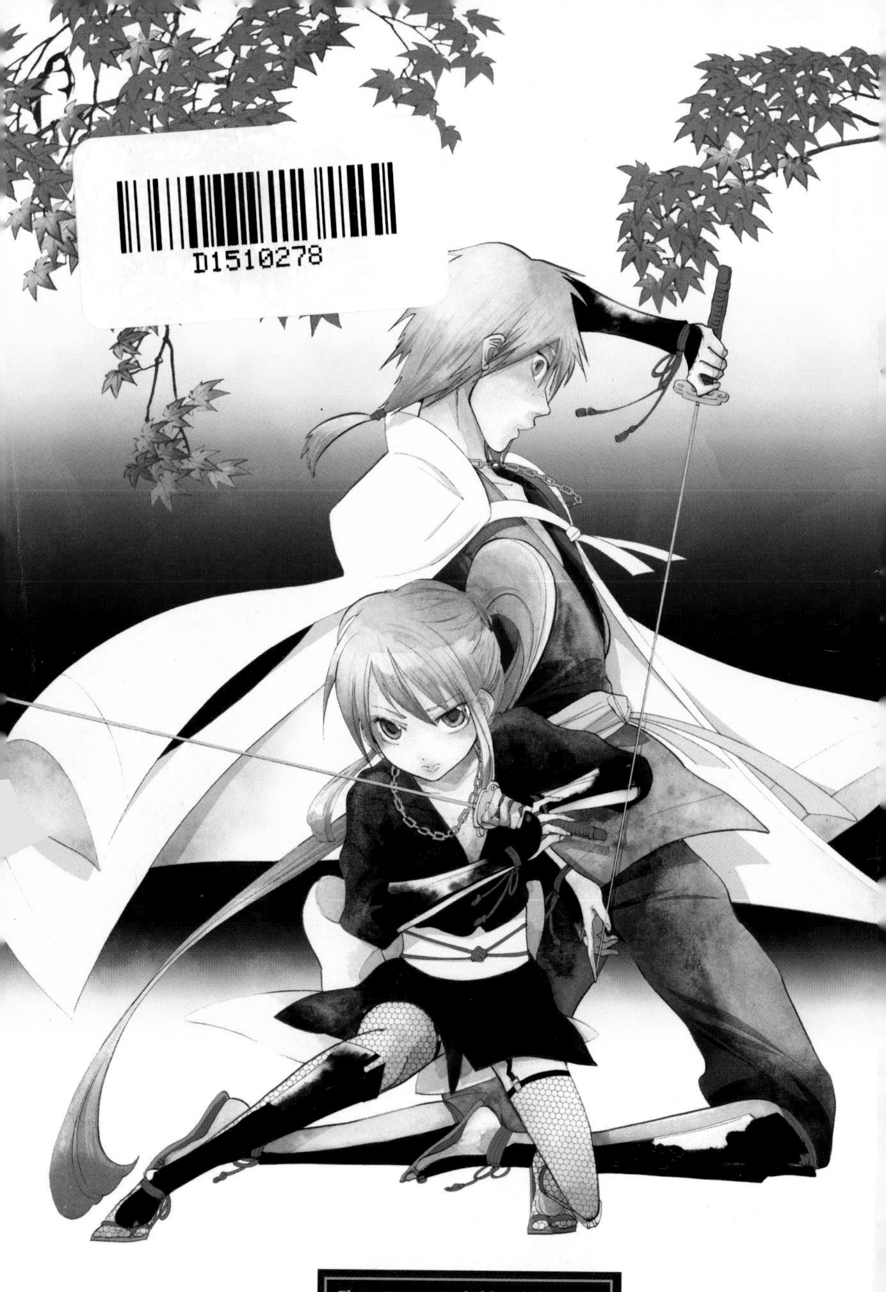

The strongest bride on earth.

Sumomomo Momomo. 2

Shinobu Ohtaka

CONTENTS

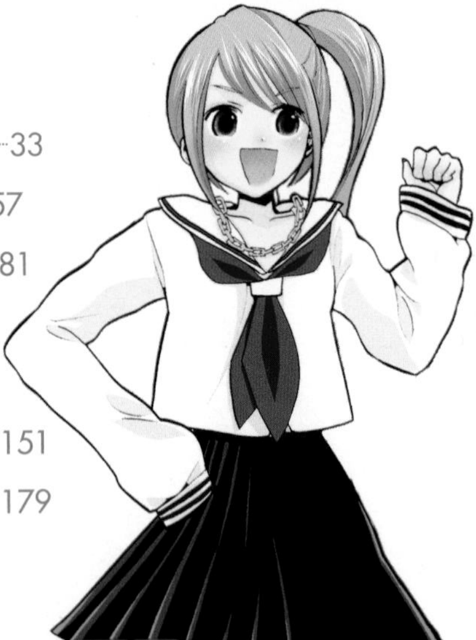

SUMOMOMO, MOMOMO

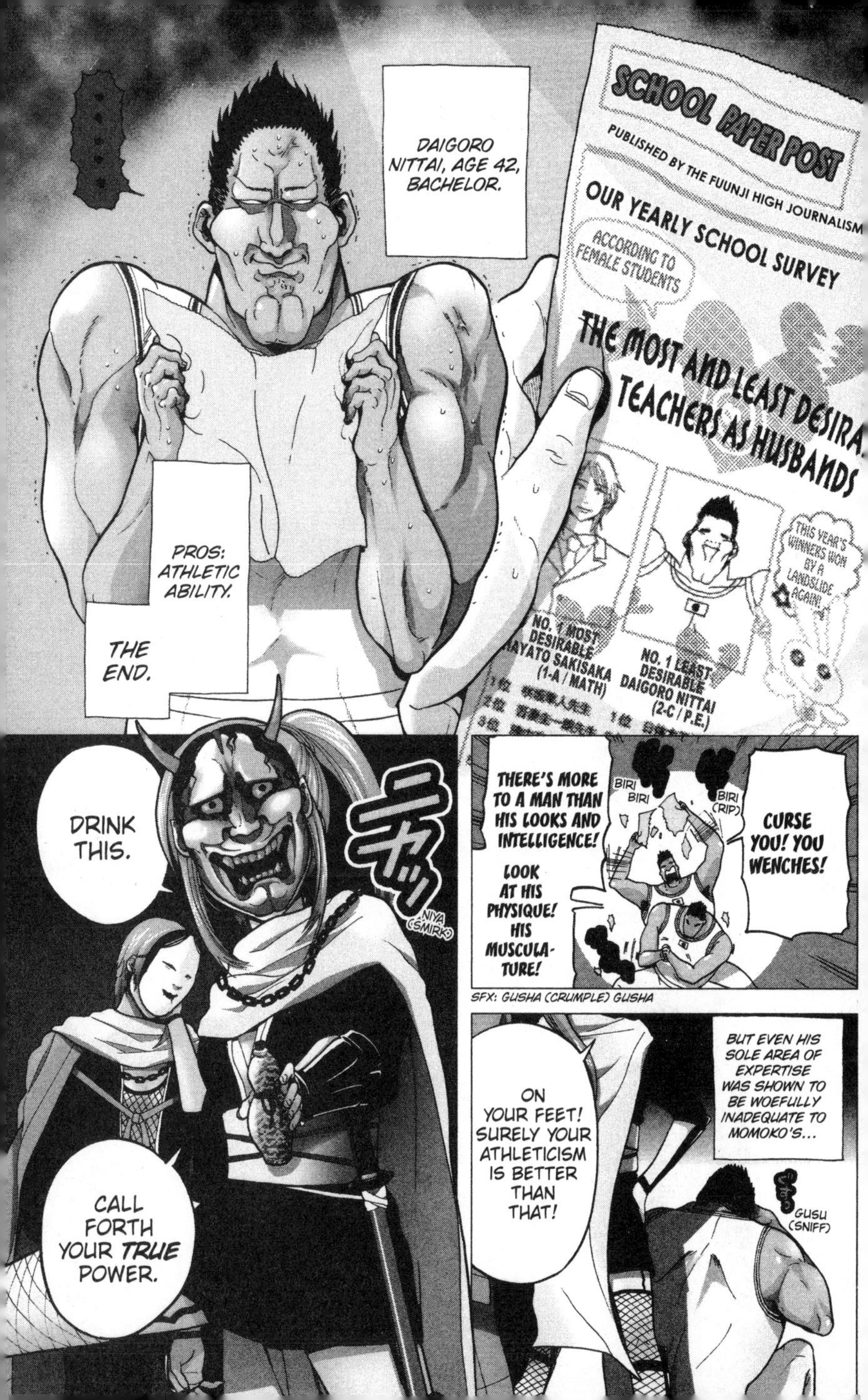
SCHOOL PAPER POST
PUBLISHED BY THE FUUNJI HIGH JOURNALISM
OUR YEARLY SCHOOL SURVEY
ACCORDING TO FEMALE STUDENTS
THE MOST AND LEAST DESIRA
TEACHERS AS HUSBANDS
THIS YEAR'S WINNERS WON BY A LANDSLIDE AGAIN!
NO. 1 MOST DESIRABLE HAYATO SAKISAKA (1-A / MATH)
NO. 1 LEAST DESIRABLE DAIGORO NITTAI (2-C / P.E.)
DAIGORO NITTAI, AGE 42, BACHELOR.
PROS: ATHLETIC ABILITY.
THE END.
THERE'S MORE TO A MAN THAN HIS LOOKS AND INTELLIGENCE!
BIRI BIRI
BIRI (RIP)
CURSE YOU! YOU WENCHES!
LOOK AT HIS PHYSIQUE! HIS MUSCULATURE!
SFX: GUSHA (CRUMPLE) GUSHA
BUT EVEN HIS SOLE AREA OF EXPERTISE WAS SHOWN TO BE WOEFULLY INADEQUATE TO MOMOKO'S...
ON YOUR FEET! SURELY YOUR ATHLETICISM IS BETTER THAN THAT!
GUSU (SNIFF)
NIYA (SMIRK)
DRINK THIS.
CALL FORTH YOUR TRUE POWER.

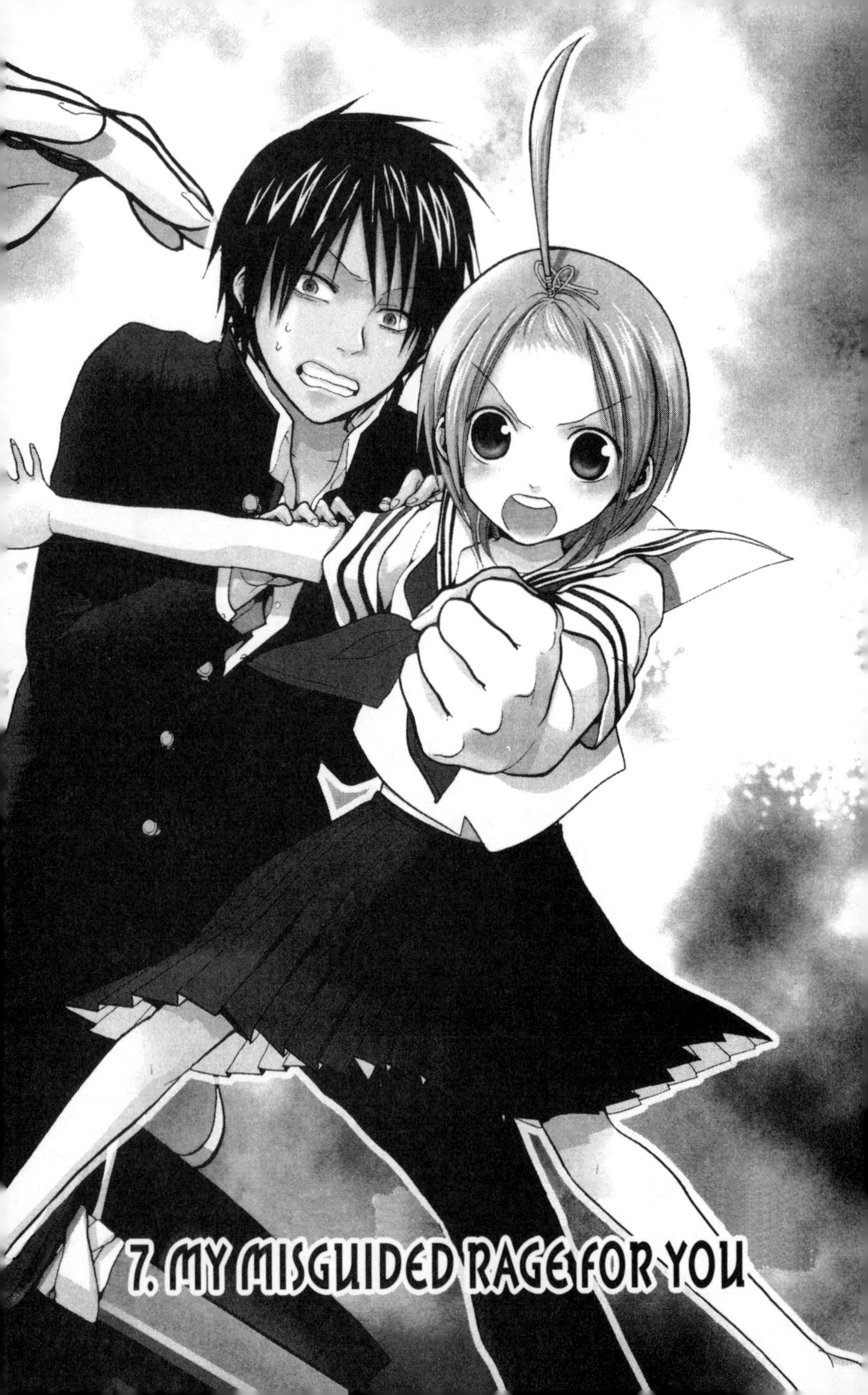
7. MY MISGUIDED RAGE FOR YOU

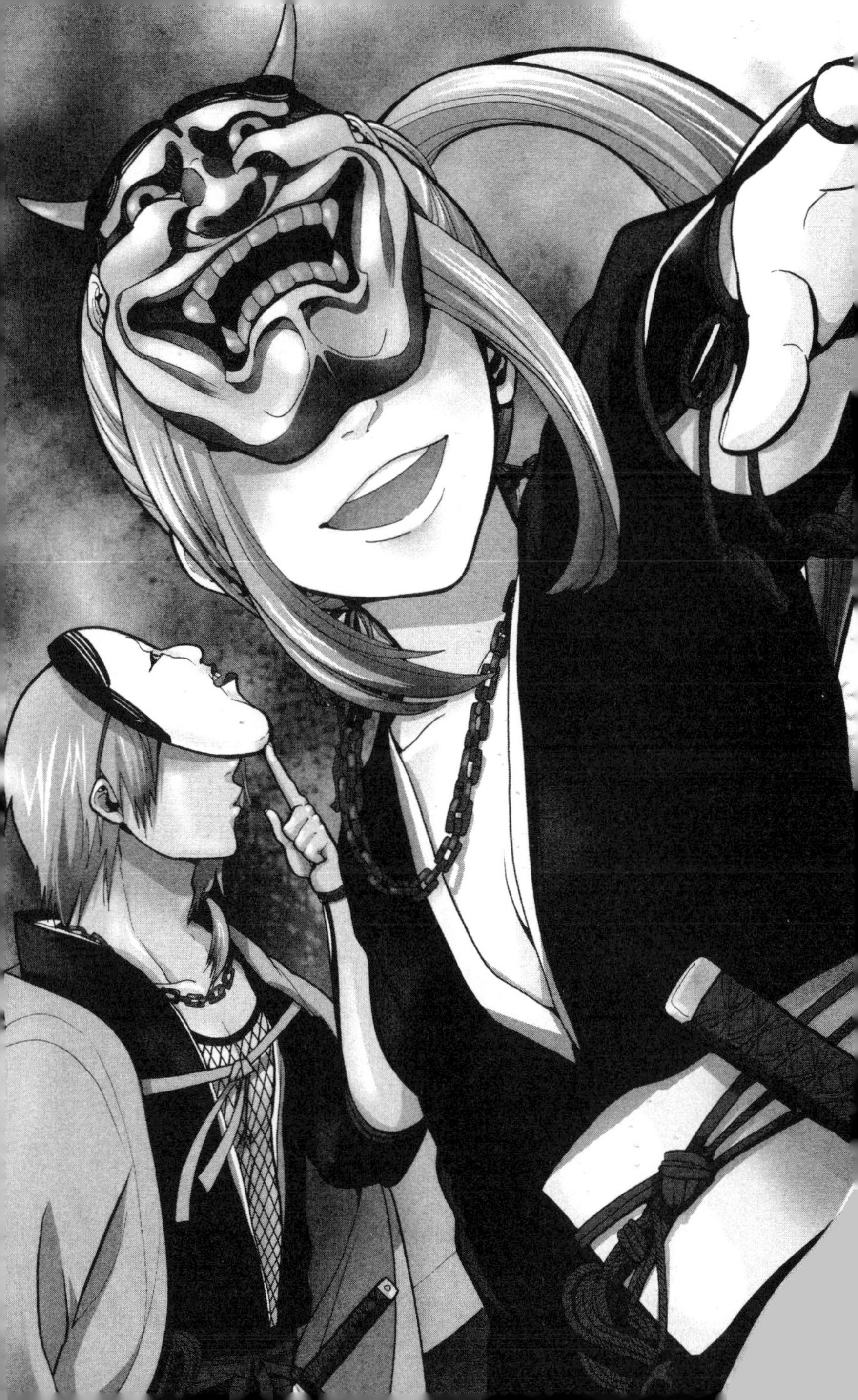

ズビュウ!!
ZUBYUWA
(ZBOWW)

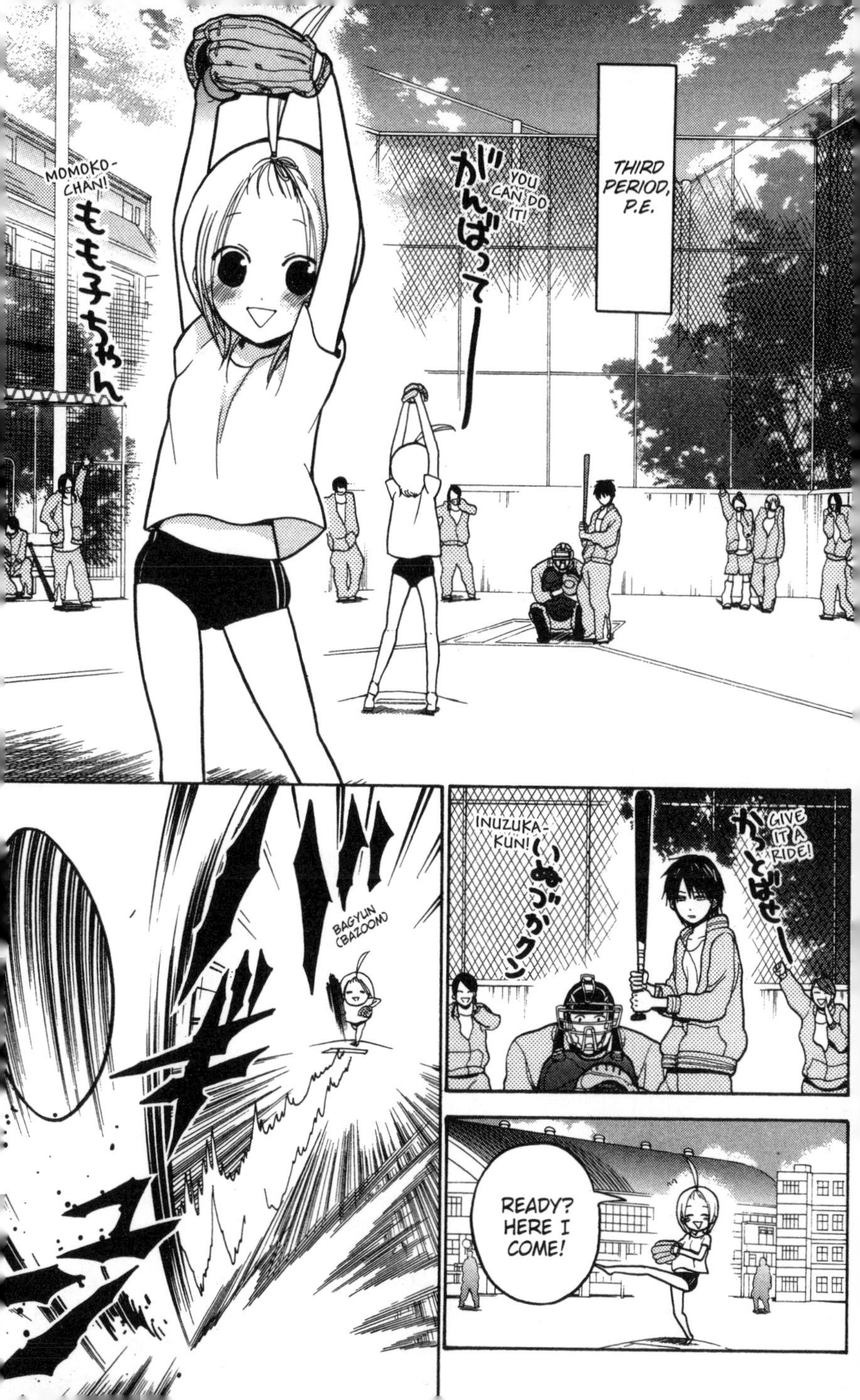

THIRD PERIOD, P.E.
がんばってーー
YOU CAN DO IT!
もも子ちゃん
MOMOKO-CHAN!
かっとばせー
GIVE IT A RIDE!
いぬづかクン
INUZUKA-KUN!
READY? HERE I COME!
BAGYUN (BAZOOM)

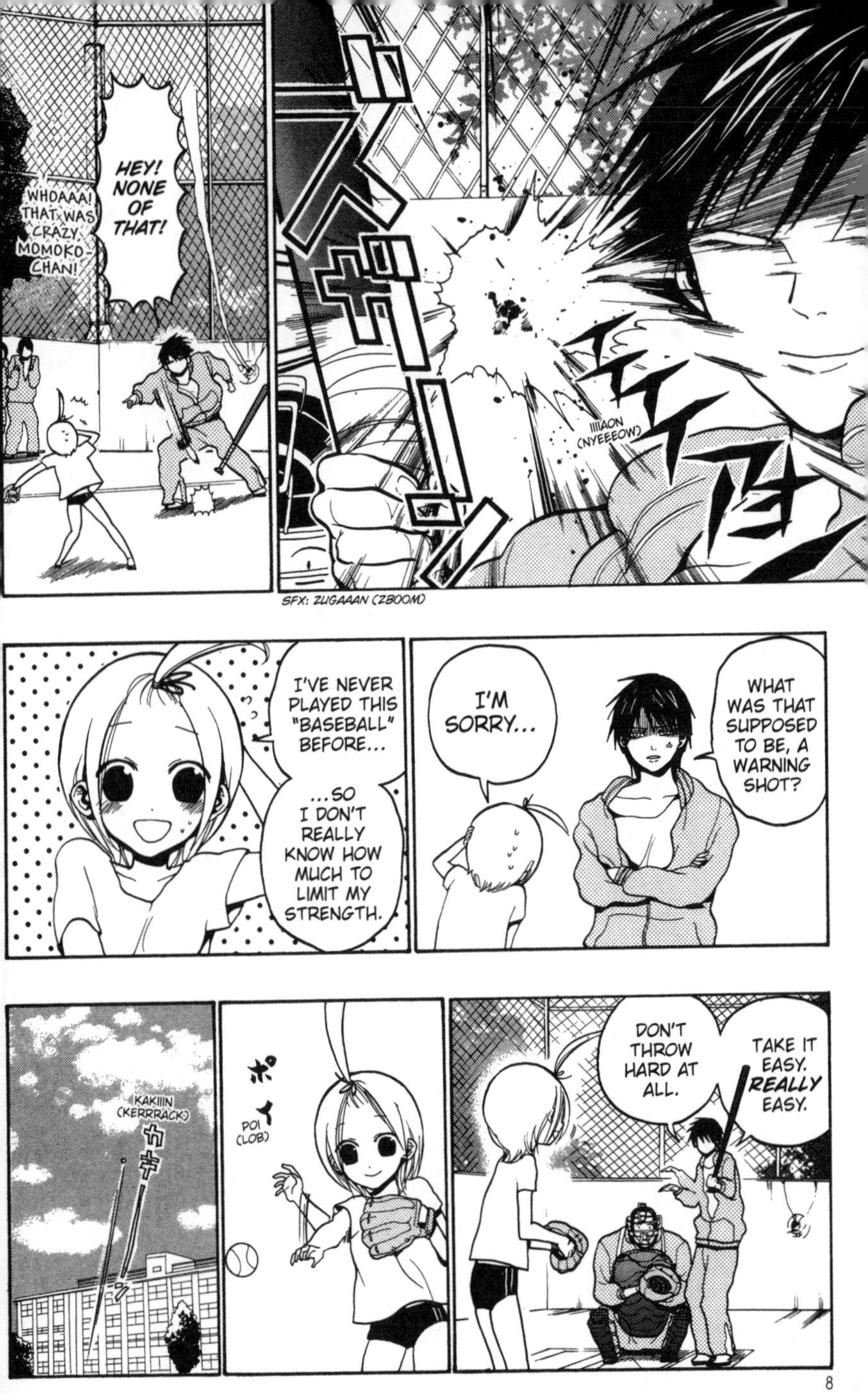
IIIIAON (NYEEEOW)
HEY! NONE OF THAT!
WHOAAA! THAT WAS CRAZY, MOMOKO-CHAN!
SFX: ZUGAAAN (ZBOOM)
WHAT WAS THAT SUPPOSED TO BE, A WARNING SHOT?
I'M SORRY...
I'VE NEVER PLAYED THIS "BASEBALL" BEFORE...
...SO I DON'T REALLY KNOW HOW MUCH TO LIMIT MY STRENGTH.
TAKE IT EASY. **REALLY** EASY.
DON'T THROW HARD AT ALL.
POI (LOB)
KAKIIIN (KERRRACK)

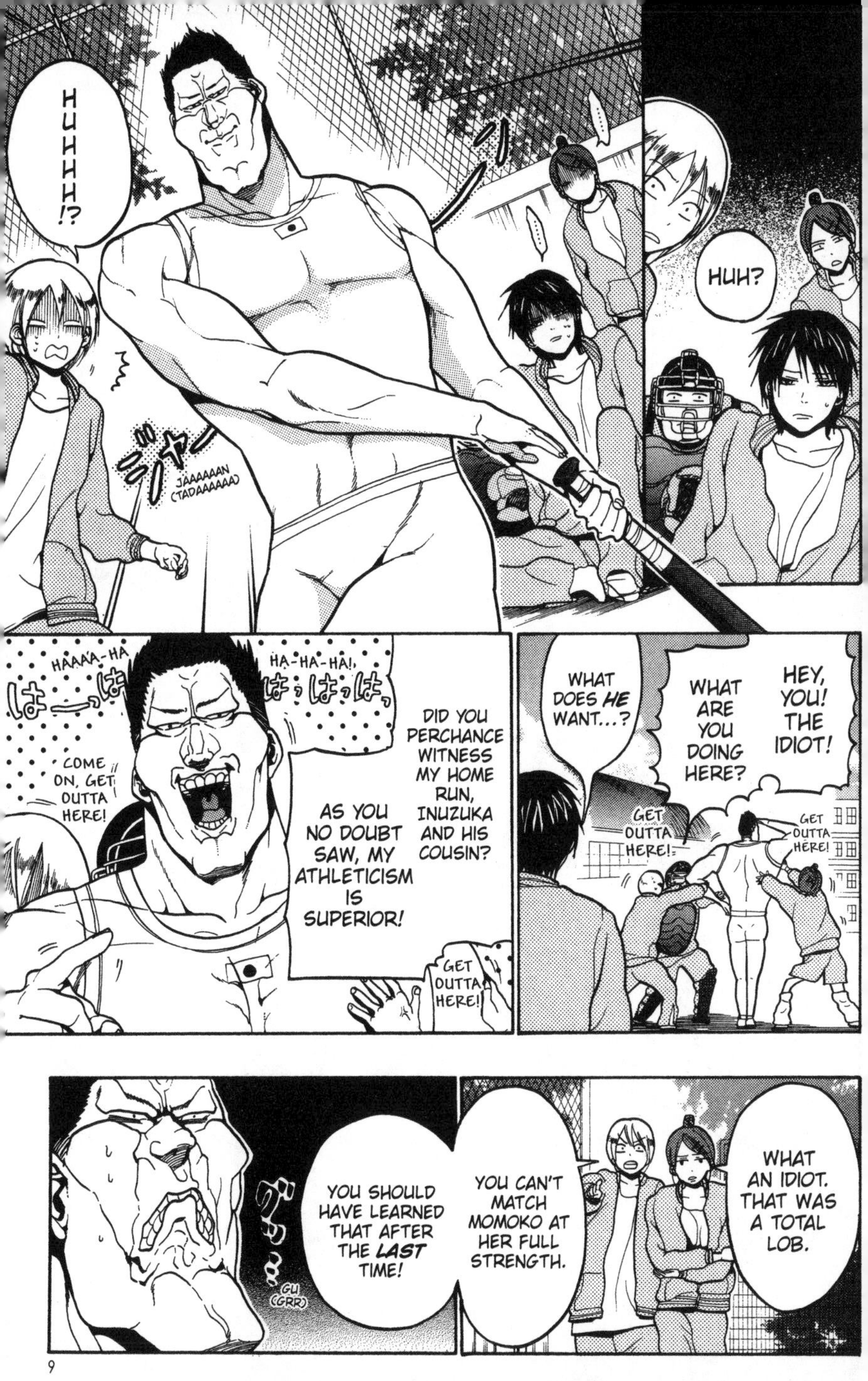

HUH?
HUHHHH!?
...
...
JAAAAAAN (TADAAAAAA)
HEY, YOU! THE IDIOT!
WHAT ARE YOU DOING HERE?
WHAT DOES *HE* WANT...?
GET OUTTA HERE!
GET OUTTA HERE!
HA-HA-HA!,
DID YOU PERCHANCE WITNESS MY HOME RUN, INUZUKA AND HIS COUSIN?
AS YOU NO DOUBT SAW, MY ATHLETICISM IS SUPERIOR!
HAAAA-HA
COME ON, GET OUTTA HERE!
GET OUTTA HERE!
WHAT AN IDIOT. THAT WAS A TOTAL LOB.
YOU CAN'T MATCH MOMOKO AT HER FULL STRENGTH.
YOU SHOULD HAVE LEARNED THAT AFTER THE *LAST* TIME!
GU (GRR)

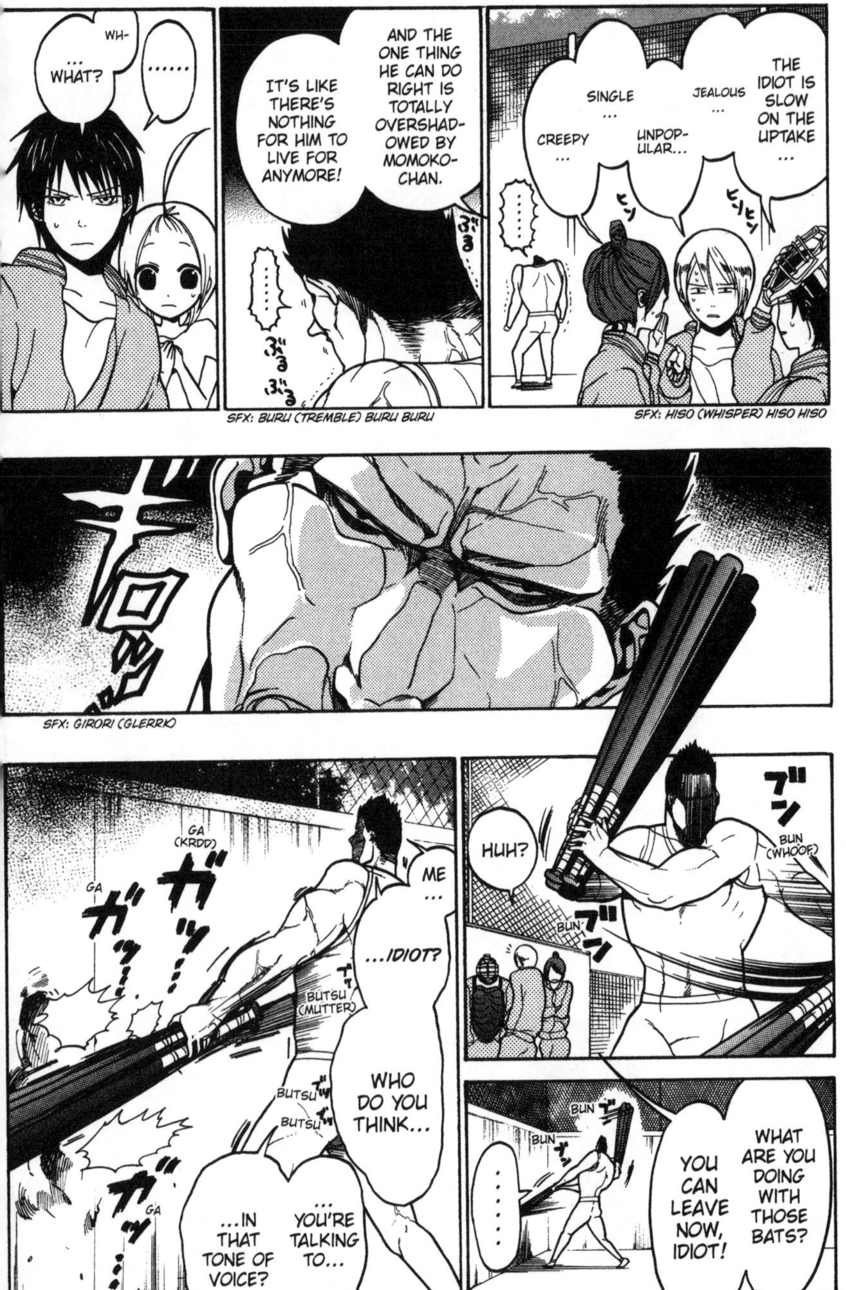
THE IDIOT IS SLOW ON THE UPTAKE...
JEALOUS...
UNPOPULAR...
SINGLE...
CREEPY...
......
AND THE ONE THING HE CAN DO RIGHT IS TOTALLY OVERSHADOWED BY MOMOKO-CHAN.
IT'S LIKE THERE'S NOTHING FOR HIM TO LIVE FOR ANYMORE!
......
......
WH- ... WHAT?
SFX: HISO (WHISPER) HISO HISO
SFX: BURU (TREMBLE) BURU BURU
SFX: GIRORI (GLERRK)
BUN (WHOOF)
HUH?
BUN
WHAT ARE YOU DOING WITH THOSE BATS?
YOU CAN LEAVE NOW, IDIOT!
BUN
BUN
......
ME ...
...IDIOT?
BUTSU (MUTTER)
WHO DO YOU THINK...
BUTSU
BUTSU
GA (KRDD)
GA
... YOU'RE TALKING TO...
...IN THAT TONE OF VOICE?
GA

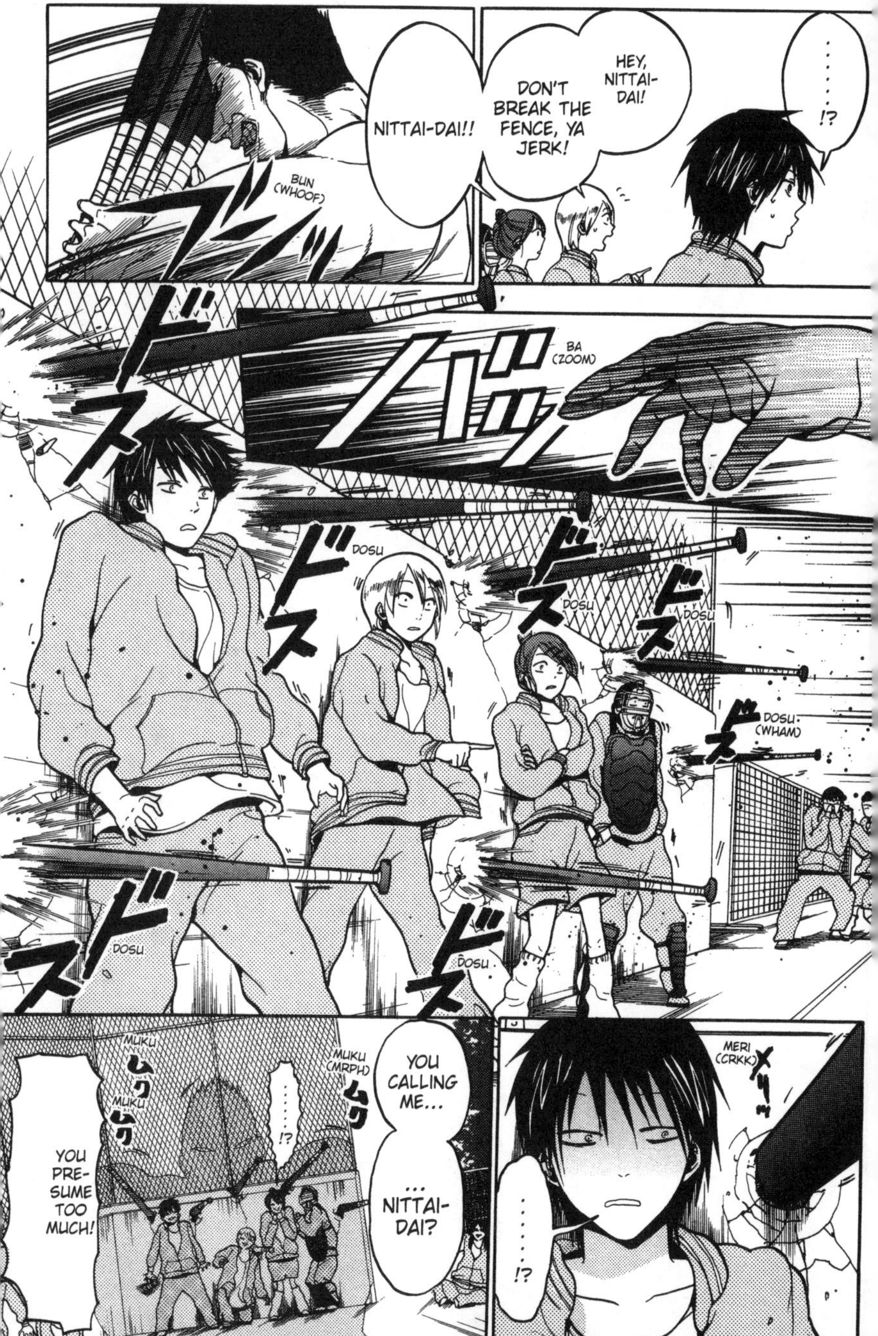
......!?
HEY, NITTAI-DAI!
DON'T BREAK THE FENCE, YA JERK!
NITTAI-DAI!!
BUN (WHOOF)
BA (ZOOM)
DOSU
DOSU
DOSU (WHAM)
DOSU
DOSU
DOSU
MERI (CRKK)
......!?
YOU CALLING ME...
...NITTAI-DAI?
MUKU (MRPH)
......!?
MUKU
MUKU
YOU PRE-SUME TOO MUCH!

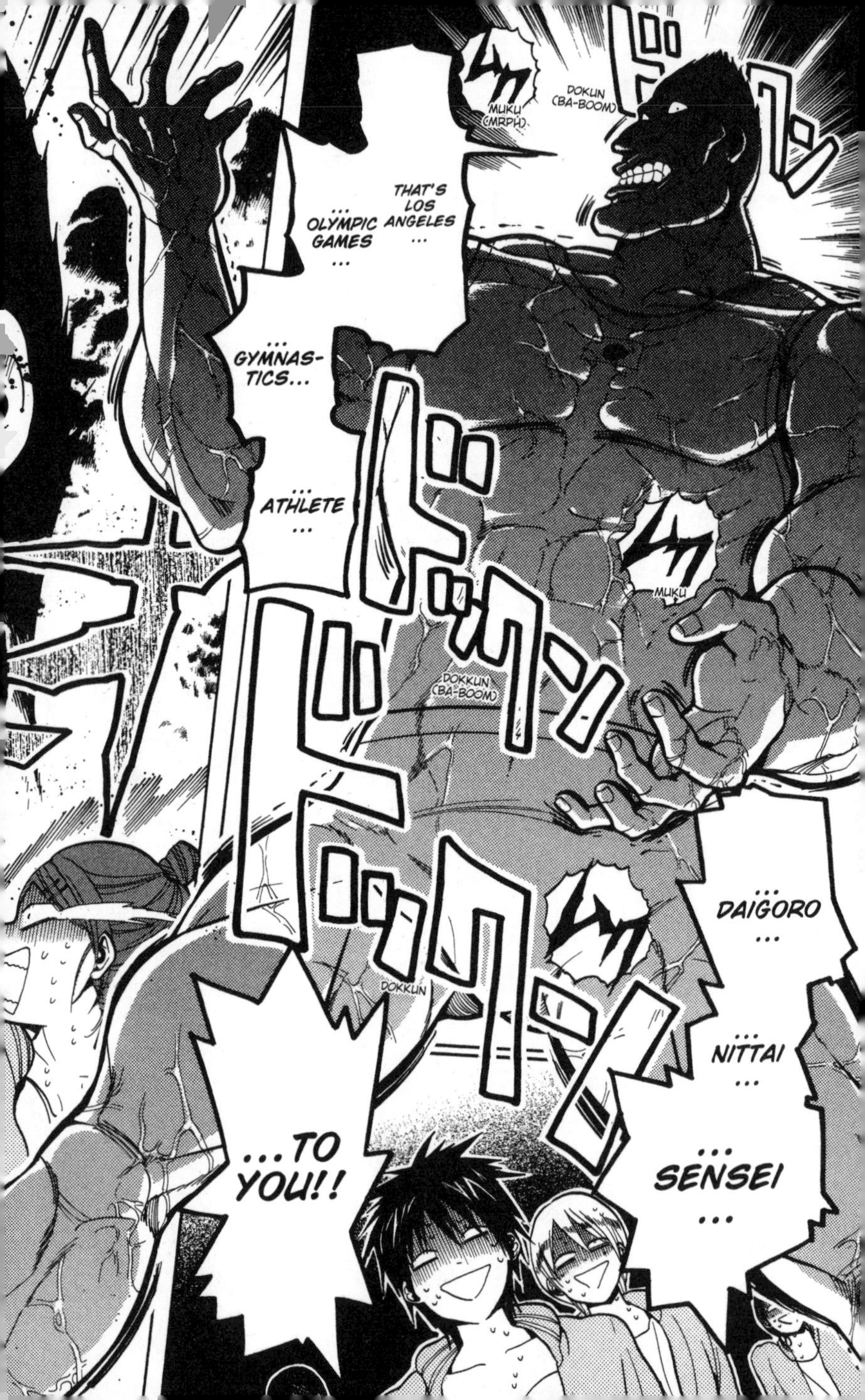
DOKUN (BA-BOOM)
MUKU (MRPH)
THAT'S LOS ANGELES ...
... OLYMPIC GAMES ...
... GYMNAS-TICS...
... ATHLETE ...
MUKU
DOKKUN (BA-BOOM)
DOKKUN
... DAIGORO ...
... NITTAI ...
... SENSEI ...
... TO YOU!!

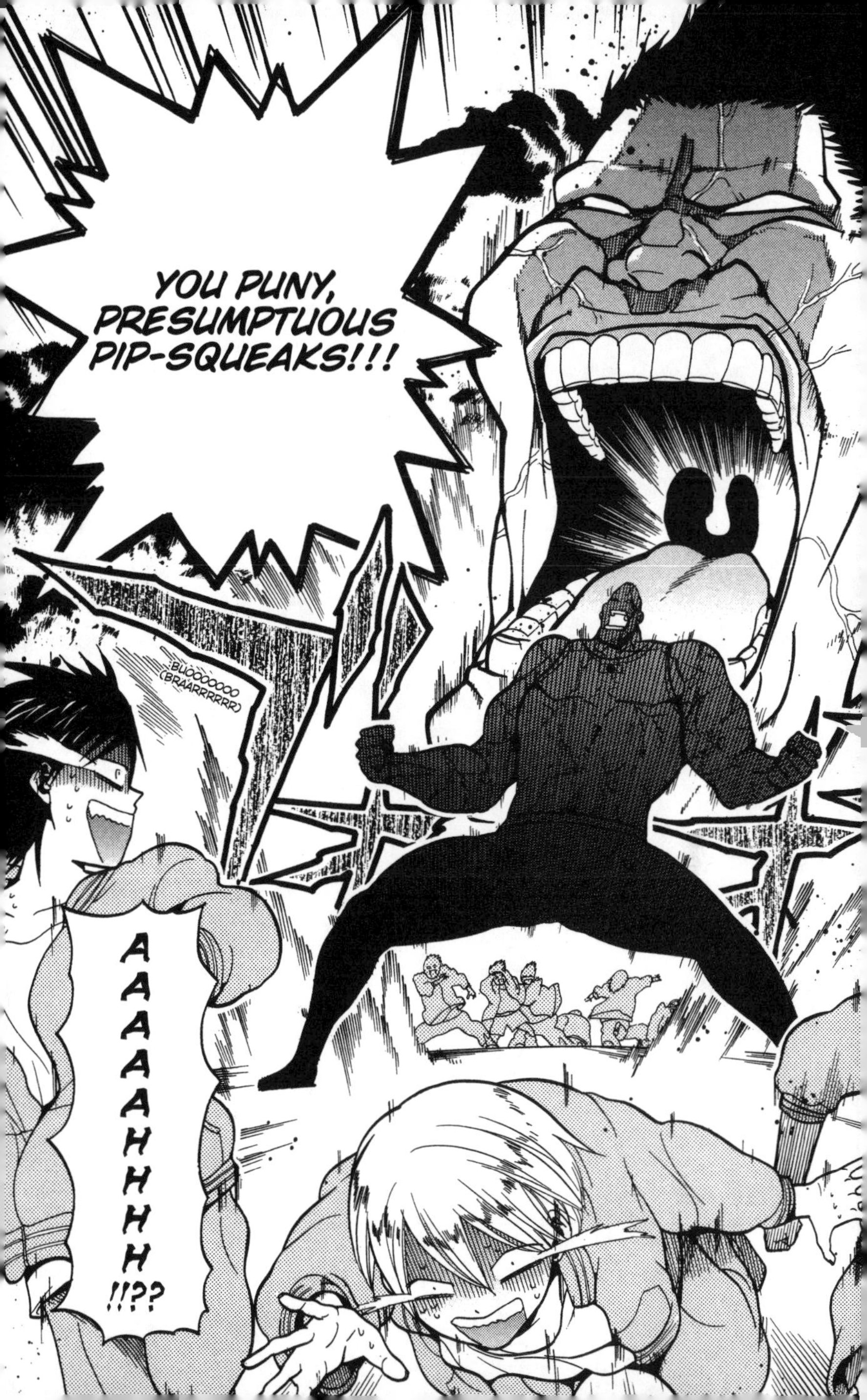
YOU PUNY, PRESUMPTUOUS PIP-SQUEAKS!!!
BUOOOOOOOO (BRAARRRRRR)
AAAAAAHHHHH!!??

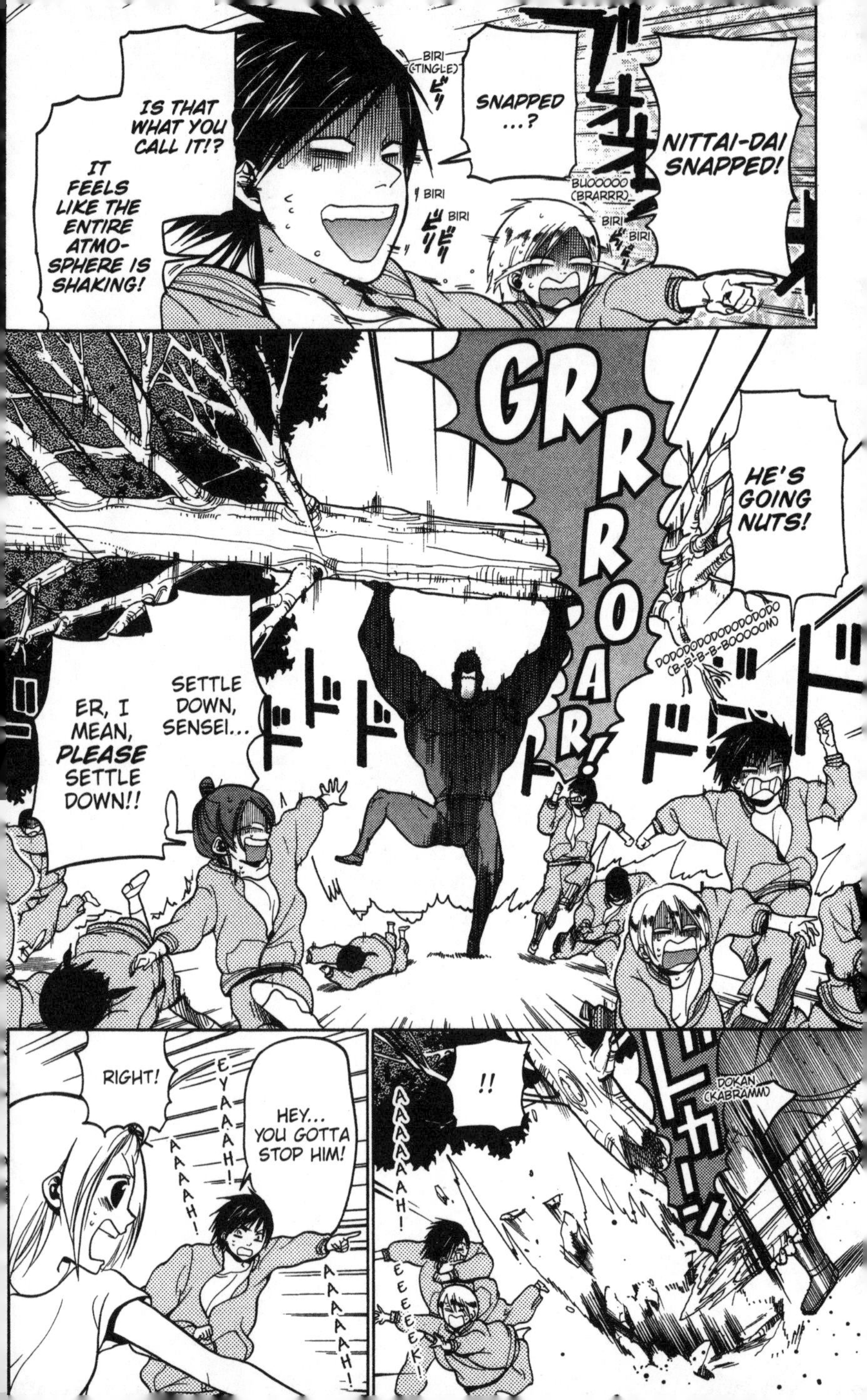
NITTAI-DAI SNAPPED!
BUOOOOO (BRARRR)
BIRI
BIRI
SNAPPED ...?
BIRI (TINGLE)
BIRI
BIRI
IS THAT WHAT YOU CALL IT!?
IT FEELS LIKE THE ENTIRE ATMO-SPHERE IS SHAKING!
HE'S GOING NUTS!
DODODODODODODODODO (B-B-B-B-BOOOOOM)
GRRROAR!
SETTLE DOWN, SENSEI...
ER, I MEAN, PLEASE SETTLE DOWN!!
DOKAN (KABRAMM)
!!
AAAAAAAH!
EEEEEEK!
HEY... YOU GOTTA STOP HIM!
EYAAAAH!
AAAAAH!
AAAAAAH!
RIGHT!

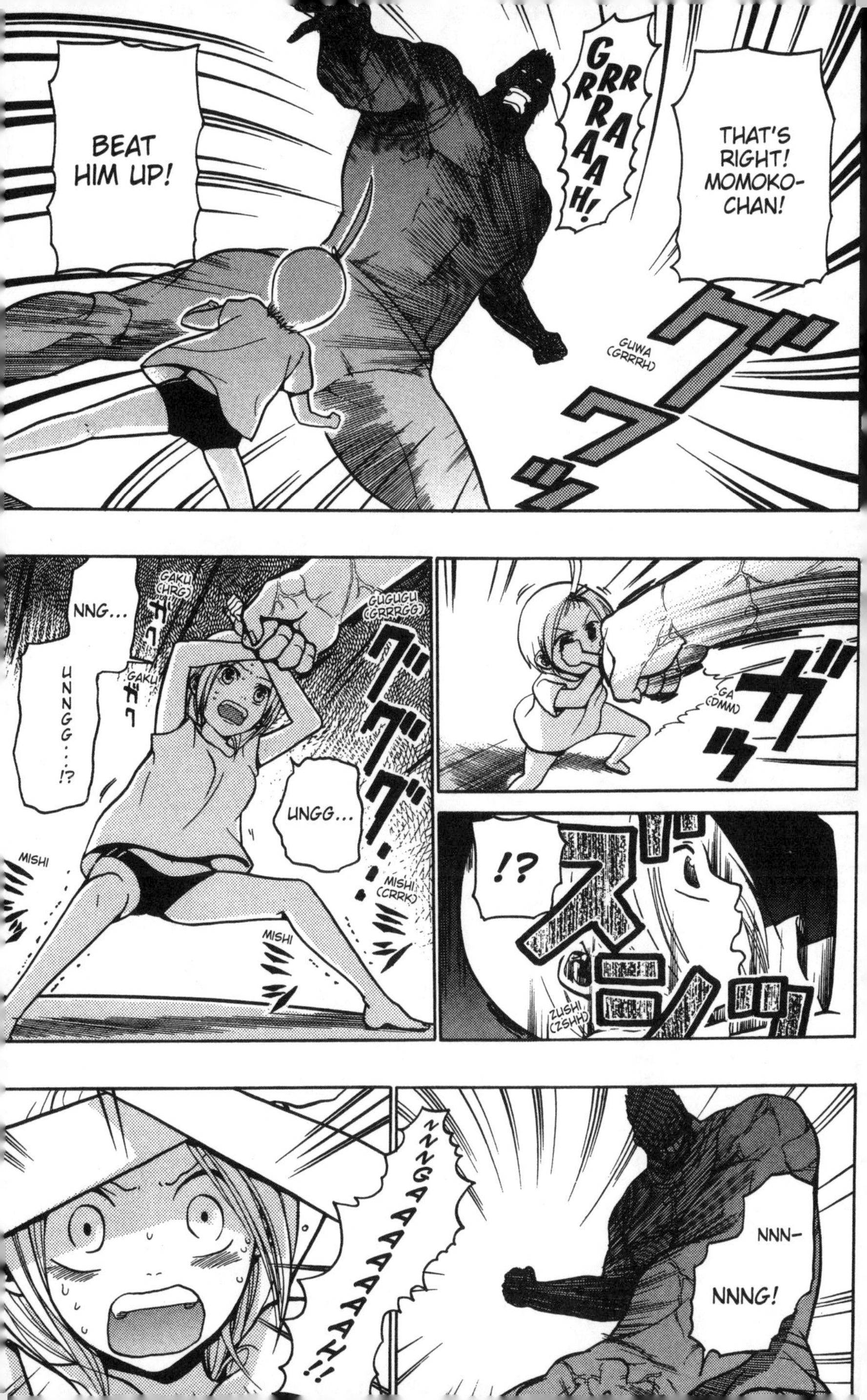
THAT'S RIGHT! MOMOKO-CHAN!
GRRRRAAAAH!
BEAT HIM UP!
GUWA (GRRRH)
GA (DMM)
!?
ZUSHI (ZSHH)
GAKU (HRG)
GUGUGU (GRRRGG)
NNG...
GAKU
UNNGG...!?
UNGG...
MISHI (CRRK)
MISHI
MISHI
NNN-
NNNG!
NNNGAAAAAAAH!!

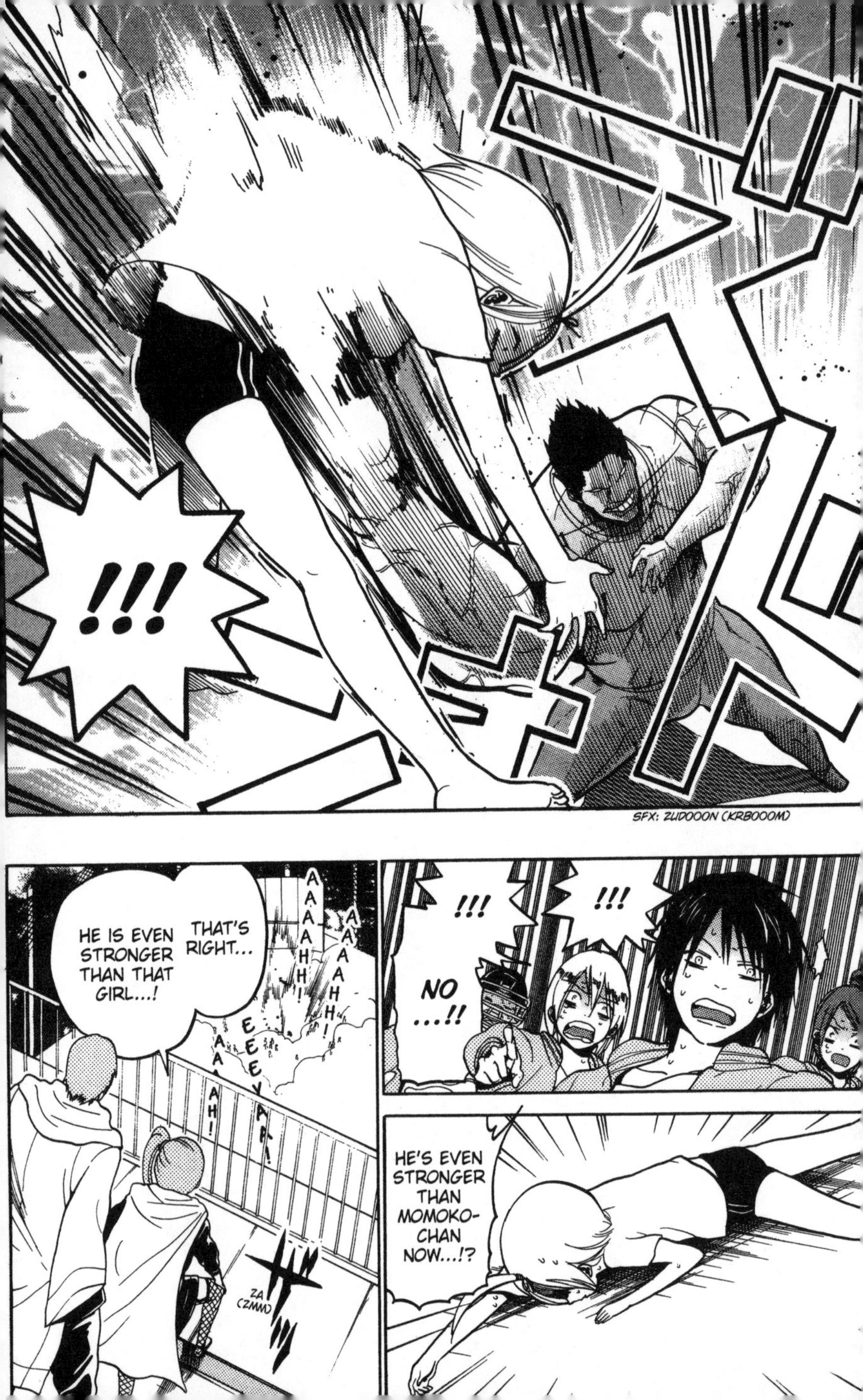
!!!
SFX: ZUDOOON (KRBOOOM)
!!!
!!!
NO ...!!
HE'S EVEN STRONGER THAN MOMOKO-CHAN NOW...!?
THAT'S RIGHT...
HE IS EVEN STRONGER THAN THAT GIRL...!
AAAAHH!
AAAAAHH!
EEEYAA!
AAAAH!
ZA (ZMM)

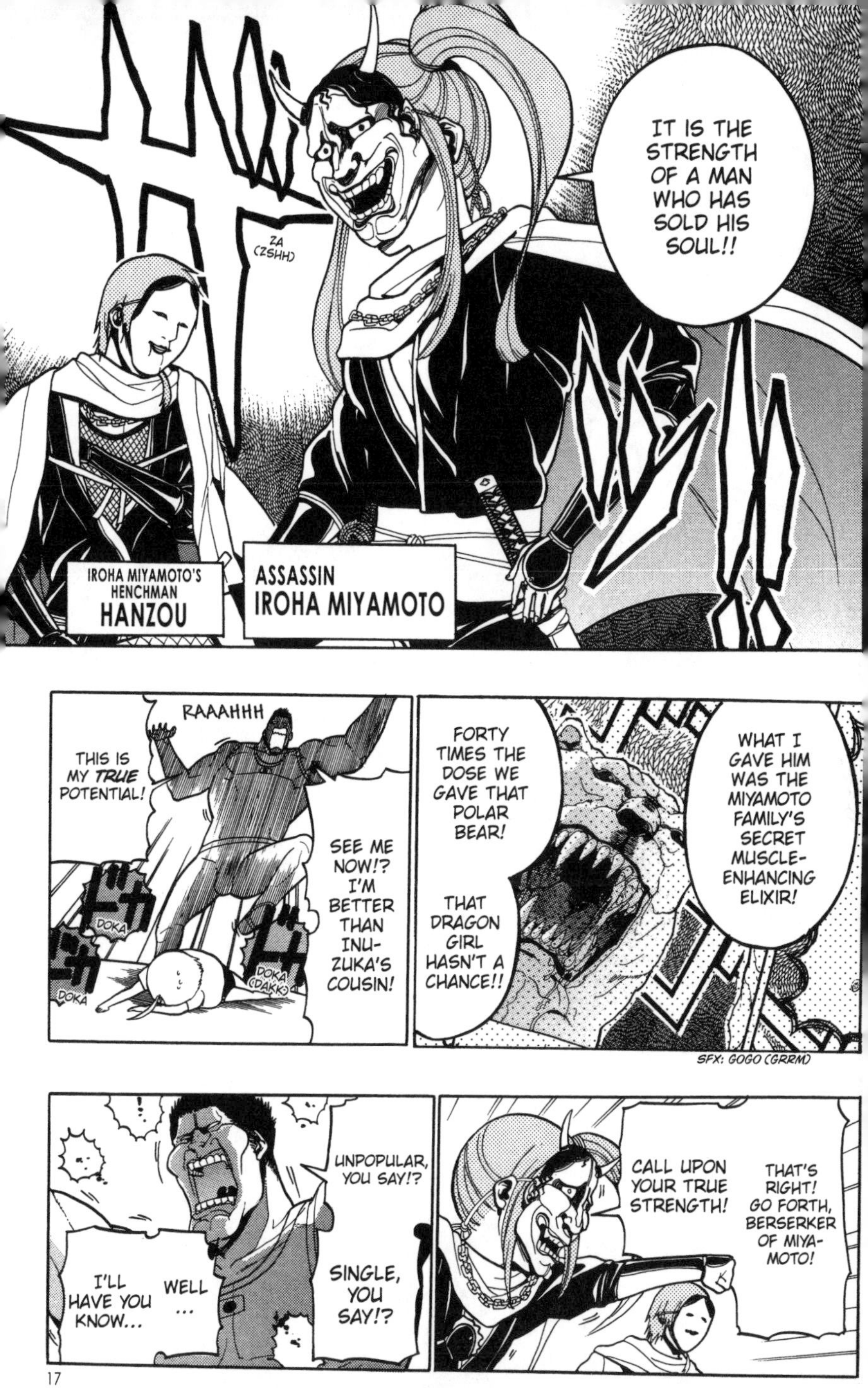
IT IS THE STRENGTH OF A MAN WHO HAS SOLD HIS SOUL!!
ZA (ZSHH)
ASSASSIN IROHA MIYAMOTO
IROHA MIYAMOTO'S HENCHMAN HANZOU
WHAT I GAVE HIM WAS THE MIYAMOTO FAMILY'S SECRET MUSCLE-ENHANCING ELIXIR!
FORTY TIMES THE DOSE WE GAVE THAT POLAR BEAR!
THAT DRAGON GIRL HASN'T A CHANCE!!
SFX: GOGO (GRRM)
RAAAHHH
THIS IS MY TRUE POTENTIAL!
SEE ME NOW!? I'M BETTER THAN INU-ZUKA'S COUSIN!
DOKA
DOKA (DAKK)
DOKA
THAT'S RIGHT! GO FORTH, BERSERKER OF MIYA-MOTO!
CALL UPON YOUR TRUE STRENGTH!
UNPOPULAR, YOU SAY!?
SINGLE, YOU SAY!?
WELL ...
I'LL HAVE YOU KNOW...

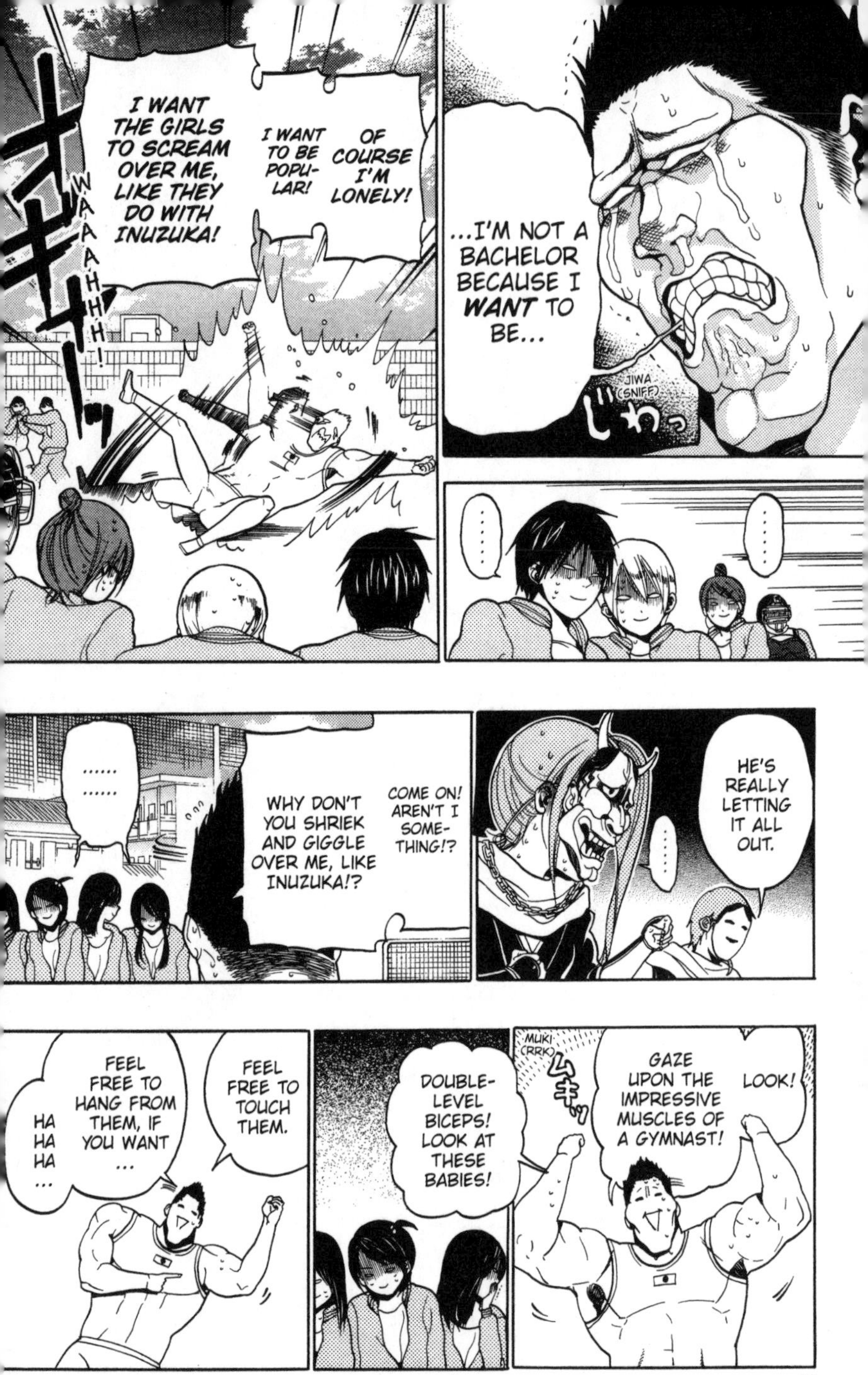
...I'M NOT A BACHELOR BECAUSE I *WANT* TO BE...
JIWA (SNIFF)
......
......
OF COURSE I'M LONELY!
I WANT TO BE POPULAR!
I WANT THE GIRLS TO SCREAM OVER ME, LIKE THEY DO WITH INUZUKA!
WAAAAHHHH!
HE'S REALLY LETTING IT ALL OUT.
......
COME ON! AREN'T I SOMETHING!?
WHY DON'T YOU SHRIEK AND GIGGLE OVER ME, LIKE INUZUKA!?
....
LOOK!
GAZE UPON THE IMPRESSIVE MUSCLES OF A GYMNAST!
MUKI (RRK)
DOUBLE-LEVEL BICEPS! LOOK AT THESE BABIES!
FEEL FREE TO TOUCH THEM.
FEEL FREE TO HANG FROM THEM, IF YOU WANT...
HA HA HA...

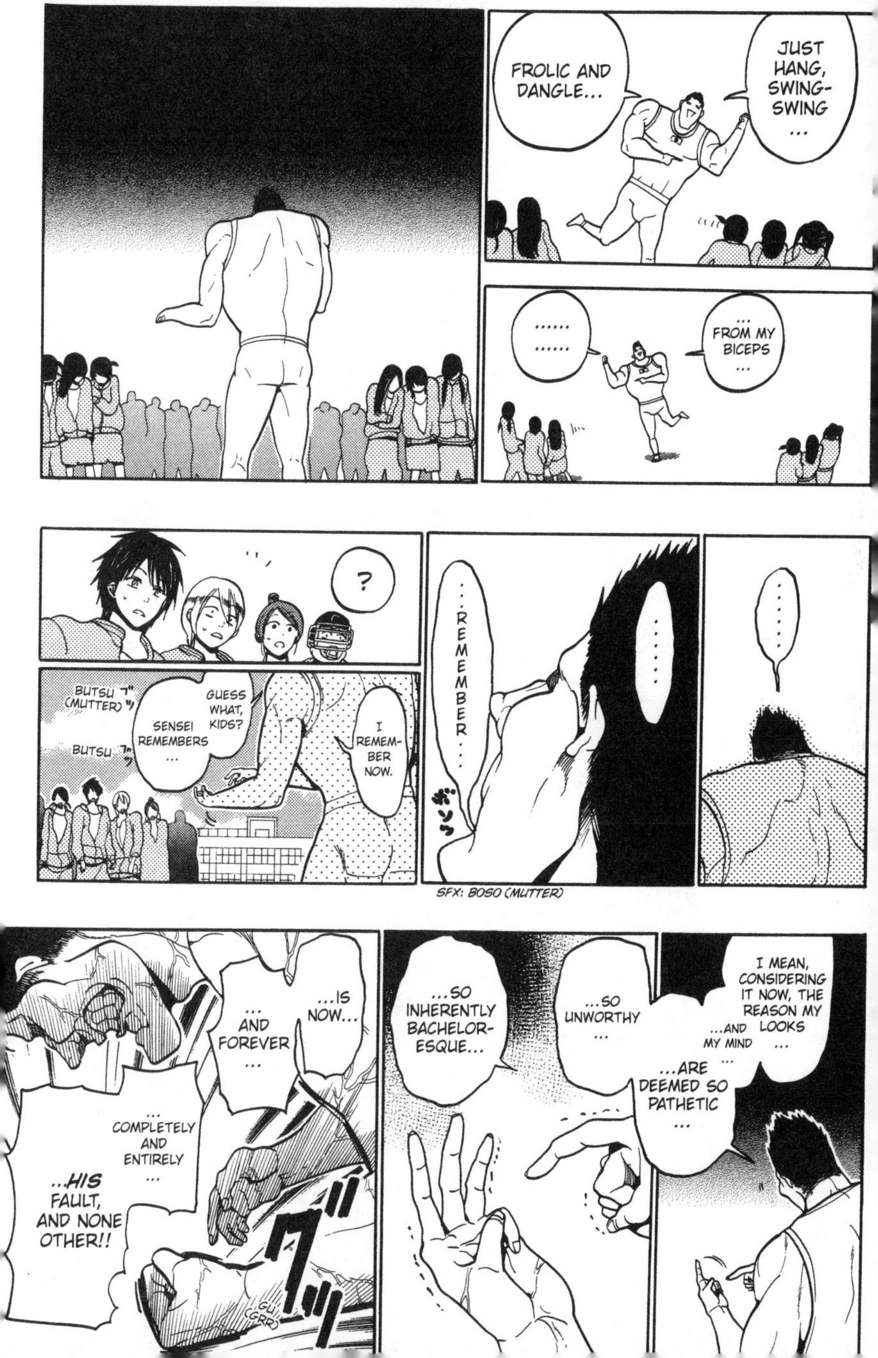
JUST HANG, SWING-SWING...
FROLIC AND DANGLE...
...FROM MY BICEPS...
......
......
......
...REMEMBER...
ボソッ
?
I REMEMBER NOW.
GUESS WHAT, KIDS?
SENSEI REMEMBERS...
BUTSU (MUTTER)
BUTSU
SFX: BOSO (MUTTER)
I MEAN, CONSIDERING IT NOW, THE REASON MY LOOKS...
...AND MY MIND...
...ARE DEEMED SO PATHETIC...
...SO UNWORTHY...
...SO INHERENTLY BACHELOR-ESQUE...
...IS NOW...
...AND FOREVER...
...COMPLETELY AND ENTIRELY...
...HIS FAULT, AND NONE OTHER!!
GU (GRR)

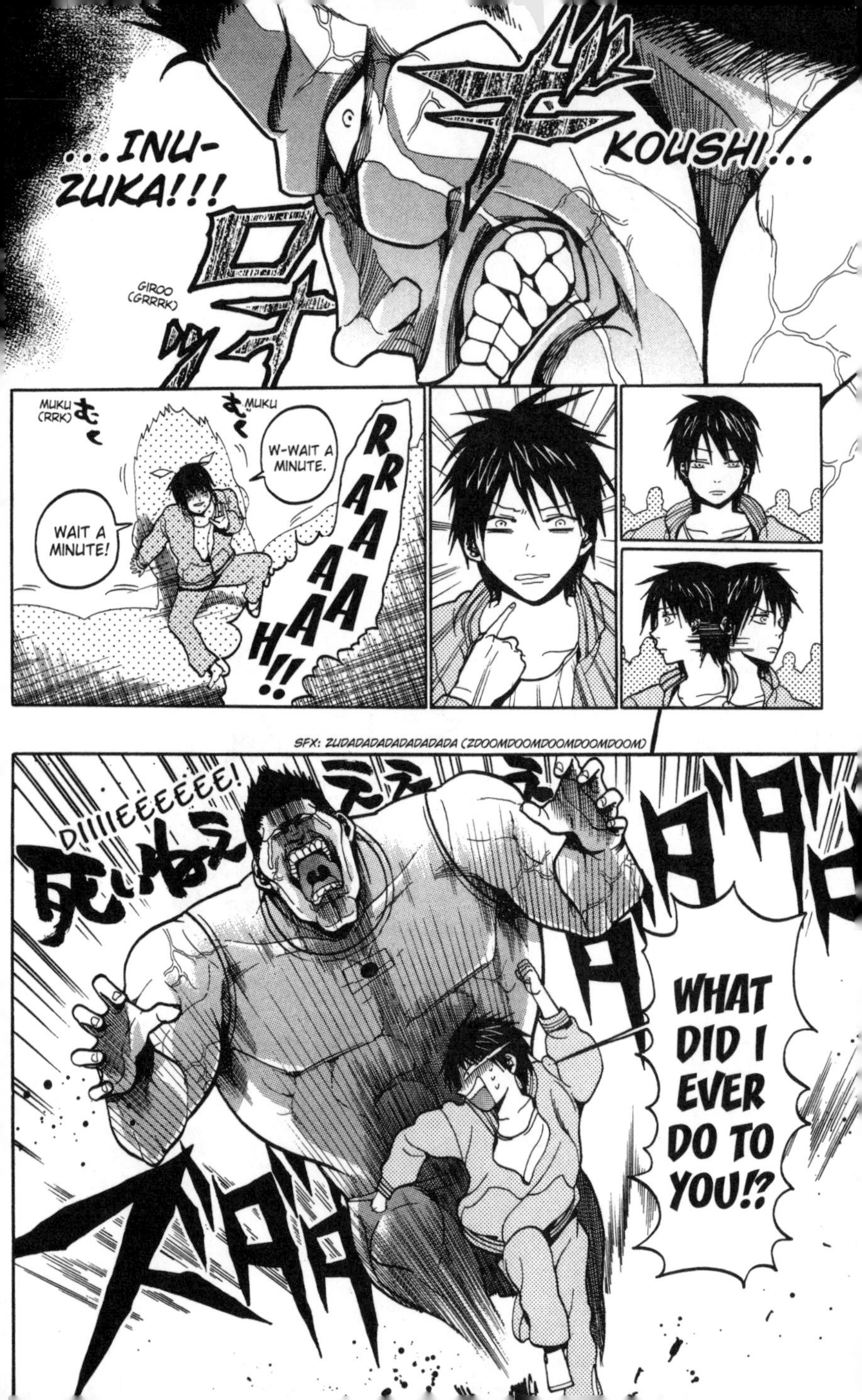
KOUSHI...
...INU-ZUKA!!!
GIROO (GRRRK)
RRAAAAAAH!!
W-WAIT A MINUTE.
MUKU
MUKU (RRK)
WAIT A MINUTE!
SFX: ZUDADADADADADADADA (ZDOOMDOOMDOOMDOOMDOOM)
DIIIIEEEEEE!
WHAT DID I EVER DO TO YOU!?

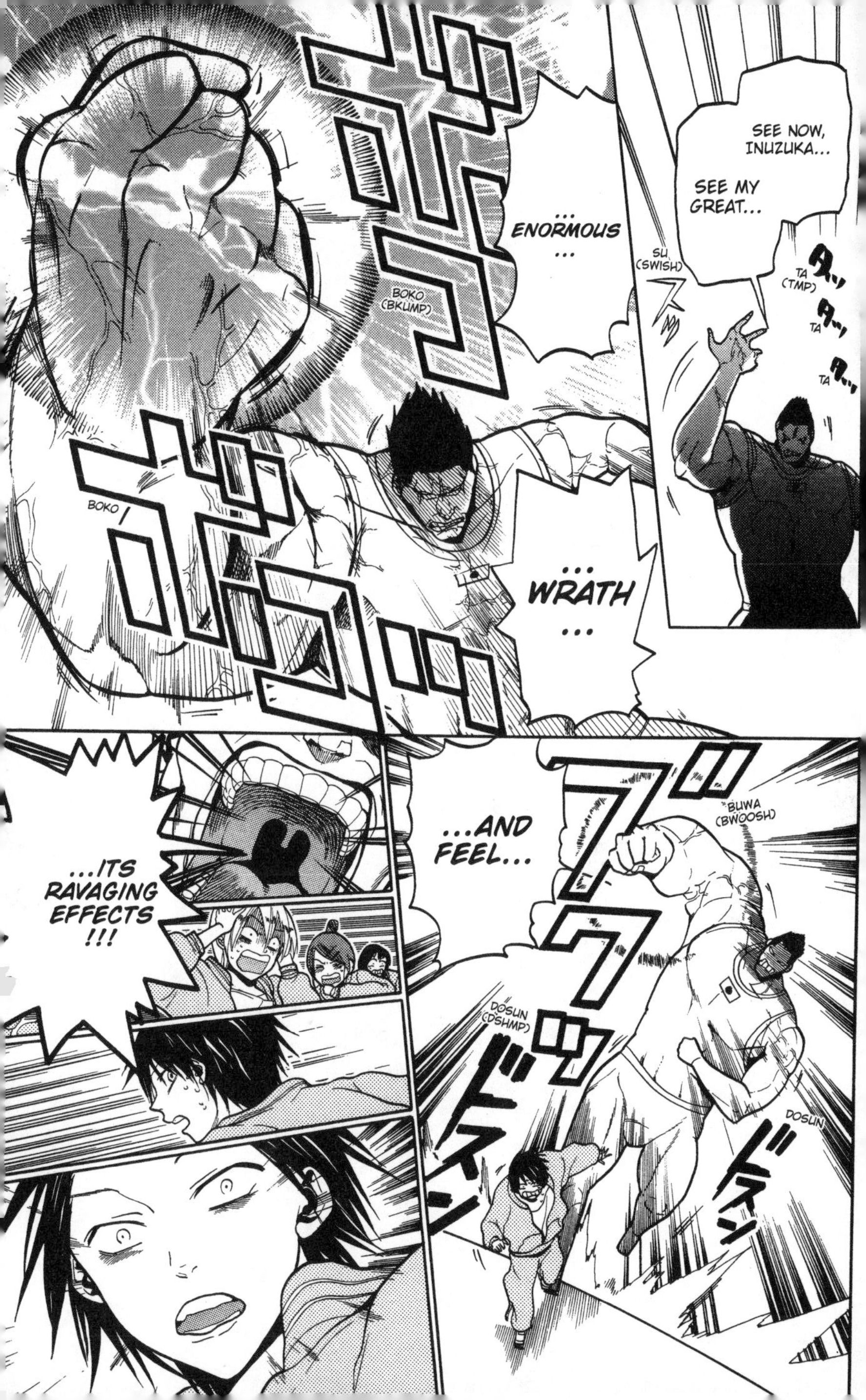
SEE NOW, INUZUKA...
SEE MY GREAT...
SU (SWISH)
TA (TMP)
TA
TA
...ENORMOUS...
BOKO (BKUMP)
BOKO
...WRATH...
...AND FEEL...
BUWA (BWOOSH)
DOSUN (DSHMP)
DOSUN
...ITS RAVAGING EFFECTS!!!

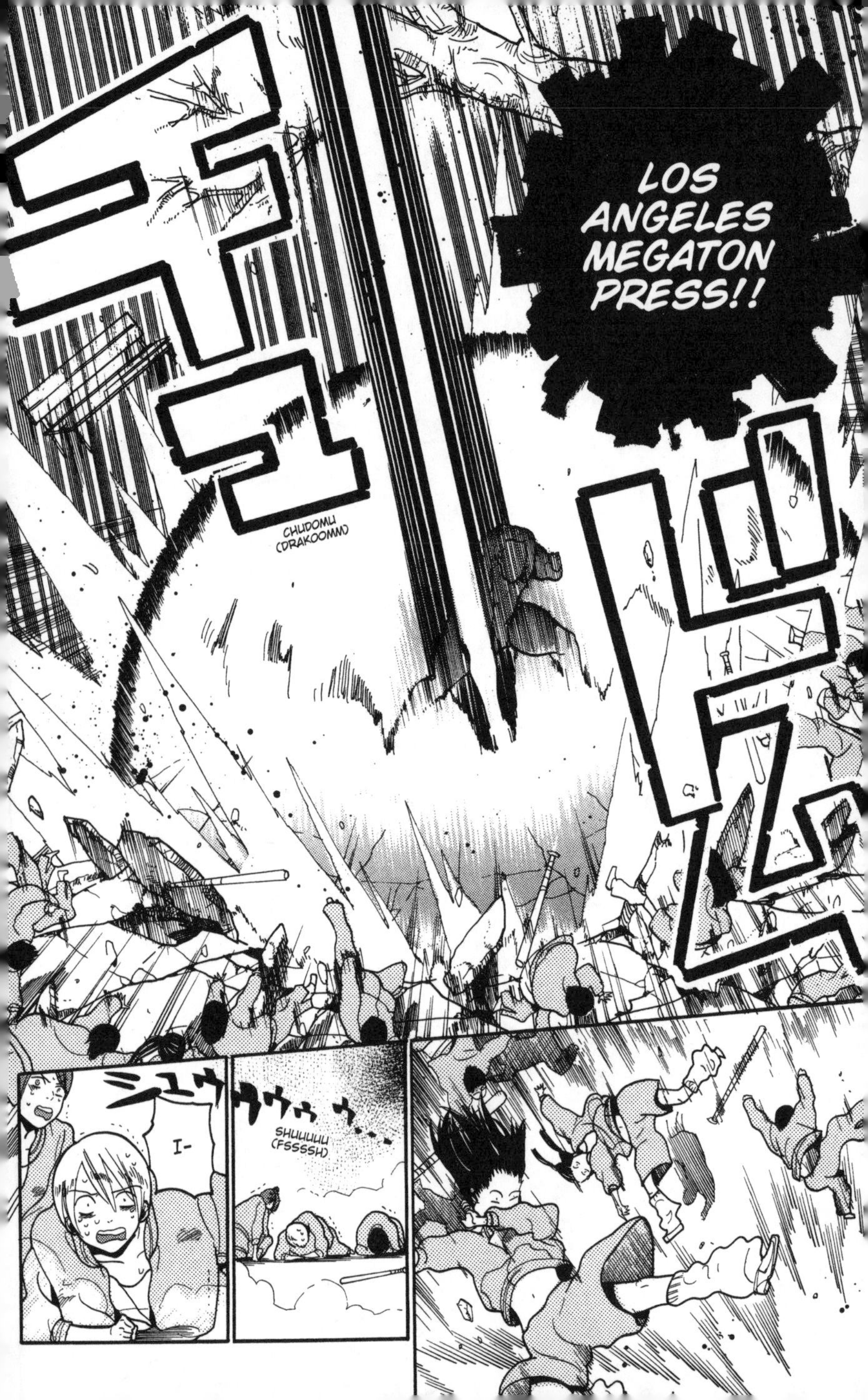
LOS ANGELES MEGATON PRESS!!
CHUDOMU (DRAKOOMM)
SHUUUUU (FSSSSH)
I-

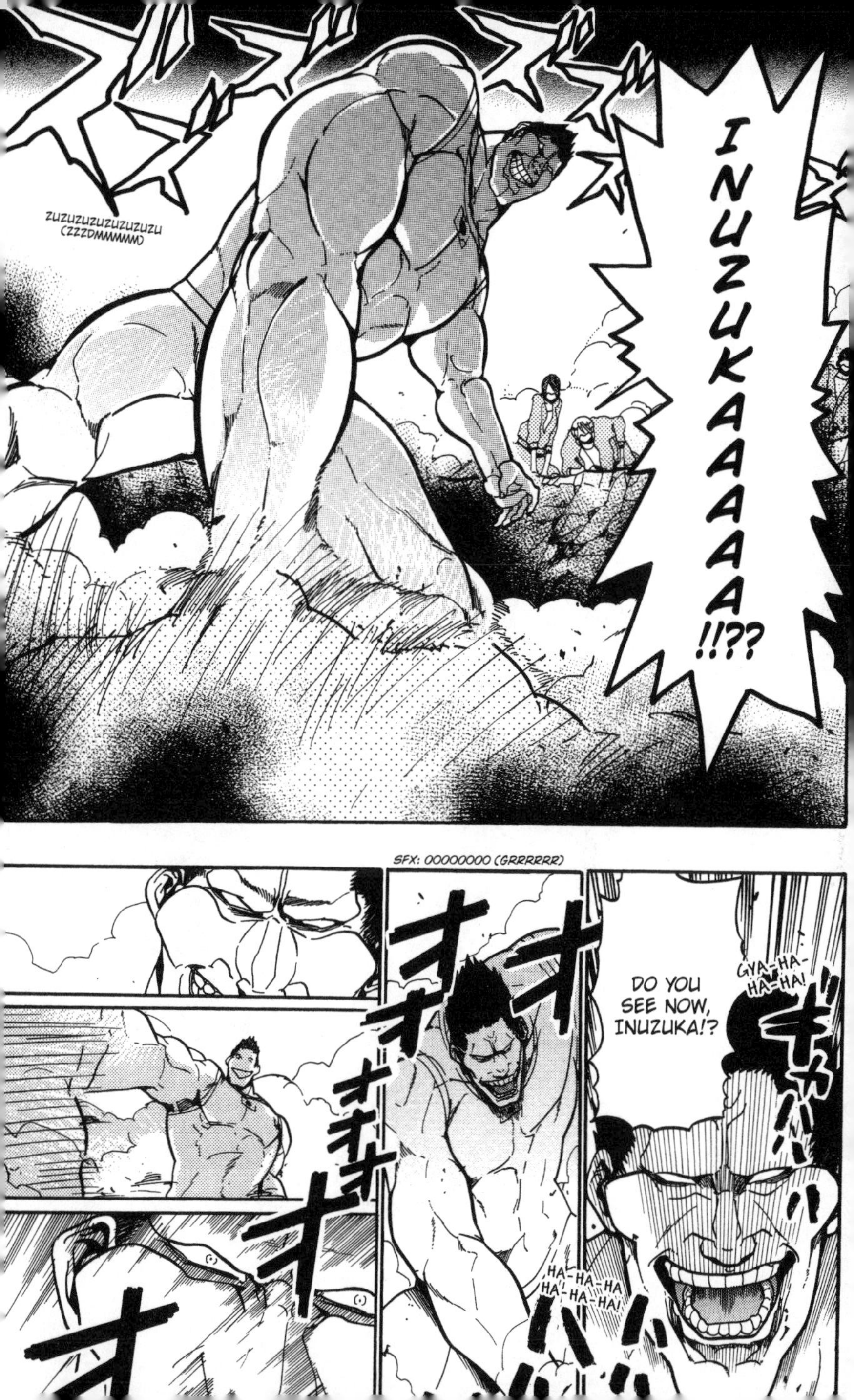
INUZUKAAAAA!!??
ZUZUZUZUZUZUZUZU
(ZZZDMMMMMM)
SFX: OOOOOOO (GRRRRRR)
GYA-HA-HA-HA!
DO YOU SEE NOW, INUZUKA!?
HA-HA-HA HA-HA-HA!

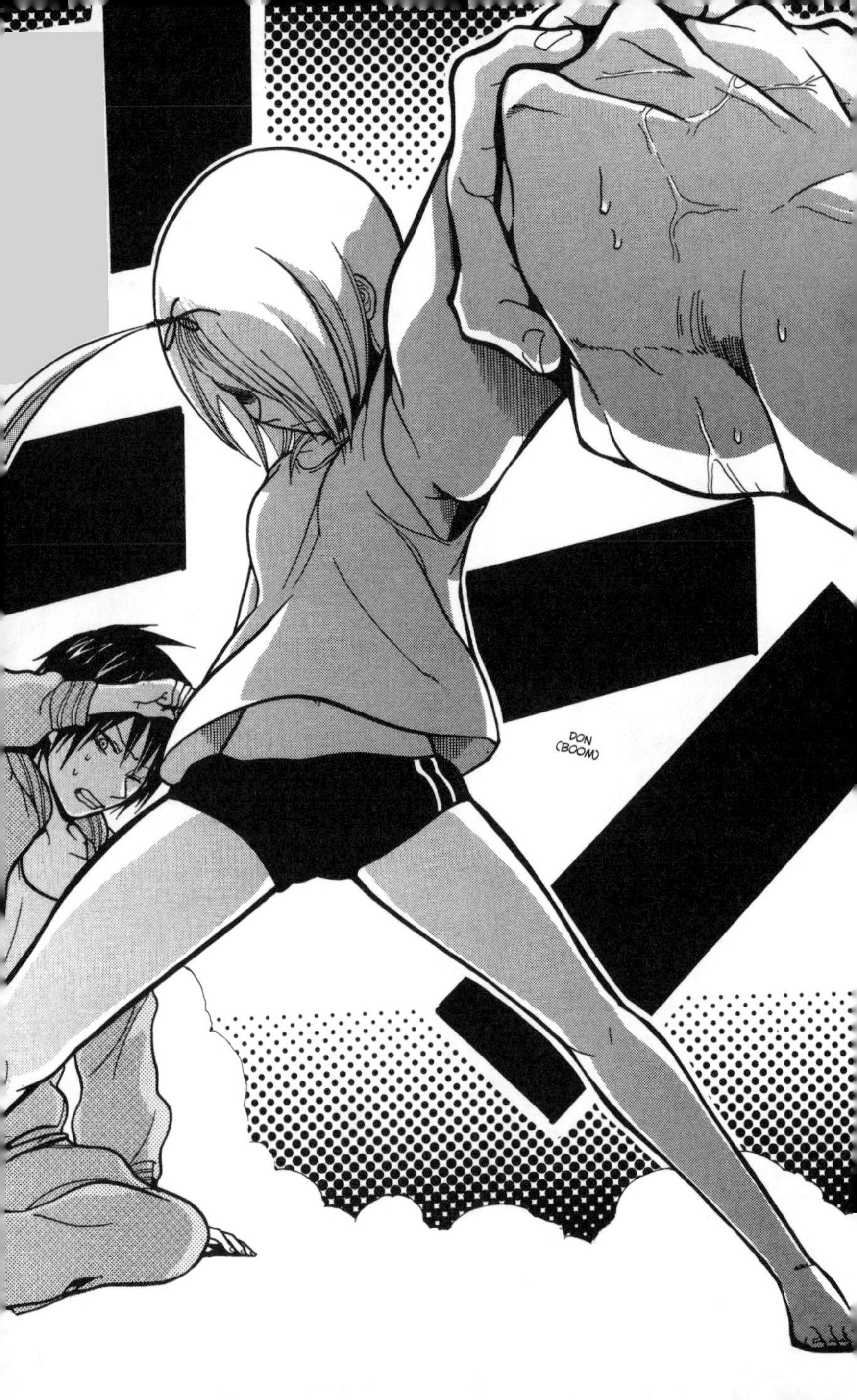
DON
(BOOM)

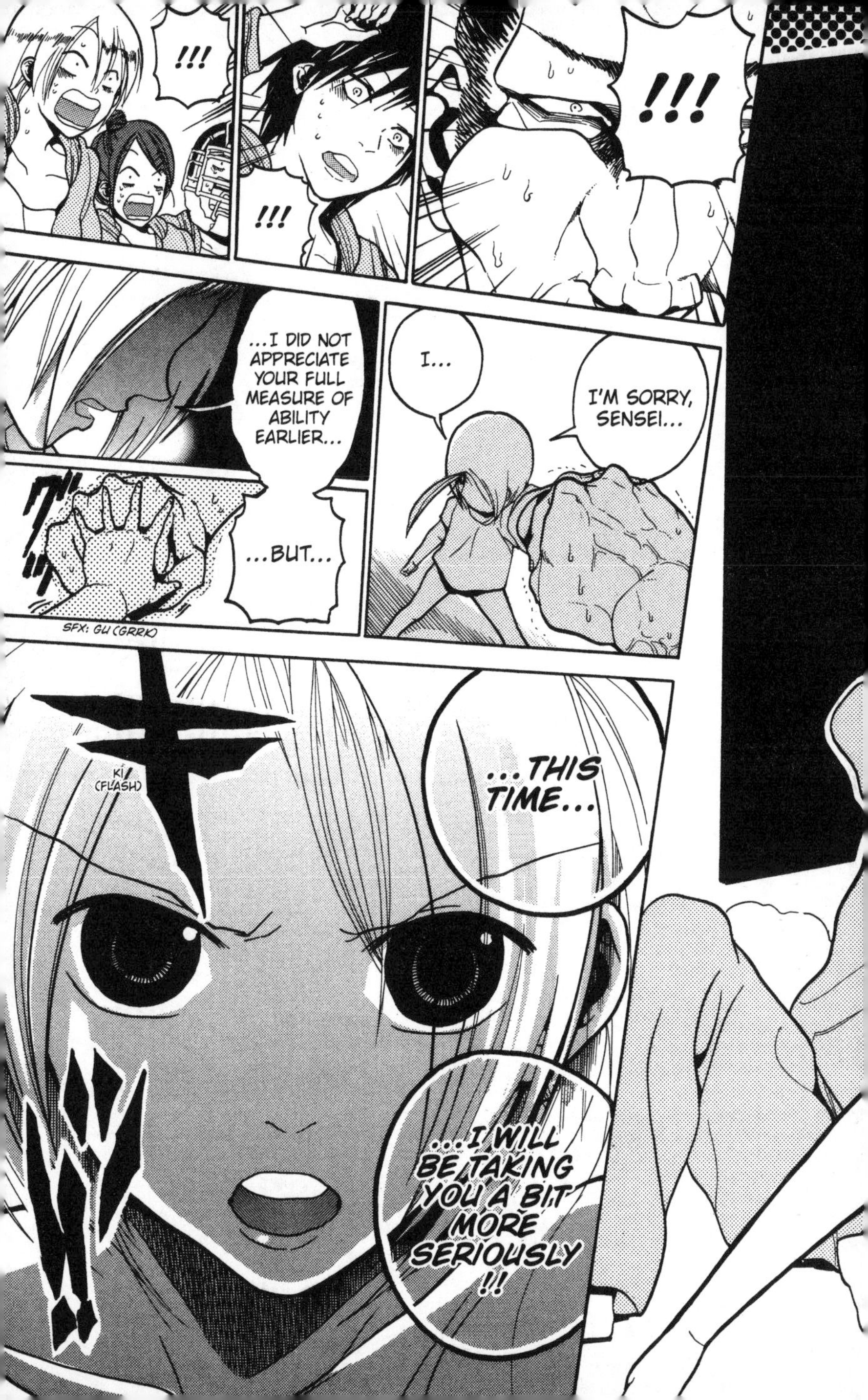
!!!
!!!
!!!
I...
I'M SORRY, SENSEI...
...I DID NOT APPRECIATE YOUR FULL MEASURE OF ABILITY EARLIER...
...BUT...
SFX: GU (GRRK)
...THIS TIME...
KI (FLASH)
...I WILL BE TAKING YOU A BIT MORE SERIOUSLY!!

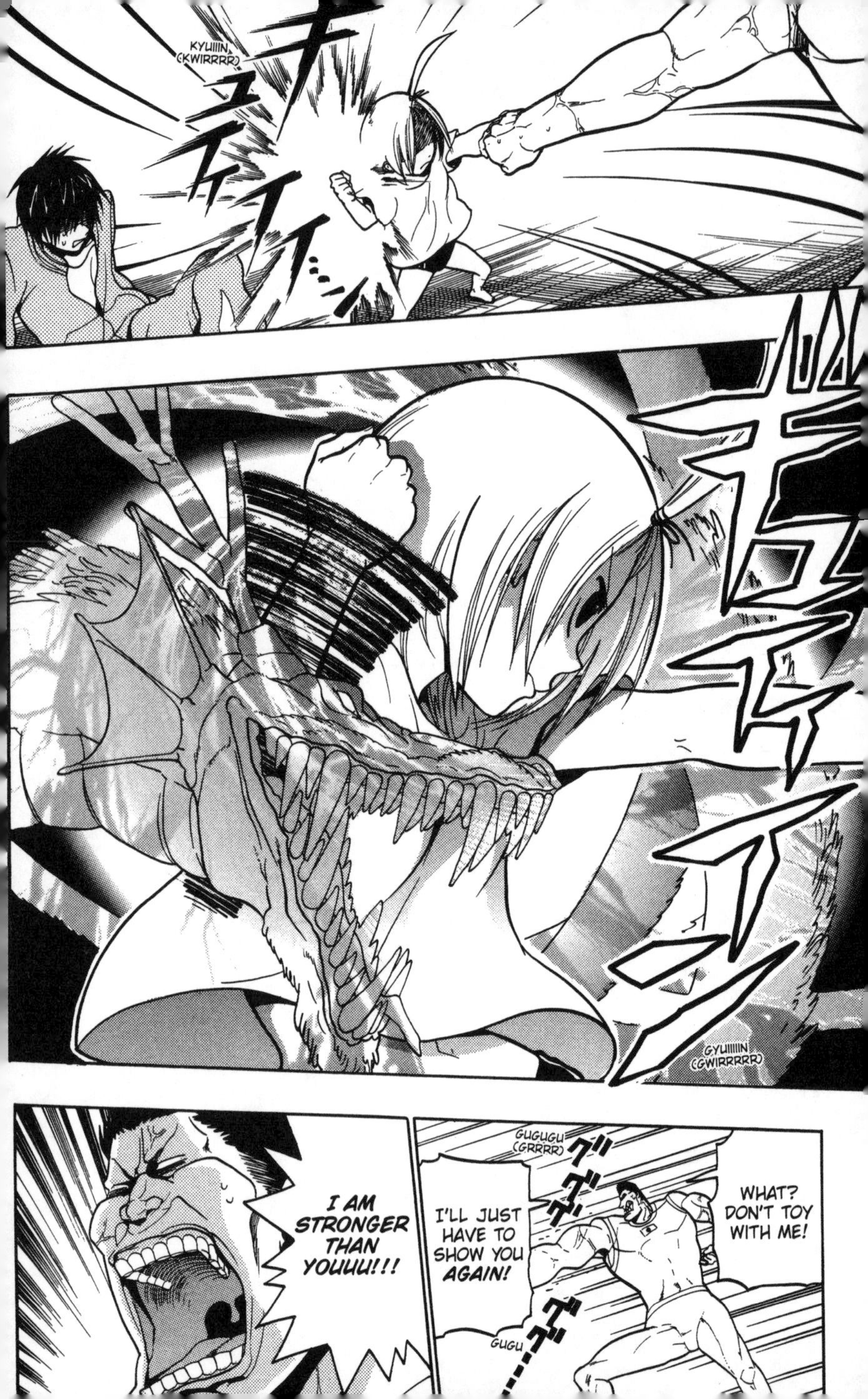
KYUIIIN (KWIRRRR)
GYUIIIIN (GWIRRRRR)
GUGUGU (GRRRR)
WHAT? DON'T TOY WITH ME!
I'LL JUST HAVE TO SHOW YOU AGAIN!
GUGU
I AM STRONGER THAN YOUUU!!!

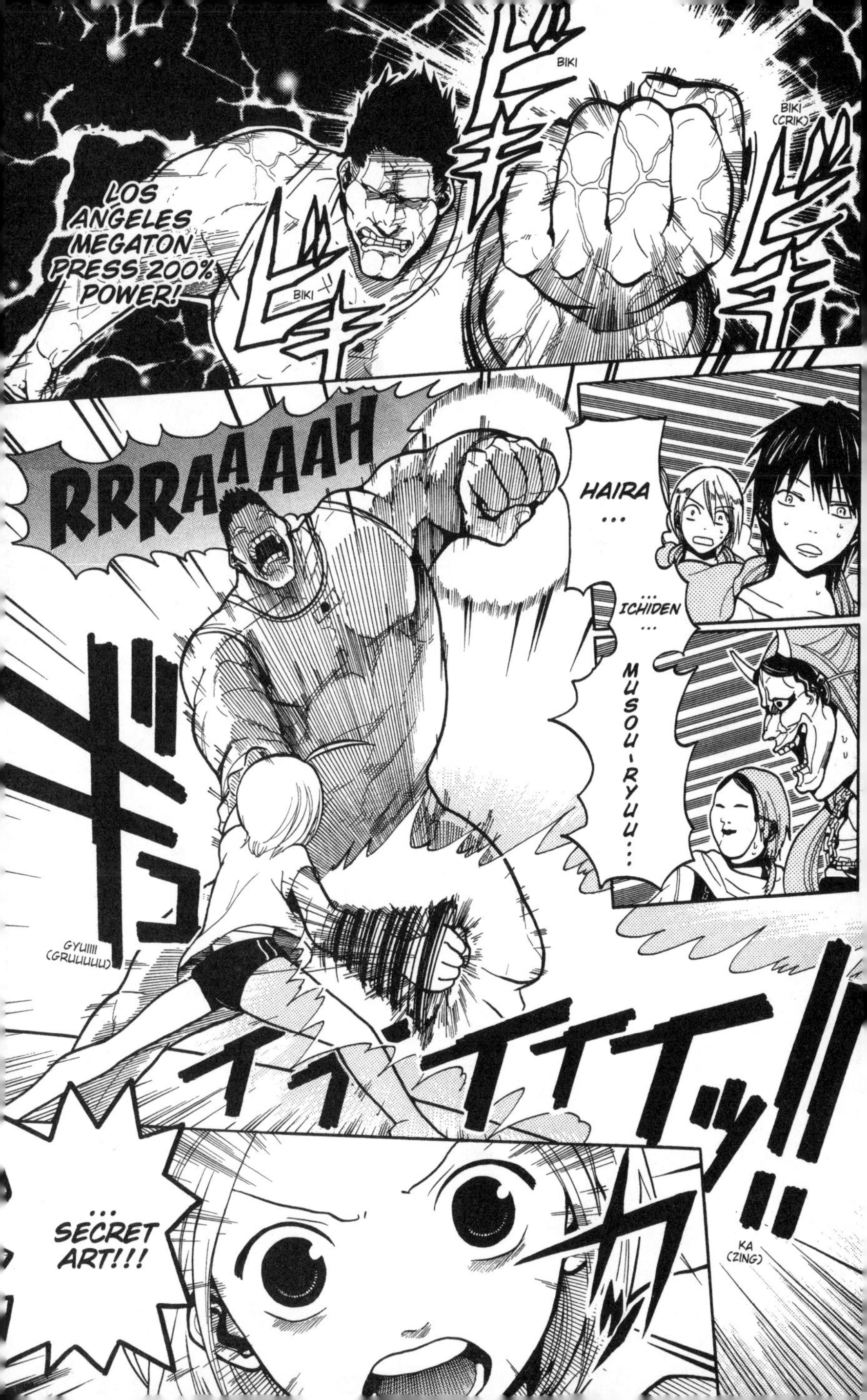
BIKI (CRIK)
BIKI
LOS ANGELES MEGATON PRESS 200% POWER!
BIKI
HAIRA ...
... ICHIDEN ...
MUSOU-RYUU...
RRRAAAAH
GYUIIII (GRUUUUUU)
KA (ZING)
... SECRET ART!!!

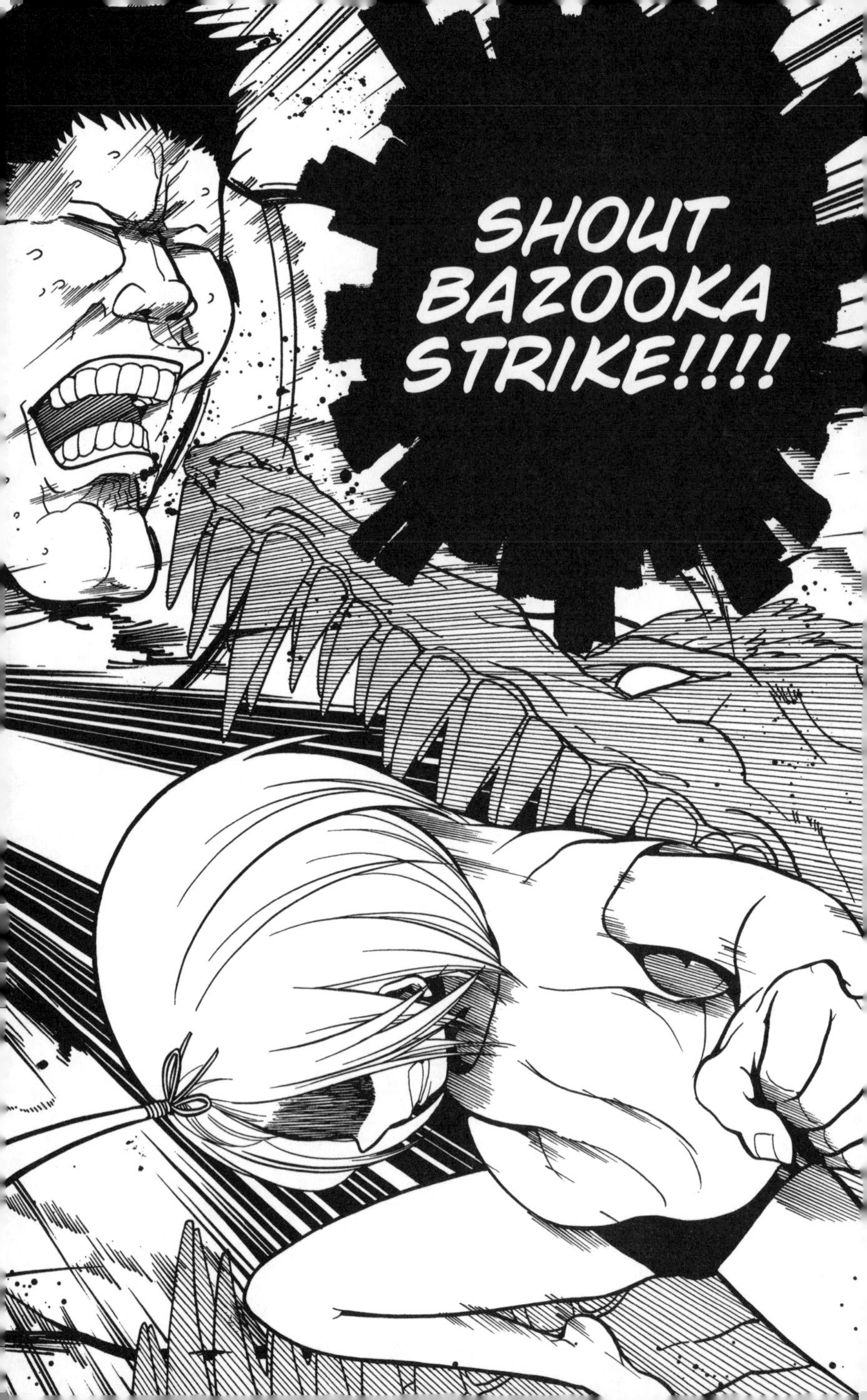
SHOUT BAZOOKA STRIKE!!!!

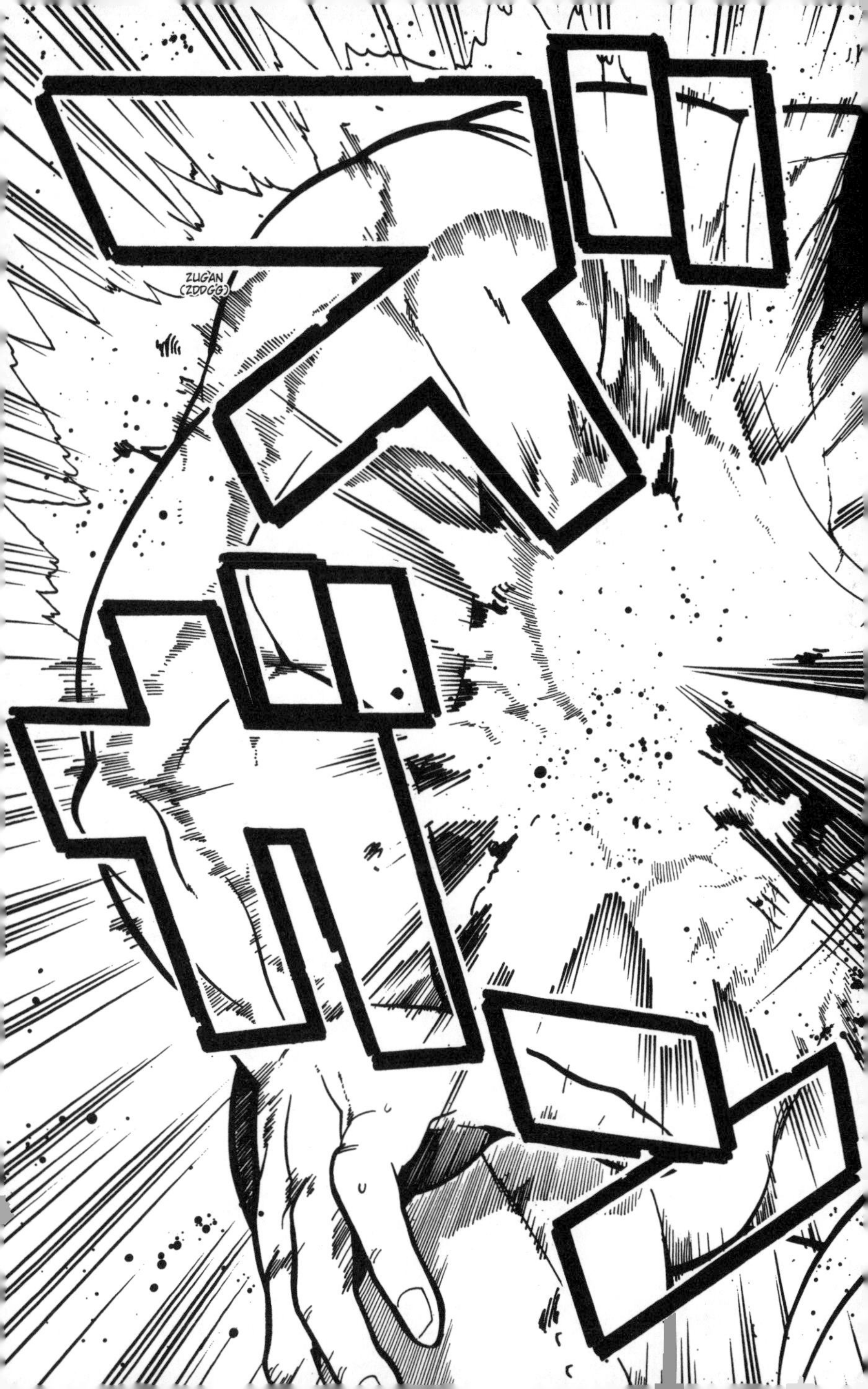
ズガン
ZUGAN
(ZDDGG)

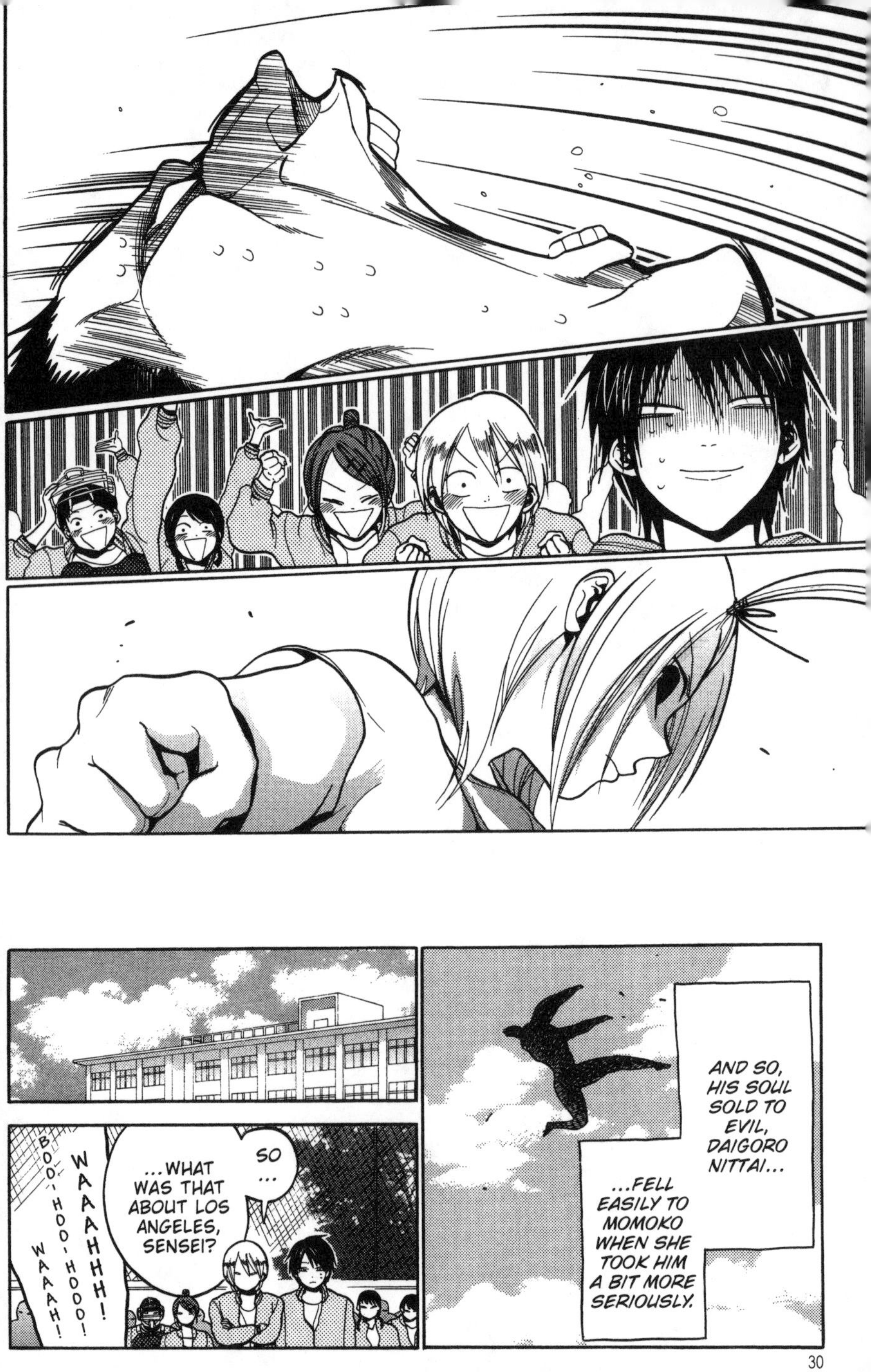
AND SO, HIS SOUL SOLD TO EVIL, DAIGORO NITTAI...
...FELL EASILY TO MOMOKO WHEN SHE TOOK HIM A BIT MORE SERIOUSLY.
SO ...
...WHAT WAS THAT ABOUT LOS ANGELES, SENSEI?
WAAAAHHH!
BOO-HOO-HOOO!
WAAAH!

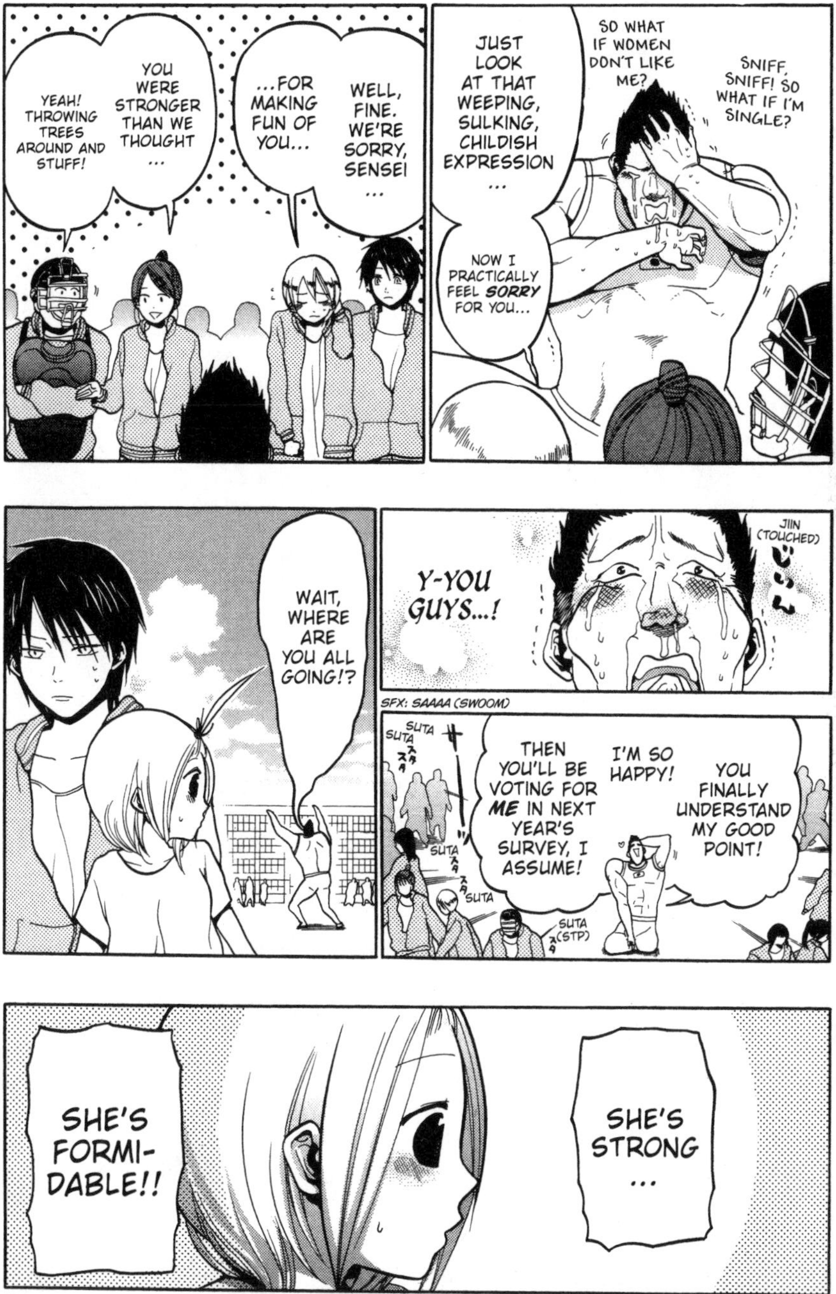
SNIFF, SNIFF! SO WHAT IF I'M SINGLE?
SO WHAT IF WOMEN DON'T LIKE ME?
JUST LOOK AT THAT WEEPING, SULKING, CHILDISH EXPRESSION ...
NOW I PRACTICALLY FEEL SORRY FOR YOU...
WELL, FINE. WE'RE SORRY, SENSEI ...
...FOR MAKING FUN OF YOU...
YOU WERE STRONGER THAN WE THOUGHT ...
YEAH! THROWING TREES AROUND AND STUFF!
JIIN (TOUCHED)
Y-YOU GUYS...!
SFX: SAAAA (SWOOM)
YOU FINALLY UNDERSTAND MY GOOD POINT!
I'M SO HAPPY!
THEN YOU'LL BE VOTING FOR ME IN NEXT YEAR'S SURVEY, I ASSUME!
SUTA SUTA
SUTA
SUTA
SUTA (STP)
WAIT, WHERE ARE YOU ALL GOING!?
SHE'S STRONG ...
SHE'S FORMIDABLE!!

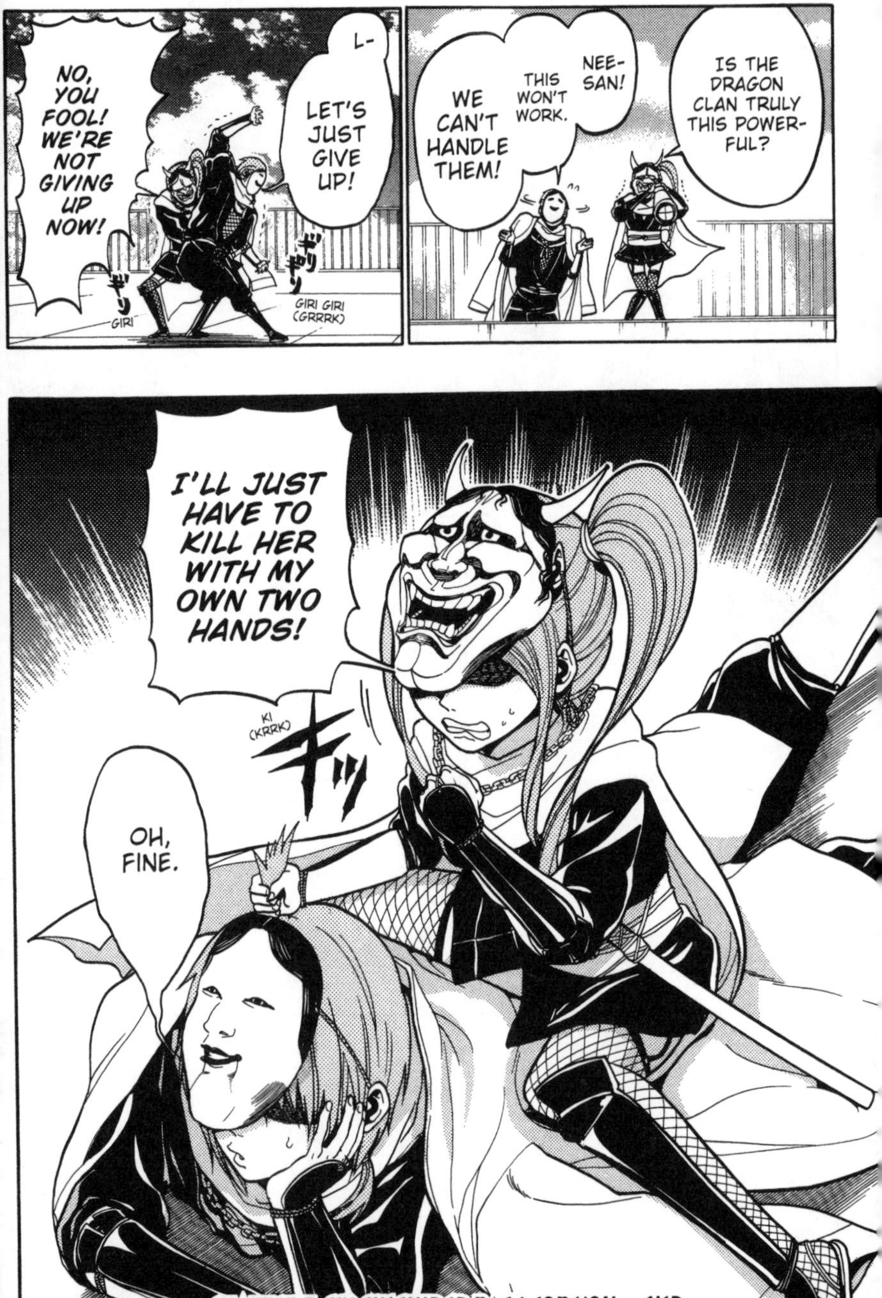
IS THE DRAGON CLAN TRULY THIS POWER-FUL?
NEE-SAN!
THIS WON'T WORK.
WE CAN'T HANDLE THEM!
L-
LET'S JUST GIVE UP!
GIRI GIRI (GRRRK)
NO, YOU FOOL! WE'RE NOT GIVING UP NOW!
GIRI
I'LL JUST HAVE TO KILL HER WITH MY OWN TWO HANDS!
KI (KRRK)
OH, FINE.
CHAPTER 7: MY MISGUIDED RAGE FOR YOU – END

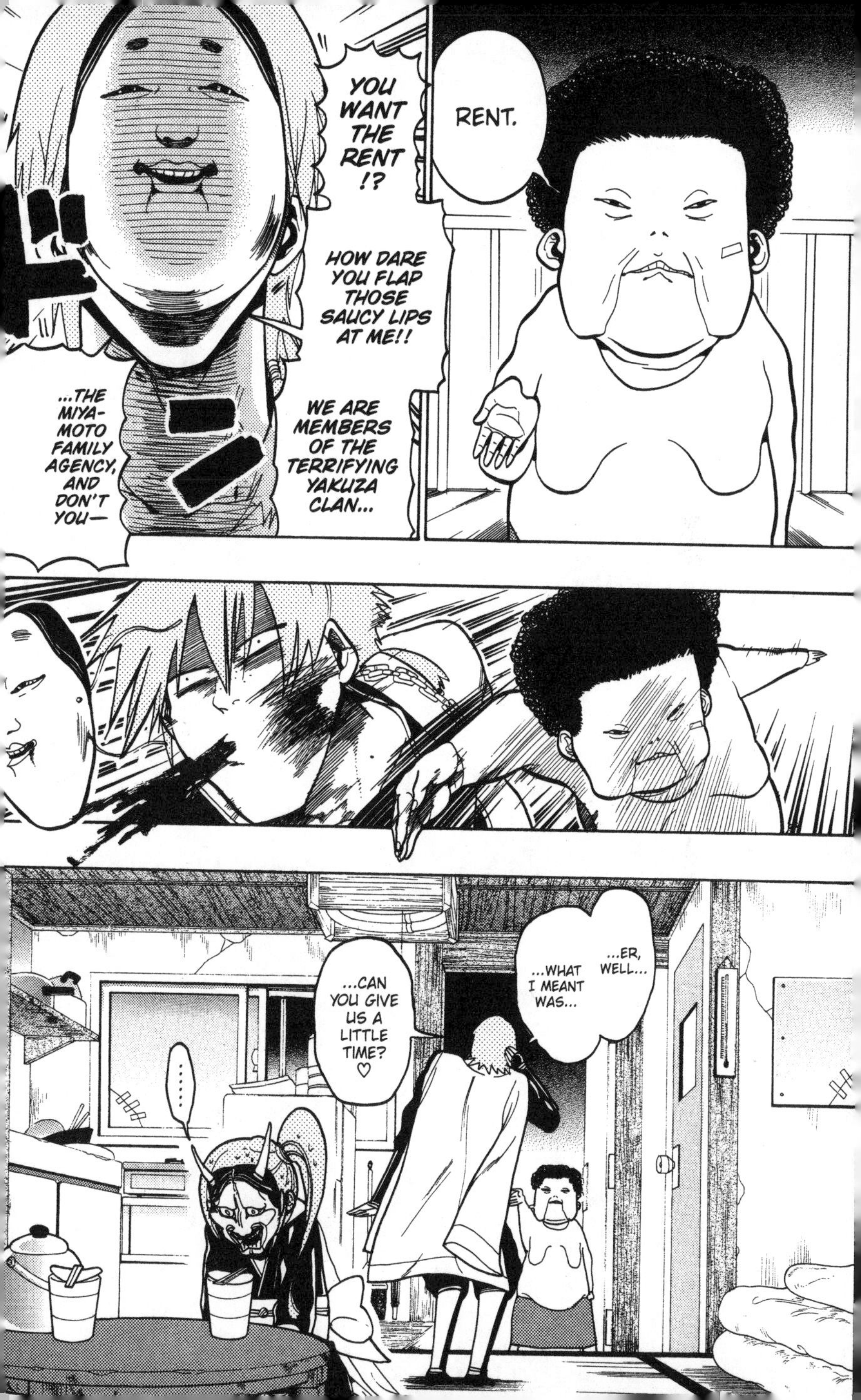
RENT.
YOU WANT THE RENT!?
HOW DARE YOU FLAP THOSE SAUCY LIPS AT ME!!
WE ARE MEMBERS OF THE TERRIFYING YAKUZA CLAN...
...THE MIYAMOTO FAMILY AGENCY, AND DON'T YOU—
...ER, WELL...
...WHAT I MEANT WAS...
...CAN YOU GIVE US A LITTLE TIME? ♡
......

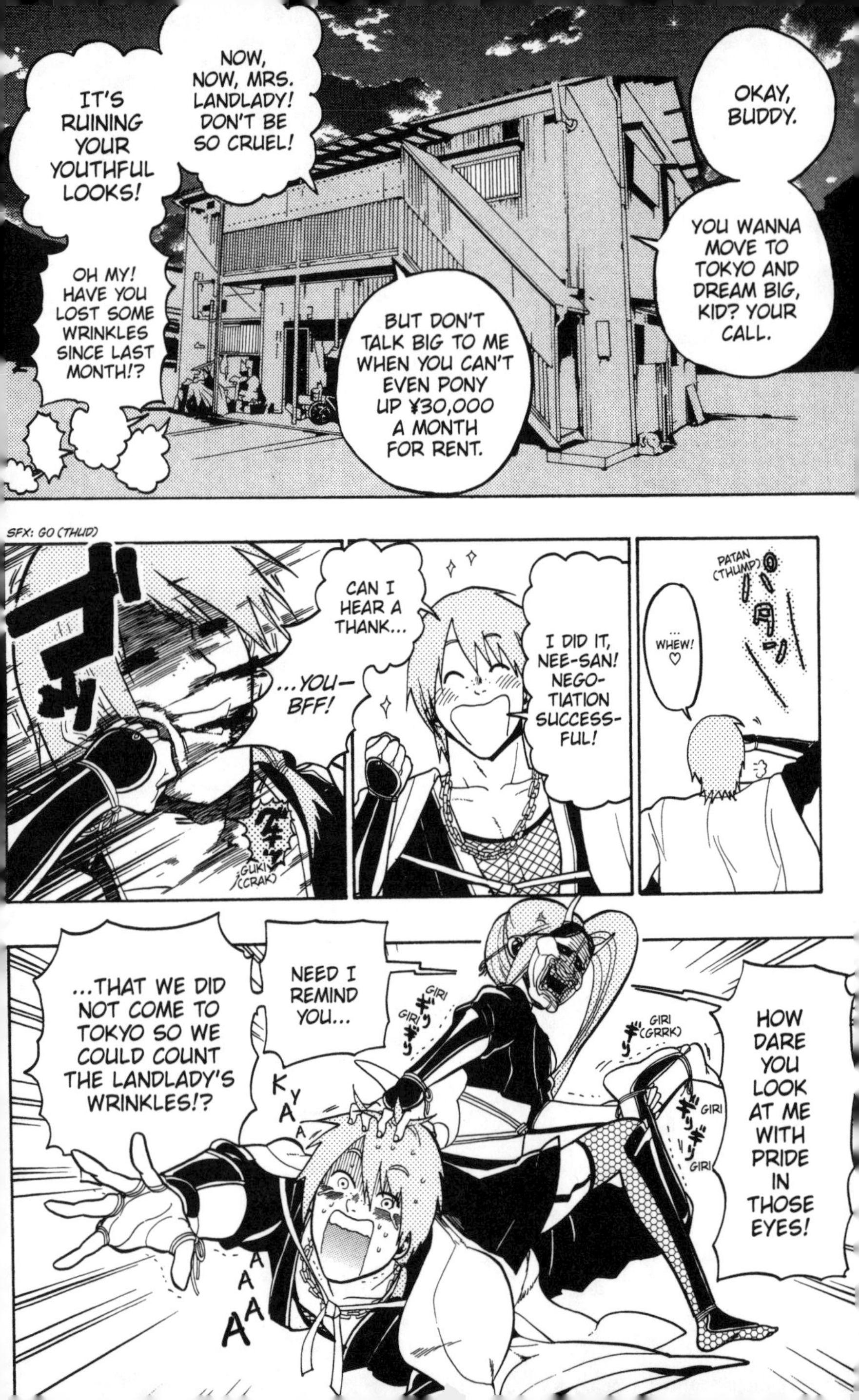
OKAY, BUDDY.
YOU WANNA MOVE TO TOKYO AND DREAM BIG, KID? YOUR CALL.
BUT DON'T TALK BIG TO ME WHEN YOU CAN'T EVEN PONY UP ¥30,000 A MONTH FOR RENT.
NOW, NOW, MRS. LANDLADY! DON'T BE SO CRUEL!
IT'S RUINING YOUR YOUTHFUL LOOKS!
OH MY! HAVE YOU LOST SOME WRINKLES SINCE LAST MONTH!?
SFX: GO (THUD)
PATAN (THUMP)
... WHEW! ♡
I DID IT, NEE-SAN! NEGO-TIATION SUCCESS-FUL!
CAN I HEAR A THANK...
...YOU— BFF!
GUKI (CRAK)
HOW DARE YOU LOOK AT ME WITH PRIDE IN THOSE EYES!
GIRI (GRRK)
GIRI GIRI
GIRI GIRI
NEED I REMIND YOU...
...THAT WE DID NOT COME TO TOKYO SO WE COULD COUNT THE LANDLADY'S WRINKLES!?
KYAAAAAAA

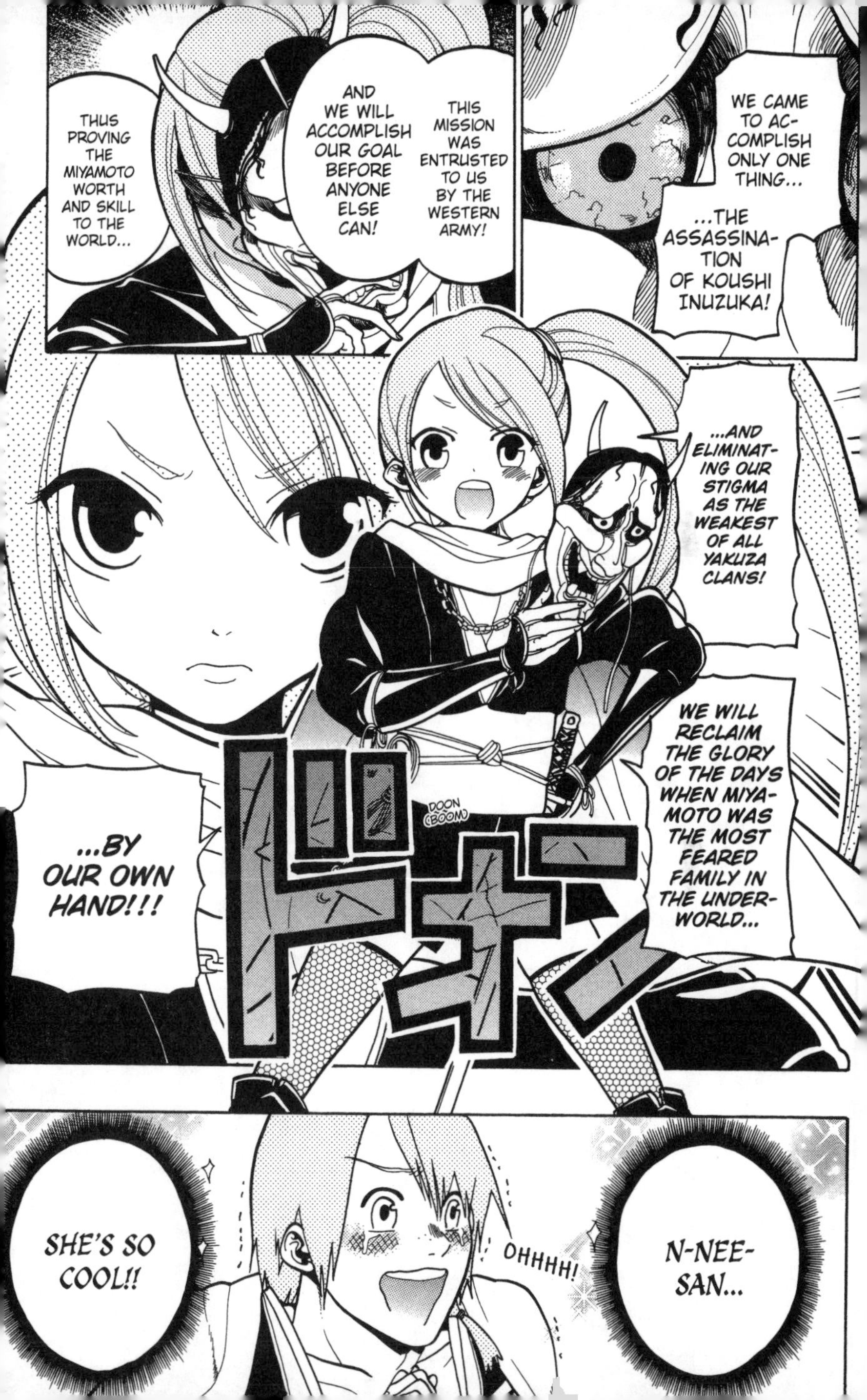
WE CAME TO ACCOMPLISH ONLY ONE THING...
...THE ASSASSINATION OF KOUSHI INUZUKA!
THIS MISSION WAS ENTRUSTED TO US BY THE WESTERN ARMY!
AND WE WILL ACCOMPLISH OUR GOAL BEFORE ANYONE ELSE CAN!
THUS PROVING THE MIYAMOTO WORTH AND SKILL TO THE WORLD...
...AND ELIMINATING OUR STIGMA AS THE WEAKEST OF ALL YAKUZA CLANS!
WE WILL RECLAIM THE GLORY OF THE DAYS WHEN MIYAMOTO WAS THE MOST FEARED FAMILY IN THE UNDERWORLD...
DOON (BOOM)
...BY OUR OWN HAND!!!
N-NEE-SAN...
OHHHH!
SHE'S SO COOL!!

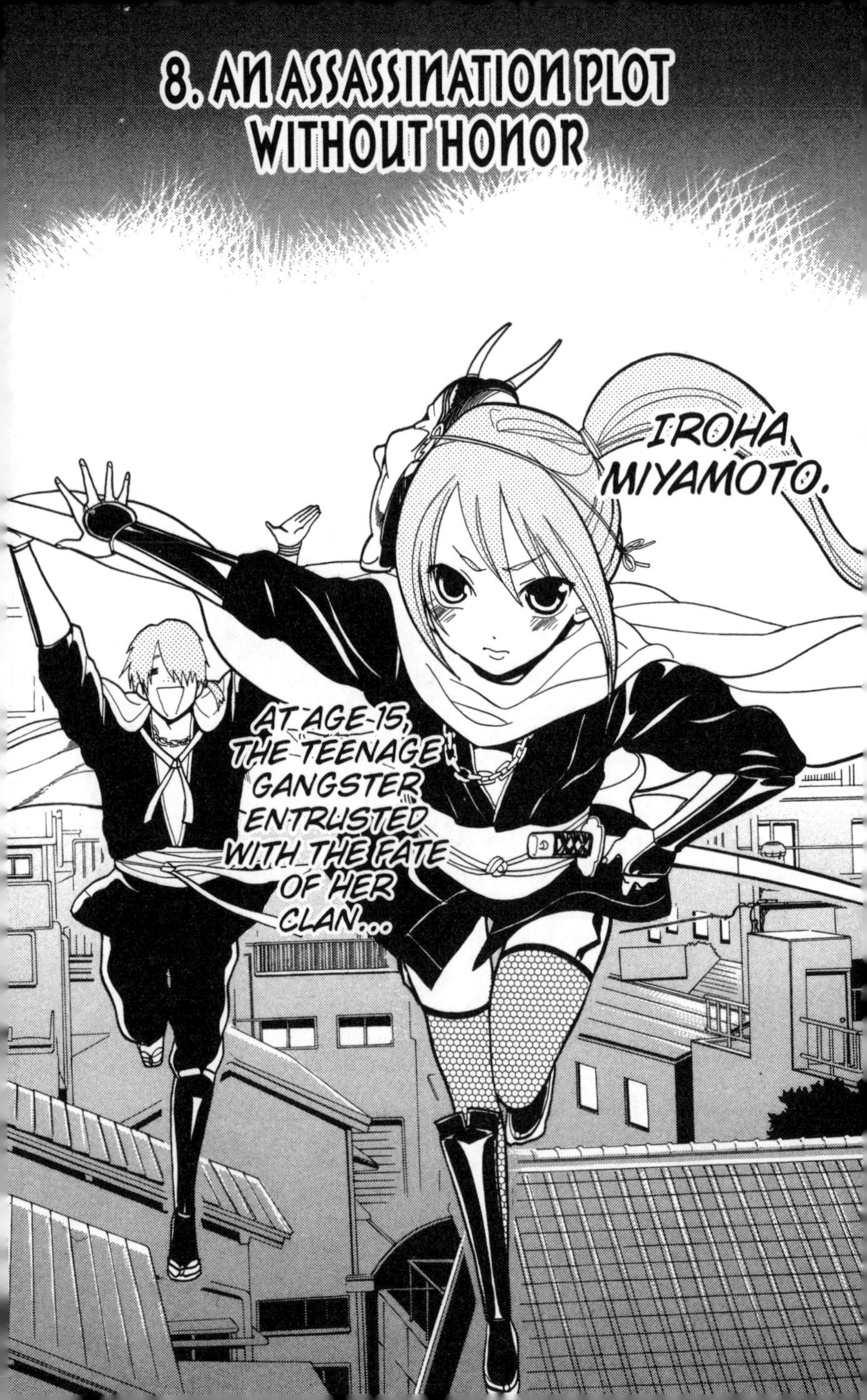
8. AN ASSASSINATION PLOT WITHOUT HONOR
IROHA MIYAMOTO.
AT AGE 15, THE TEENAGE GANGSTER ENTRUSTED WITH THE FATE OF HER CLAN...

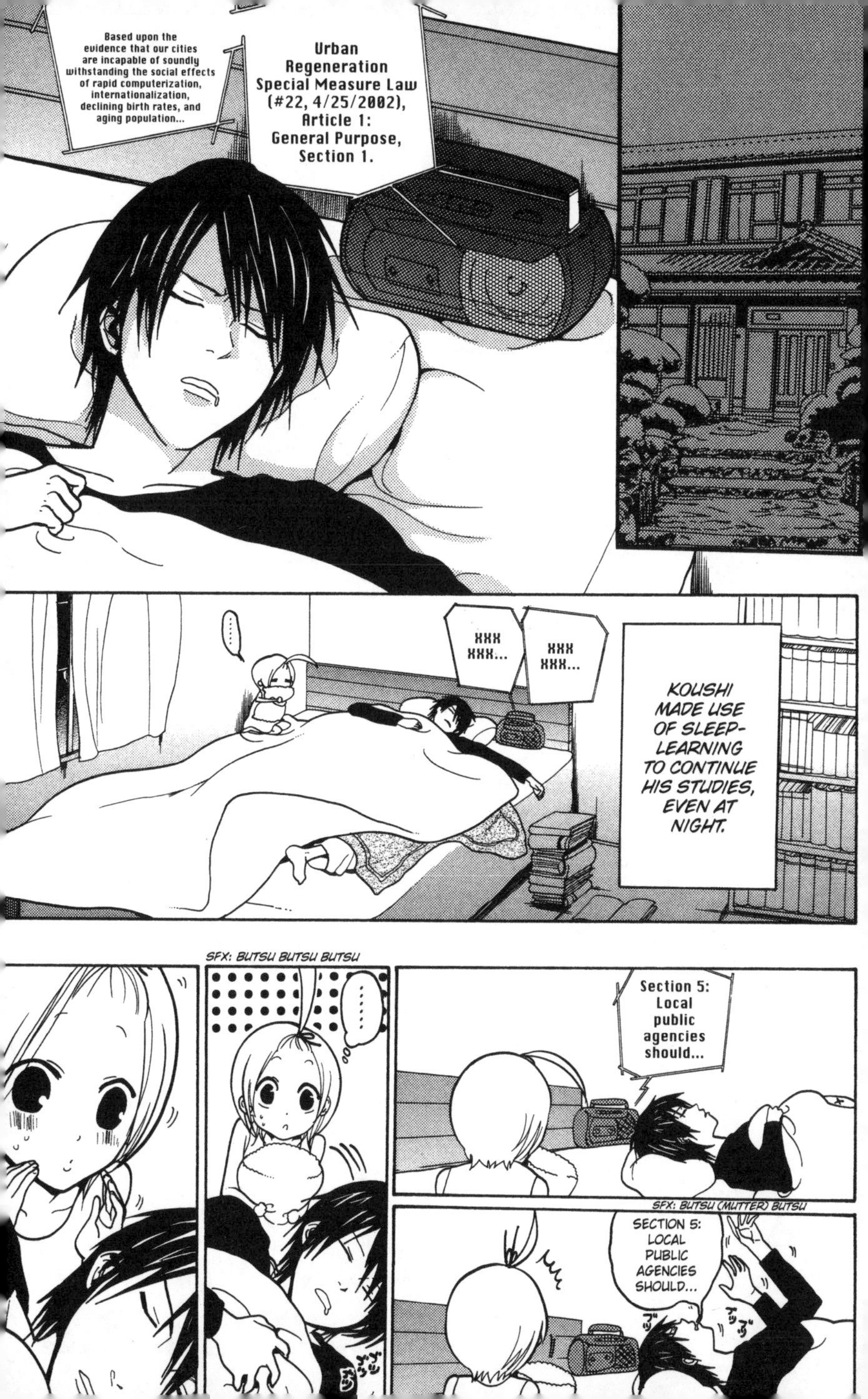
Urban Regeneration Special Measure Law (#22, 4/25/2002), Article 1: General Purpose, Section 1.
Based upon the evidence that our cities are incapable of soundly withstanding the social effects of rapid computerization, internationalization, declining birth rates, and aging population...
KOUSHI MADE USE OF SLEEP-LEARNING TO CONTINUE HIS STUDIES, EVEN AT NIGHT.
XXX XXX...
XXX XXX...
......
Section 5: Local public agencies should...
SFX: BUTSU (MUTTER) BUTSU
SECTION 5: LOCAL PUBLIC AGENCIES SHOULD...
SFX: BUTSU BUTSU BUTSU
......

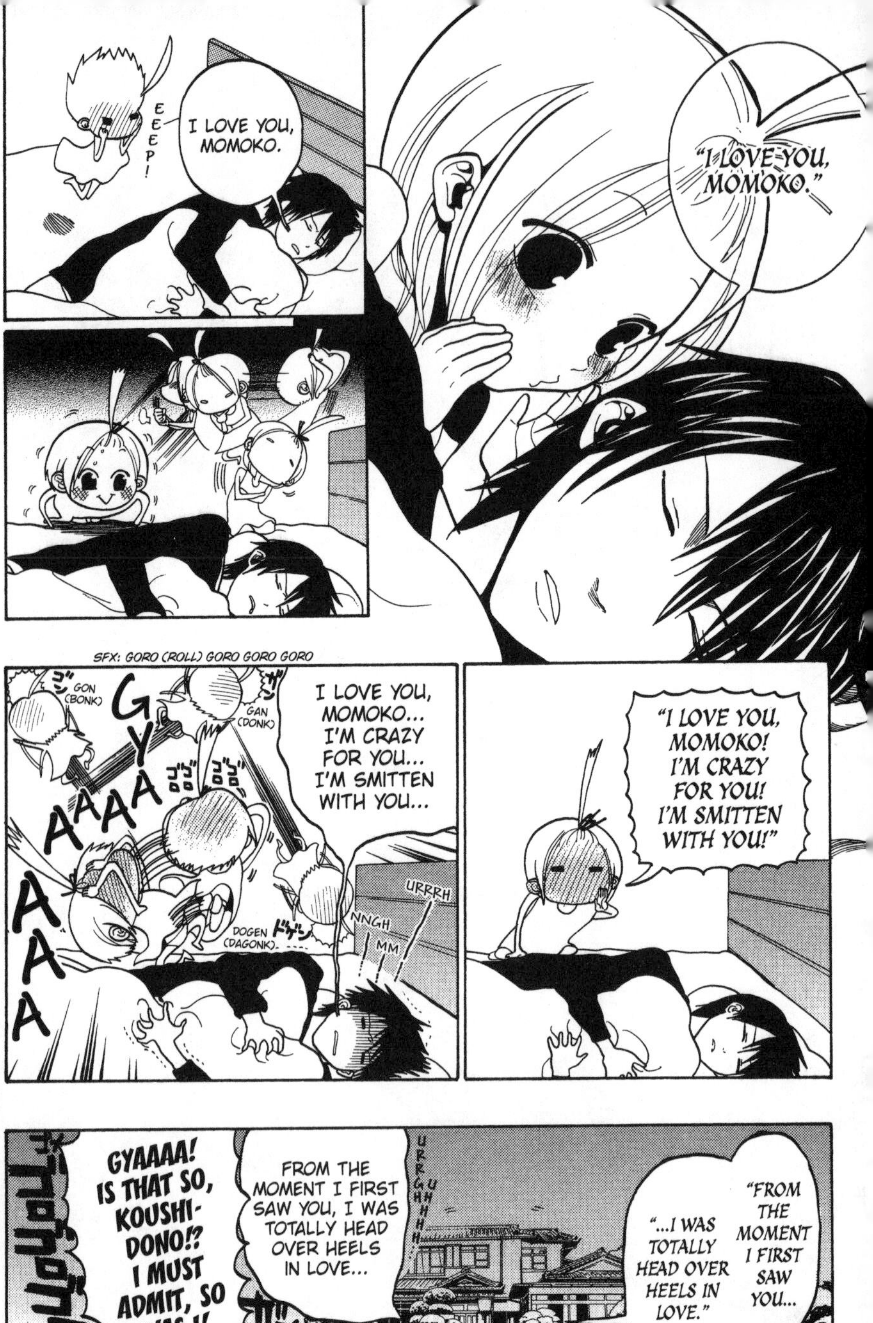
"I LOVE YOU, MOMOKO."
I LOVE YOU, MOMOKO.
EEEEP!
SFX: GORO (ROLL) GORO GORO GORO
"I LOVE YOU, MOMOKO! I'M CRAZY FOR YOU! I'M SMITTEN WITH YOU!"
GAN (DONK)
I LOVE YOU, MOMOKO... I'M CRAZY FOR YOU... I'M SMITTEN WITH YOU...
GON (BONK)
GYAAAAAAA
URRRH
NNGH
MM
DOGEN (DAGONK)
"FROM THE MOMENT I FIRST SAW YOU...
"...I WAS TOTALLY HEAD OVER HEELS IN LOVE."
URRGH UHHHHH
FROM THE MOMENT I FIRST SAW YOU, I WAS TOTALLY HEAD OVER HEELS IN LOVE...
GYAAAA! IS THAT SO, KOUSHI-DONO!? I MUST ADMIT, SO WAS I! ♡

SFX (L-R): GON GOROGOROGOROGORO / GAN GON GAKON

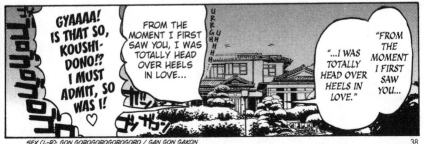

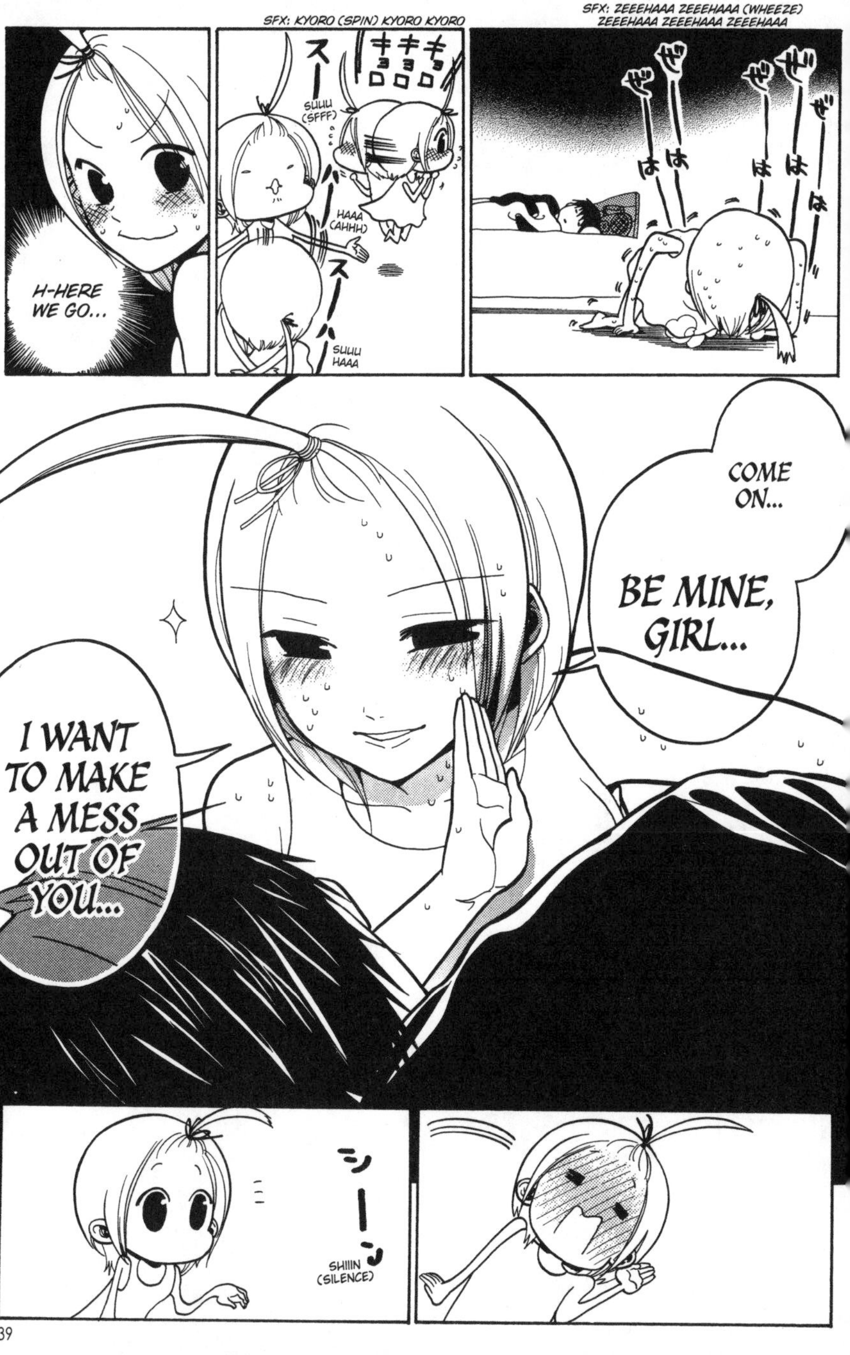
SFX: ZEEEHAAA ZEEEHAAA (WHEEZE)
ZEEEHAAA ZEEEHAAA ZEEEHAAA
SFX: KYORO (SPIN) KYORO KYORO
SUUU (SFFF)
HAAA (AHHH)
SUUU HAAA
H-HERE WE GO...
COME ON...
BE MINE, GIRL...
I WANT TO MAKE A MESS OUT OF YOU...
SHIIIN (SILENCE)

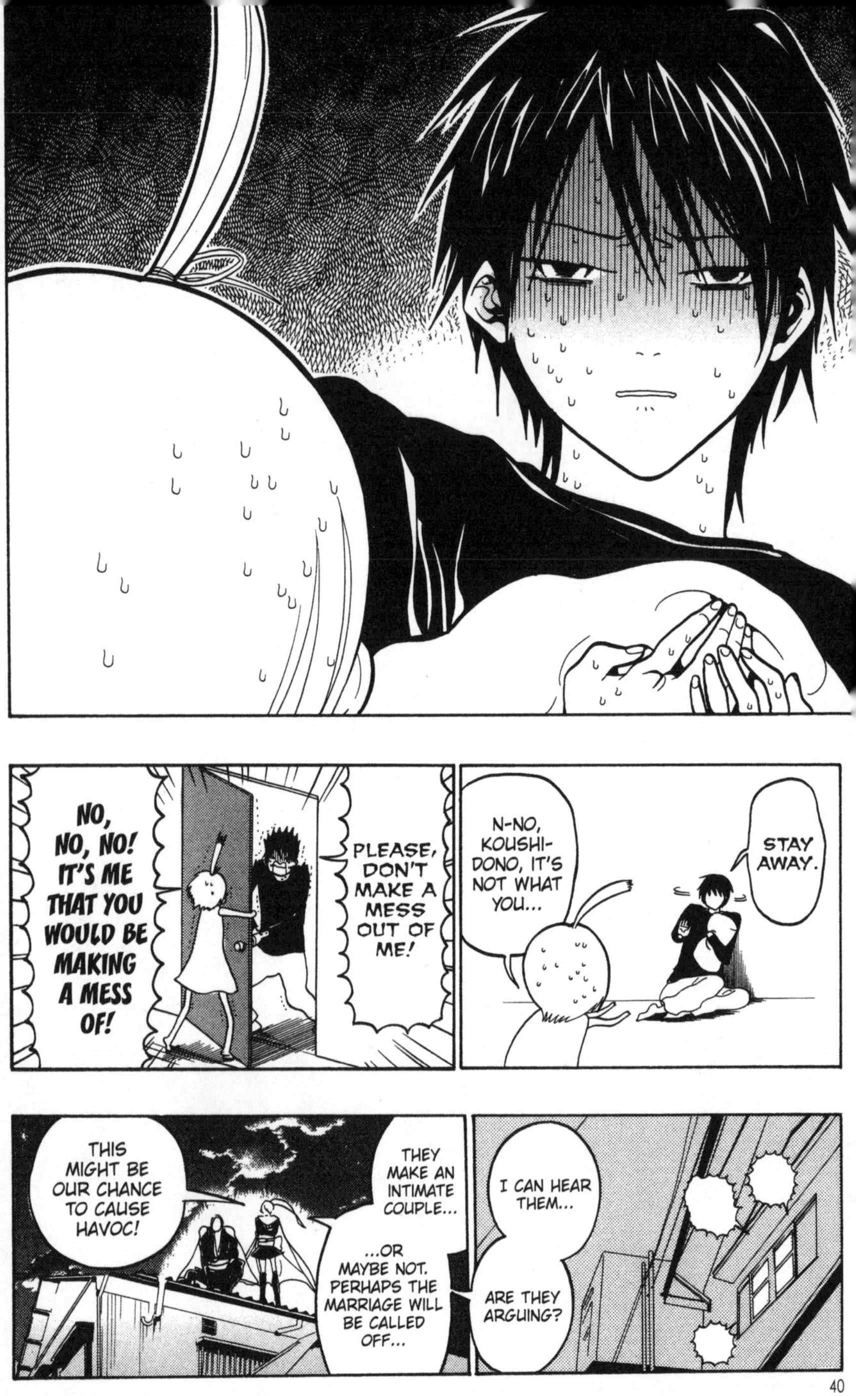
STAY AWAY.
N-NO, KOUSHI-DONO, IT'S NOT WHAT YOU...
PLEASE, DON'T MAKE A MESS OUT OF ME!
NO, NO, NO! IT'S ME THAT YOU WOULD BE MAKING A MESS OF!
I CAN HEAR THEM...
ARE THEY ARGUING?
THEY MAKE AN INTIMATE COUPLE...
...OR MAYBE NOT. PERHAPS THE MARRIAGE WILL BE CALLED OFF...
THIS MIGHT BE OUR CHANCE TO CAUSE HAVOC!

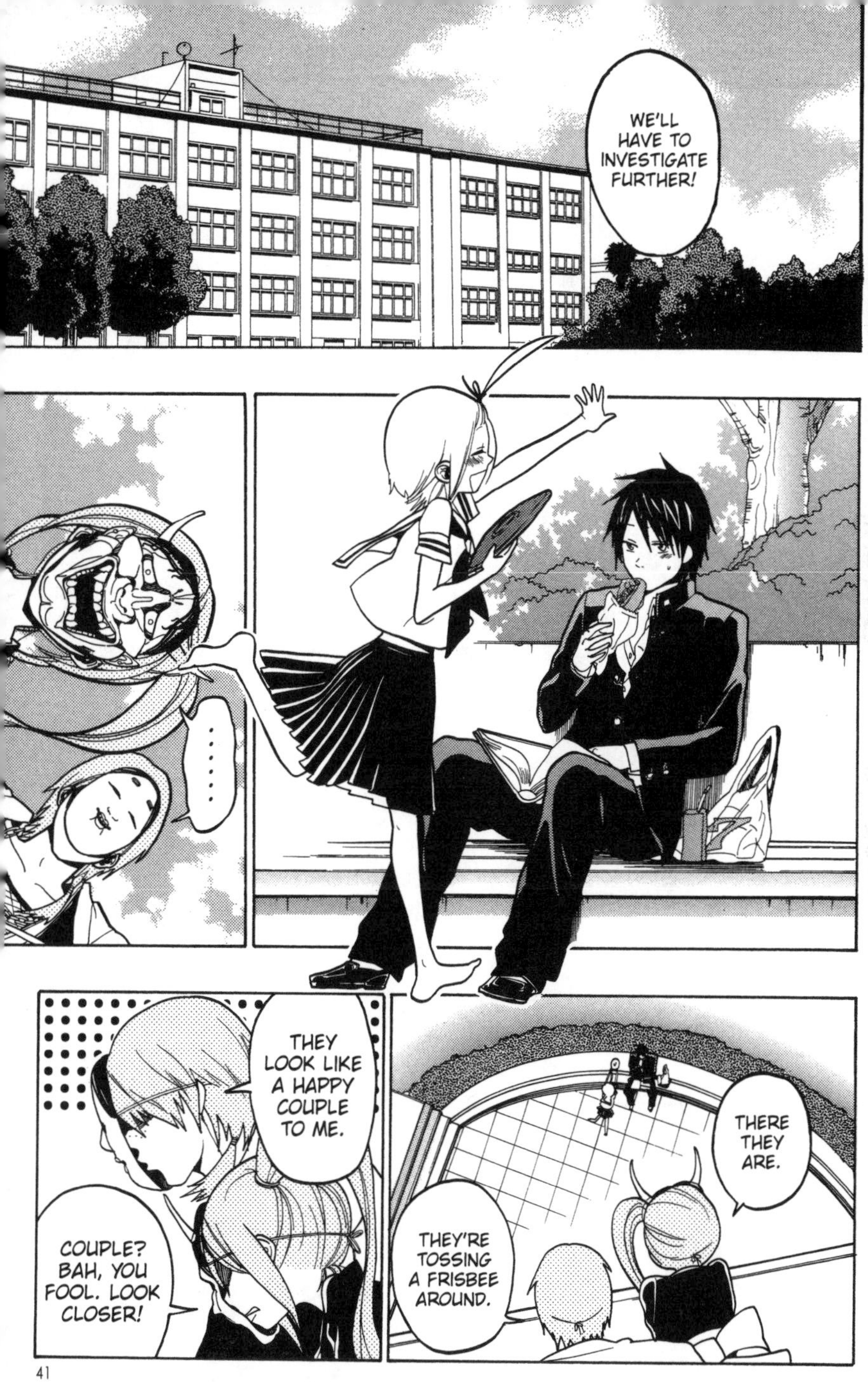
WE'LL HAVE TO INVESTIGATE FURTHER!
......
THERE THEY ARE.
THEY'RE TOSSING A FRISBEE AROUND.
THEY LOOK LIKE A HAPPY COUPLE TO ME.
COUPLE? BAH, YOU FOOL. LOOK CLOSER!

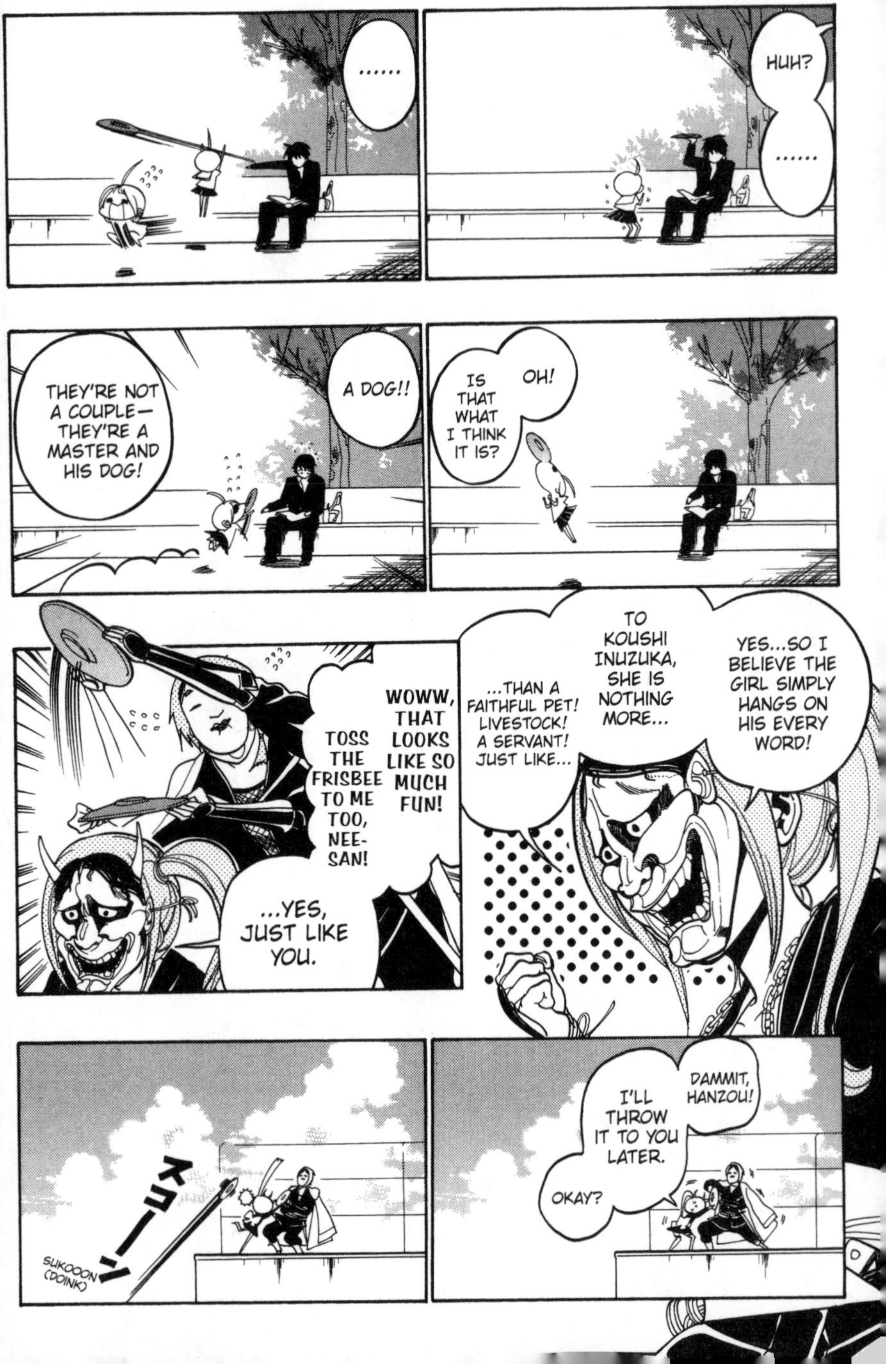
HUH?
......
......
OH!
IS THAT WHAT I THINK IT IS?
A DOG!!
THEY'RE NOT A COUPLE— THEY'RE A MASTER AND HIS DOG!
YES...SO I BELIEVE THE GIRL SIMPLY HANGS ON HIS EVERY WORD!
TO KOUSHI INUZUKA, SHE IS NOTHING MORE...
...THAN A FAITHFUL PET! LIVESTOCK! A SERVANT! JUST LIKE...
WOWW, THAT LOOKS LIKE SO MUCH FUN!
TOSS THE FRISBEE TO ME TOO, NEE-SAN!
...YES, JUST LIKE YOU.
DAMMIT, HANZOU!
I'LL THROW IT TO YOU LATER.
OKAY?
SUKOOON (DOINK)

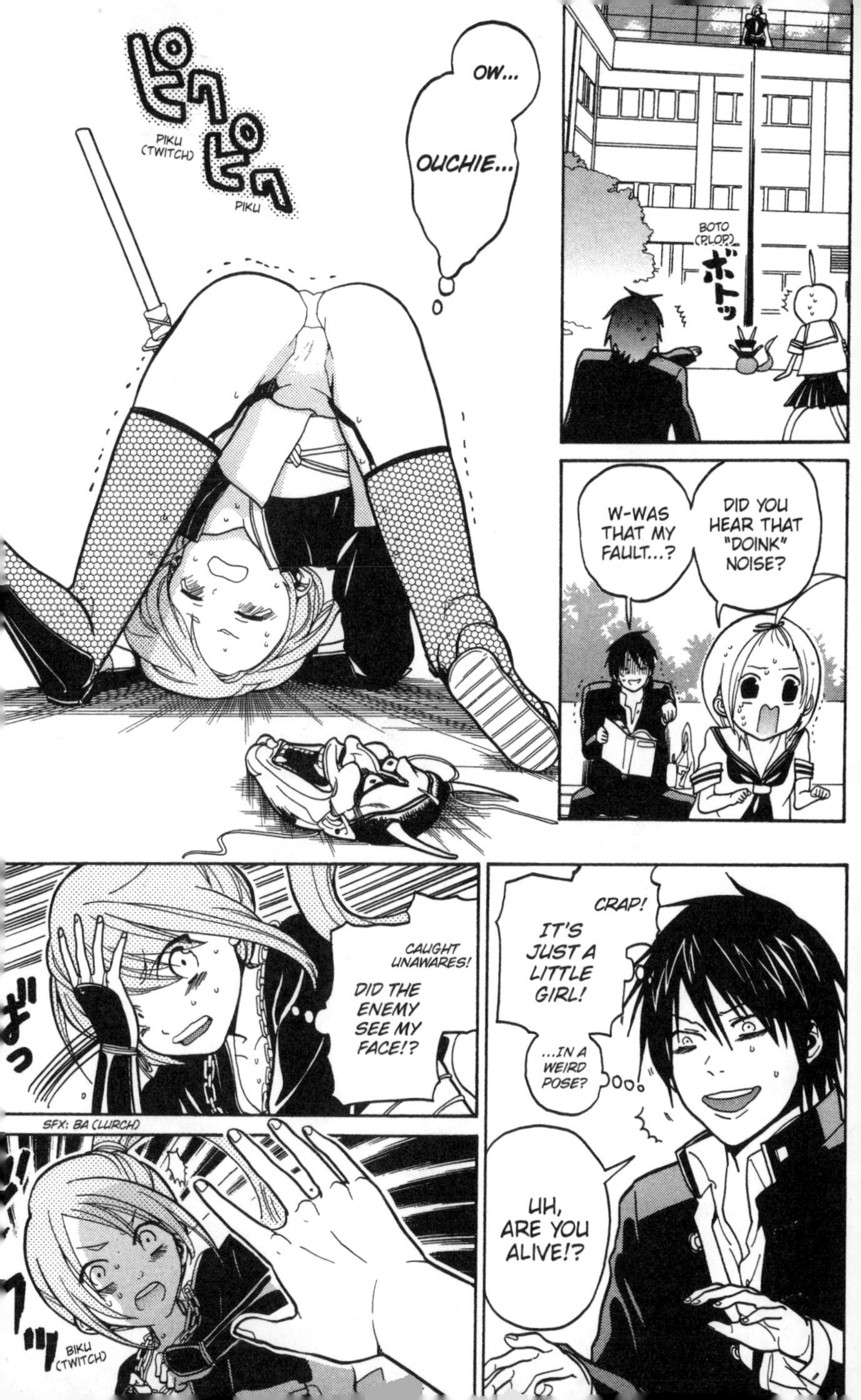
BOTO (PLOP)
DID YOU HEAR THAT "DOINK" NOISE?
W-WAS THAT MY FAULT...?
OW...
OUCHIE...
PIKU (TWITCH)
PIKU
CRAP!
IT'S JUST A LITTLE GIRL!
...IN A WEIRD POSE?
UH, ARE YOU ALIVE!?
CAUGHT UNAWARES!
DID THE ENEMY SEE MY FACE!?
SFX: BA (LURCH)
BIKU (TWITCH)

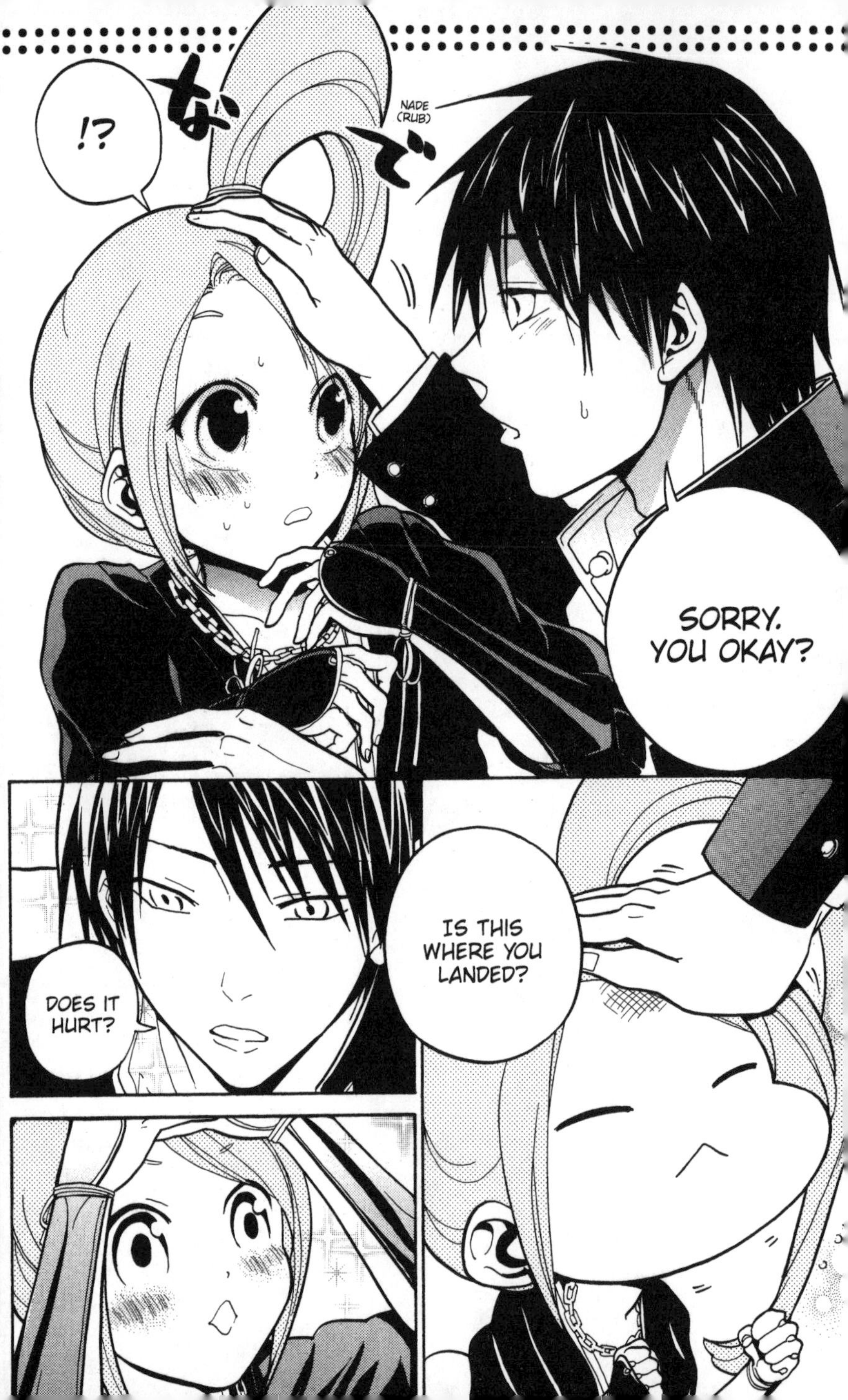
なで
NADE (RUB)
!?
SORRY. YOU OKAY?
IS THIS WHERE YOU LANDED?
DOES IT HURT?

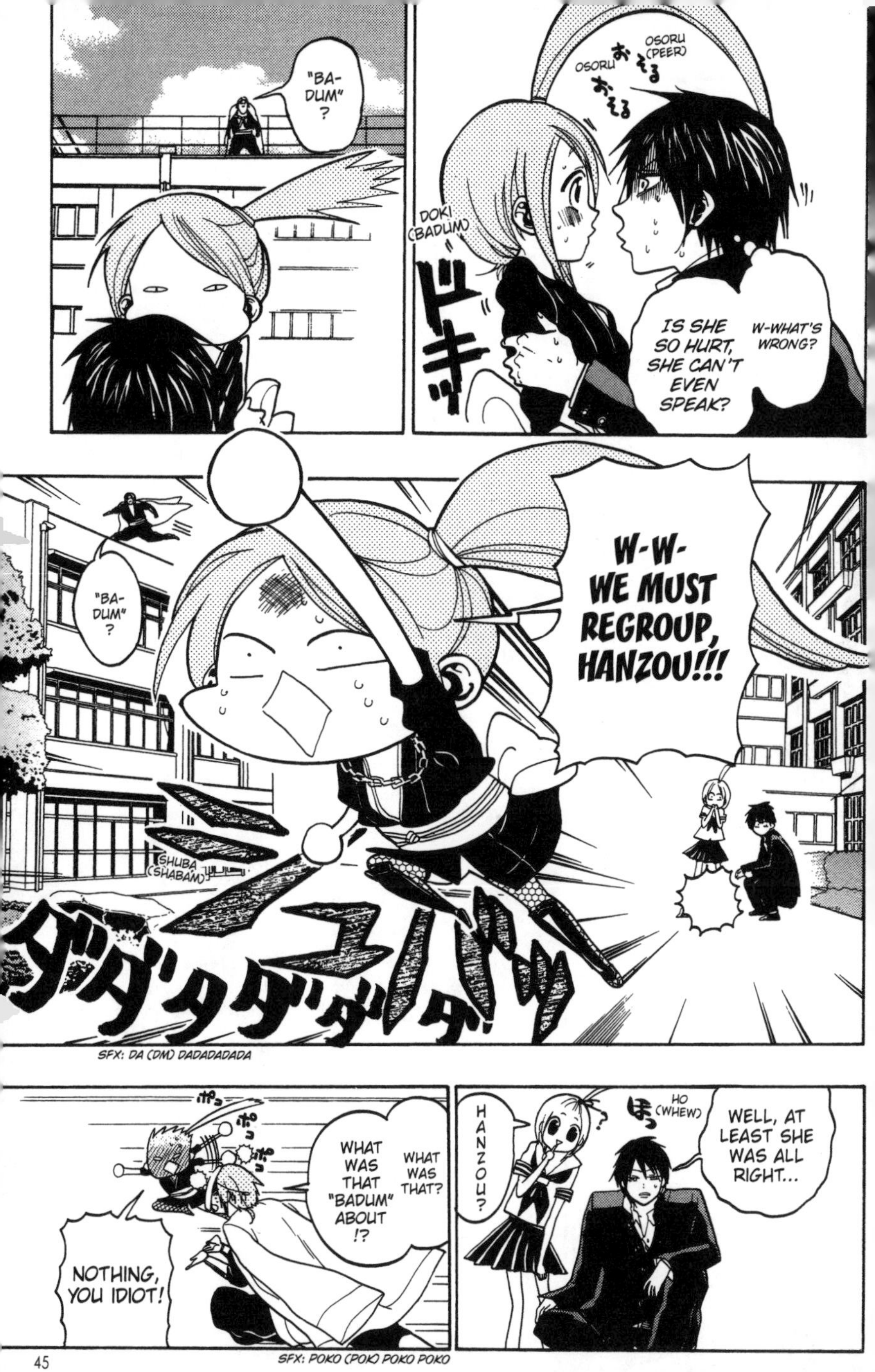
OSORU (PEER)
OSORU
DOKI (BADUM)
W-WHAT'S WRONG?
IS SHE SO HURT, SHE CAN'T EVEN SPEAK?
"BA-DUM"?
W-W-WE MUST REGROUP, HANZOU!!!
"BA-DUM"?
SHUBA (SHABAM)
SFX: DA (DM) DADADADADA
HANZOU?
HO (WHEW)
WELL, AT LEAST SHE WAS ALL RIGHT...
WHAT WAS THAT?
WHAT WAS THAT "BADUM" ABOUT!?
NOTHING, YOU IDIOT!
SFX: POKO (POK) POKO POKO

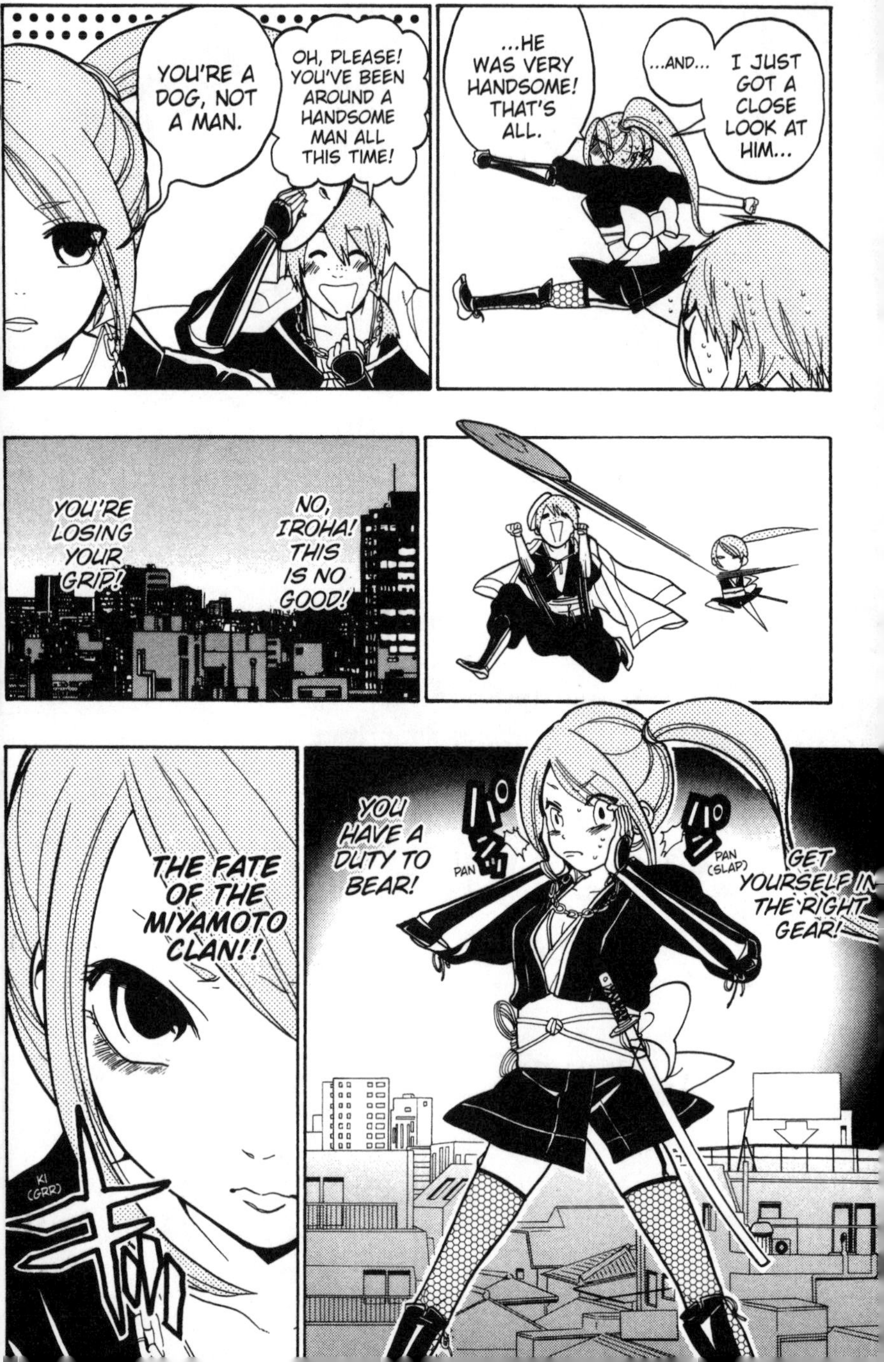
I JUST GOT A CLOSE LOOK AT HIM...
...AND...
...HE WAS VERY HANDSOME! THAT'S ALL.
OH, PLEASE! YOU'VE BEEN AROUND A HANDSOME MAN ALL THIS TIME!
YOU'RE A DOG, NOT A MAN.
NO, IROHA! THIS IS NO GOOD!
YOU'RE LOSING YOUR GRIP!
GET YOURSELF IN THE RIGHT GEAR!
PAN (SLAP)
PAN
YOU HAVE A DUTY TO BEAR!
THE FATE OF THE MIYAMOTO CLAN!!
KI (GRR)

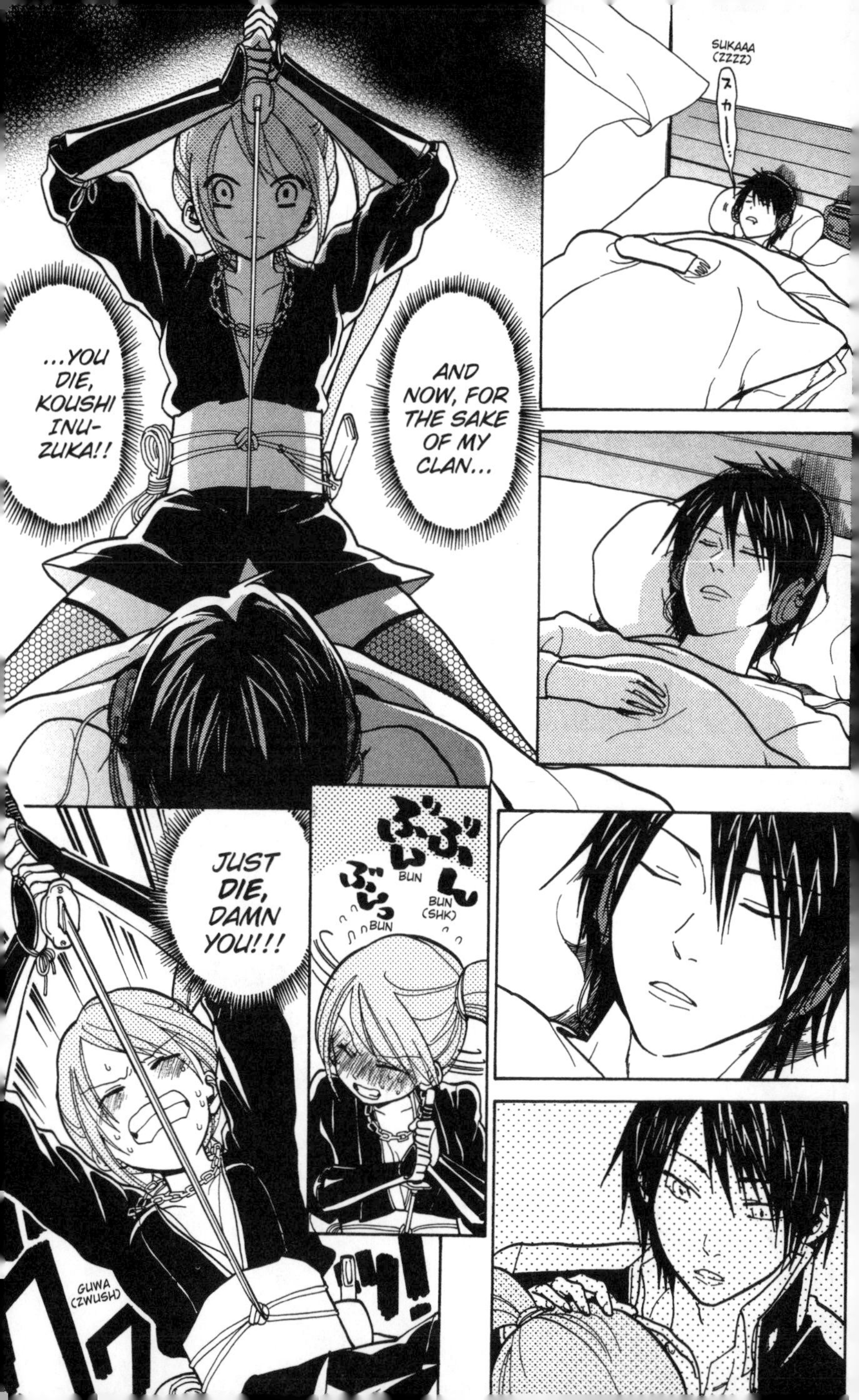
SUKAAA (ZZZZ)
スカー…
AND NOW, FOR THE SAKE OF MY CLAN...
...YOU DIE, KOUSHI INU-ZUKA!!
ぶんぶん
BUN
BUN (SHK)
ぶんっ
BUN
JUST DIE, DAMN YOU!!!
GUWA (ZWUSH)

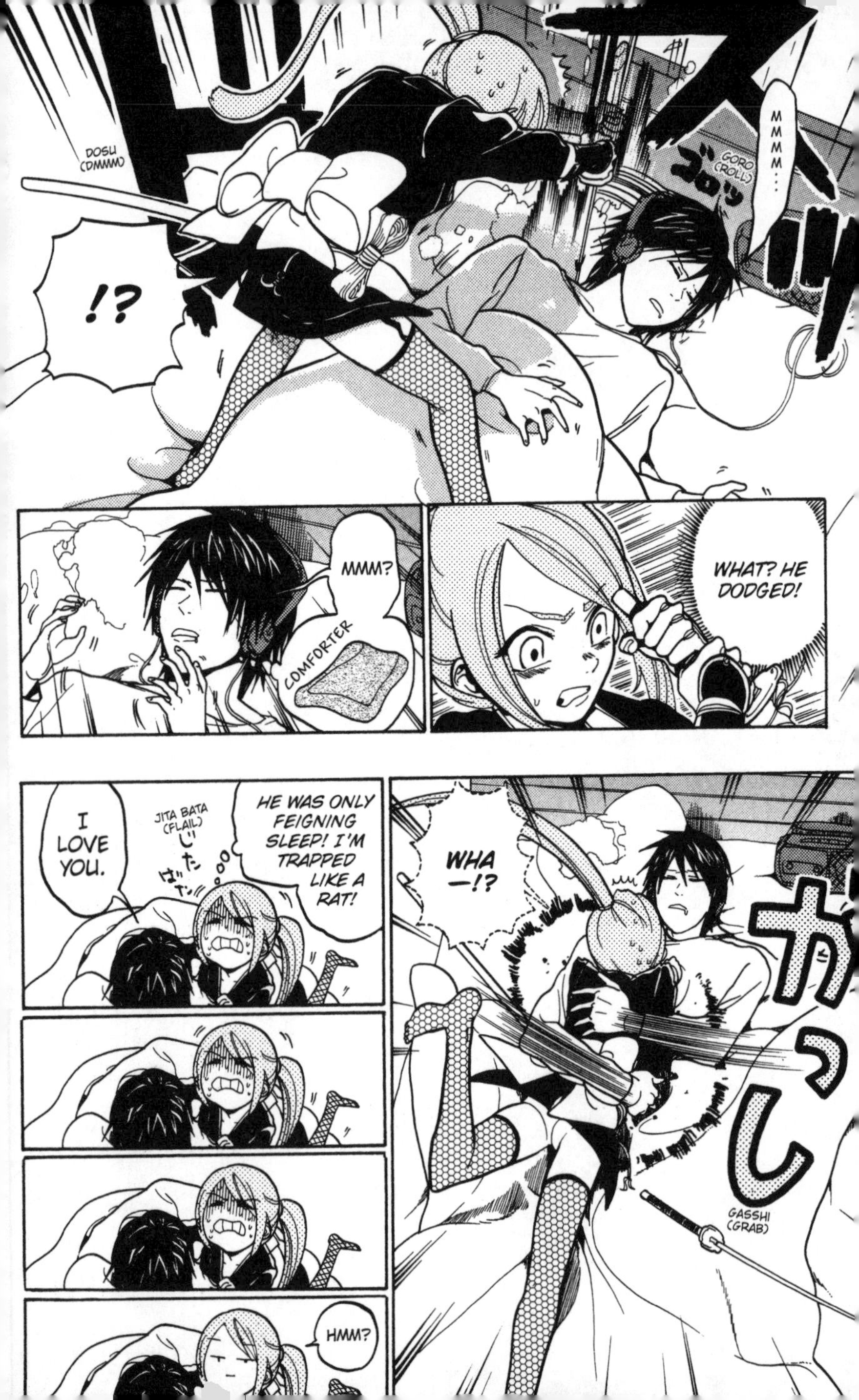
MMMM...
GORO (ROLL)
ゴロッ
DOSU (DMMM)
!?
WHAT? HE DODGED!
MMM?
COMFORTER
WHA—!?
がっし
GASSHI (GRAB)
HE WAS ONLY FEIGNING SLEEP! I'M TRAPPED LIKE A RAT!
JITA BATA (FLAIL)
じたばた
I LOVE YOU.
HMM?

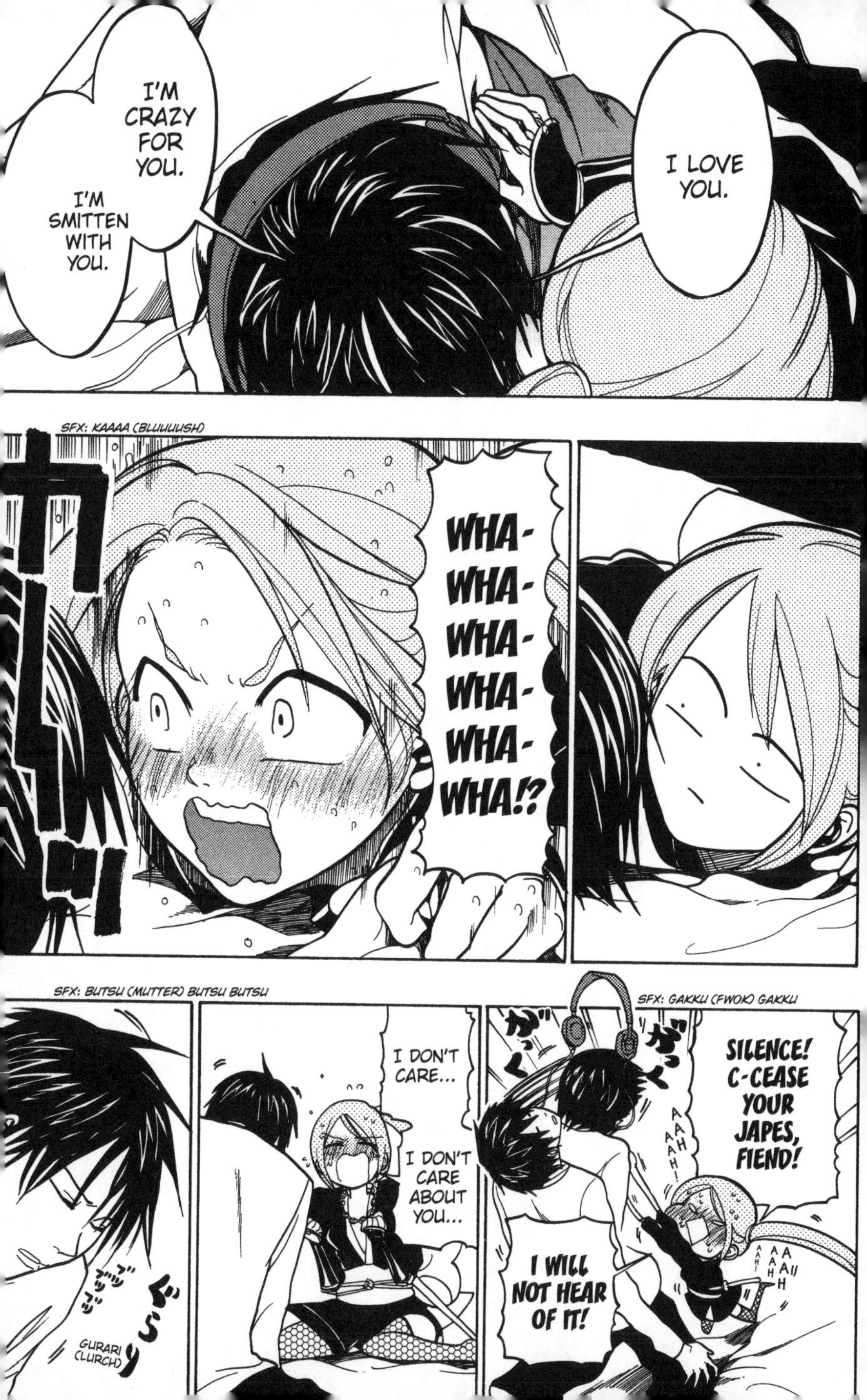
I LOVE YOU.
I'M CRAZY FOR YOU.
I'M SMITTEN WITH YOU.
SFX: KAAAA (BLUUUUSH)
WHA-WHA-WHA-WHA-WHA-WHA!?
SFX: GAKKU (FWOK) GAKKU
SILENCE! C-CEASE YOUR JAPES, FIEND!
AAH AAH AAH!
AAH! AAH AAH AAH
I WILL NOT HEAR OF IT!
I DON'T CARE...
I DON'T CARE ABOUT YOU...
SFX: BUTSU (MUTTER) BUTSU BUTSU
GURARI (LURCH)

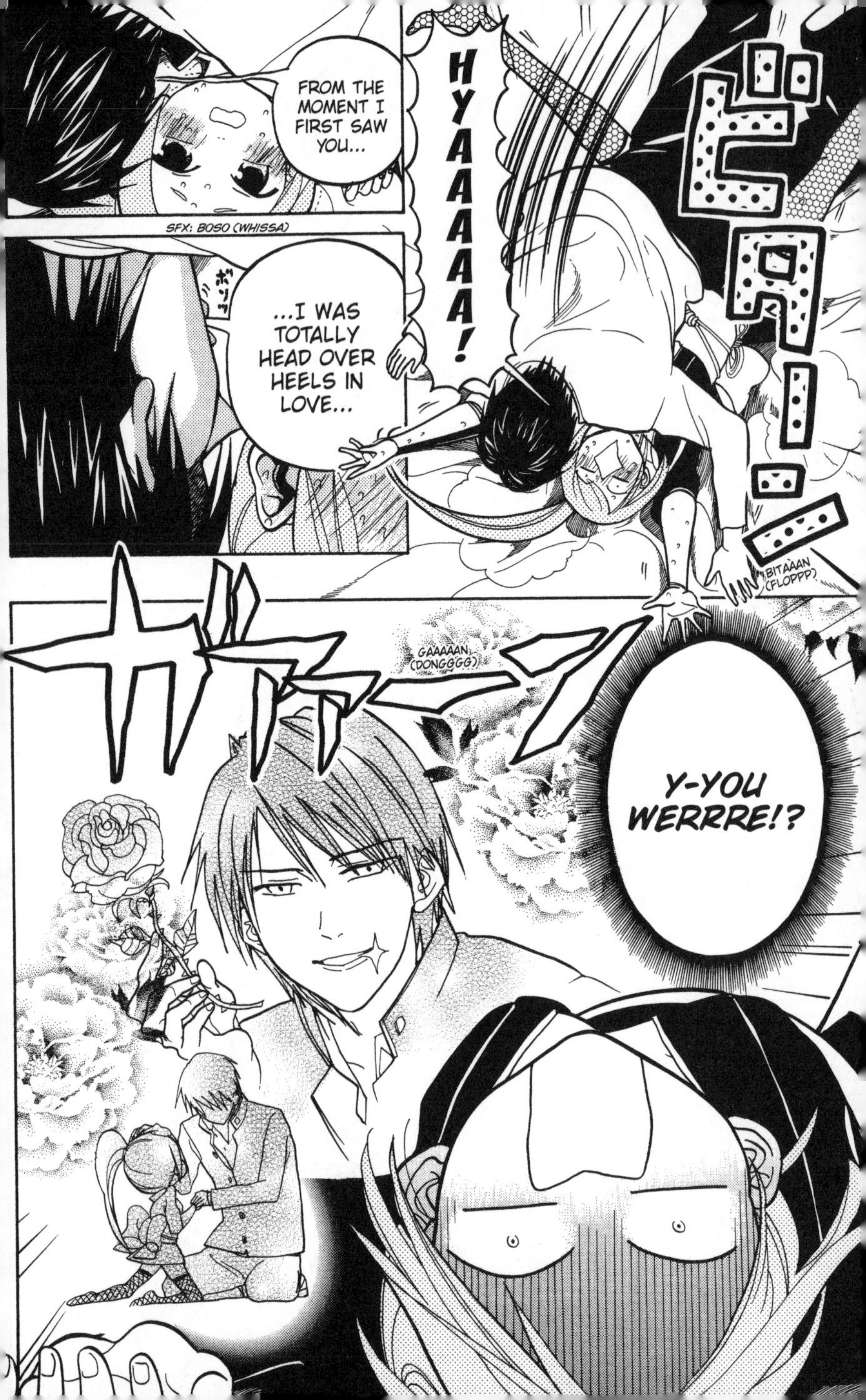
HYAAAAA!
BITAAAN (FLOPPP)
FROM THE MOMENT I FIRST SAW YOU...
SFX: BOSO (WHISSA)
...I WAS TOTALLY HEAD OVER HEELS IN LOVE...
GAAAAAN (DONGGGG)
Y-YOU WERRRE!?

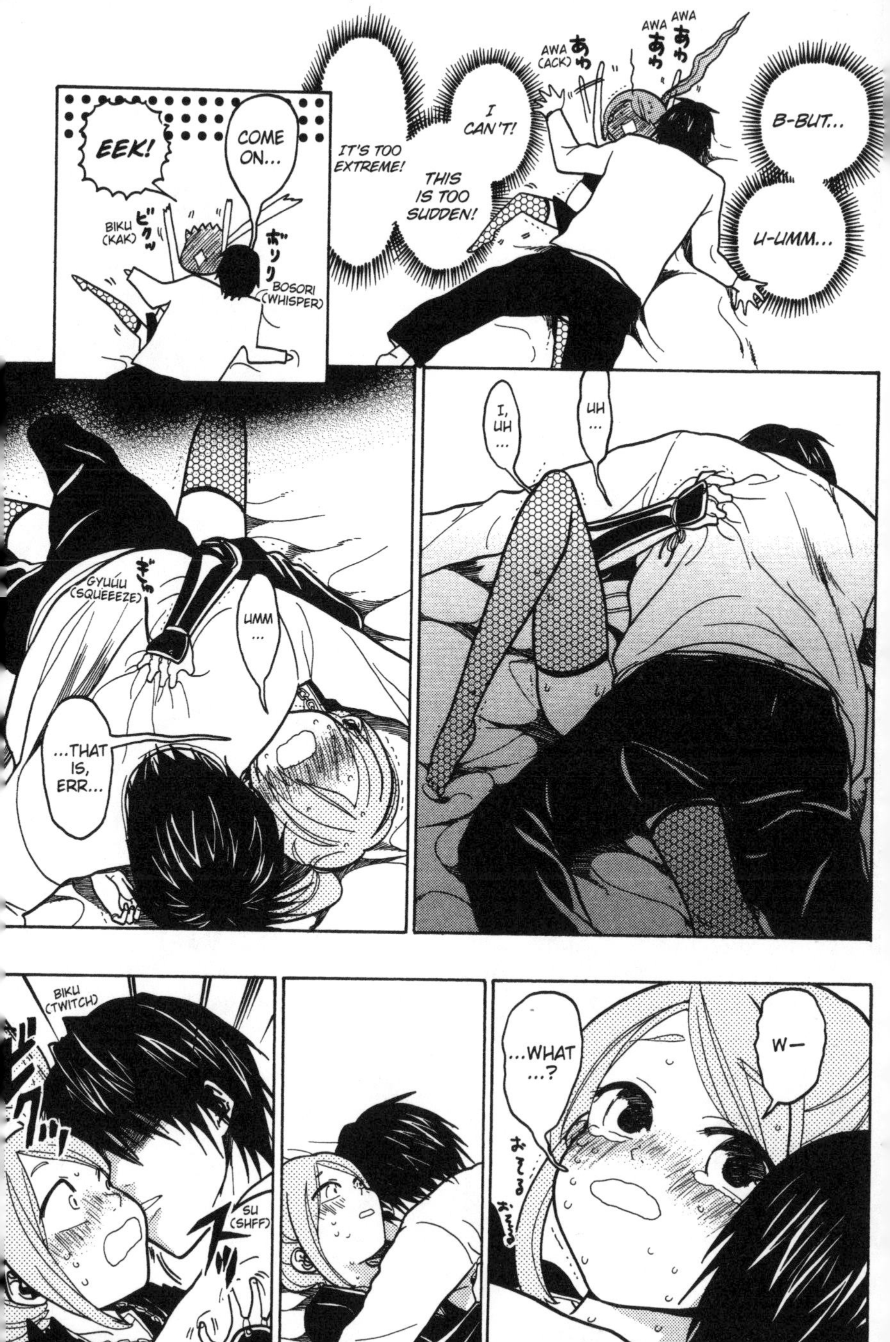
AWA あゎ
AWA あゎ
AWA (ACK) あゎ
B-BUT...
U-UMM...
I CAN'T!
THIS IS TOO SUDDEN!
IT'S TOO EXTREME!
COME ON...
EEK!
BOSORI (WHISPER) ボソリ
BIKU (KAK) ビクッ
UH ...
I, UH ...
UMM ...
GYUUU (SQUEEEZE) ぎゅ
...THAT IS, ERR...
W—
...WHAT ...?
おそる
おそる
BIKU (TWITCH) ビクッ
SU (SHFF)

SFX: OSORU (PEER) OSORU

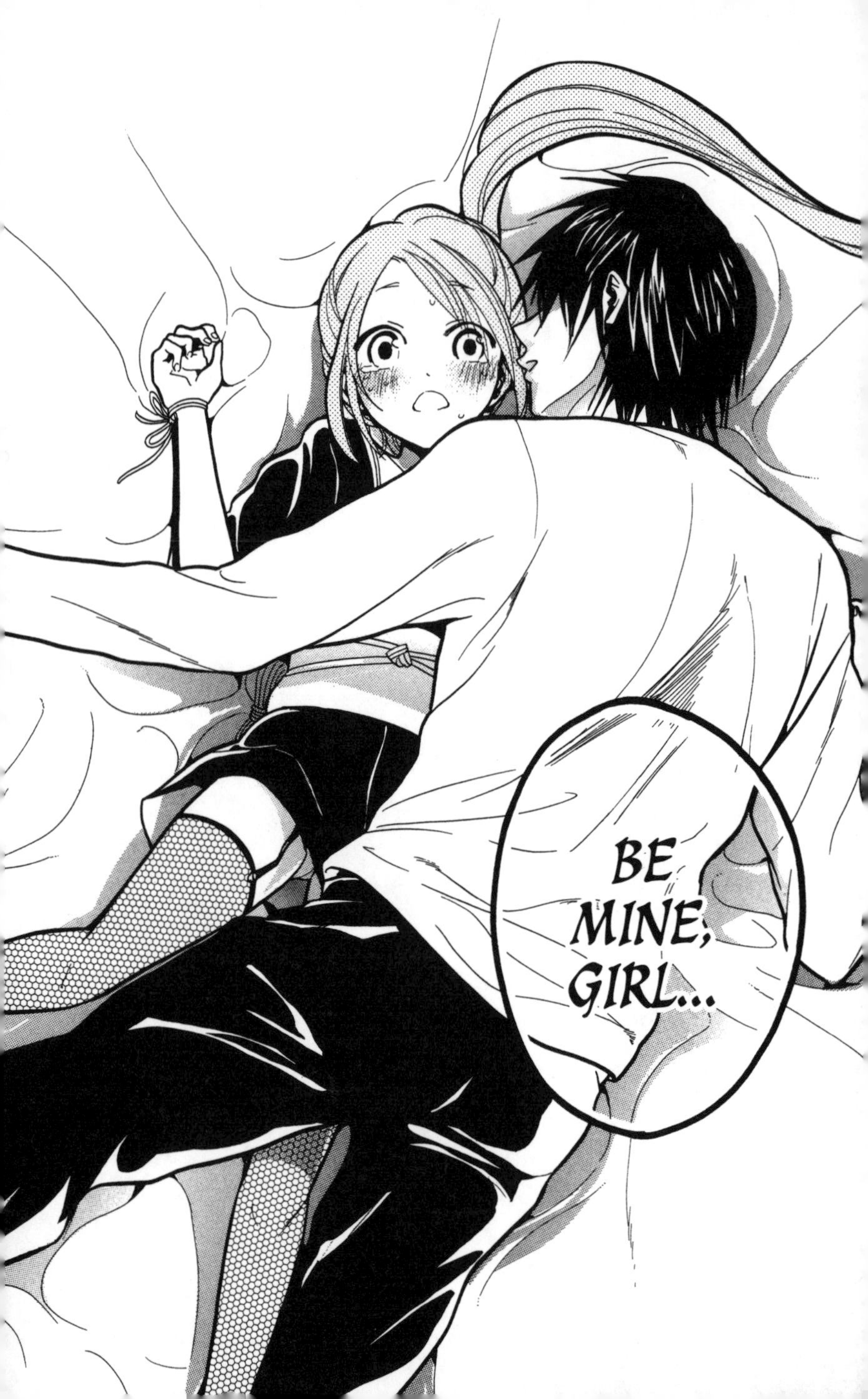
BE MINE, GIRL...

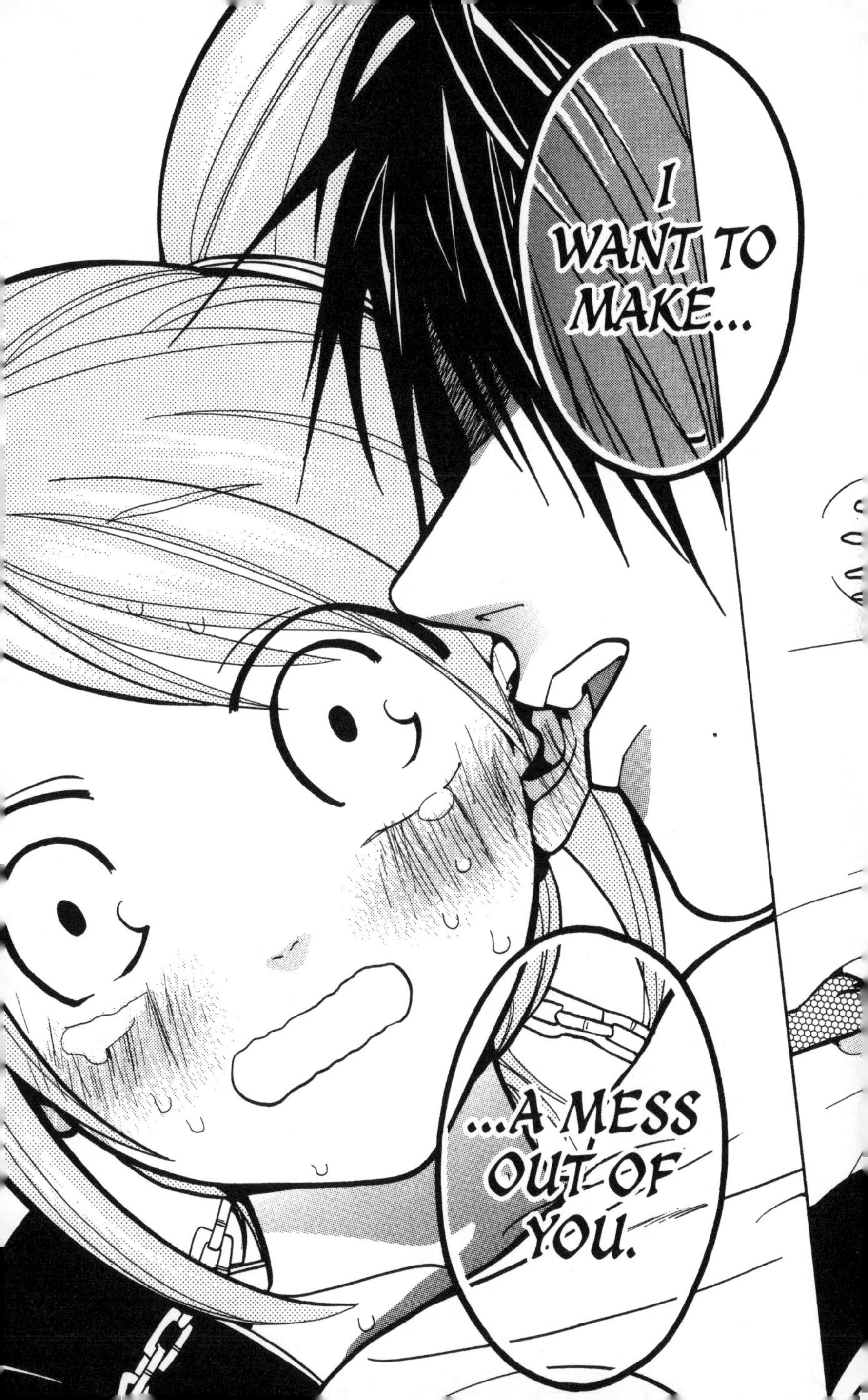
I WANT TO MAKE...
...A MESS OUT OF YOU.

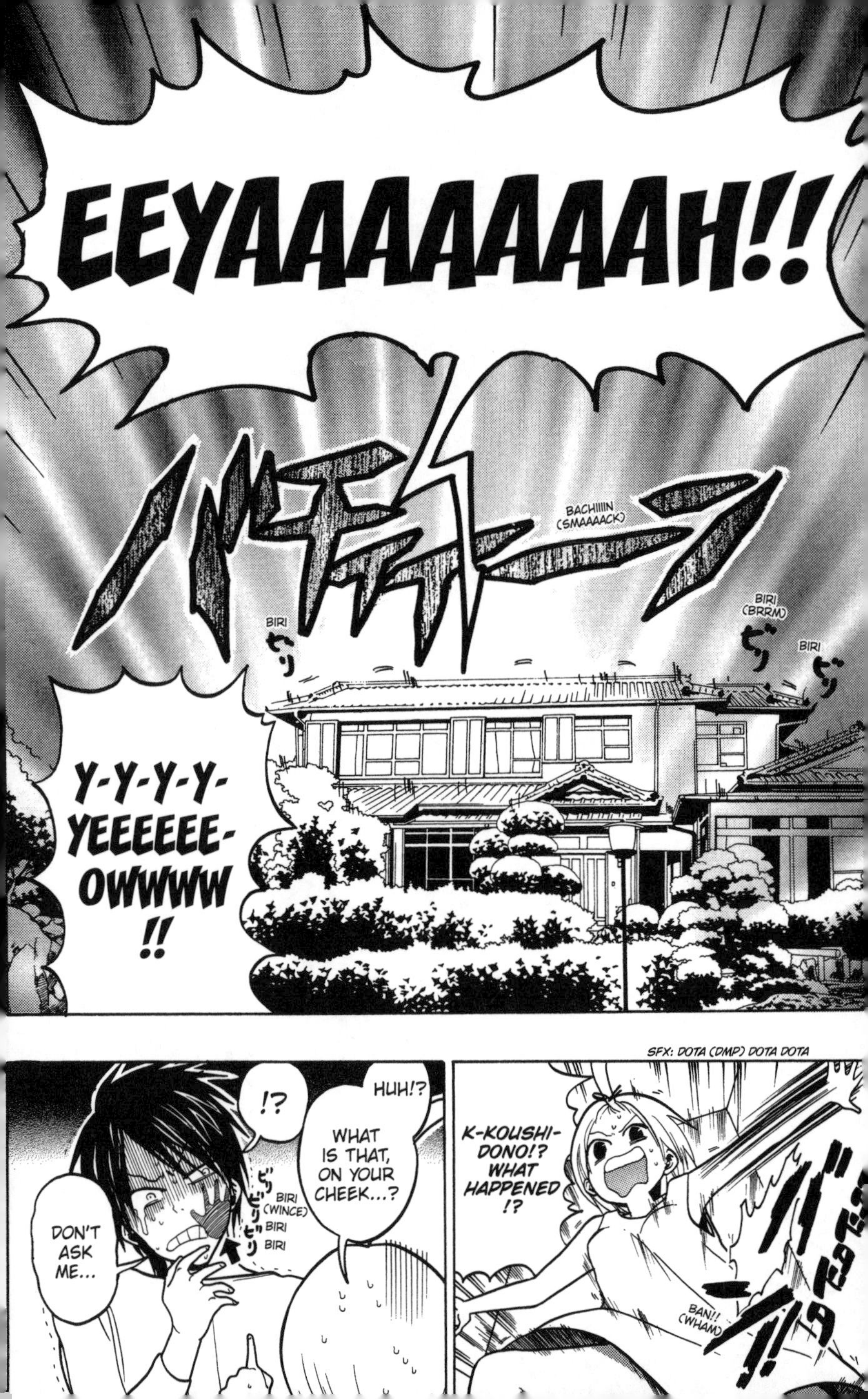
EEYAAAAAAAAH!!
BACHIIIIN (SMAAAACK)
BIRI (BRRM)
BIRI
BIRI
Y-Y-Y-Y-YEEEEEE-OWWWW!!
SFX: DOTA (DMP) DOTA DOTA
K-KOUSHI-DONO!? WHAT HAPPENED!?
BAN!! (WHAM)
HUH!?
WHAT IS THAT, ON YOUR CHEEK...?
!?
BIRI (WINCE) BIRI BIRI
DON'T ASK ME...

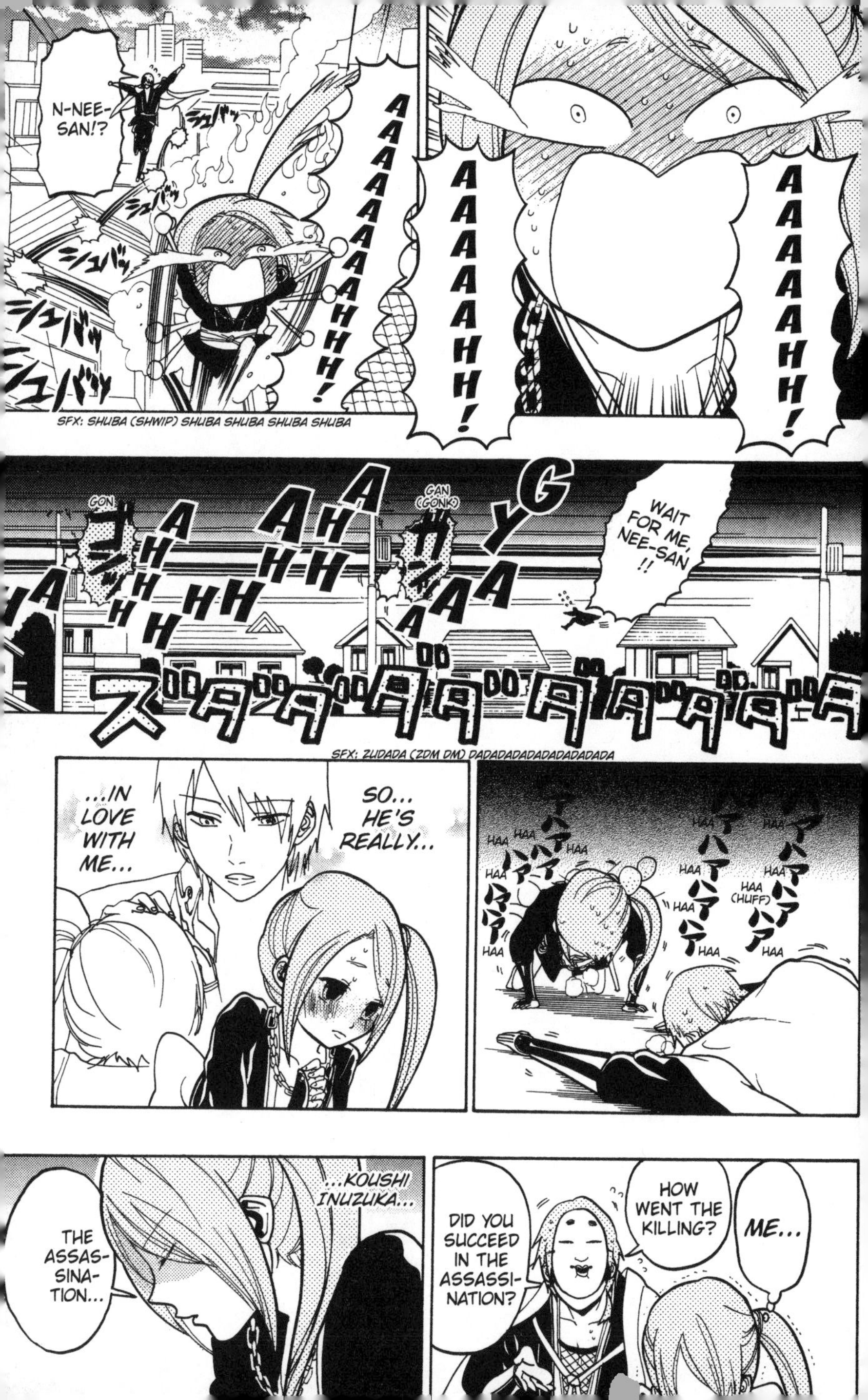

AAAAAAAHH!
AAAAAAAHH!
AAAAAAAAAAHHH!
N-NEE-SAN!?
SFX: SHUBA (SHWIP) SHUBA SHUBA SHUBA SHUBA
WAIT FOR ME, NEE-SAN!!
GYAAAAA
GAN (GONK)
AHHHHH
AHHHHHH
GON
SFX: ZUDADA (ZDM DM) DADADADADADADADADADA
HAA HAA HAA HAA HAA
HAA HAA (HUFF) HAA HAA HAA
SO... HE'S REALLY...
...IN LOVE WITH ME...
ME...
HOW WENT THE KILLING?
DID YOU SUCCEED IN THE ASSASSINATION?
...KOUSHI INUZUKA...
THE ASSAS-SINA-TION...

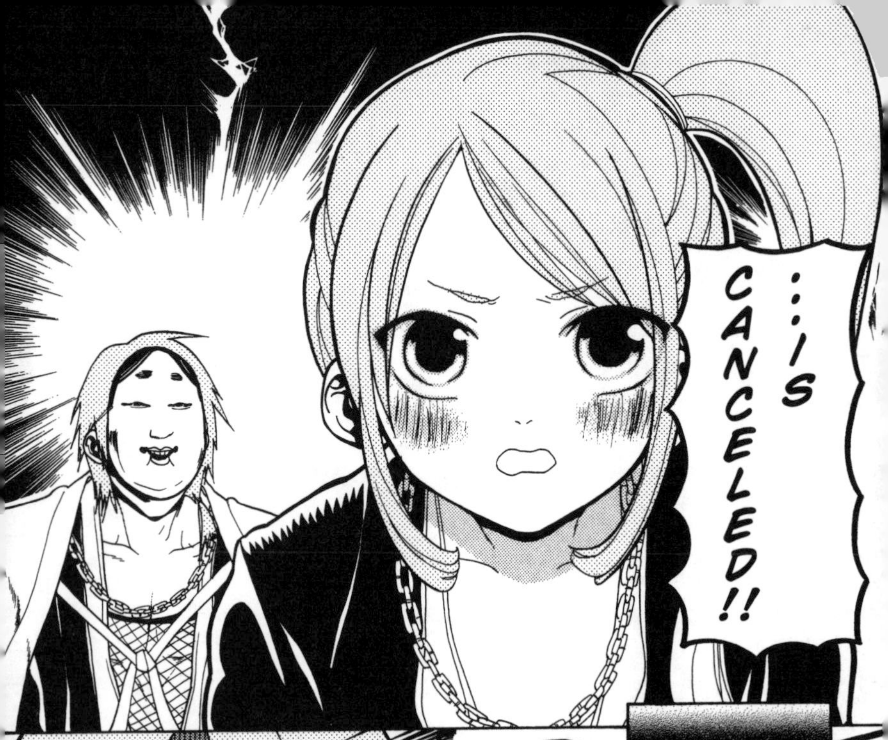
...IS CANCELED!!
WHAAAAAT!!??
PISHÄA (CRAAKK)

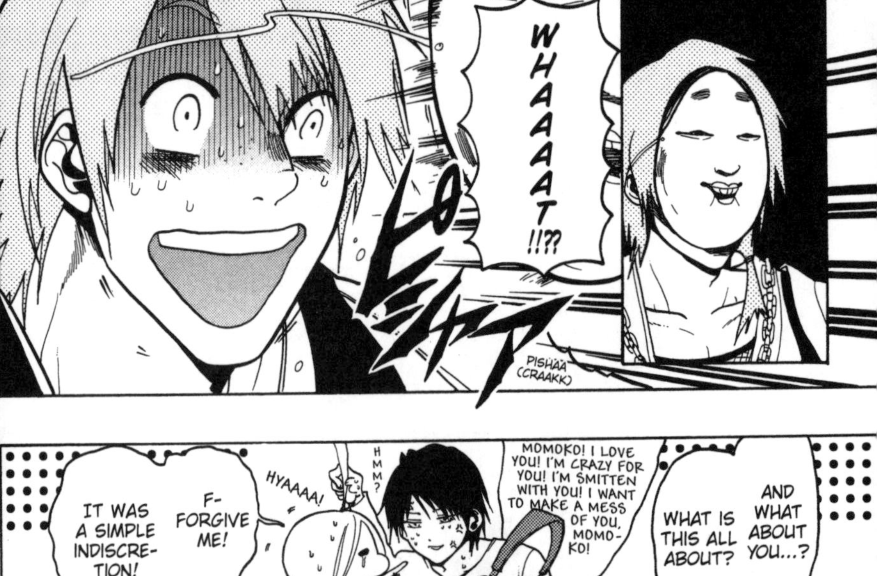
AND WHAT ABOUT YOU...?
WHAT IS THIS ALL ABOUT?
MOMOKO! I LOVE YOU! I'M CRAZY FOR YOU! I'M SMITTEN WITH YOU! I WANT TO MAKE A MESS OF YOU, MOMOKO!
HMM?
HYAAAA!
F-FORGIVE ME!
IT WAS A SIMPLE INDISCRE-TION!

CHAPTER 8. AN ASSASSINATION PLOT WITHOUT HONOR – END

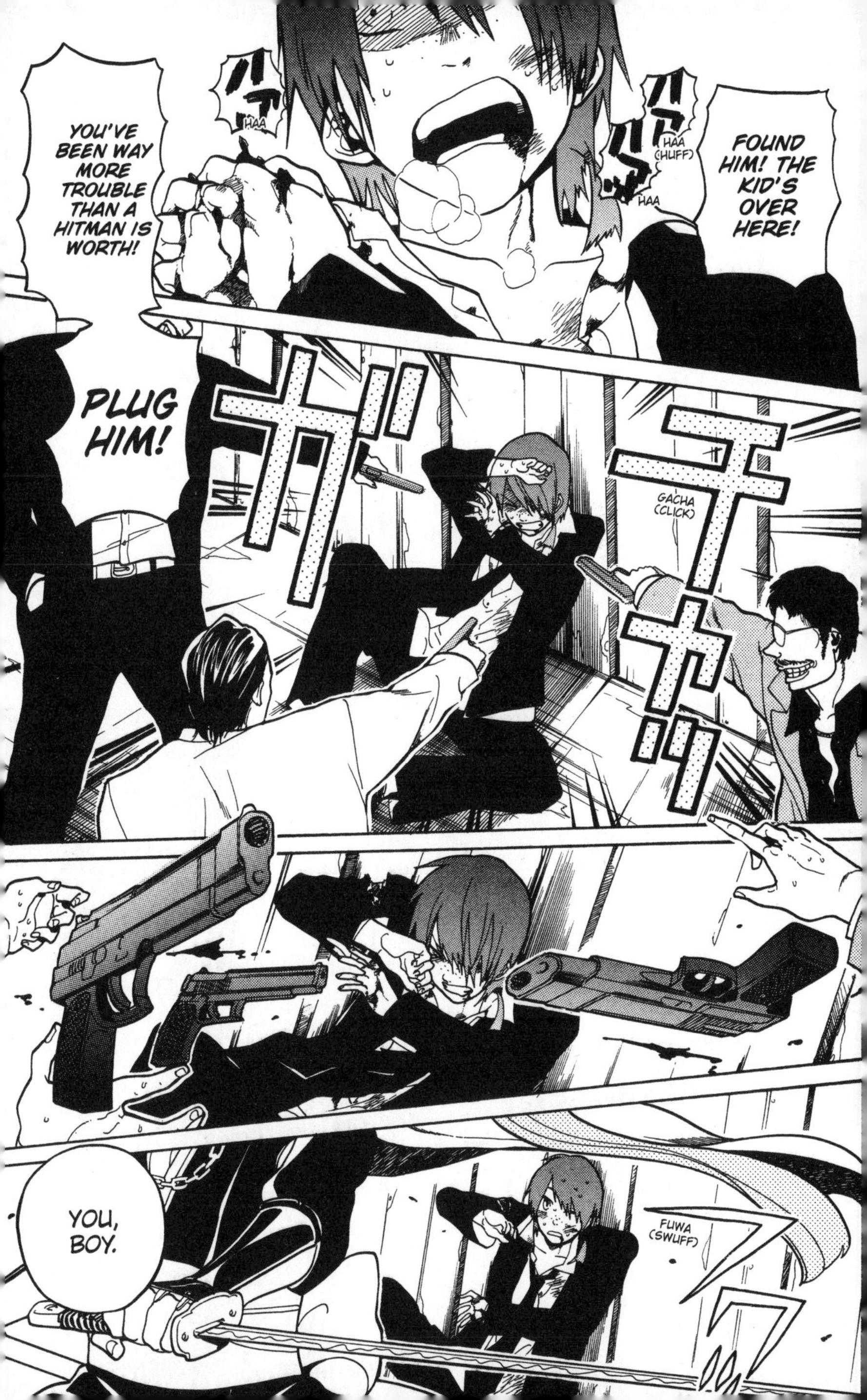
FOUND HIM! THE KID'S OVER HERE!
HAA (HUFF)
HAA
HAA
YOU'VE BEEN WAY MORE TROUBLE THAN A HITMAN IS WORTH!
GACHA (CLICK)
PLUG HIM!
FUWA (SWUFF)
YOU, BOY.

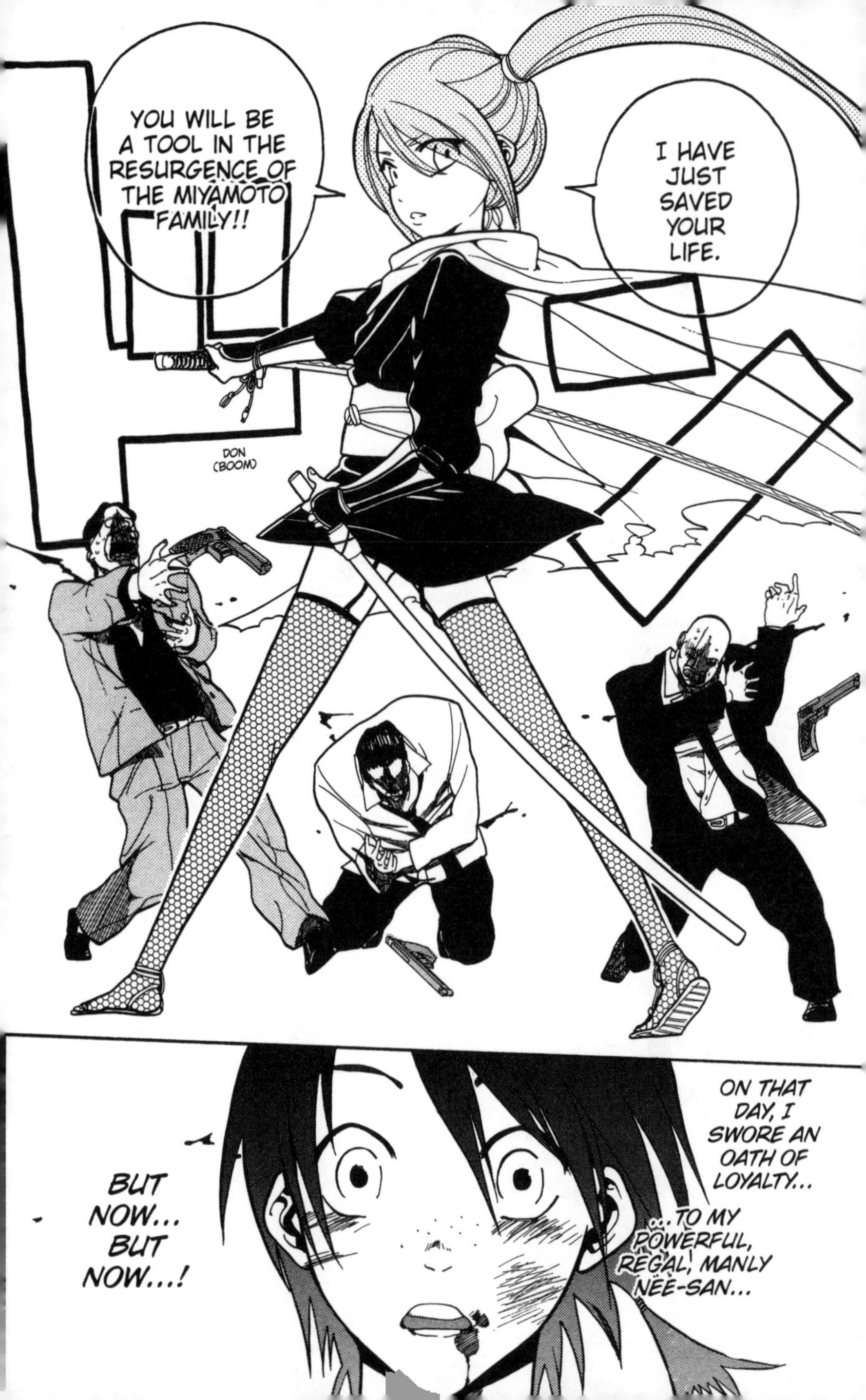
I HAVE JUST SAVED YOUR LIFE.
YOU WILL BE A TOOL IN THE RESURGENCE OF THE MIYAMOTO FAMILY!!
DON (BOOM)
ON THAT DAY, I SWORE AN OATH OF LOYALTY...
...TO MY POWERFUL, REGAL, MANLY NÉE-SAN...
BUT NOW... BUT NOW...!

9. HOW LONG CAN THE PET DOG "STAY"?

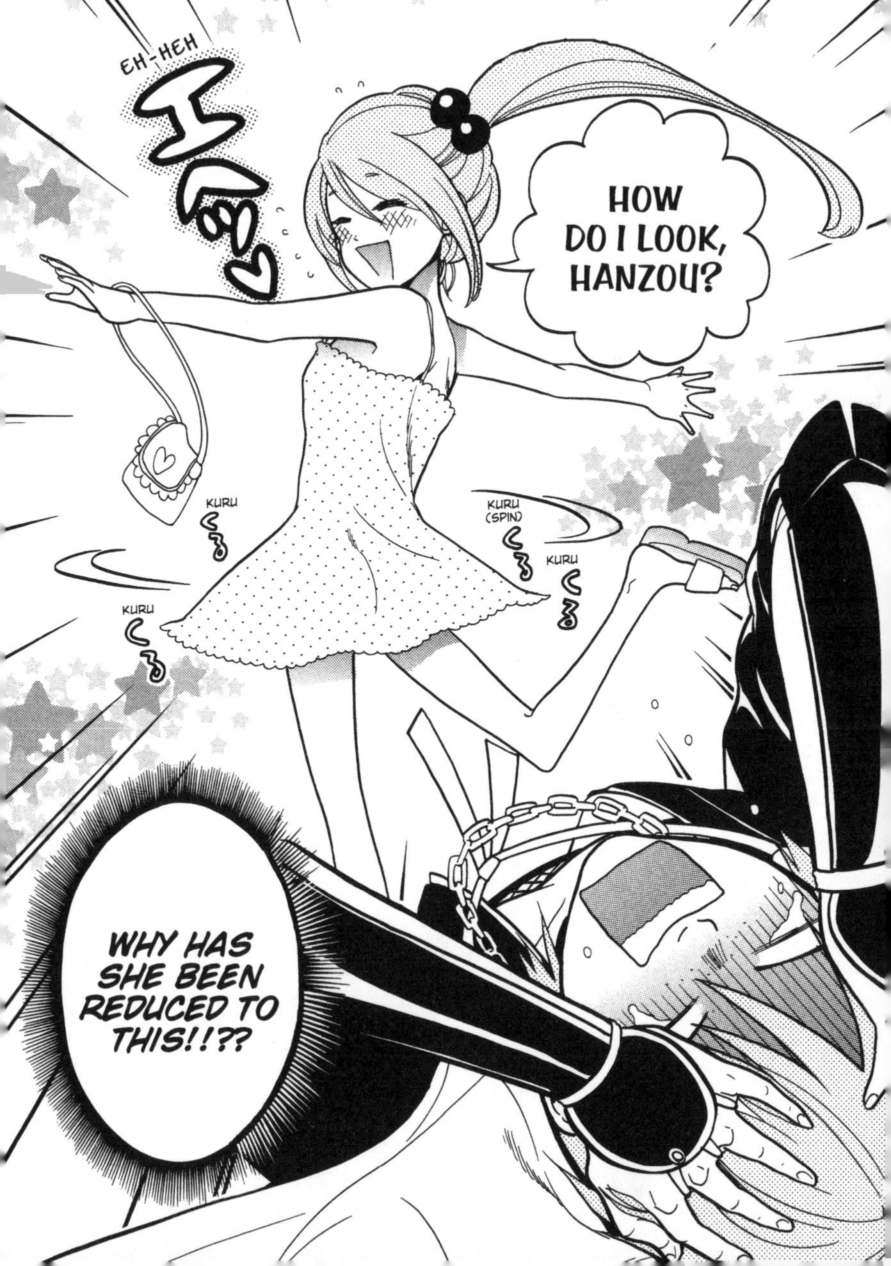
HOW DO I LOOK, HANZOU?
EH-HEH
KURU (SPIN)
KURU
KURU
KURU
WHY HAS SHE BEEN REDUCED TO THIS!!??

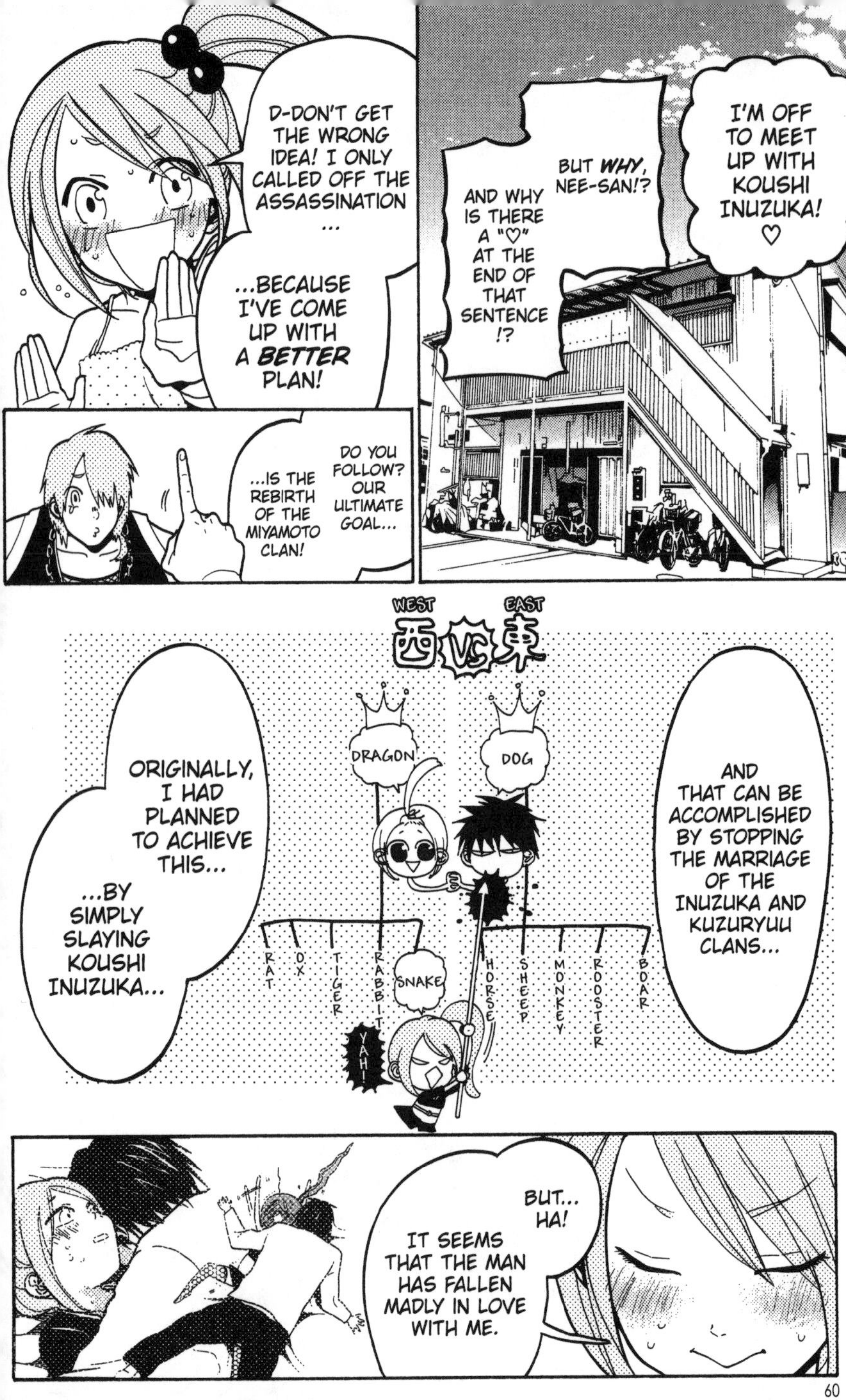
I'M OFF TO MEET UP WITH KOUSHI INUZUKA! ♡
BUT *WHY*, NEE-SAN!?
AND WHY IS THERE A "♡" AT THE END OF THAT SENTENCE!?
D-DON'T GET THE WRONG IDEA! I ONLY CALLED OFF THE ASSASSINATION ...
...BECAUSE I'VE COME UP WITH A *BETTER* PLAN!
DO YOU FOLLOW? OUR ULTIMATE GOAL...
...IS THE REBIRTH OF THE MIYAMOTO CLAN!
WEST 西 VS 東 EAST
AND THAT CAN BE ACCOMPLISHED BY STOPPING THE MARRIAGE OF THE INUZUKA AND KUZURYUU CLANS...
DRAGON
DOG
RAT
OX
TIGER
RABBIT
SNAKE
HORSE
SHEEP
MONKEY
ROOSTER
BOAR
YAH!
ORIGINALLY, I HAD PLANNED TO ACHIEVE THIS...
...BY SIMPLY SLAYING KOUSHI INUZUKA...
BUT... HA!
IT SEEMS THAT THE MAN HAS FALLEN MADLY IN LOVE WITH ME.

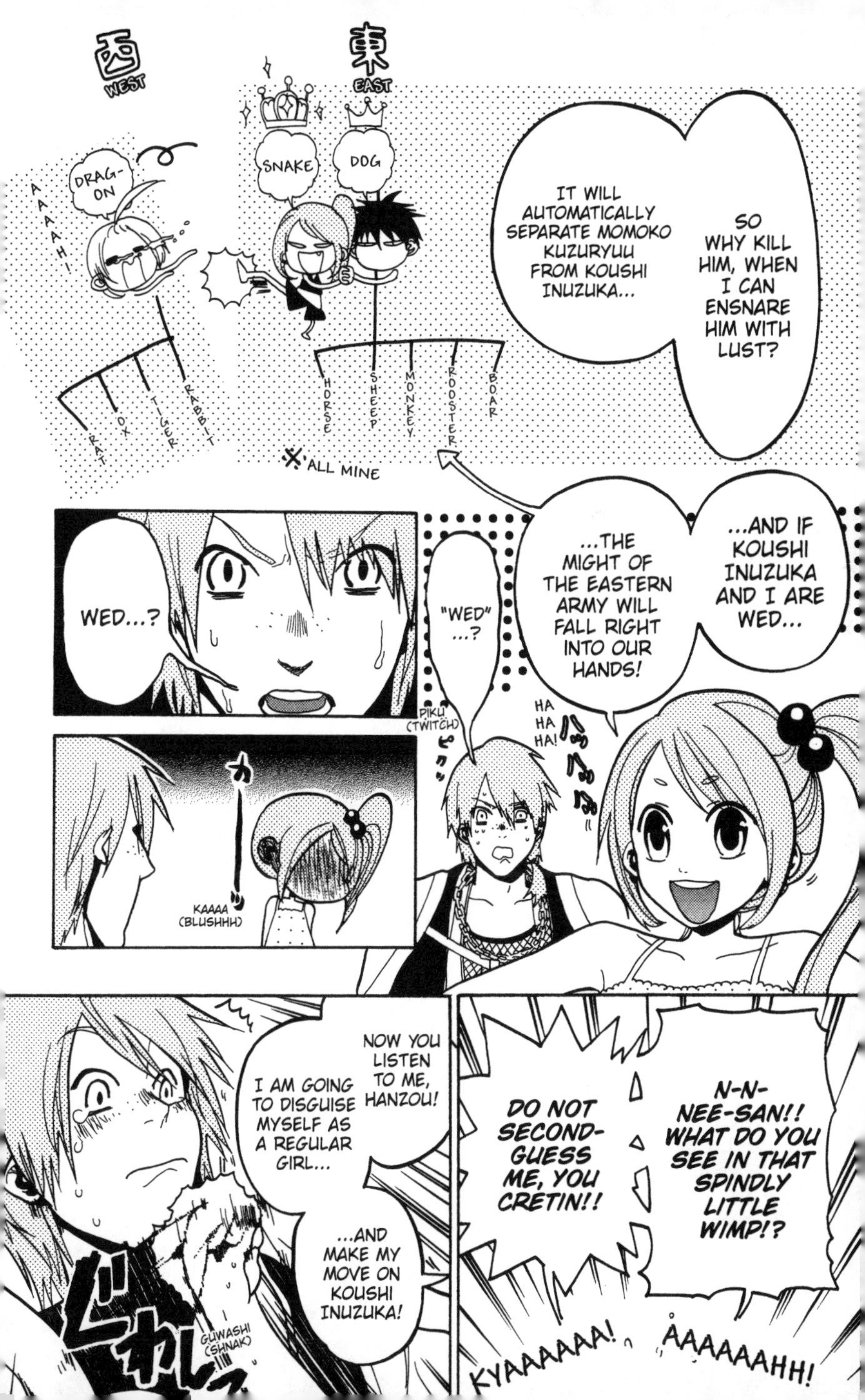
SO WHY KILL HIM, WHEN I CAN ENSNARE HIM WITH LUST?
IT WILL AUTOMATICALLY SEPARATE MOMOKO KUZURYUU FROM KOUSHI INUZUKA...
EAST
DOG
SNAKE
HORSE
SHEEP
MONKEY
ROOSTER
BOAR
WEST
DRAG-ON
AAAAAH!
RAT
OX
TIGER
RABBIT
※ALL MINE
...AND IF KOUSHI INUZUKA AND I ARE WED...
...THE MIGHT OF THE EASTERN ARMY WILL FALL RIGHT INTO OUR HANDS!
HA HA HA!
"WED" ...?
PIKU (TWITCH)
WED...?
KAAAA (BLUSHHH)
N-N-NEE-SAN!! WHAT DO YOU SEE IN THAT SPINDLY LITTLE WIMP!?
DO NOT SECOND-GUESS ME, YOU CRETIN!!
AAAAAAAH!
KYAAAAAA!
NOW YOU LISTEN TO ME, HANZOU!
I AM GOING TO DISGUISE MYSELF AS A REGULAR GIRL...
...AND MAKE MY MOVE ON KOUSHI INUZUKA!
GUWASHI (SHNAK)

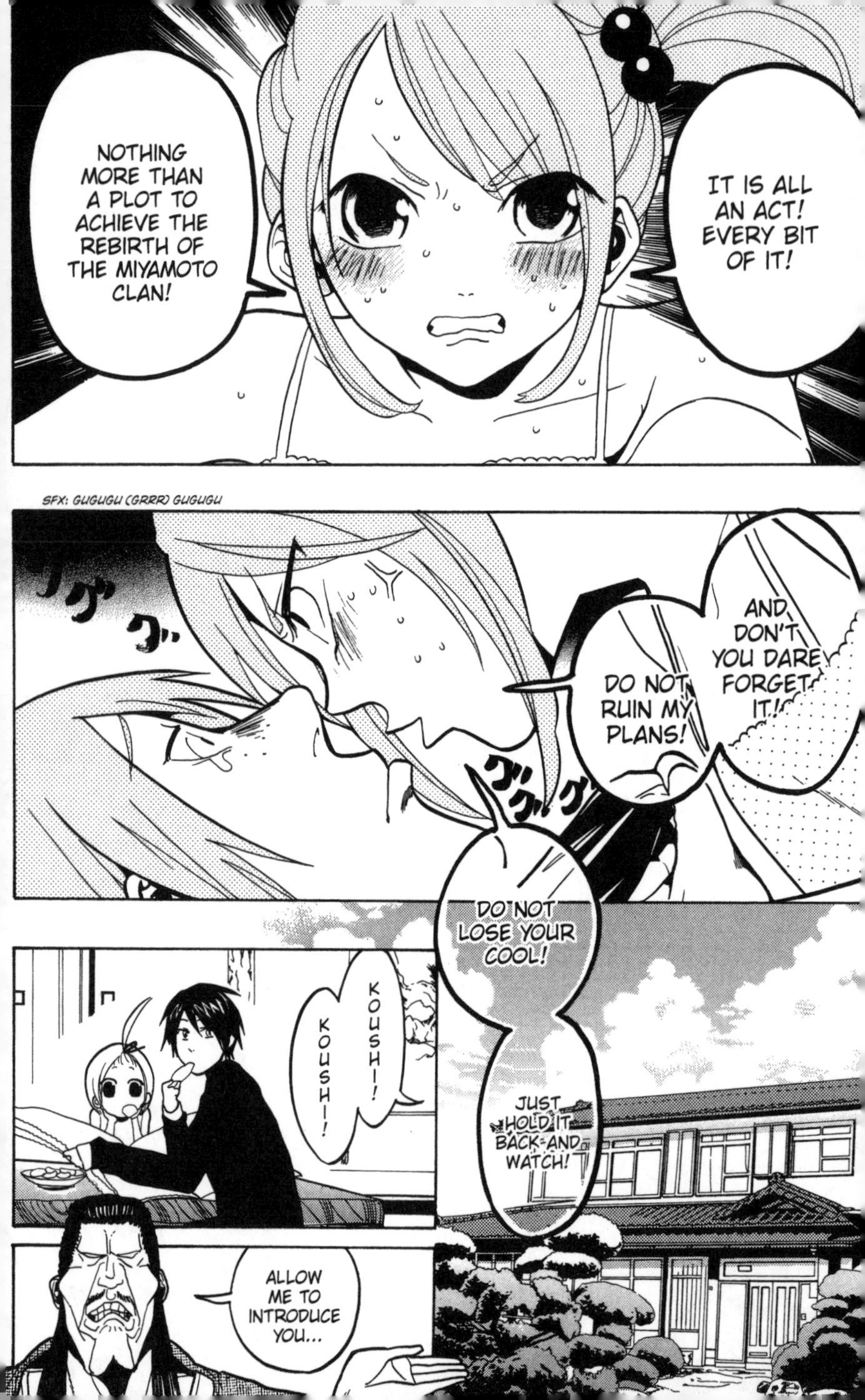
IT IS ALL AN ACT! EVERY BIT OF IT!
NOTHING MORE THAN A PLOT TO ACHIEVE THE REBIRTH OF THE MIYAMOTO CLAN!
SFX: GUGUGU (GRRR) GUGUGU
AND DON'T YOU DARE FORGET IT!
DO NOT RUIN MY PLANS!
DO NOT LOSE YOUR COOL!
JUST HOLD IT BACK AND WATCH!
KOUSH! KOUSH!
ALLOW ME TO INTRODUCE YOU...

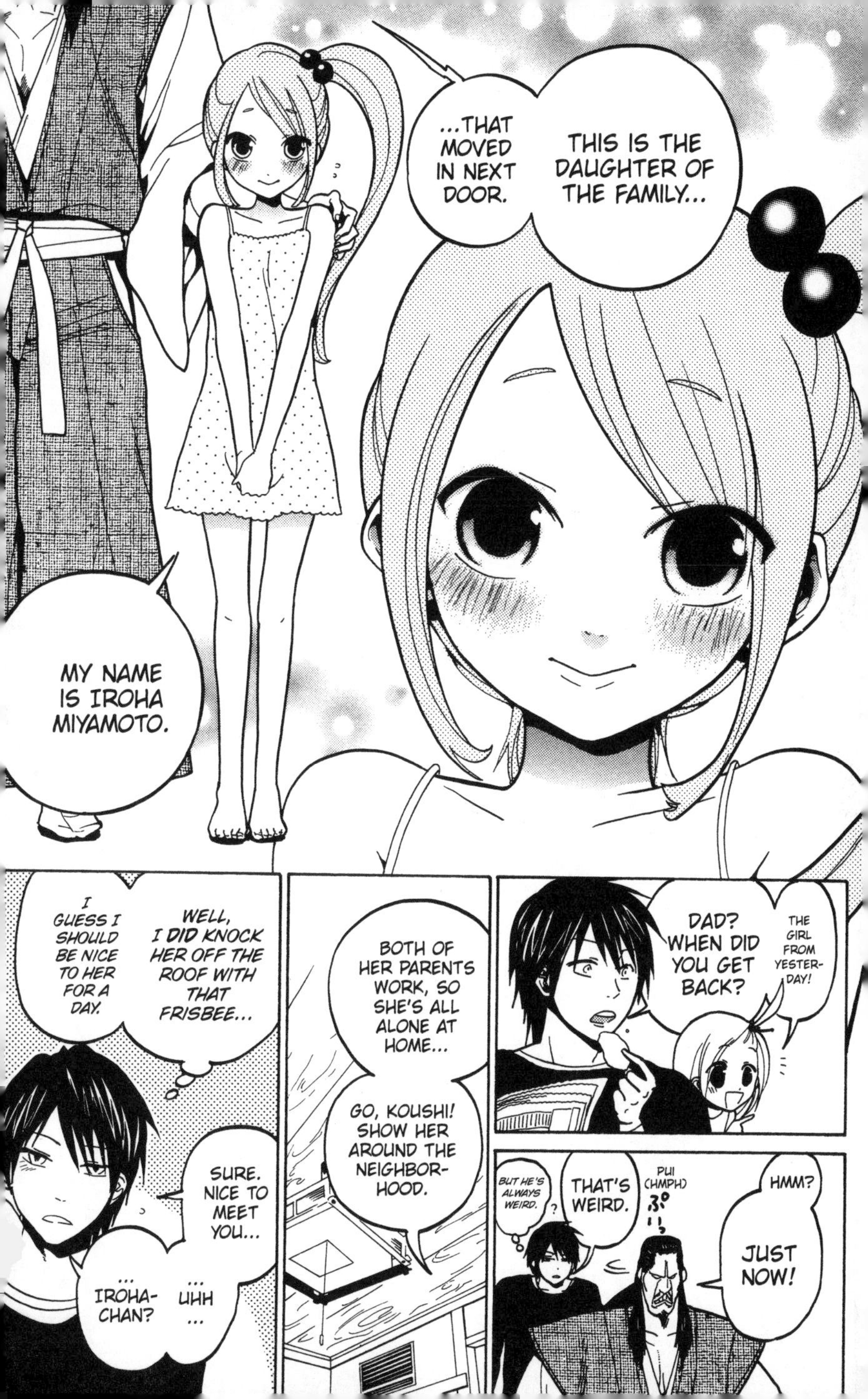

THIS IS THE DAUGHTER OF THE FAMILY...
...THAT MOVED IN NEXT DOOR.
MY NAME IS IROHA MIYAMOTO.
THE GIRL FROM YESTER-DAY!
DAD? WHEN DID YOU GET BACK?
HMM?
JUST NOW!
PUI (HMPH)
THAT'S WEIRD.
BUT HE'S ALWAYS WEIRD.
BOTH OF HER PARENTS WORK, SO SHE'S ALL ALONE AT HOME...
GO, KOUSHI! SHOW HER AROUND THE NEIGHBOR-HOOD.
WELL, I *DID* KNOCK HER OFF THE ROOF WITH THAT FRISBEE...
I GUESS I SHOULD BE NICE TO HER FOR A DAY.
SURE. NICE TO MEET YOU...
...UHH...
...IROHA-CHAN?

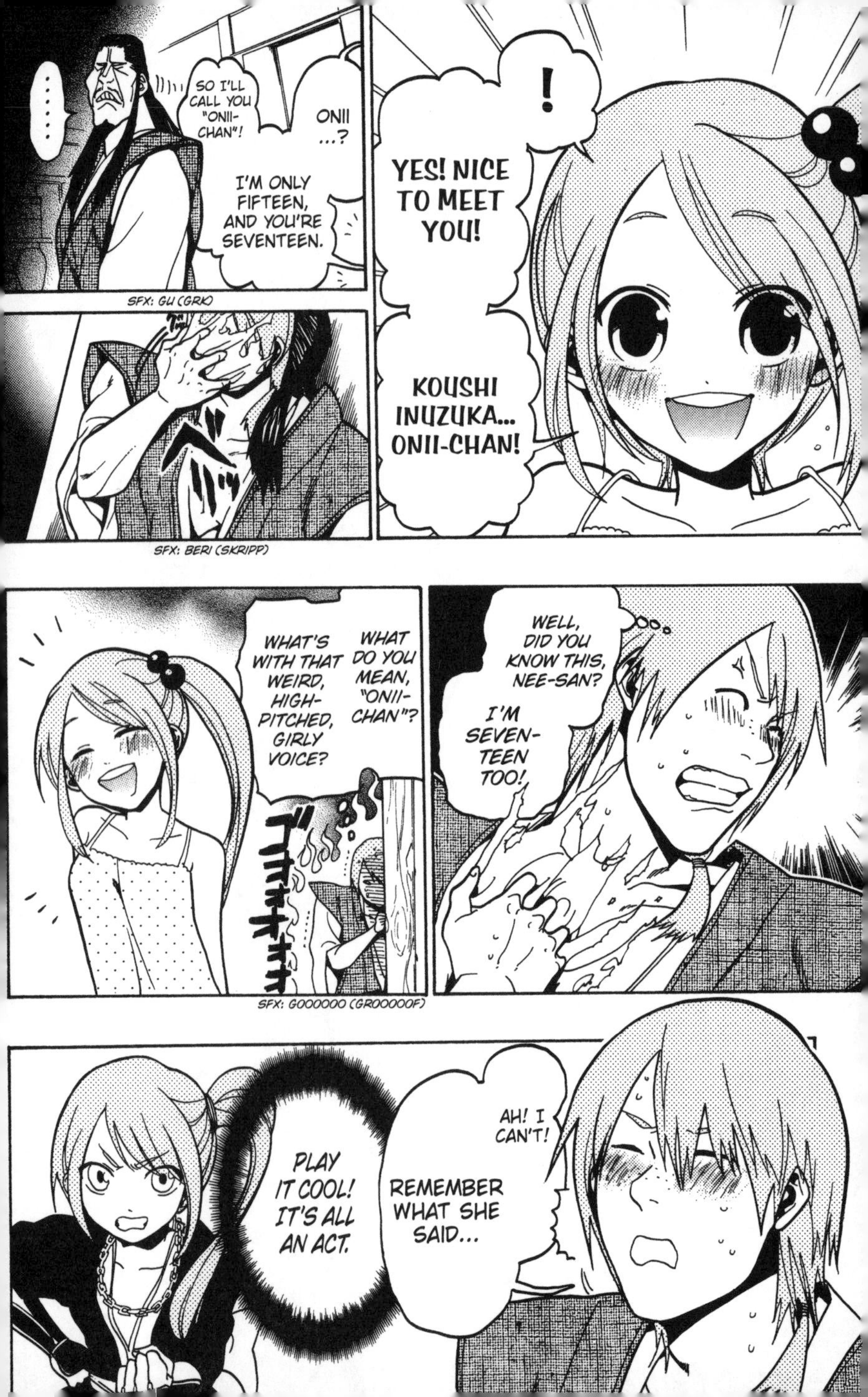
!
YES! NICE TO MEET YOU!
KOUSHI INUZUKA... ONII-CHAN!
ONII ...?
I'M ONLY FIFTEEN, AND YOU'RE SEVENTEEN.
SO I'LL CALL YOU "ONII-CHAN"!
......
SFX: GU (GRK)
SFX: BERI (SKRIPP)
WELL, DID YOU KNOW THIS, NEE-SAN?
I'M SEVENTEEN TOO!
WHAT DO YOU MEAN, "ONII-CHAN"?
WHAT'S WITH THAT WEIRD, HIGH-PITCHED, GIRLY VOICE?
SFX: GOOOOOO (GROOOOOF)
AH! I CAN'T!
REMEMBER WHAT SHE SAID...
PLAY IT COOL! IT'S ALL AN ACT.

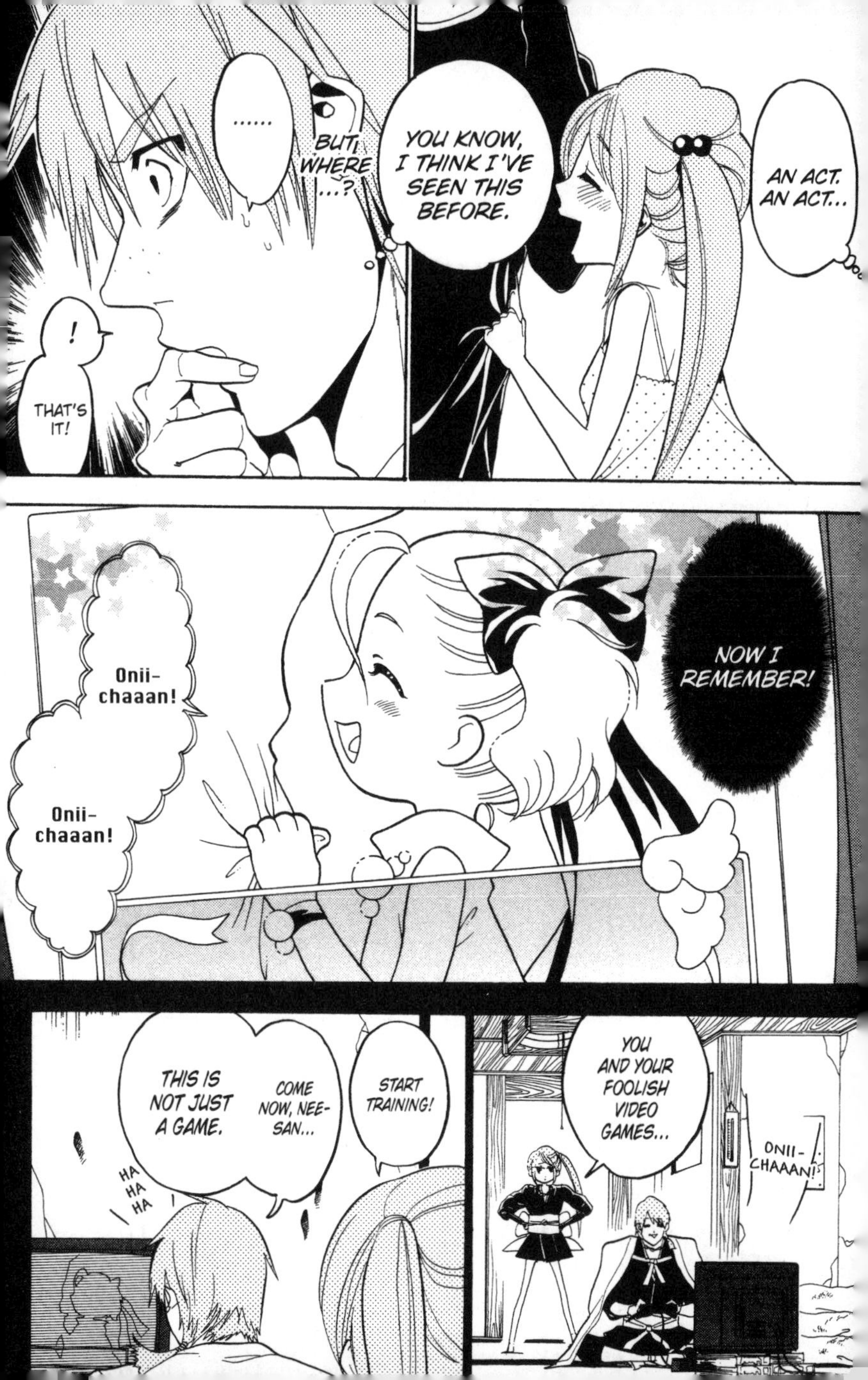
AN ACT. AN ACT...
YOU KNOW, I THINK I'VE SEEN THIS BEFORE.
......
BUT, WHERE ...?
!
THAT'S IT!
NOW I REMEMBER!
Onii-chaaan!
Onii-chaaan!
YOU AND YOUR FOOLISH VIDEO GAMES...
ONII-CHAAAN!
START TRAINING!
COME NOW, NEE-SAN...
THIS IS NOT JUST A GAME.
HA HA HA

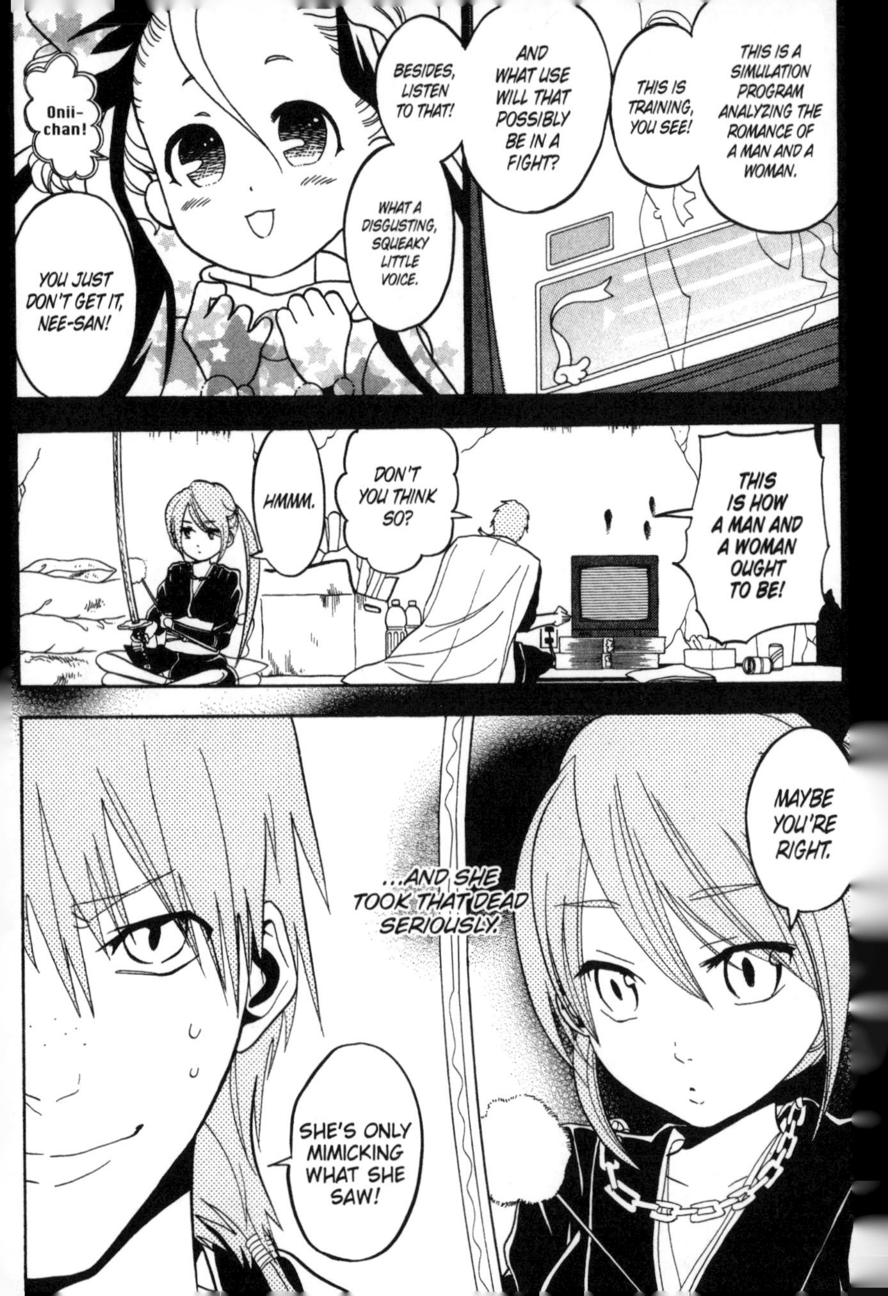
THIS IS A SIMULATION PROGRAM ANALYZING THE ROMANCE OF A MAN AND A WOMAN.
THIS IS TRAINING, YOU SEE!
AND WHAT USE WILL THAT POSSIBLY BE IN A FIGHT?
BESIDES, LISTEN TO THAT!
WHAT A DISGUSTING, SQUEAKY LITTLE VOICE.
Onii-chan!
YOU JUST DON'T GET IT, NEE-SAN!
THIS IS HOW A MAN AND A WOMAN OUGHT TO BE!
DON'T YOU THINK SO?
HMMM.
MAYBE YOU'RE RIGHT.
...AND SHE TOOK THAT DEAD SERIOUSLY.
SHE'S ONLY MIMICKING WHAT SHE SAW!

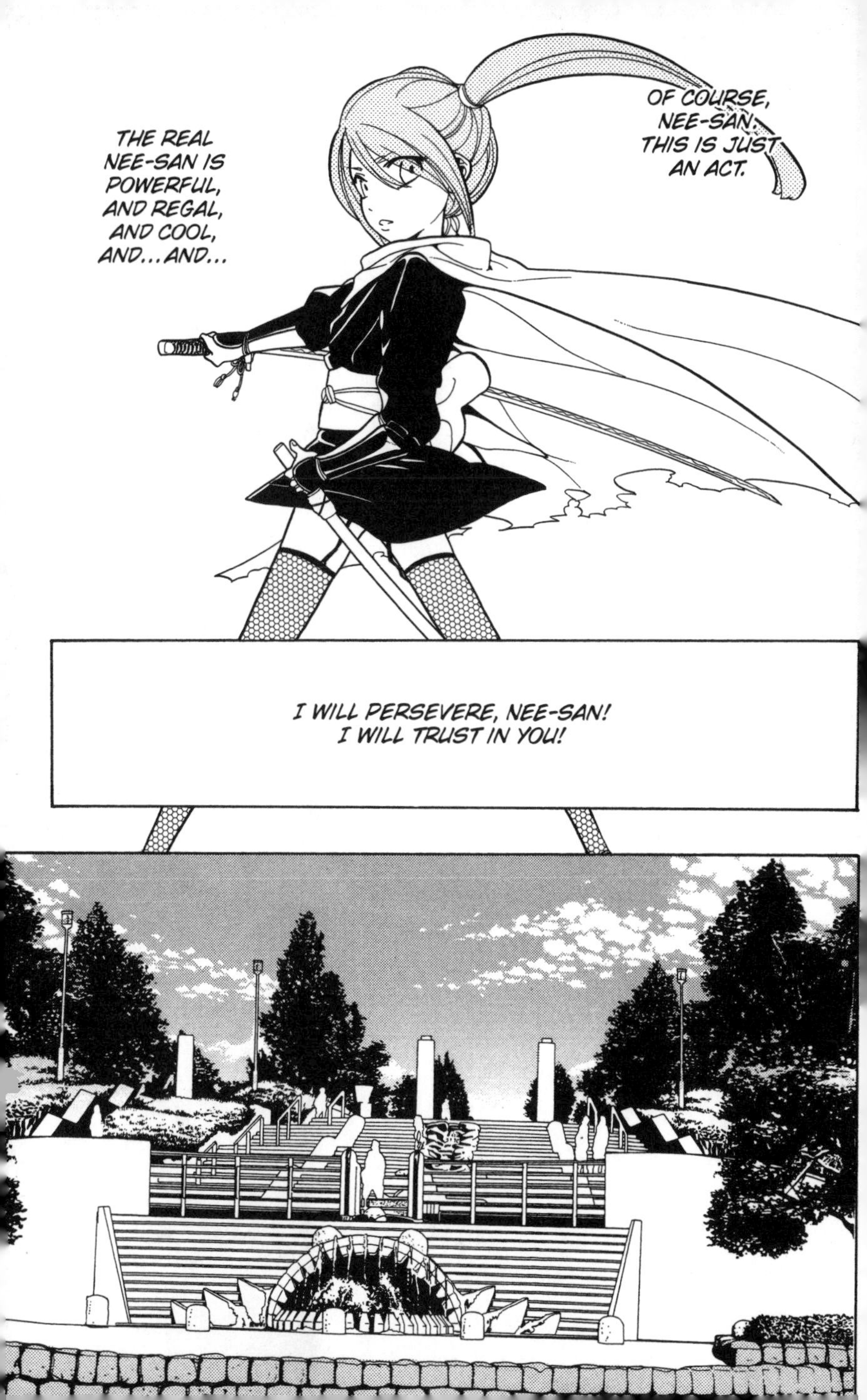
OF COURSE, NEE-SAN. THIS IS JUST AN ACT.
THE REAL NEE-SAN IS POWERFUL, AND REGAL, AND COOL, AND... AND...
I WILL PERSEVERE, NEE-SAN! I WILL TRUST IN YOU!

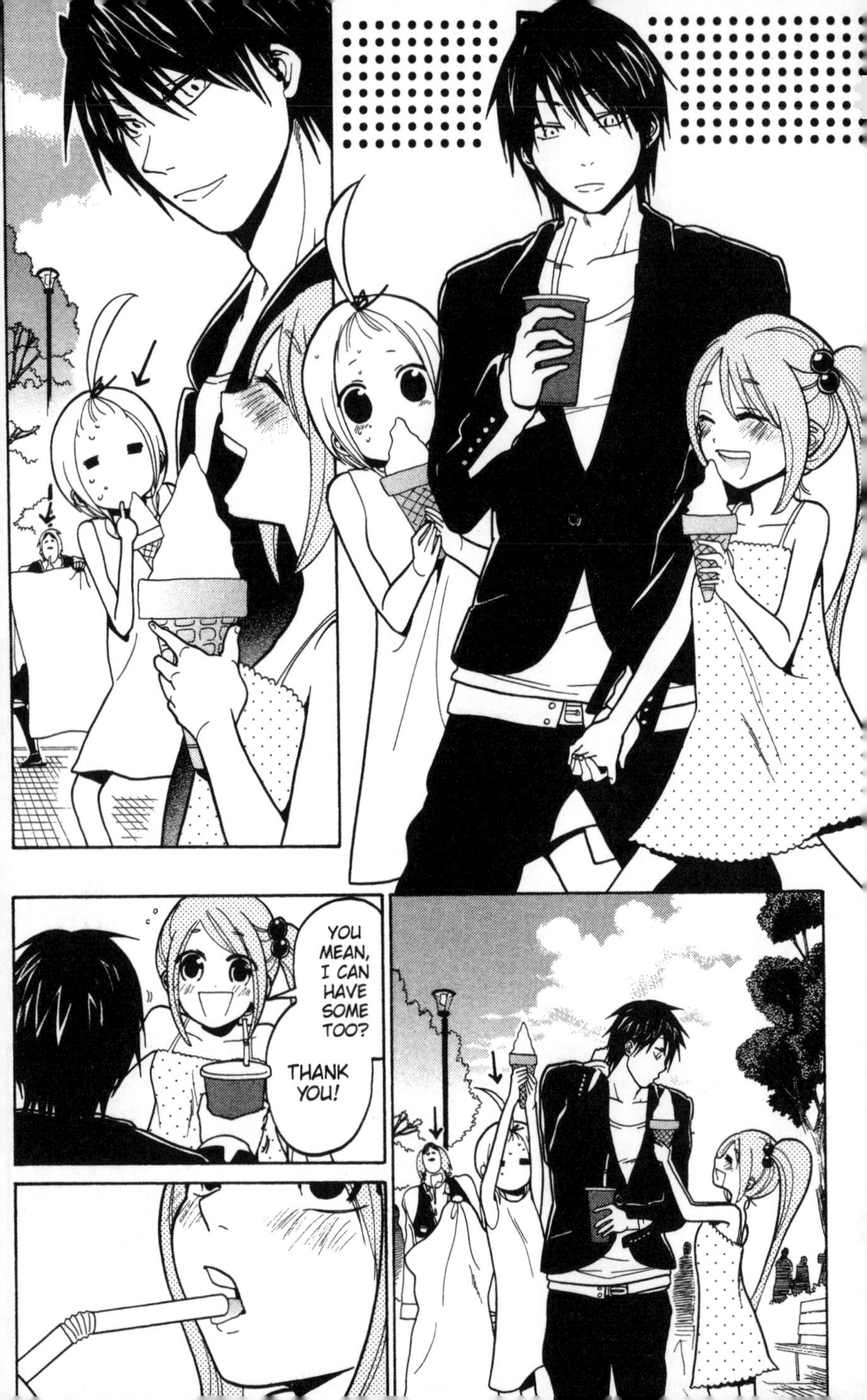
YOU MEAN, I CAN HAVE SOME TOO?
THANK YOU!

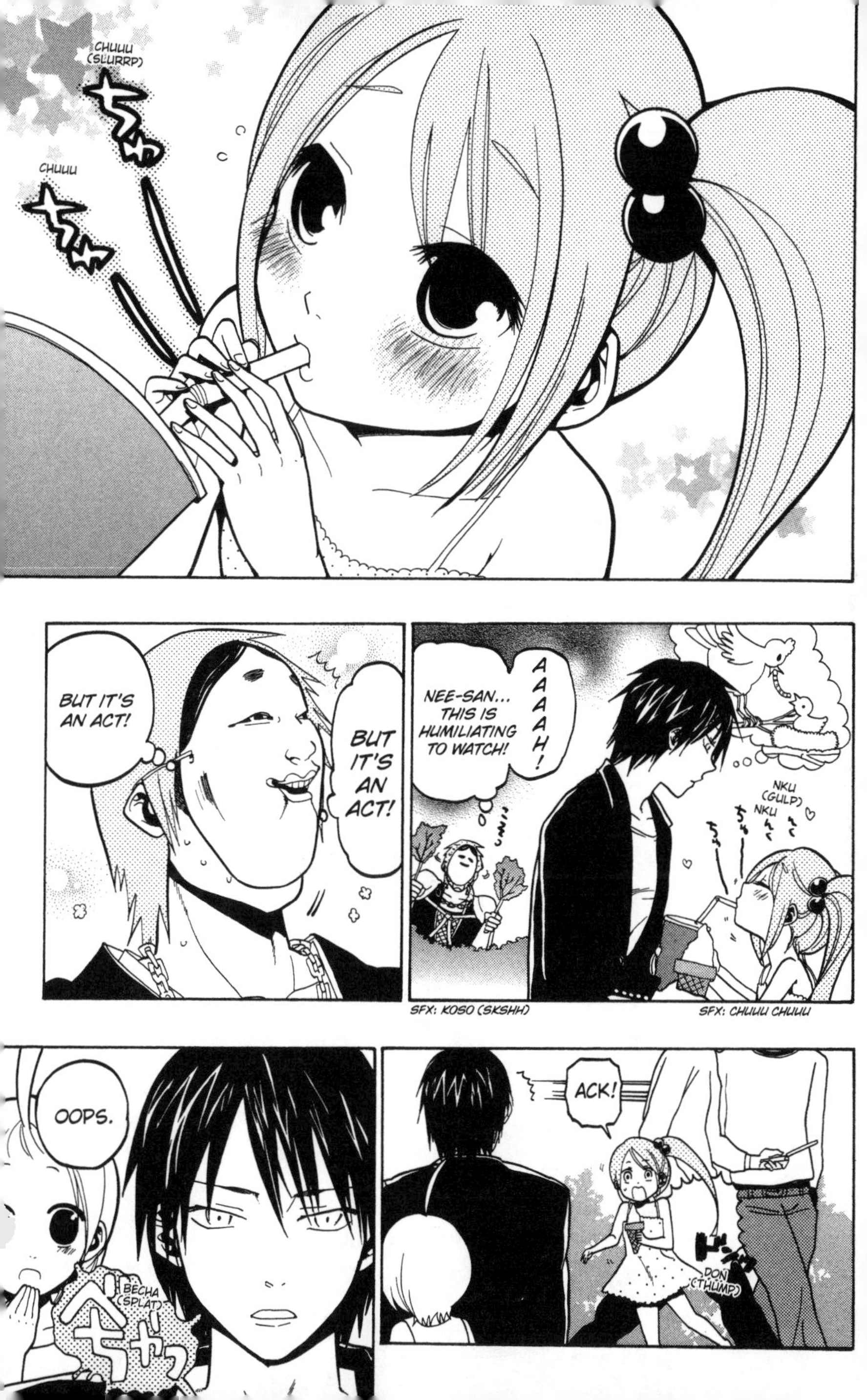
CHUUU (SLURRP)
CHUUU
AAAAH!
NEE-SAN... THIS IS HUMILIATING TO WATCH!
NKU (GULP) NKU
SFX: CHUUU CHUUU
SFX: KOSO (SKSHH)
BUT IT'S AN ACT!
BUT IT'S AN ACT!
ACK!
DON (THUMP)
OOPS.
BECHA (SPLAT)

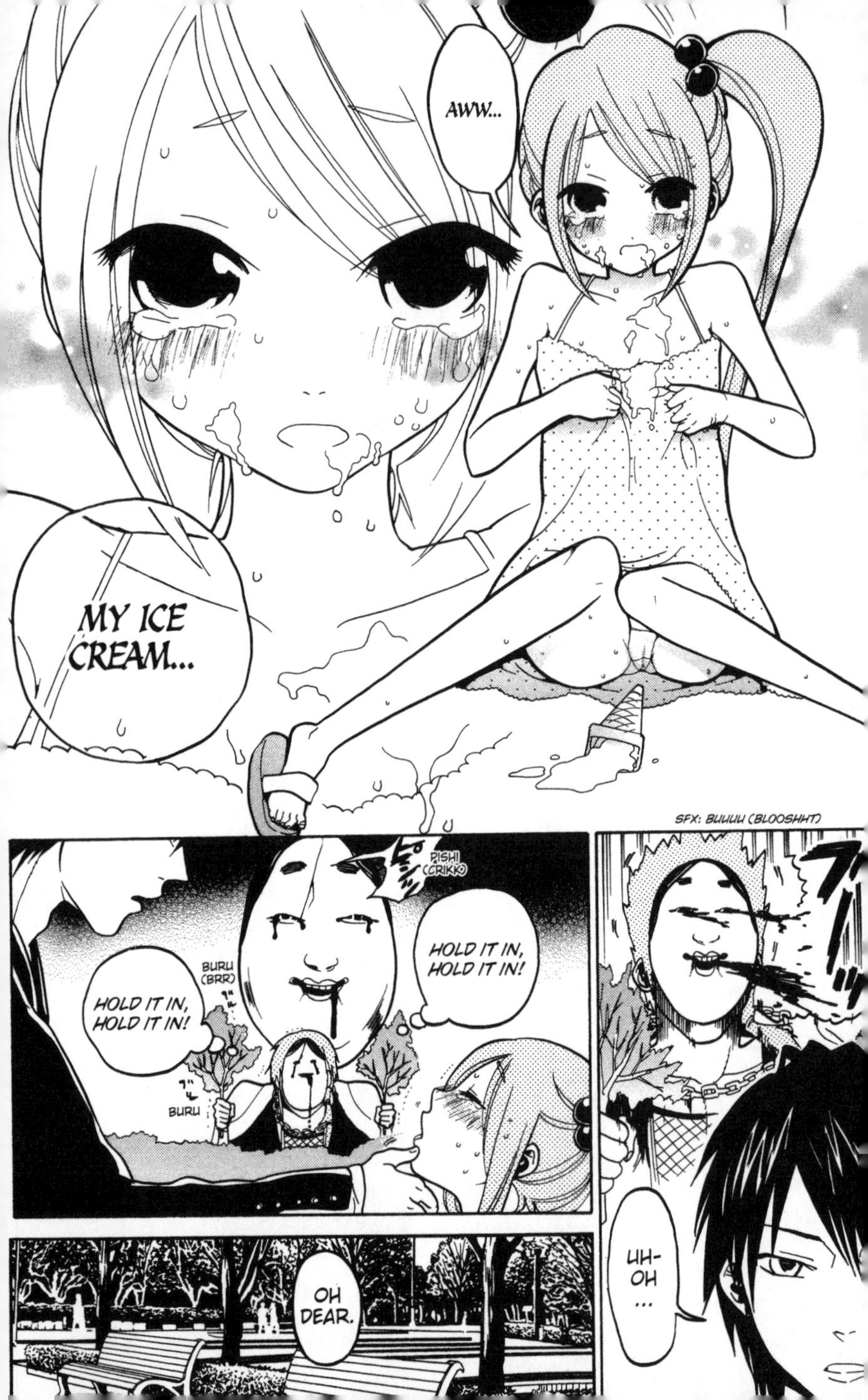
AWW...
MY ICE CREAM...
SFX: BUUUU (BLOOSHHT)
UH-OH ...
PISHI (CRIKK)
HOLD IT IN, HOLD IT IN!
BURU (BRR)
HOLD IT IN, HOLD IT IN!
BURU
OH DEAR.

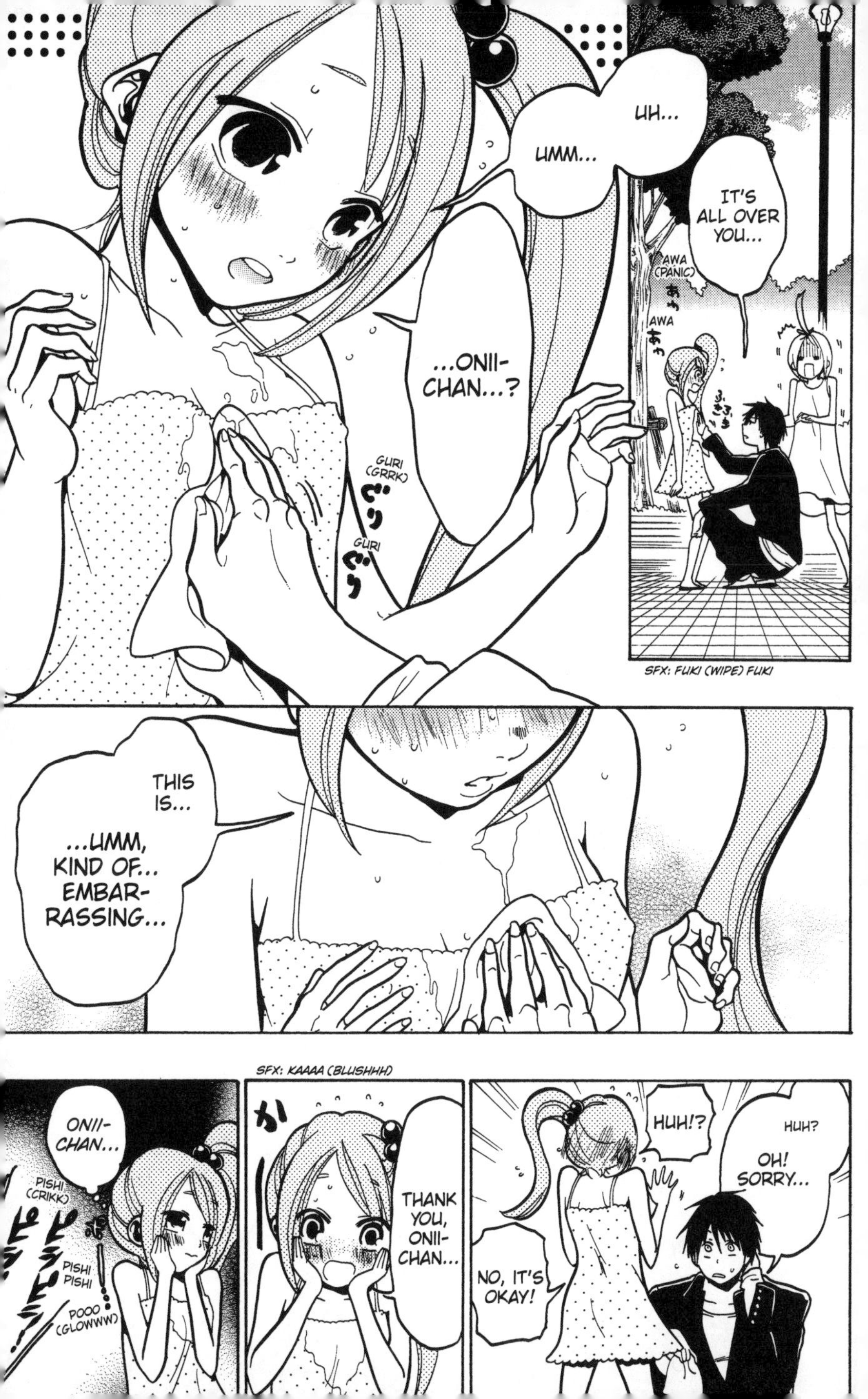
IT'S ALL OVER YOU...
AWA (PANIC)
AWA
SFX: FUKI (WIPE) FUKI
UH...
UMM...
...ONII-CHAN...?
GURI (GRRK)
GURI
THIS IS...
...UMM, KIND OF... EMBARRASSING...
HUH!?
HUH?
OH! SORRY...
NO, IT'S OKAY!
SFX: KAAAA (BLUSHHH)
THANK YOU, ONII-CHAN...
ONII-CHAN...
PISHI (CRIKK)
PISHI PISHI
POOO (GLOWWW)

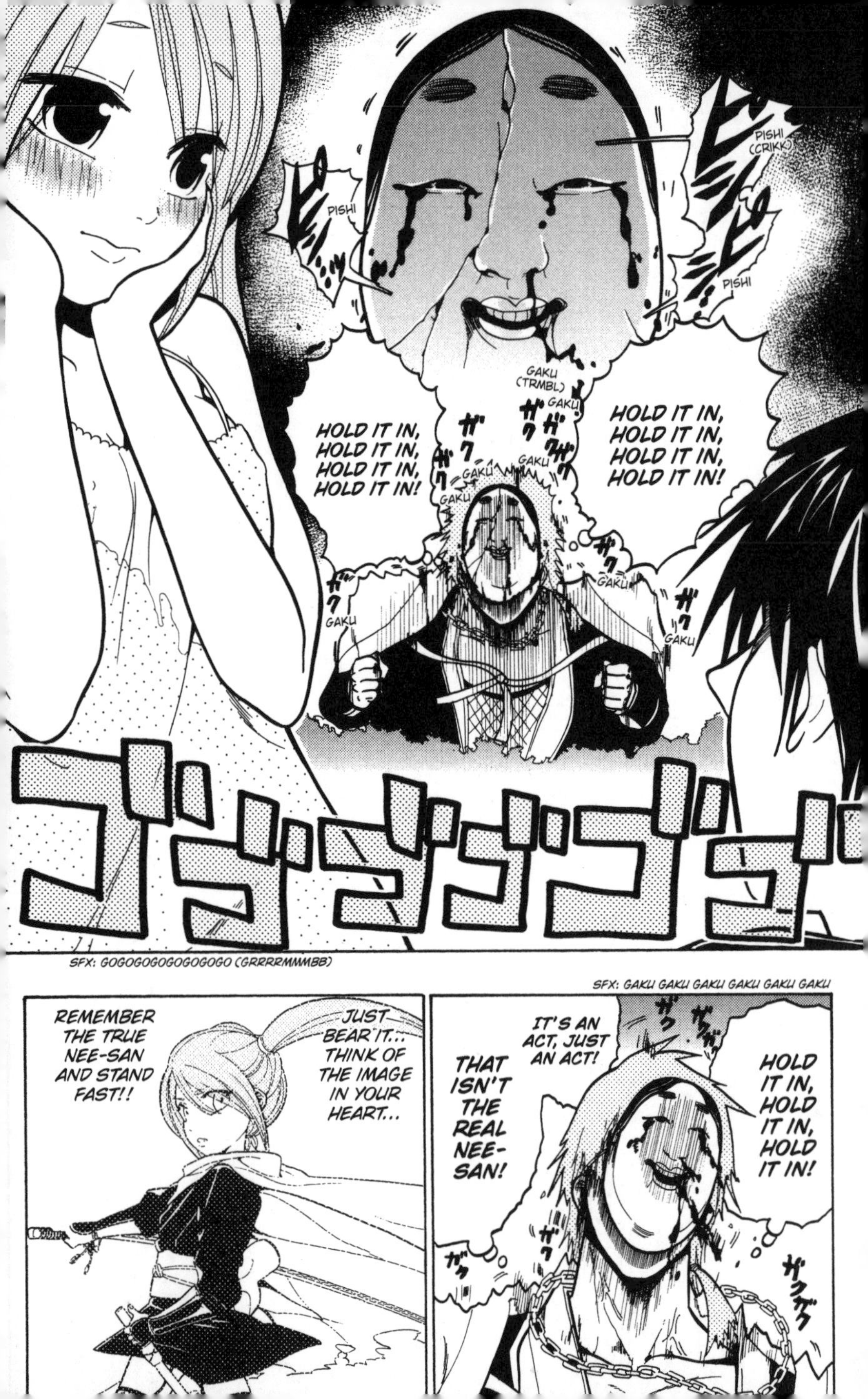

PISHI (CRIKK)
PISHI
HOLD IT IN, HOLD IT IN, HOLD IT IN, HOLD IT IN!
GAKU (TRMBL)
GAKU
GAKU
GAKU
GAKU
GAKU
GAKU
GAKU
HOLD IT IN, HOLD IT IN, HOLD IT IN, HOLD IT IN!
PISHI
SFX: GOGOGOGOGOGOGOGO (GRRRRMMMBB)
SFX: GAKU GAKU GAKU GAKU GAKU GAKU
HOLD IT IN, HOLD IT IN, HOLD IT IN!
IT'S AN ACT, JUST AN ACT!
THAT ISN'T THE REAL NEE-SAN!
JUST BEAR IT... THINK OF THE IMAGE IN YOUR HEART...
REMEMBER THE TRUE NEE-SAN AND STAND FAST!!

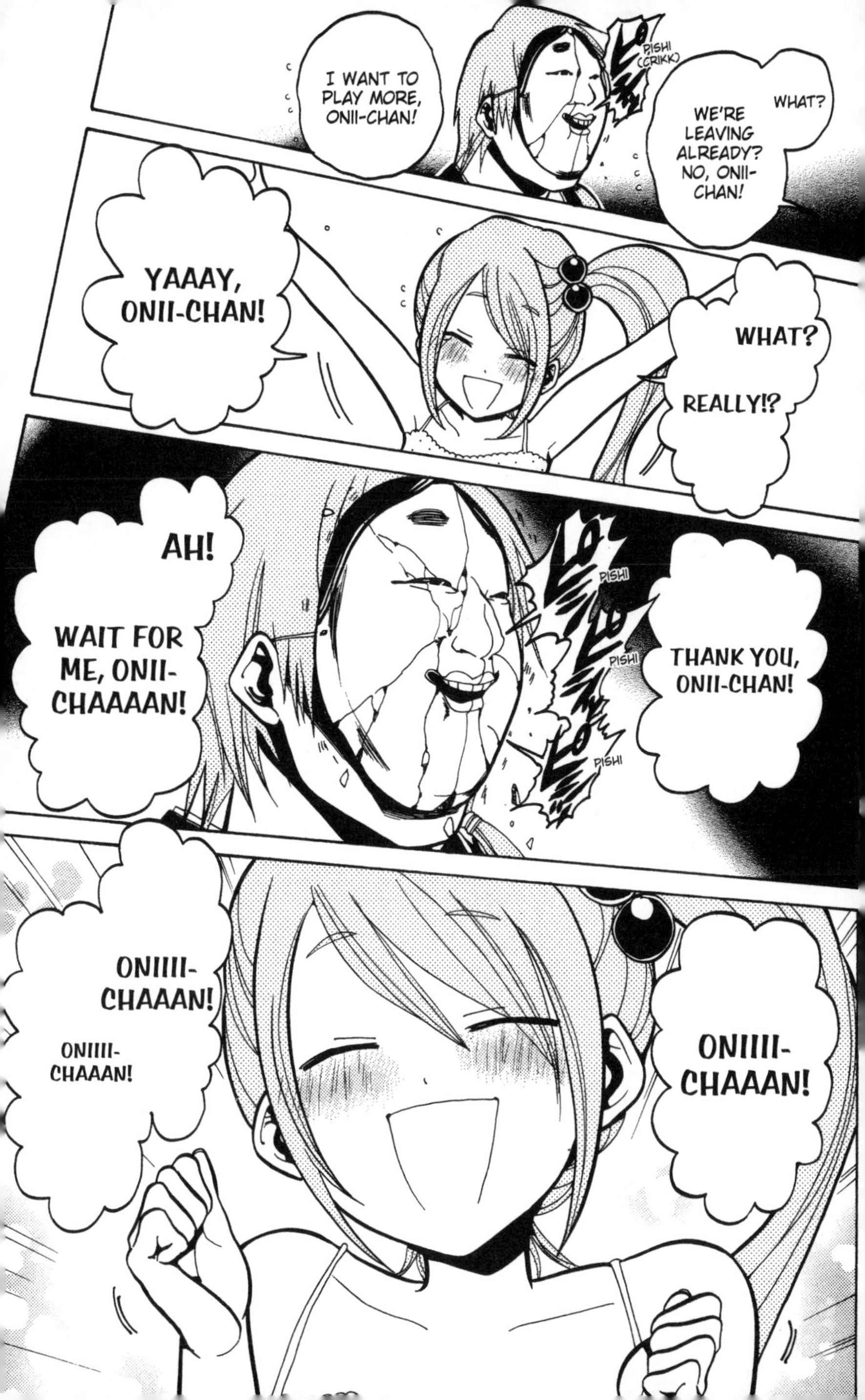
WHAT?
WE'RE LEAVING ALREADY? NO, ONII-CHAN!
PISHI (CRIKK)
I WANT TO PLAY MORE, ONII-CHAN!
WHAT?
REALLY!?
YAAAY, ONII-CHAN!
THANK YOU, ONII-CHAN!
PISHI
PISHI
PISHI
AH!
WAIT FOR ME, ONII-CHAAAAN!
ONIIII-CHAAAN!
ONIIII-CHAAAN!
ONIIII-CHAAAN!

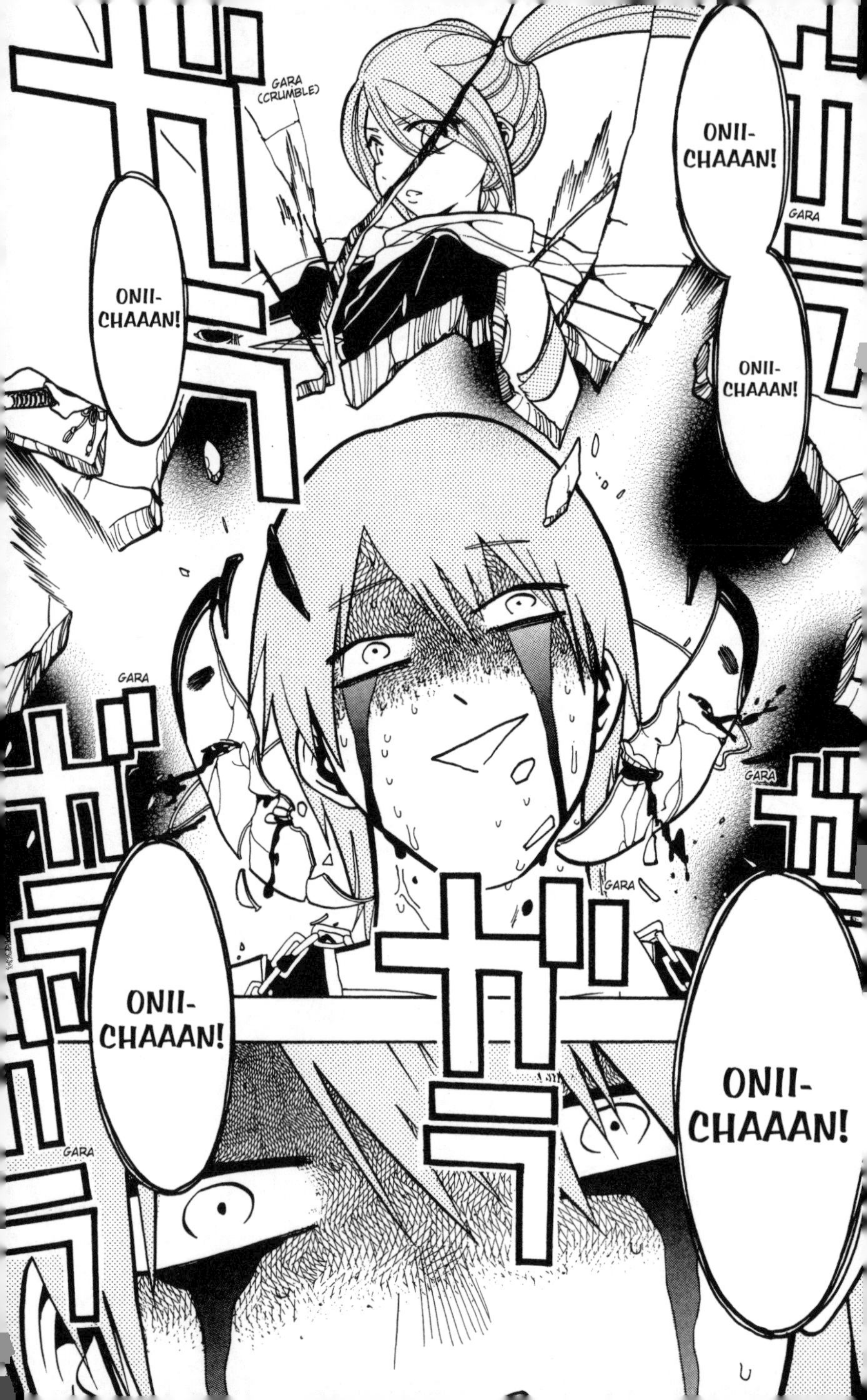
ONII-CHAAAN!
GARA
ONII-CHAAAN!
GARA (CRUMBLE)
ONII-CHAAAN!
GARA
GARA
GARA
ONII-CHAAAN!
ONII-CHAAAN!
GARA

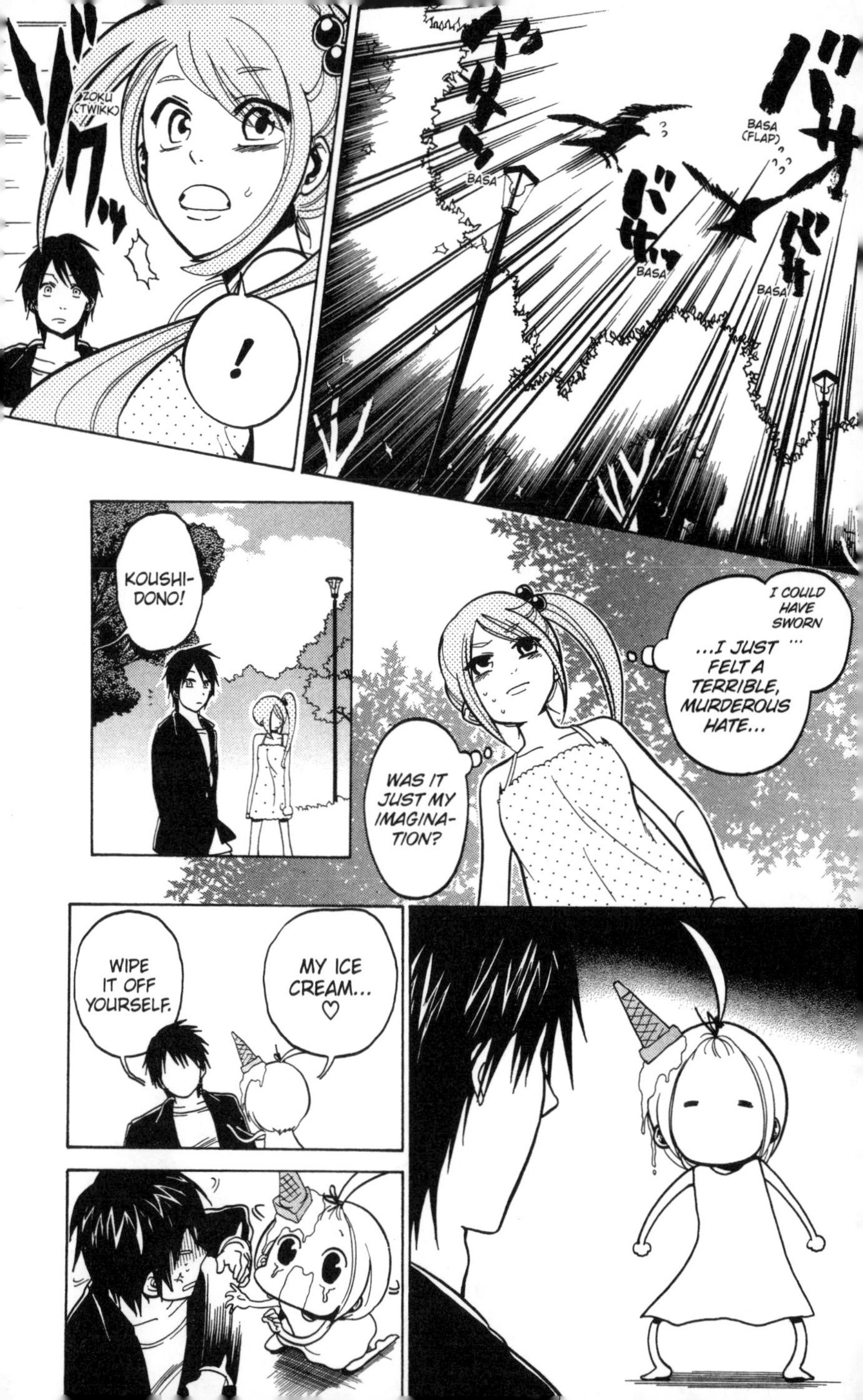
BASA (FLAP)
BASA
BASA
BASA
ZOKU (TWIKK)
!
I COULD HAVE SWORN ... ...I JUST FELT A TERRIBLE, MURDEROUS HATE...
WAS IT JUST MY IMAGINA-TION?
KOUSHI-DONO!
MY ICE CREAM... ♡
WIPE IT OFF YOURSELF.

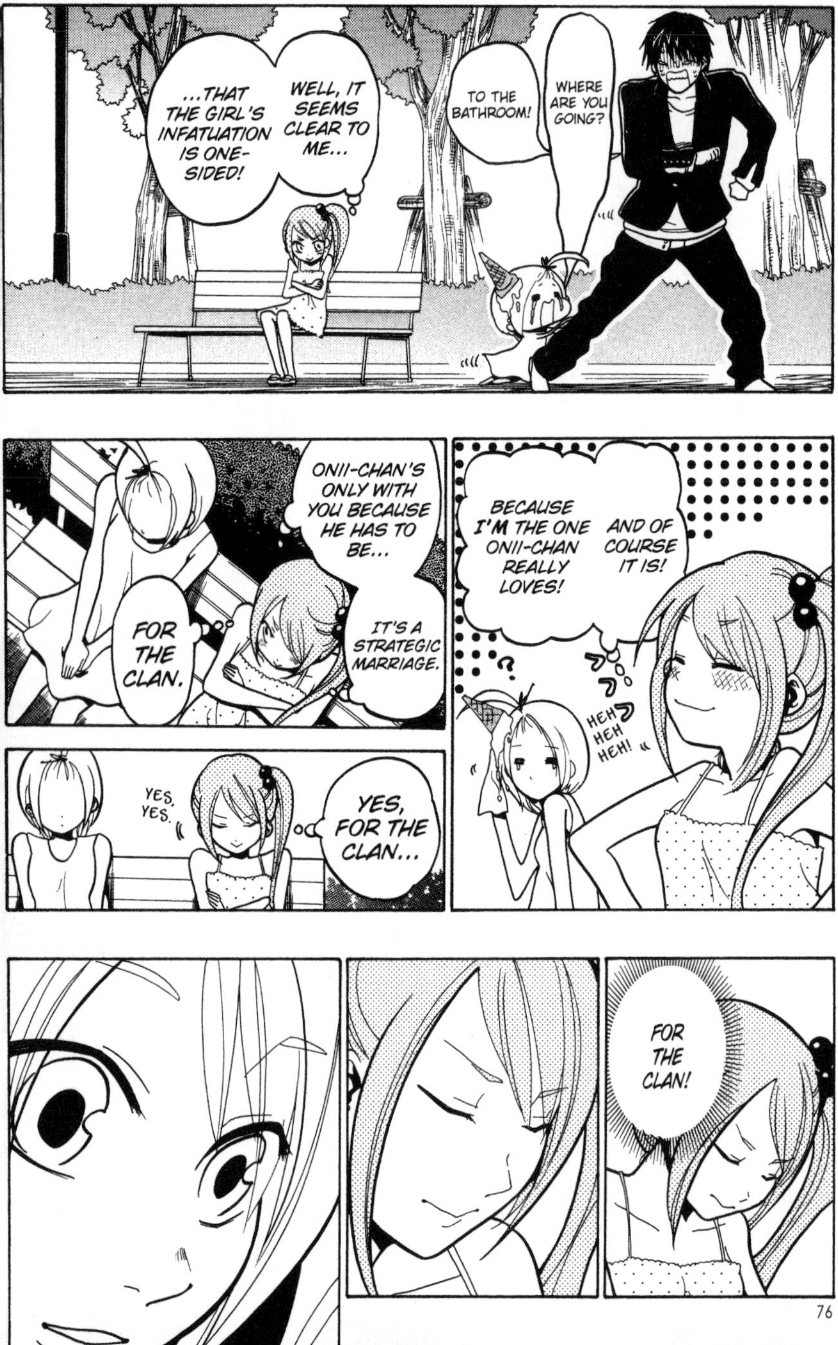
WHERE ARE YOU GOING?
TO THE BATHROOM!
WELL, IT SEEMS CLEAR TO ME...
...THAT THE GIRL'S INFATUATION IS ONE-SIDED!
AND OF COURSE IT IS!
BECAUSE I'M THE ONE ONII-CHAN REALLY LOVES!
HEH HEH HEH!
ONII-CHAN'S ONLY WITH YOU BECAUSE HE HAS TO BE...
IT'S A STRATEGIC MARRIAGE.
FOR THE CLAN.
YES, FOR THE CLAN...
YES, YES.
FOR THE CLAN!

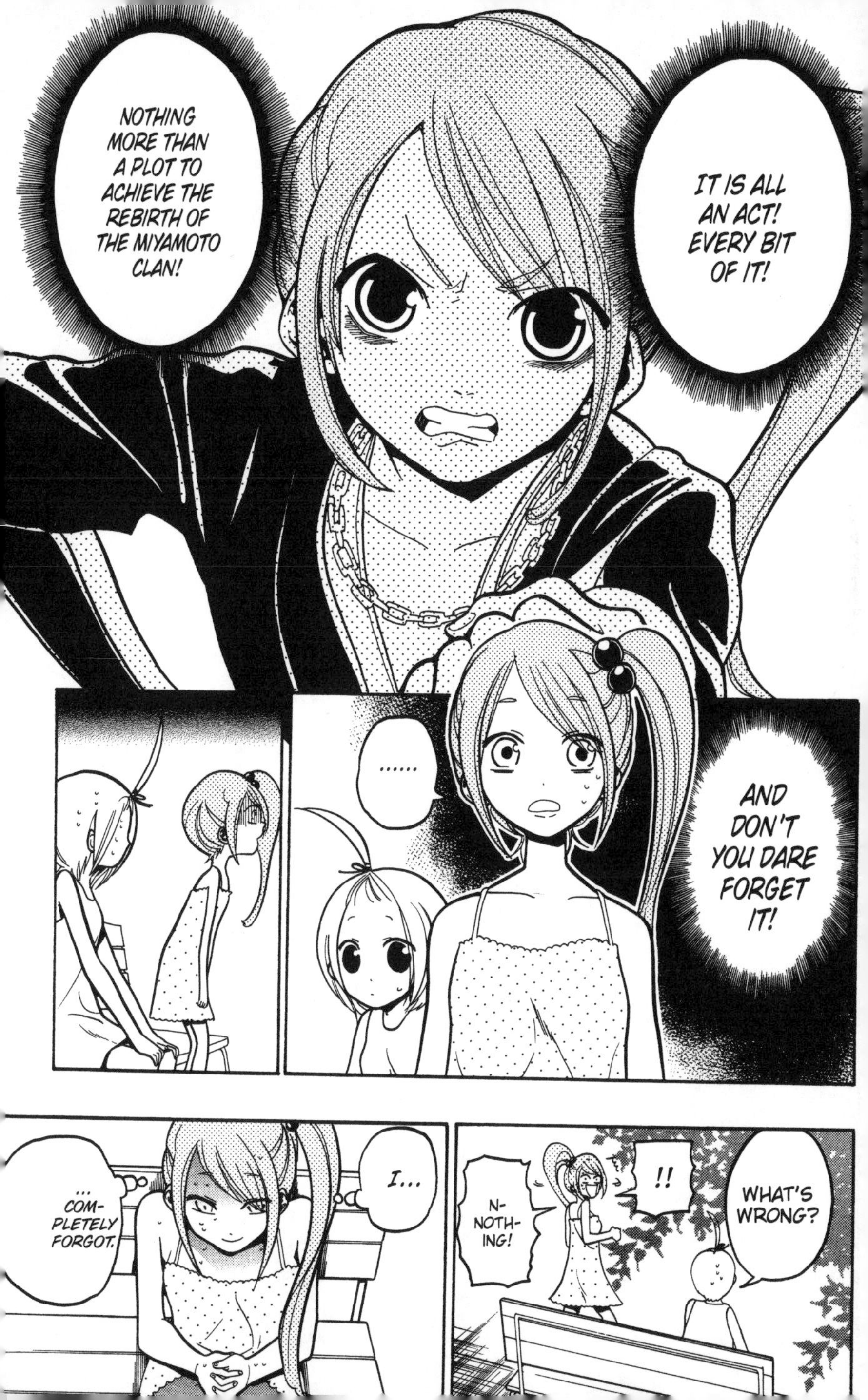
IT IS ALL AN ACT! EVERY BIT OF IT!
NOTHING MORE THAN A PLOT TO ACHIEVE THE REBIRTH OF THE MIYAMOTO CLAN!
AND DON'T YOU DARE FORGET IT!
......
WHAT'S WRONG?
!!
N-NOTHING!
I...
...COMPLETELY FORGOT.

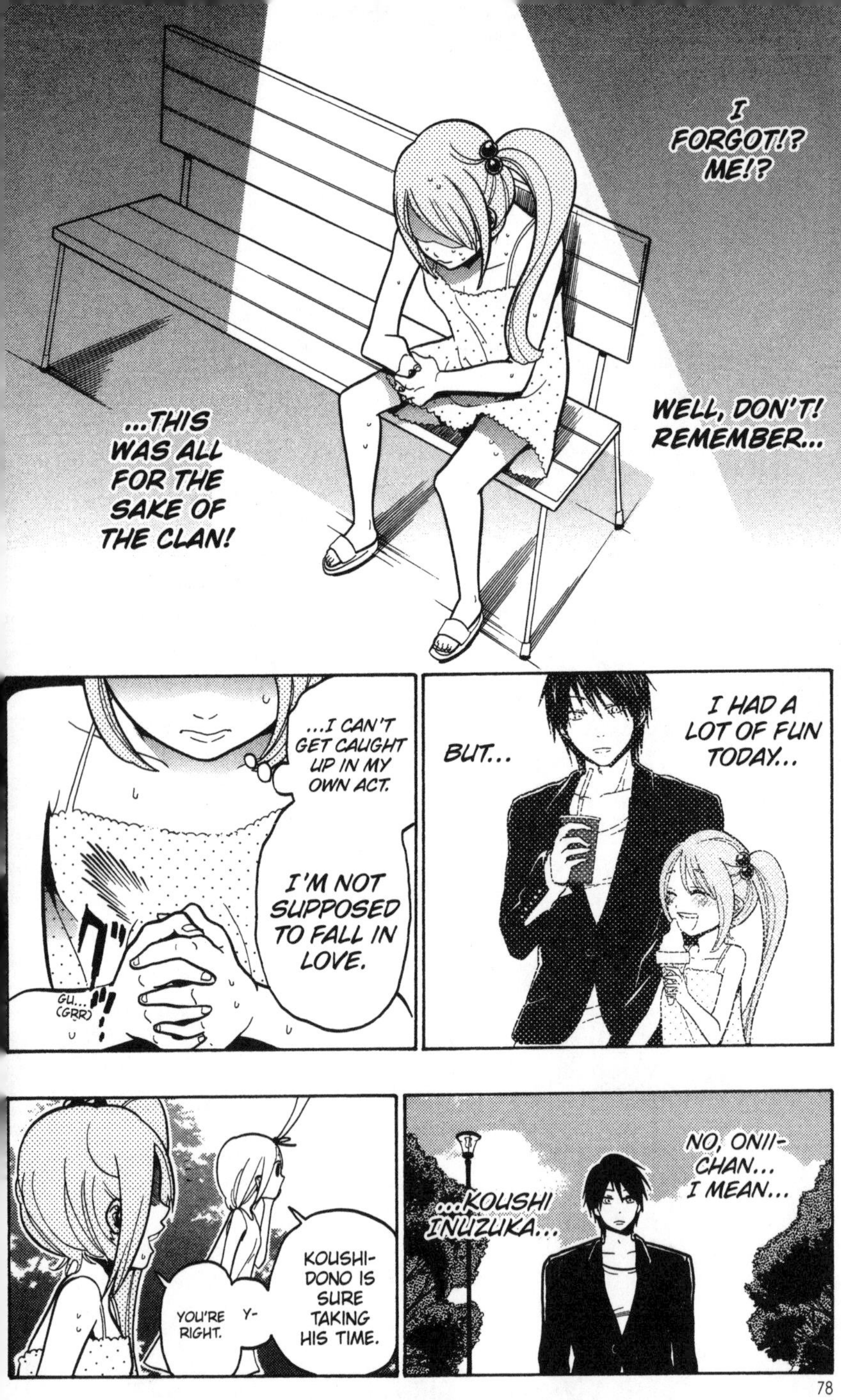
I FORGOT!? ME!?
WELL, DON'T! REMEMBER...
...THIS WAS ALL FOR THE SAKE OF THE CLAN!
I HAD A LOT OF FUN TODAY...
BUT...
...I CAN'T GET CAUGHT UP IN MY OWN ACT.
I'M NOT SUPPOSED TO FALL IN LOVE.
GU... (GRR)
NO, ONII-CHAN... I MEAN...
...KOUSHI INUZUKA...
KOUSHI-DONO IS SURE TAKING HIS TIME.
Y-
YOU'RE RIGHT.

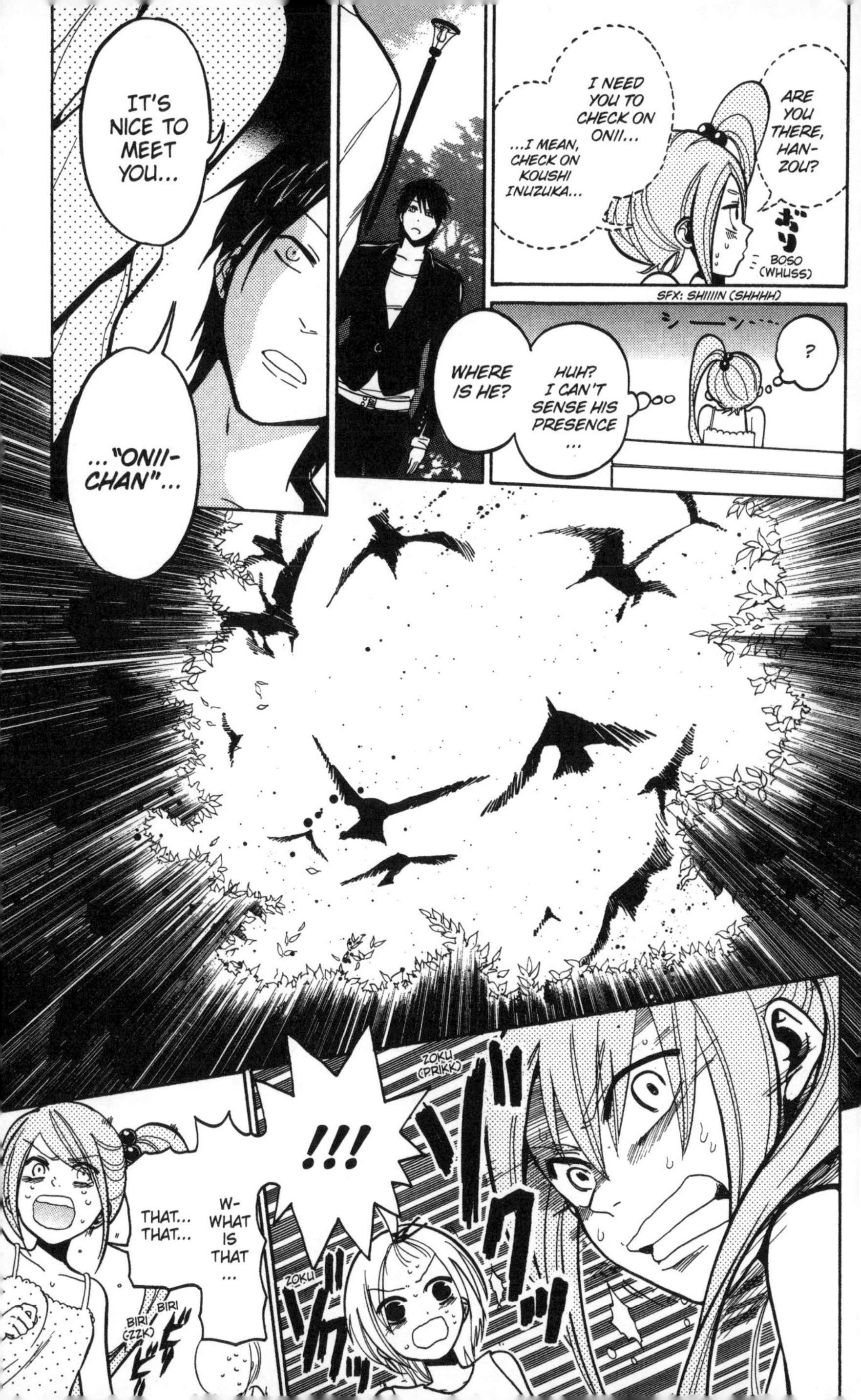
ARE YOU THERE, HAN-ZOU?
I NEED YOU TO CHECK ON ONII...
...I MEAN, CHECK ON KOUSHI INUZUKA...
BOSO (WHUSS)
SFX: SHIIIIN (SHHHH)
?
HUH? I CAN'T SENSE HIS PRESENCE ...
WHERE IS HE?
IT'S NICE TO MEET YOU...
..."ONII-CHAN"...
ZOKU (PRIKK)
!!!
ZOKU
W-WHAT IS THAT ...
THAT... THAT...
BIRI (ZZK) BIRI

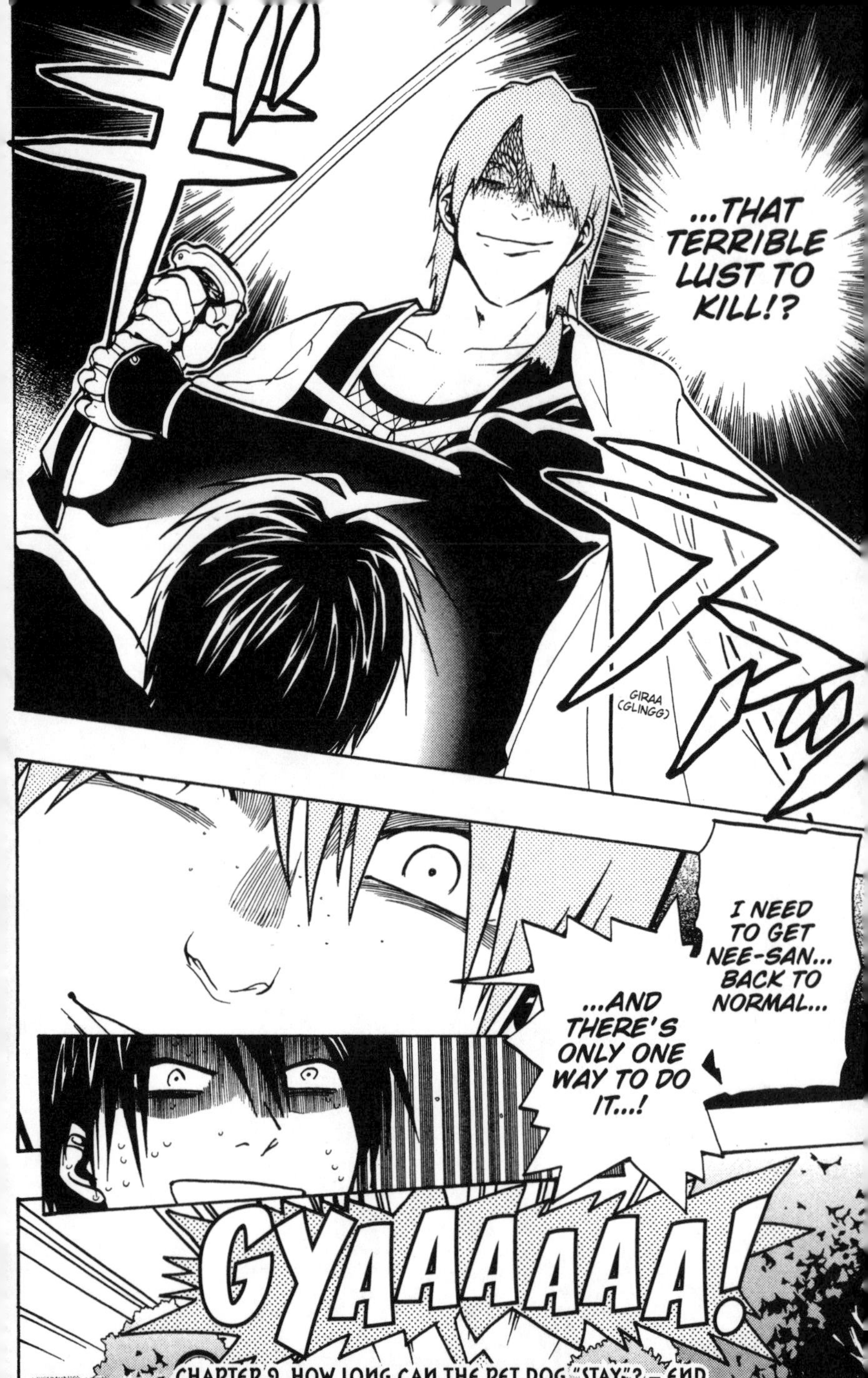
...THAT TERRIBLE LUST TO KILL!?
GIRAA (GLINGG)
I NEED TO GET NEE-SAN... BACK TO NORMAL...
...AND THERE'S ONLY ONE WAY TO DO IT...!
GYAAAAAA!
CHAPTER 9. HOW LONG CAN THE PET DOG "STAY"? – END

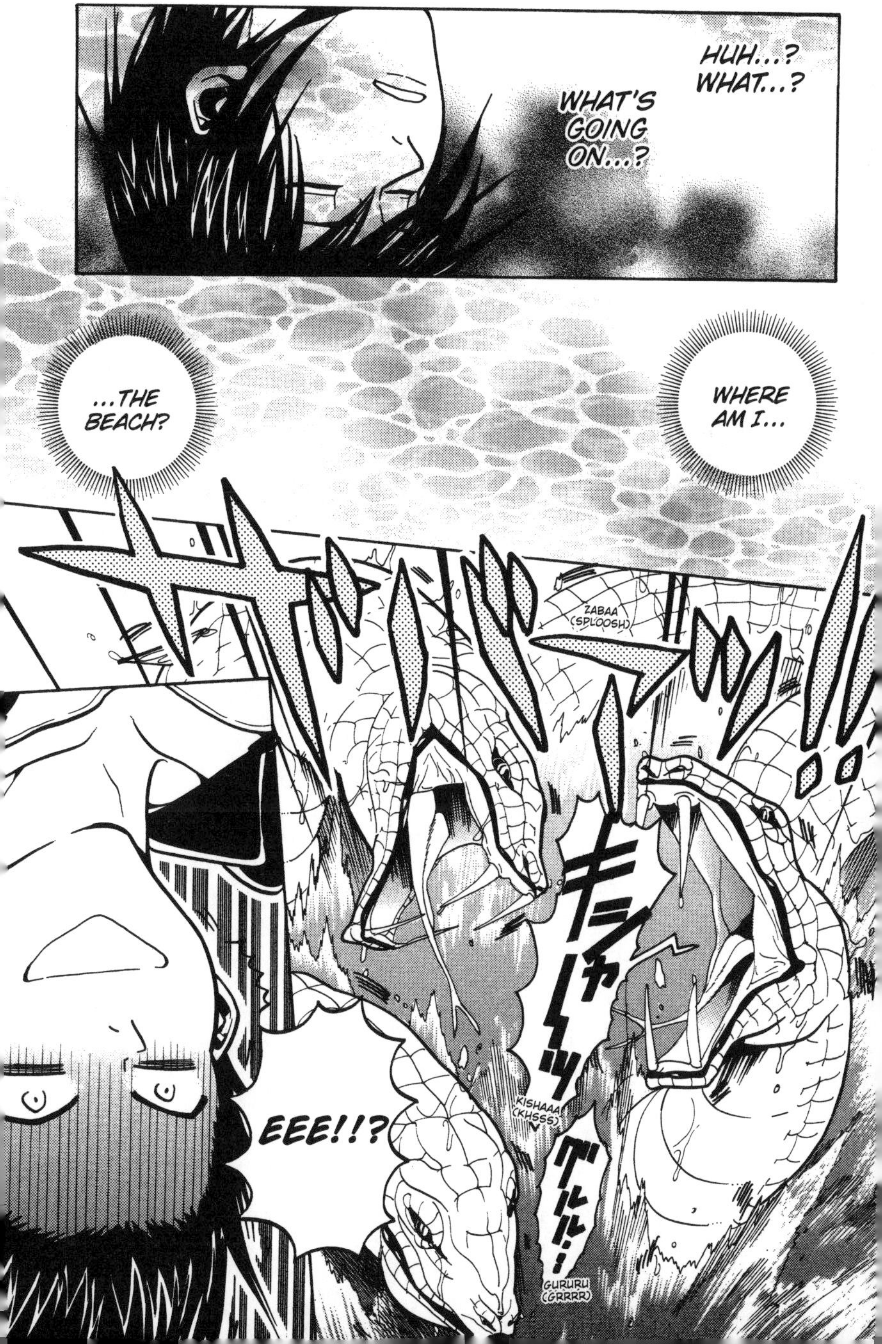
HUH...? WHAT...?
WHAT'S GOING ON...?
WHERE AM I...
...THE BEACH?
ZABAA (SPLOOSH)
KISHAAA (KHSSS)
GURURU (GRRRR)
EEE!!?

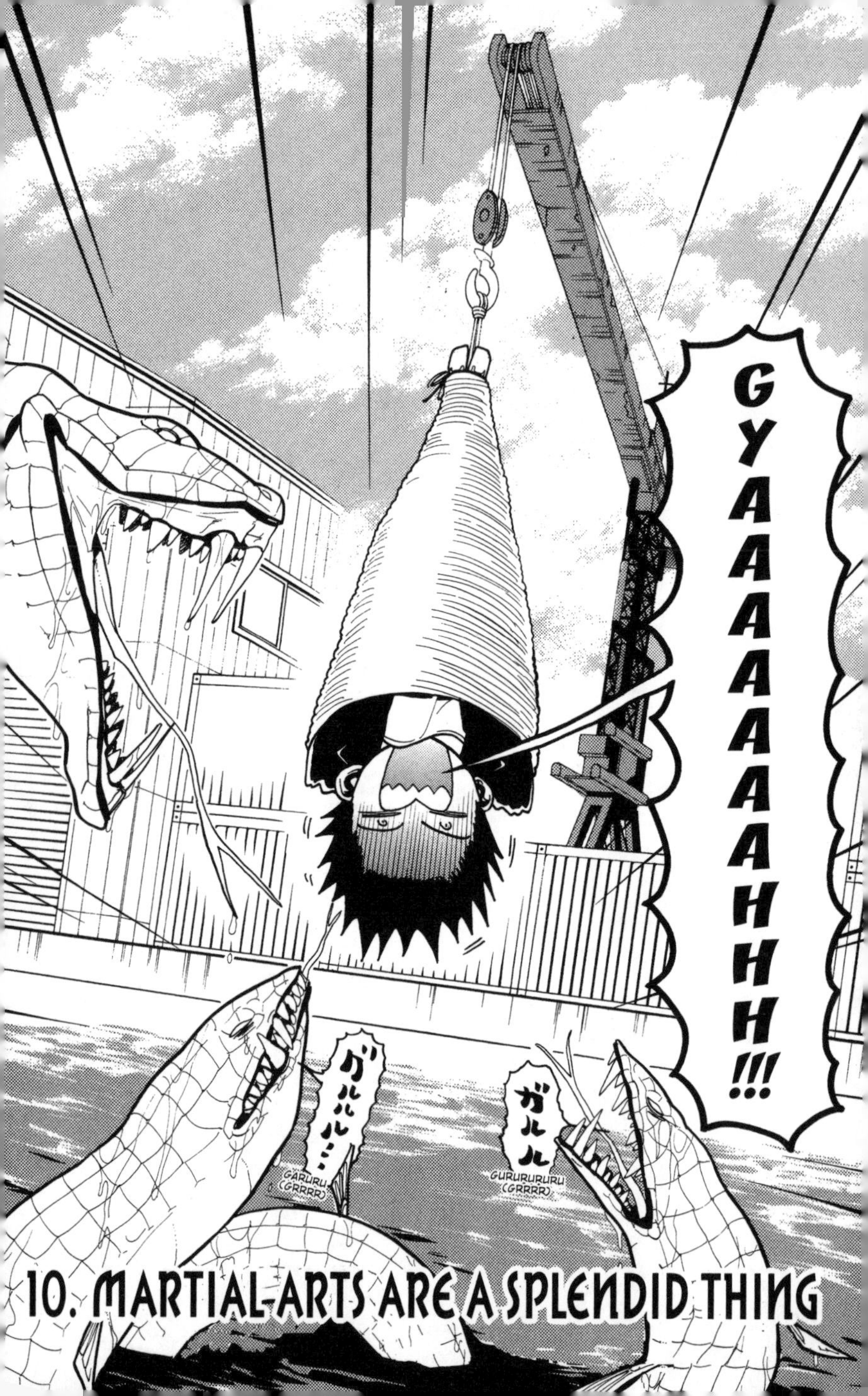
GYAAAAAAAAHHH!!!
ガルル
GURURURURU (GRRRR)
グルルル…
GARURU (GRRRR)
10. MARTIAL ARTS ARE A SPLENDID THING

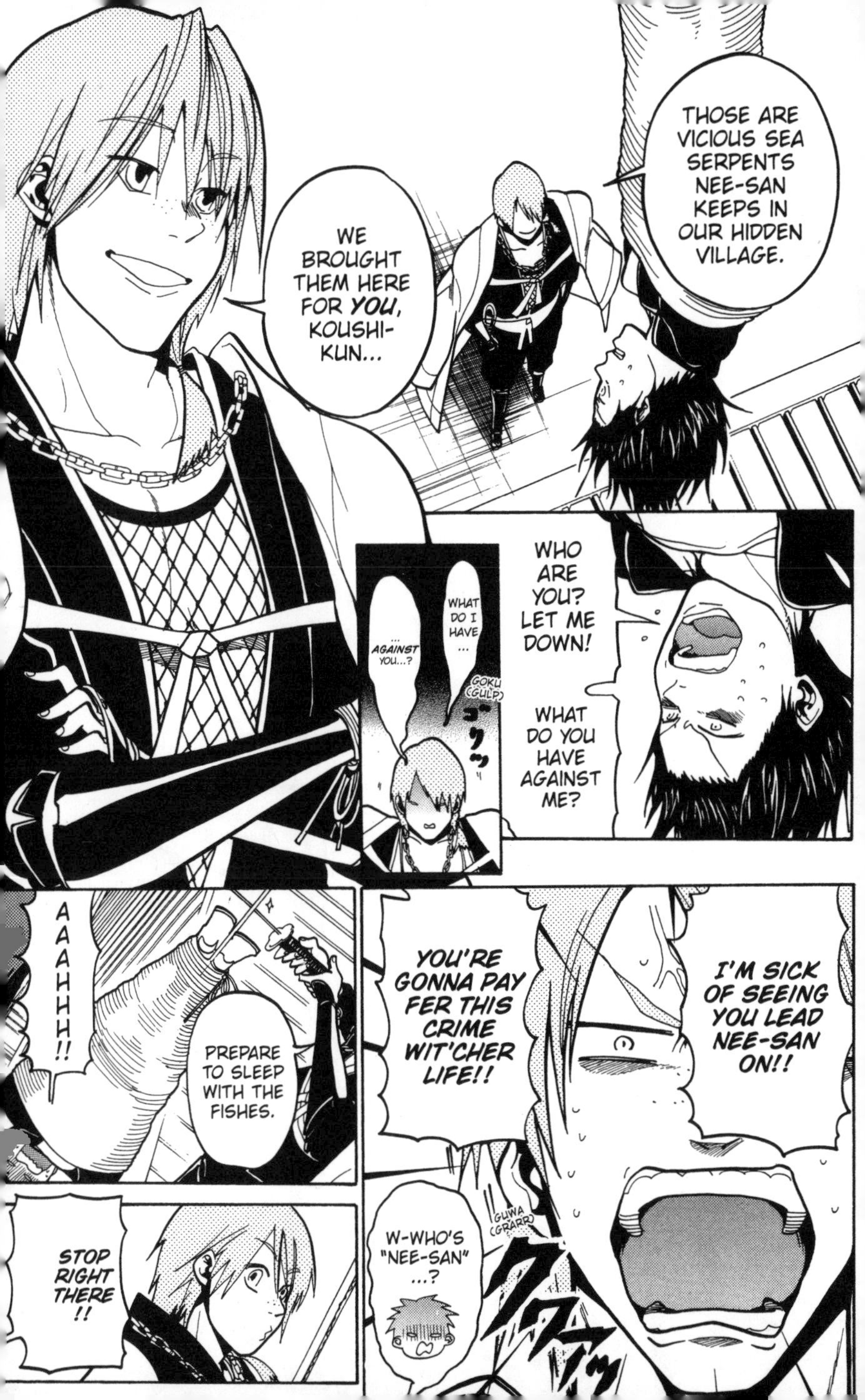
THOSE ARE VICIOUS SEA SERPENTS NEE-SAN KEEPS IN OUR HIDDEN VILLAGE.
WE BROUGHT THEM HERE FOR *YOU*, KOUSHI-KUN...
WHO ARE YOU? LET ME DOWN!
WHAT DO YOU HAVE AGAINST ME?
WHAT DO I HAVE...
...*AGAINST* YOU...?
GOKU (GULP)
I'M SICK OF SEEING YOU LEAD NEE-SAN ON!!
YOU'RE GONNA PAY FER THIS CRIME WIT'CHER LIFE!!
GUWA (GRARR)
W-WHO'S "NEE-SAN" ...?
PREPARE TO SLEEP WITH THE FISHES.
AAAAHHH!!
STOP RIGHT THERE!!

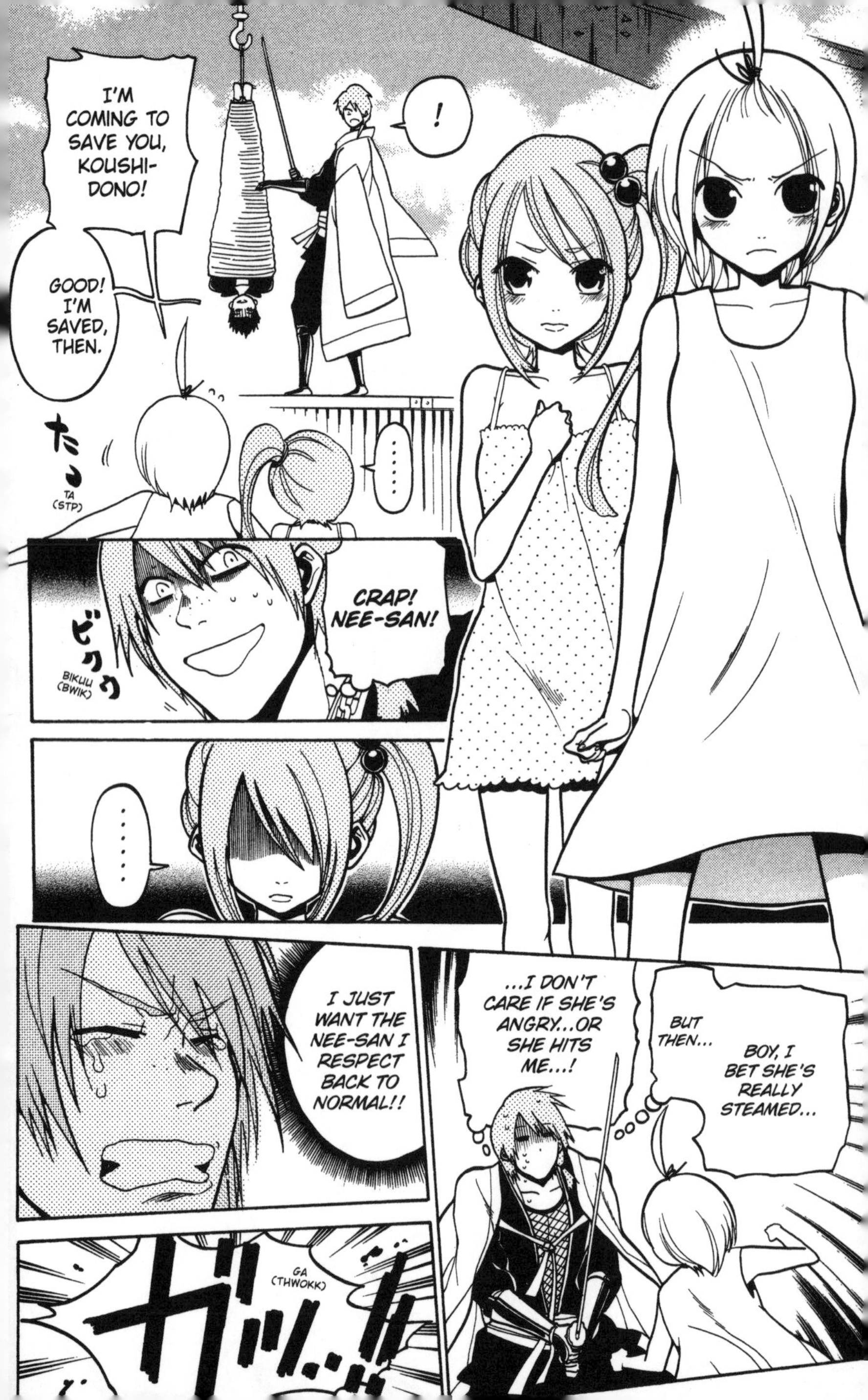
!
I'M COMING TO SAVE YOU, KOUSHI-DONO!
GOOD! I'M SAVED, THEN.
......
たっ
TA (STP)
CRAP! NEE-SAN!
ビクゥ
BIKUU (BWIK)
......
BOY, I BET SHE'S REALLY STEAMED...
BUT THEN...
...I DON'T CARE IF SHE'S ANGRY...OR SHE HITS ME...!
I JUST WANT THE NEE-SAN I RESPECT BACK TO NORMAL!!
ガツ…!!
GA (THWOKK)

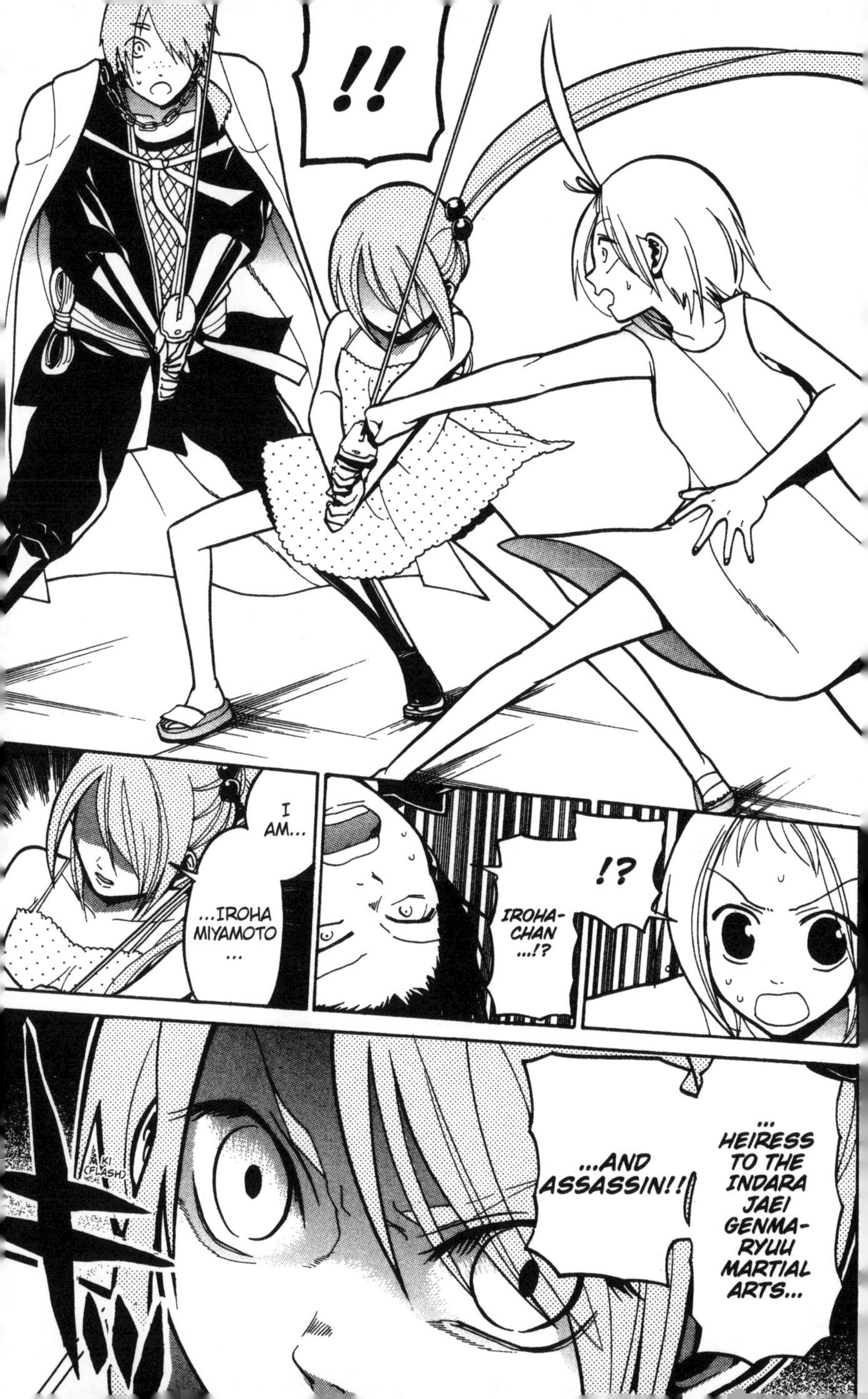
!!
!?
IROHA-CHAN ...!?
I AM...
...IROHA MIYAMOTO ...
... HEIRESS TO THE INDARA JAEI GENMA-RYUU MARTIAL ARTS...
...AND ASSASSIN!!
KI (FLASH)

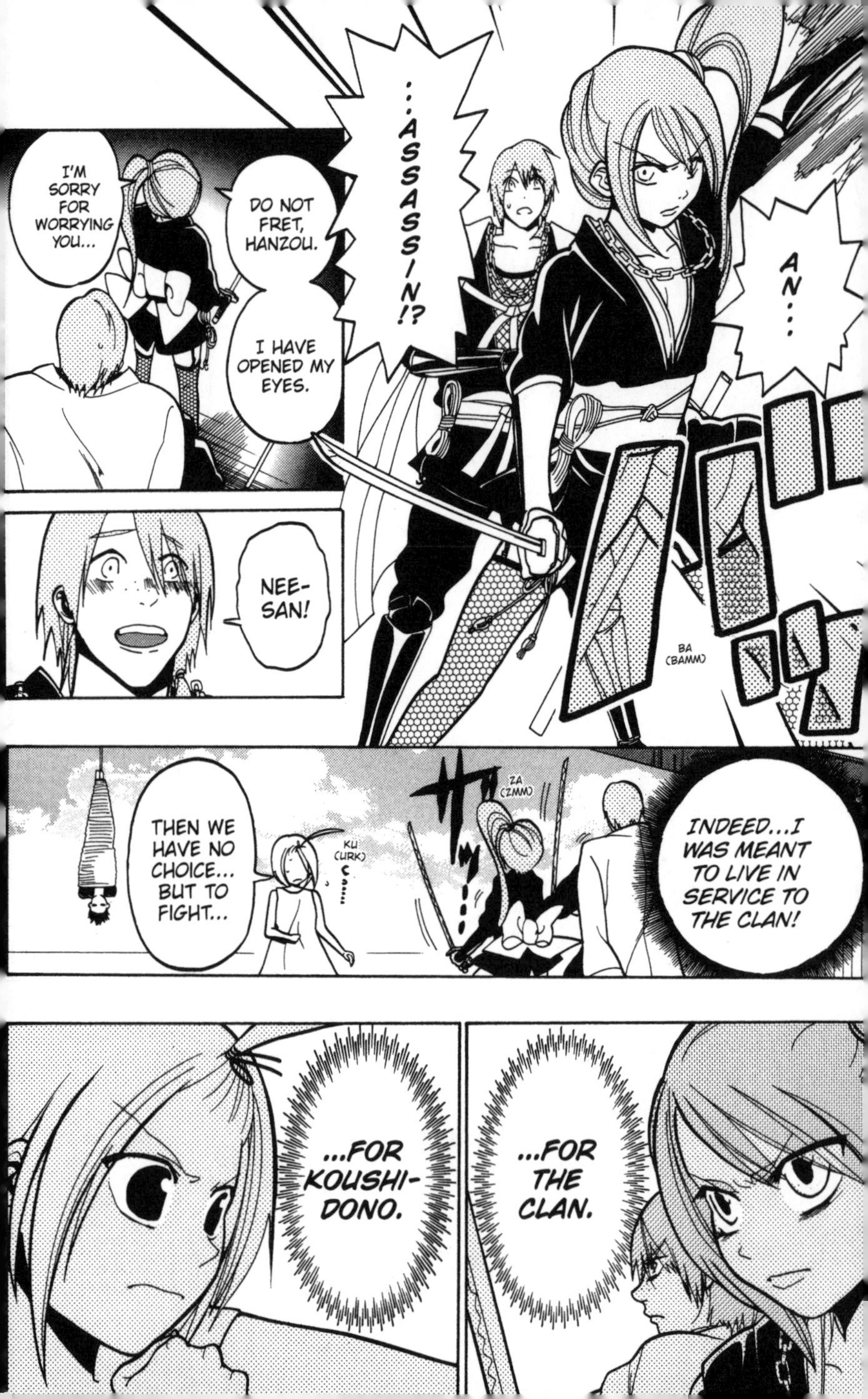
AN...
...ASSASSIN!?
BA (BAMM)
DO NOT FRET, HANZOU.
I HAVE OPENED MY EYES.
I'M SORRY FOR WORRYING YOU...
NEE-SAN!
INDEED...I WAS MEANT TO LIVE IN SERVICE TO THE CLAN!
ZA (ZMM)
KU (URK)
THEN WE HAVE NO CHOICE... BUT TO FIGHT...
...FOR THE CLAN.
...FOR KOUSHI-DONO.

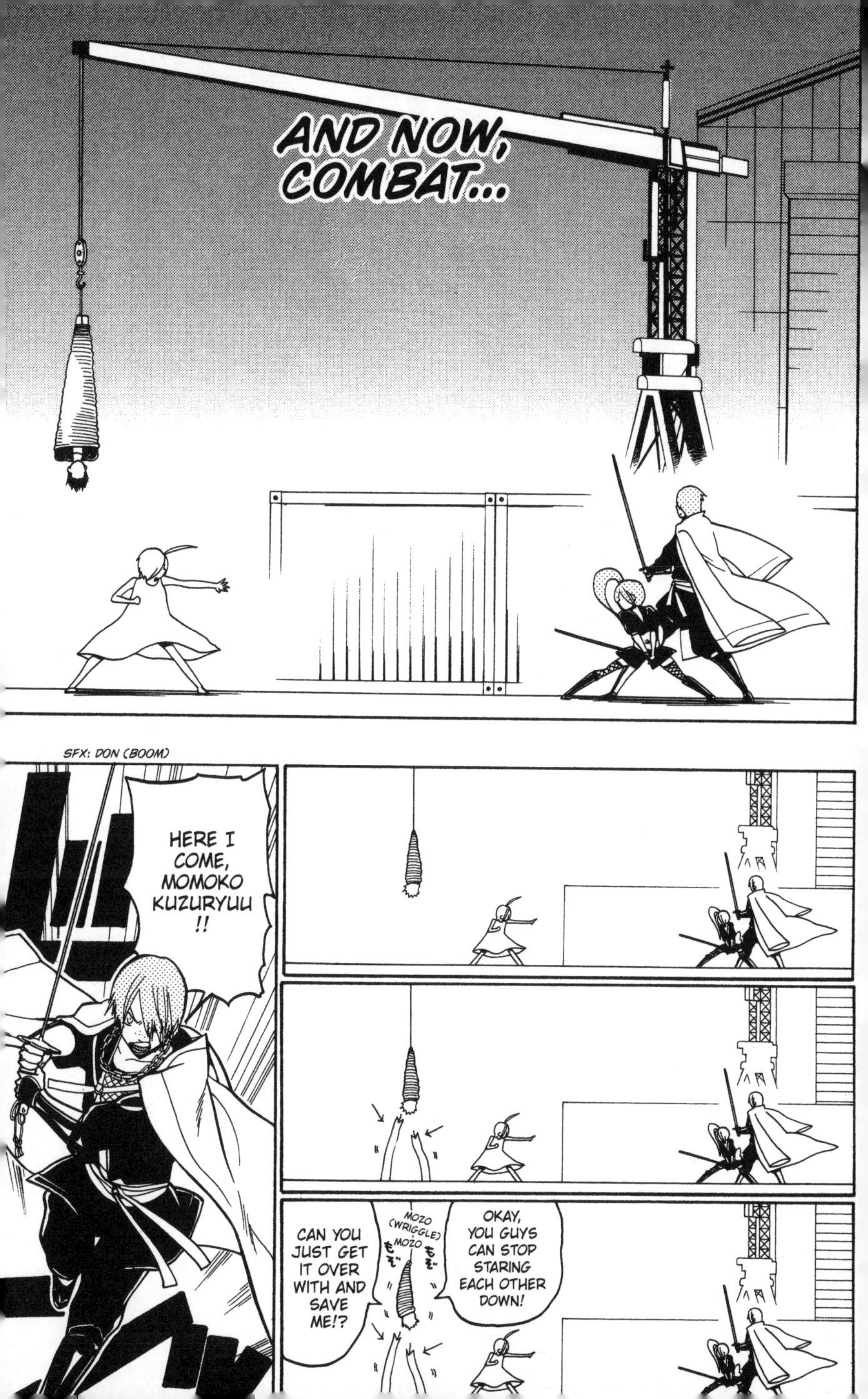
AND NOW, COMBAT...
SFX: DON (BOOM)
OKAY, YOU GUYS CAN STOP STARING EACH OTHER DOWN!
MOZO (WRIGGLE) MOZO
CAN YOU JUST GET IT OVER WITH AND SAVE ME!?
HERE I COME, MOMOKO KUZURYUU!!

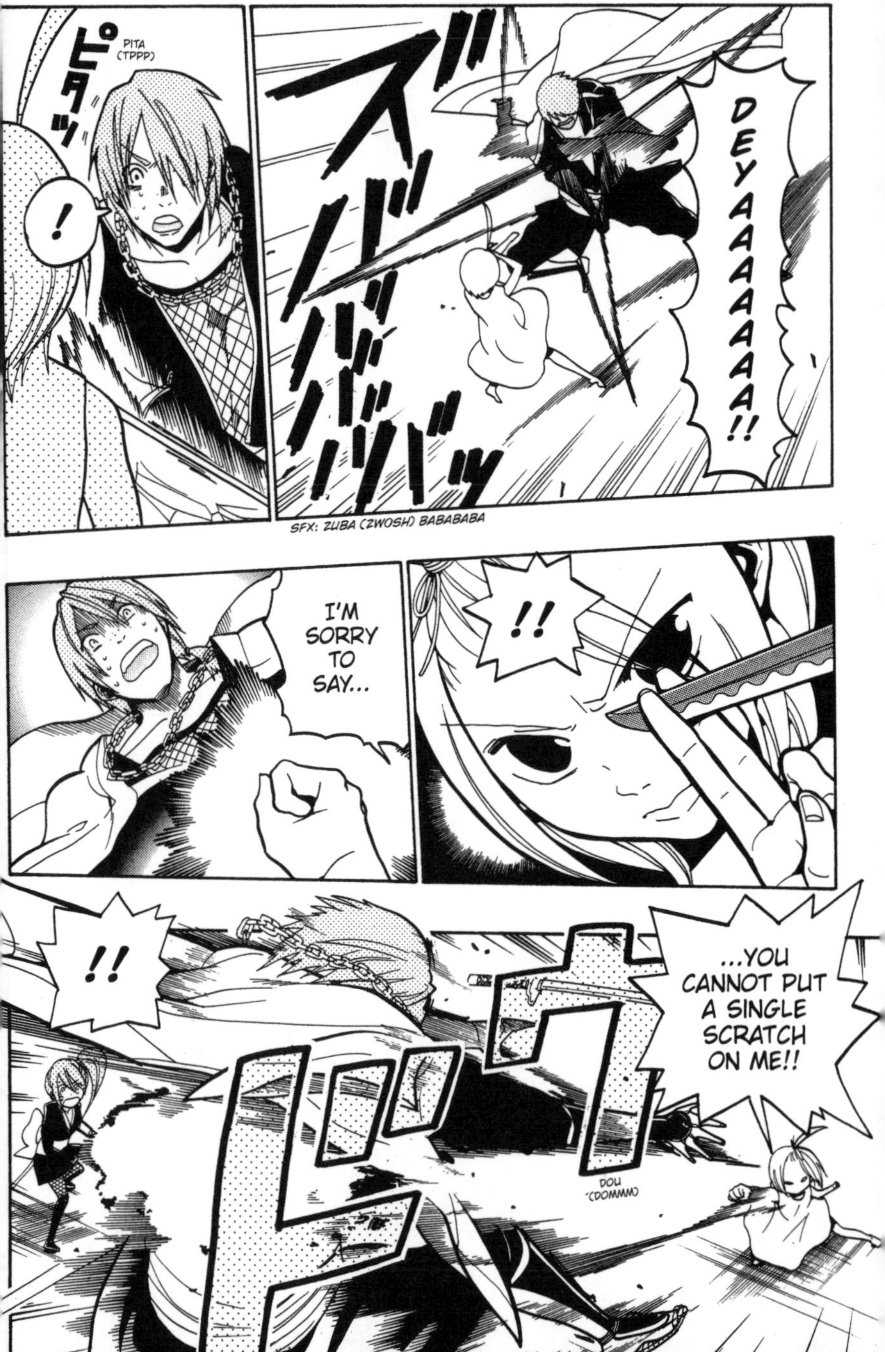
DEYAAAAAAAAAA!!
SFX: ZUBA (ZWOSH) BABABABA
PITA (TPPP)
!
!!
I'M SORRY TO SAY...
...YOU CANNOT PUT A SINGLE SCRATCH ON ME!!
!!
DOU (DOMMM)

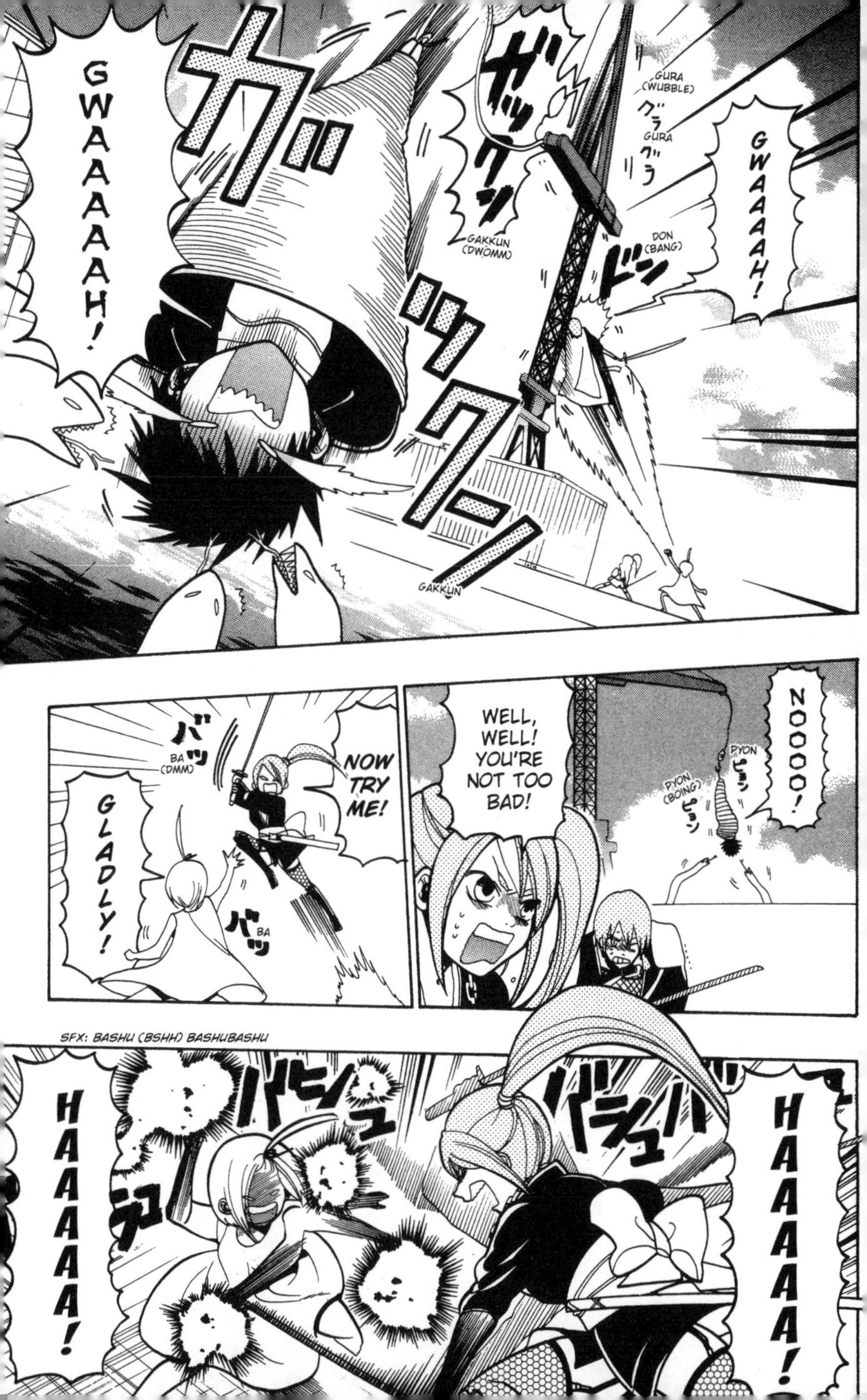
GURA (WUBBLE)
GURA
GWAAAAAH!
DON (BANG)
GAKKUN (DWOMM)
GAKKUN
GWAAAAAAH!
NOOOOO!
PYON
PYON (BOING)
WELL, WELL! YOU'RE NOT TOO BAD!
NOW TRY ME!
BA (DMM)
GLADLY!
BA
SFX: BASHU (BSHH) BASHUBASHU
HAAAAAAA!
HAAAAAAA!

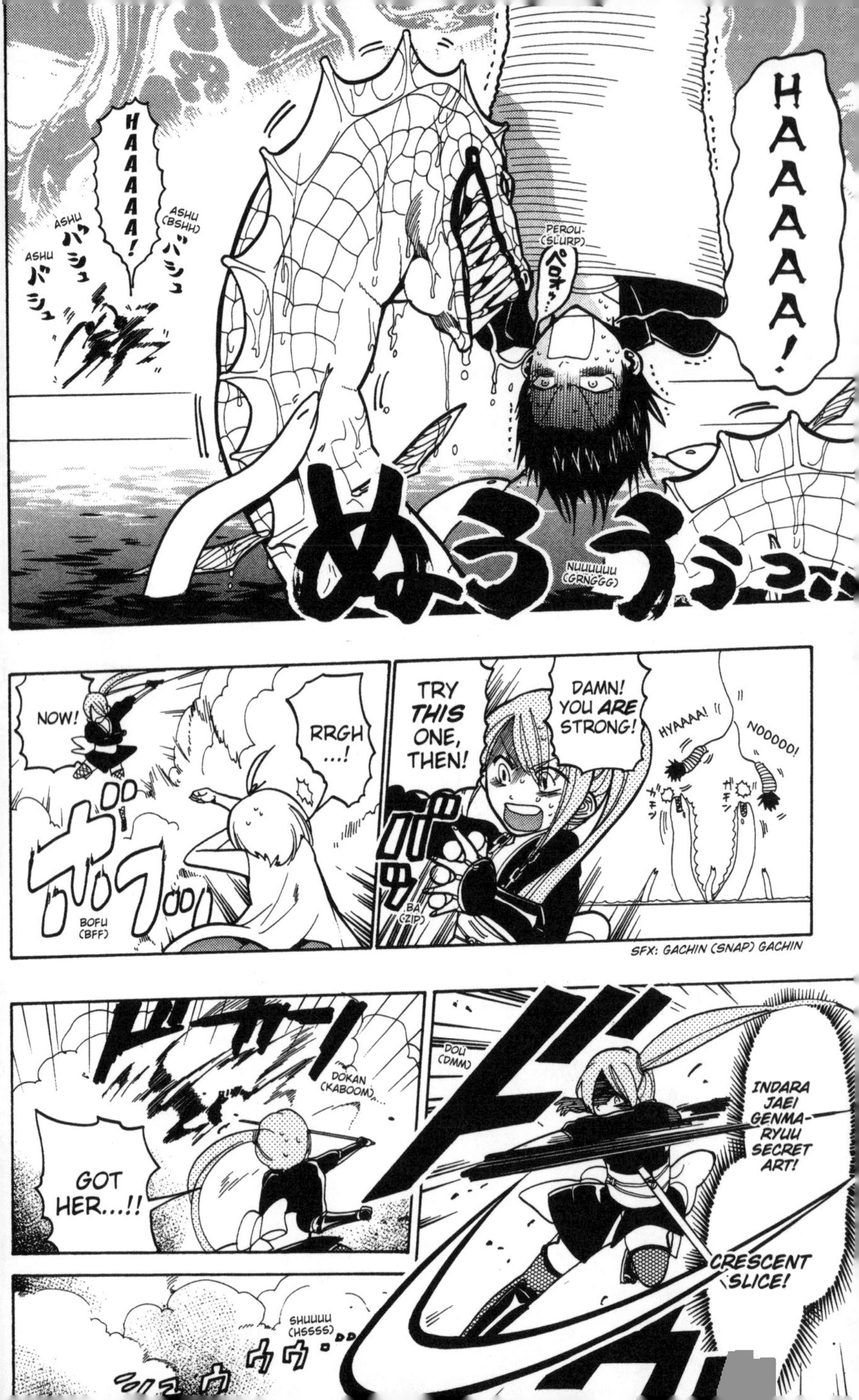
HAAAAAA!
PEROU- (SLURP) ペロォ…
ASHU (BSHH) バシュ
ASHU バシュ
ASHU バシュ
HAAAAAA!
NUUUUUU (GRNGGG) ぬろろぅっ…
NOOOOO!
HYAAAA!
DAMN! YOU ARE STRONG!
TRY THIS ONE, THEN!
BA (ZIP)
RRGH ...!
NOW!
BOFU (BFF)
SFX: GACHIN (SNAP) GACHIN
INDARA JAEI GENMA-RYUU SECRET ART!
CRESCENT SLICE!
DOU (DMM)
DOKAN (KABOOM)
GOT HER...!!
SHUUUU (HSSSS)

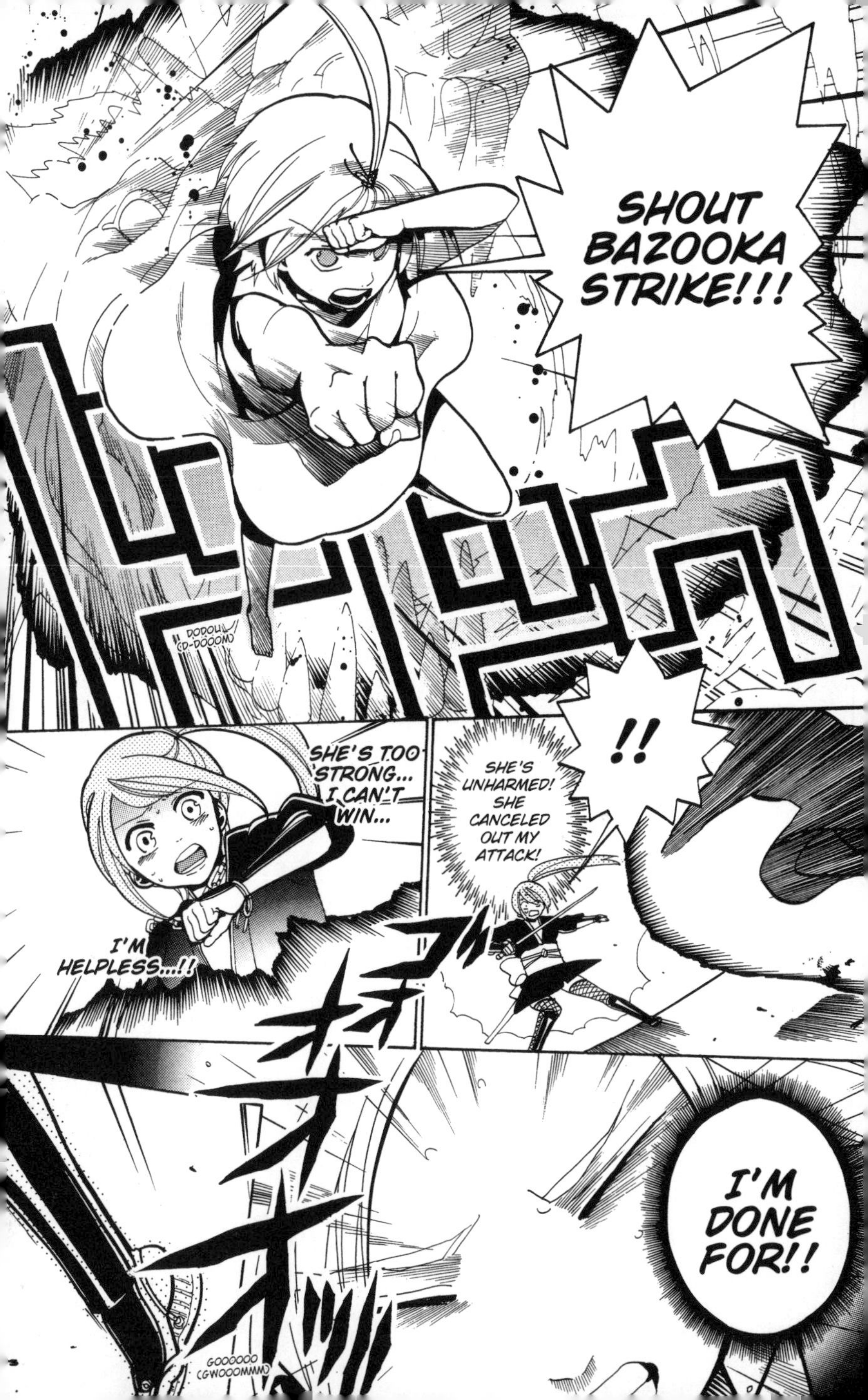
SHOUT BAZOOKA STRIKE!!!
DODOU (D-DOOOM)
!!
SHE'S UNHARMED! SHE CANCELED OUT MY ATTACK!
SHE'S TOO STRONG... I CAN'T WIN...
I'M HELPLESS...!!
I'M DONE FOR!!
GOOOOOO (GWOOOMMM)

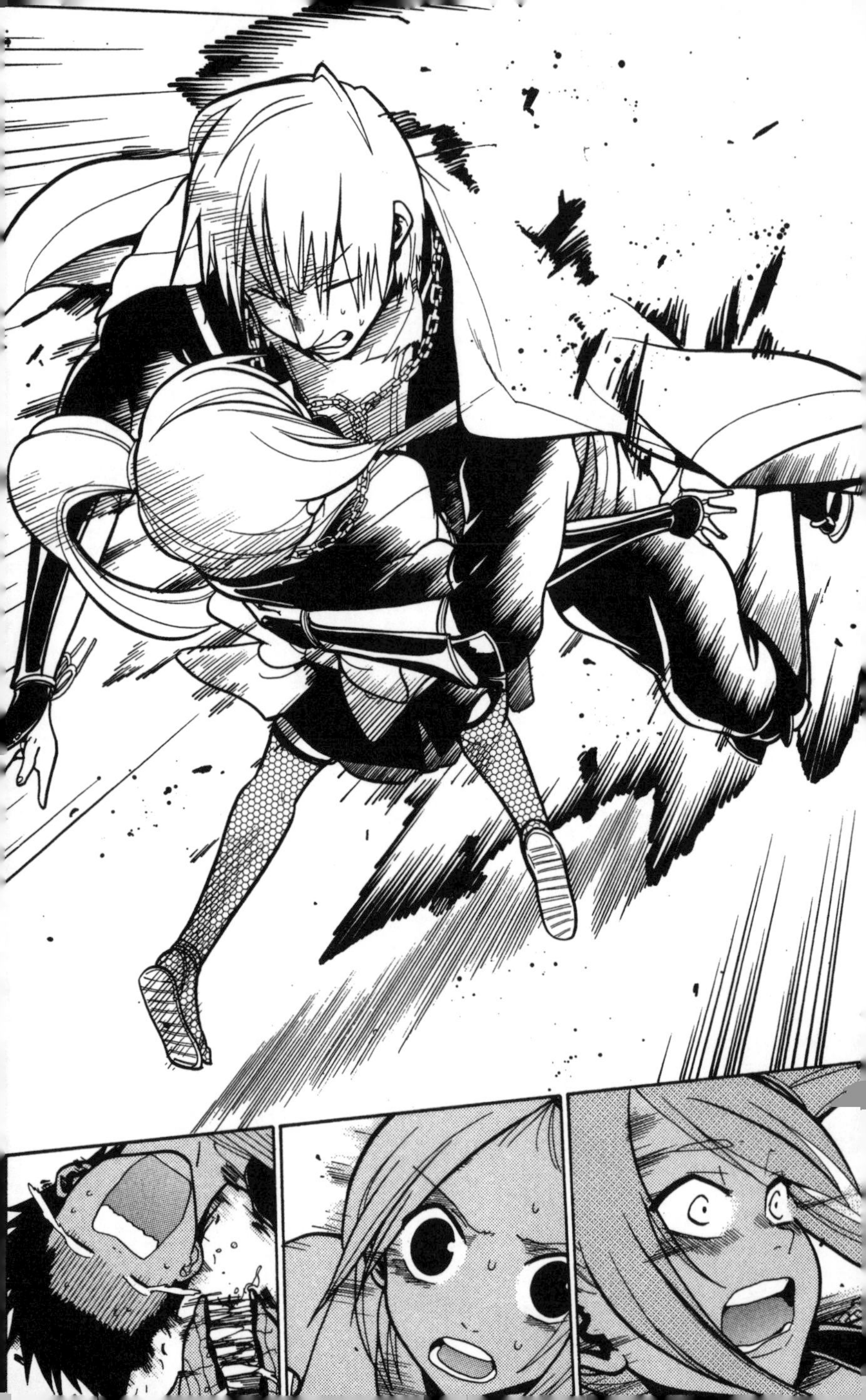

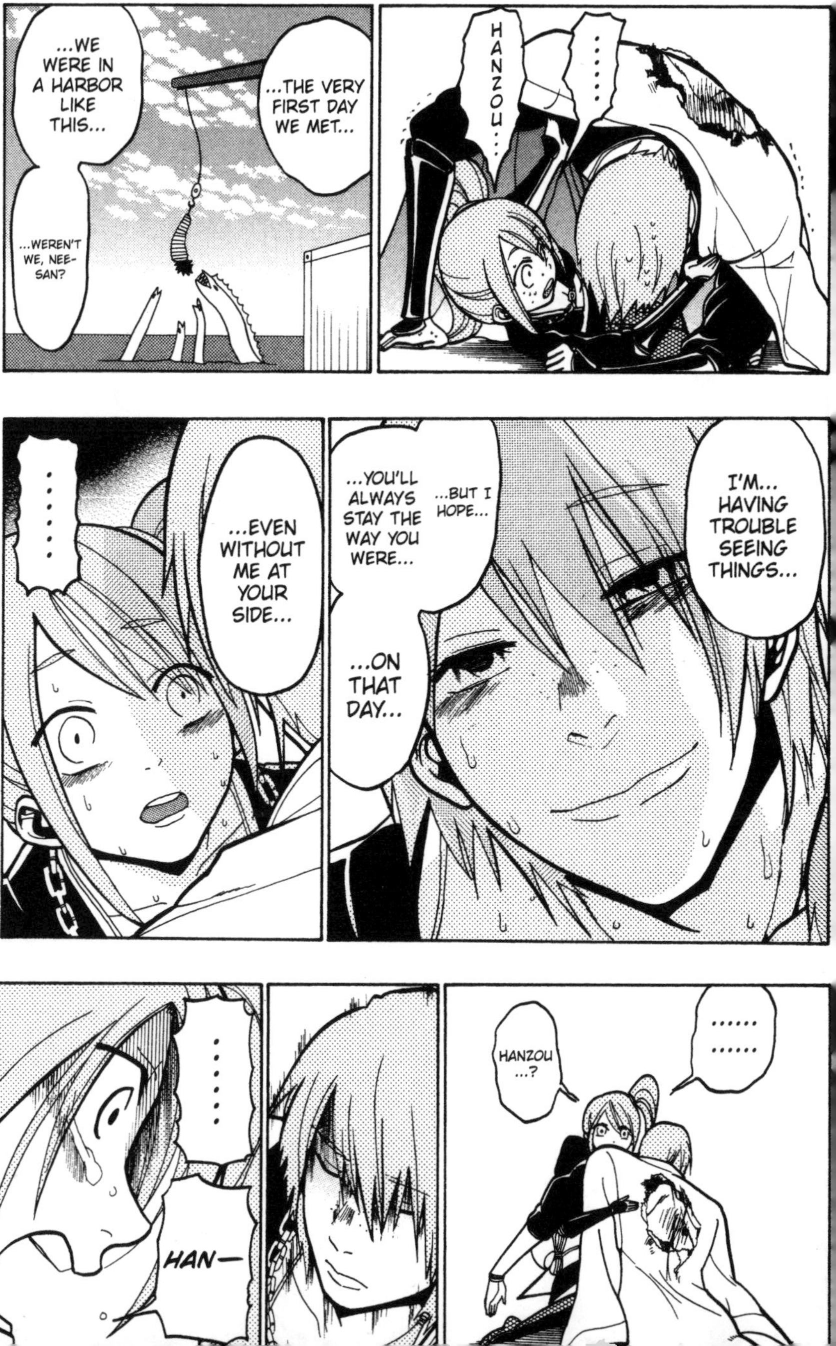
......
HANZOU...
...THE VERY FIRST DAY WE MET...
...WE WERE IN A HARBOR LIKE THIS...
...WEREN'T WE, NEE-SAN?
I'M... HAVING TROUBLE SEEING THINGS...
...BUT I HOPE...
...YOU'LL ALWAYS STAY THE WAY YOU WERE...
...ON THAT DAY...
...EVEN WITHOUT ME AT YOUR SIDE...
......
....
HANZOU ...?
......
HAN—

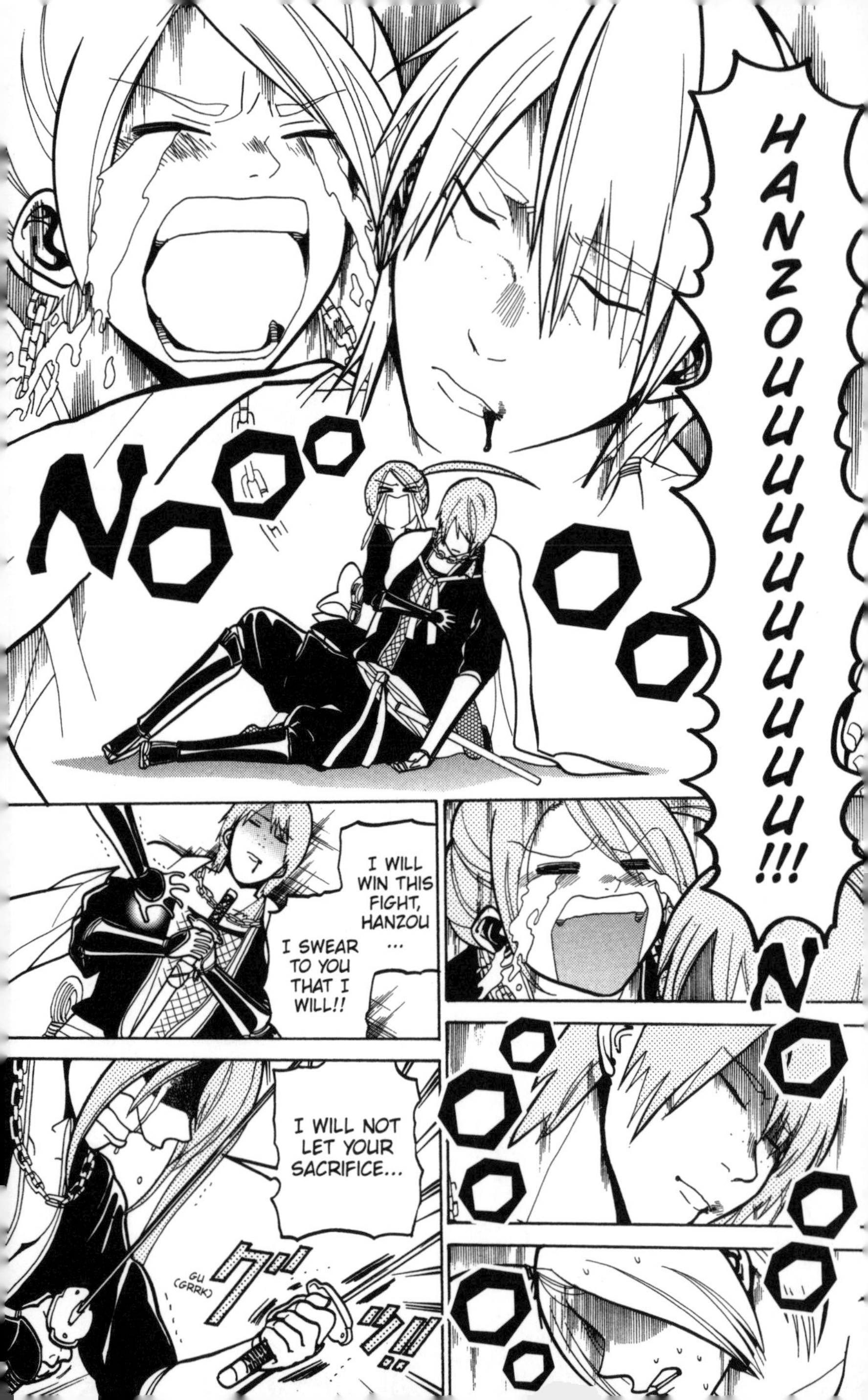
HANZOUUUUUUUUUUUUU!!!
NOOOOOO
NOOOOOOOO
I WILL WIN THIS FIGHT, HANZOU...
I SWEAR TO YOU THAT I WILL!!
I WILL NOT LET YOUR SACRIFICE...
GU (GRRK)

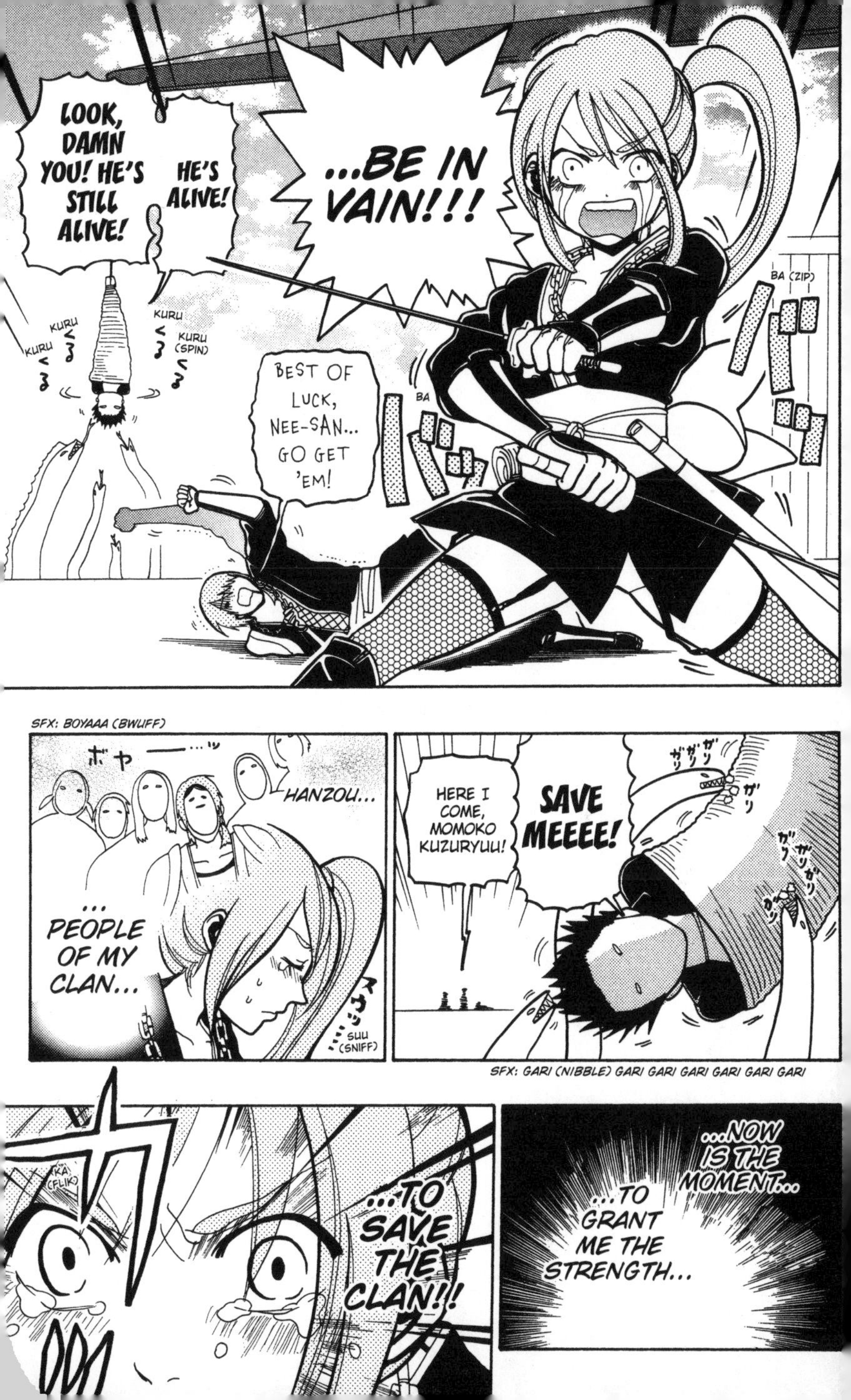
...BE IN VAIN!!!
HE'S ALIVE!
LOOK, DAMN YOU! HE'S STILL ALIVE!
BA (ZIP)
BA
KURU KURU (SPIN)
KURU
KURU
KURU
BEST OF LUCK, NEE-SAN... GO GET 'EM!
SAVE MEEEE!
HERE I COME, MOMOKO KUZURYUU!
SFX: GARI (NIBBLE) GARI GARI GARI GARI GARI GARI
SFX: BOYAAA (BWUFF)
HANZOU...
...PEOPLE OF MY CLAN...
SUU (SNIFF)
...NOW IS THE MOMENT...
...TO GRANT ME THE STRENGTH...
...TO SAVE THE CLAN!!
KA (FLIK)

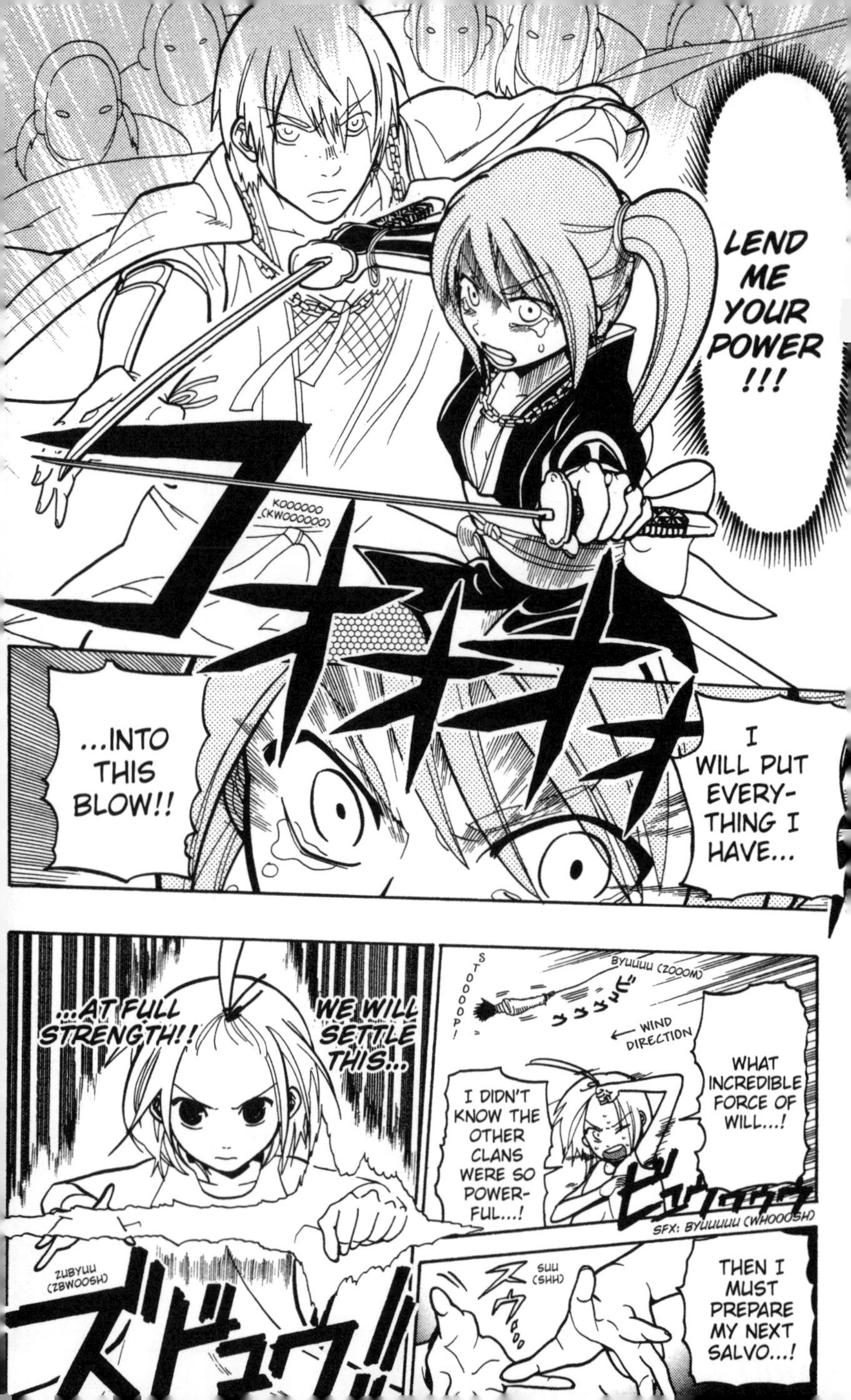
LEND ME YOUR POWER!!!
KOOOOOO (KWOOOOOO)
I WILL PUT EVERYTHING I HAVE...
...INTO THIS BLOW!!
STOOOOP!
BYUUUU (ZOOOM)
← WIND DIRECTION
WHAT INCREDIBLE FORCE OF WILL...!
I DIDN'T KNOW THE OTHER CLANS WERE SO POWERFUL...!
SFX: BYUUUUU (WHOOOSH)
WE WILL SETTLE THIS...
...AT FULL STRENGTH!!
SUU (SHH)
THEN I MUST PREPARE MY NEXT SALVO...!
ZUBYUU (ZBWOOSH)

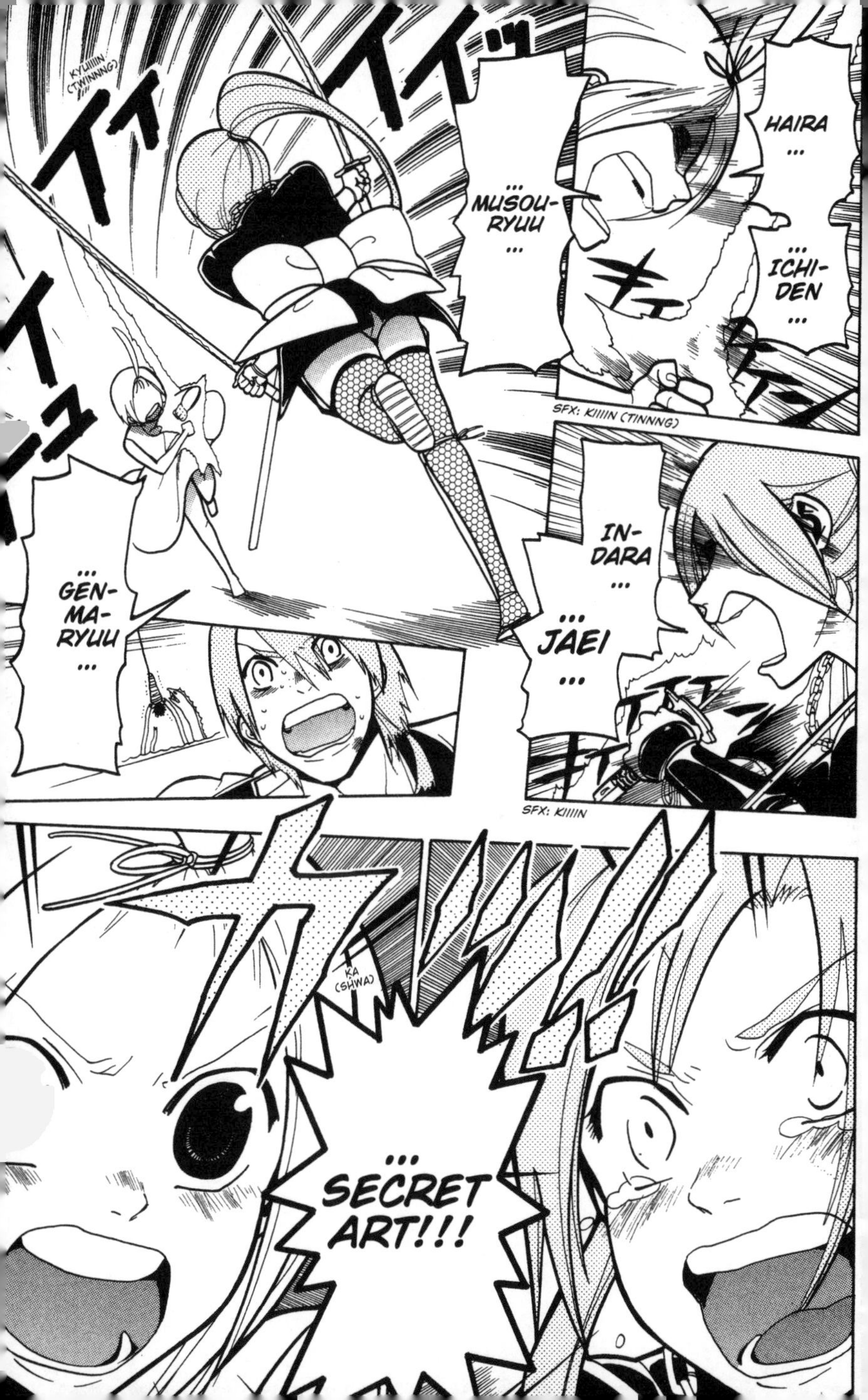

HAIRA ...
... MUSOU-RYUU ...
... ICHI-DEN ...
SFX: KIIIIN (TINNNG)
KYUIIIIN (TWINNNG)
IN-DARA ...
... JAEI ...
SFX: KIIIN
... GEN-MA-RYUU ...
KA (SHWA)
... SECRET ART!!!

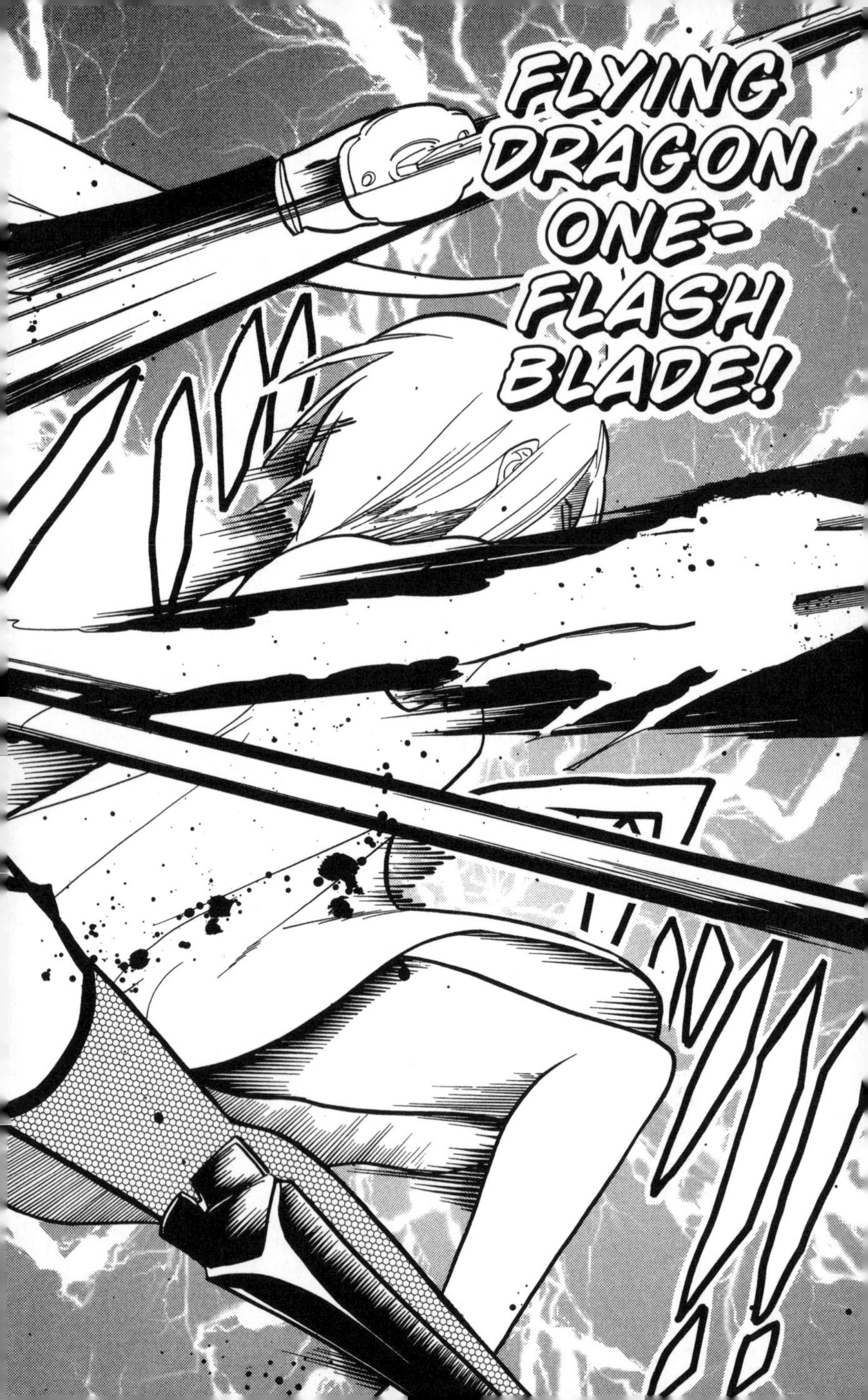
FLYING DRAGON ONE-FLASH BLADE!

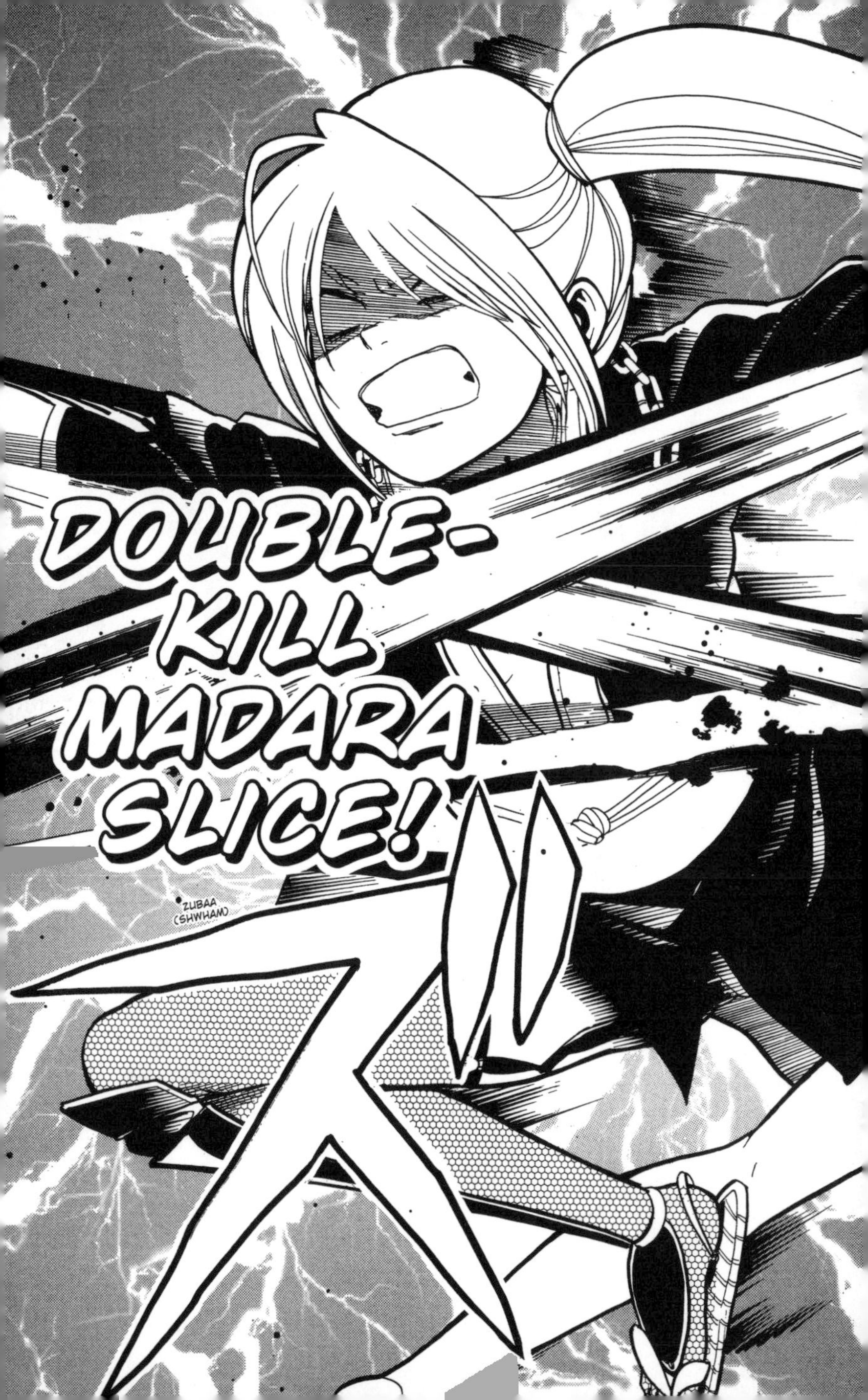
DOUBLE-KILL MADARA SLICE!
ZUBAA (SHWHAM)

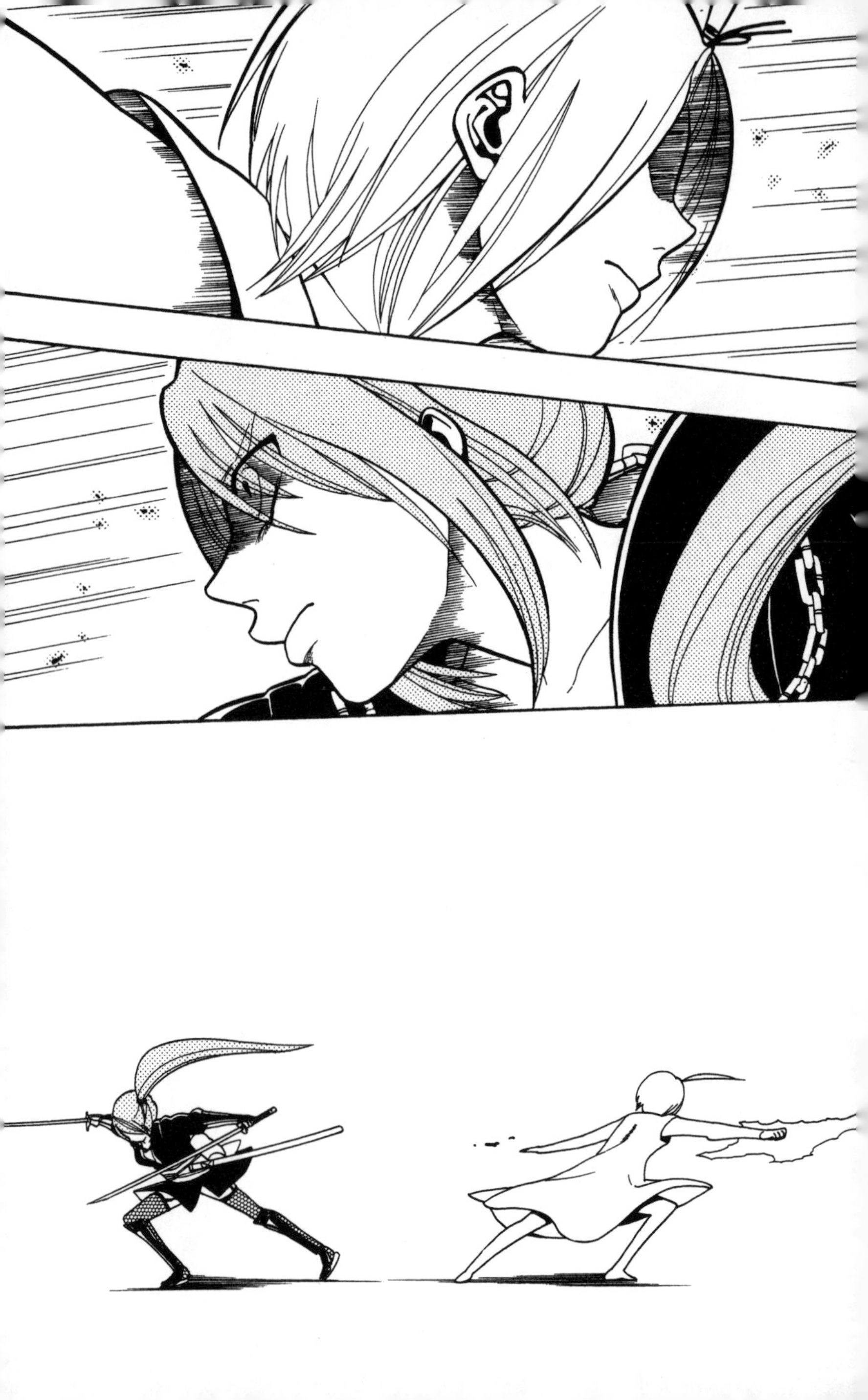

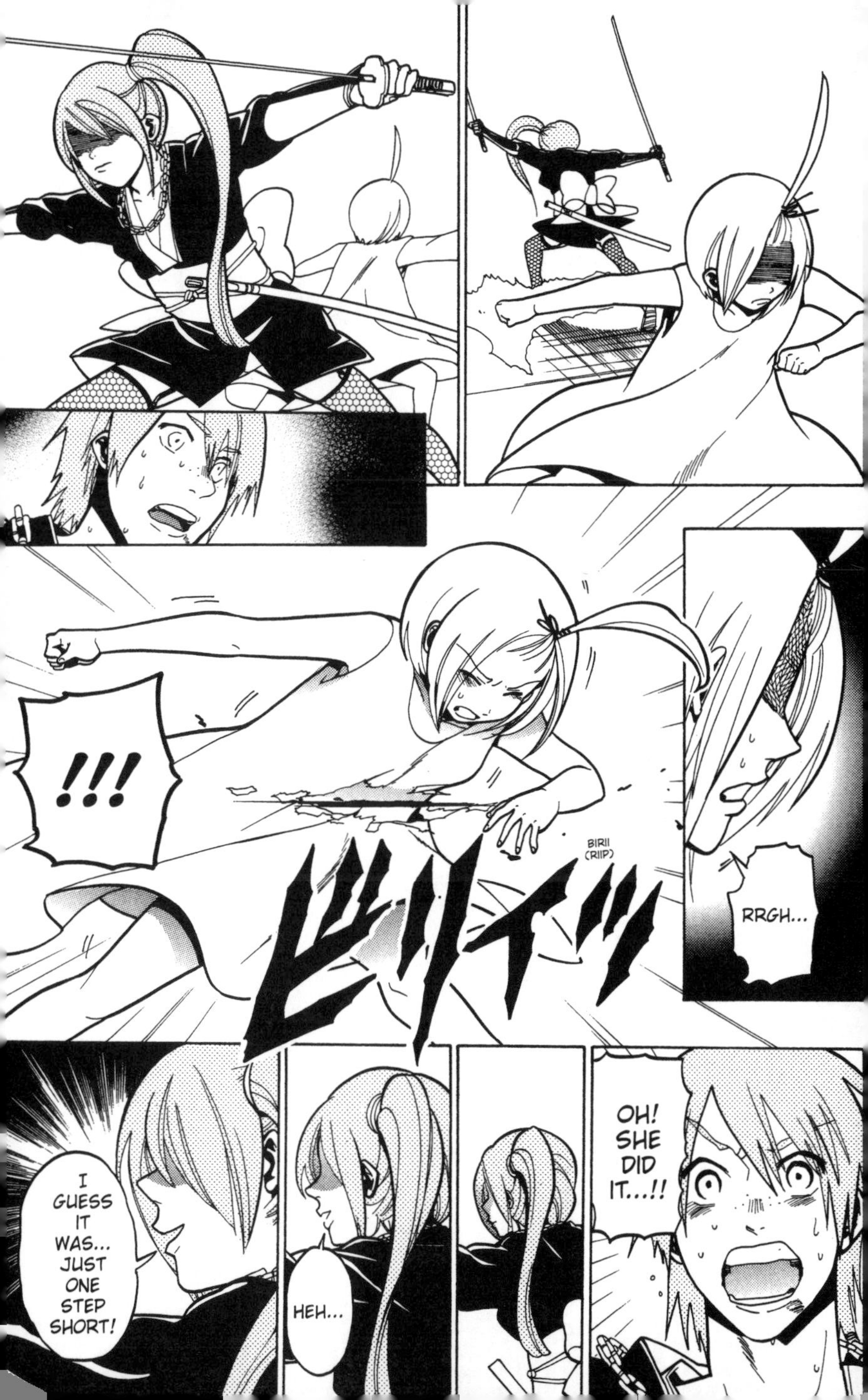
RRGH...
!!!
BIRII (RIIP)
ビリイッ
OH! SHE DID IT...!!
HEH...
I GUESS IT WAS... JUST ONE STEP SHORT!

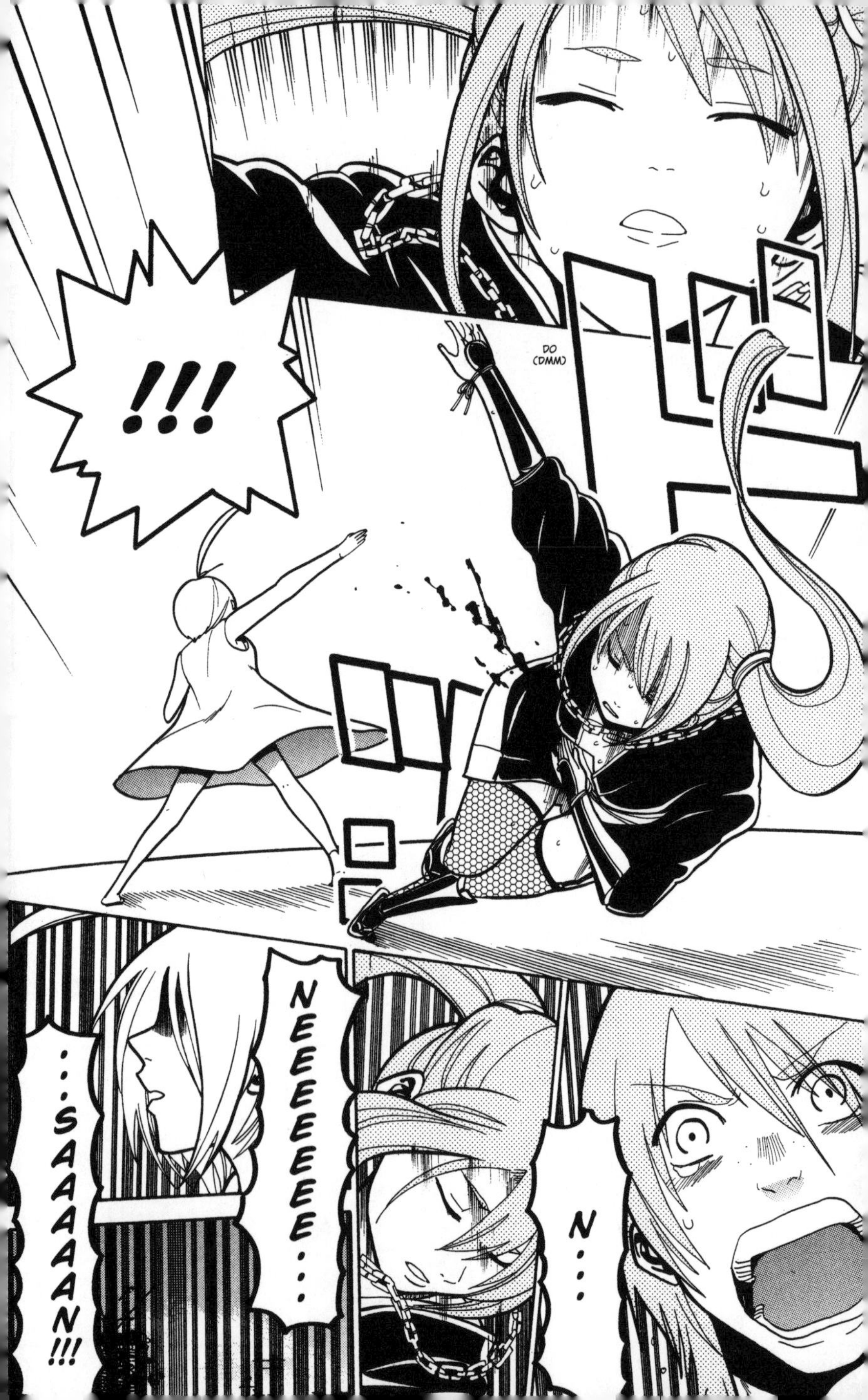
DO
(DMM)
!!!
N...
NEEEEEEEE...
...SAAAAAAN!!!

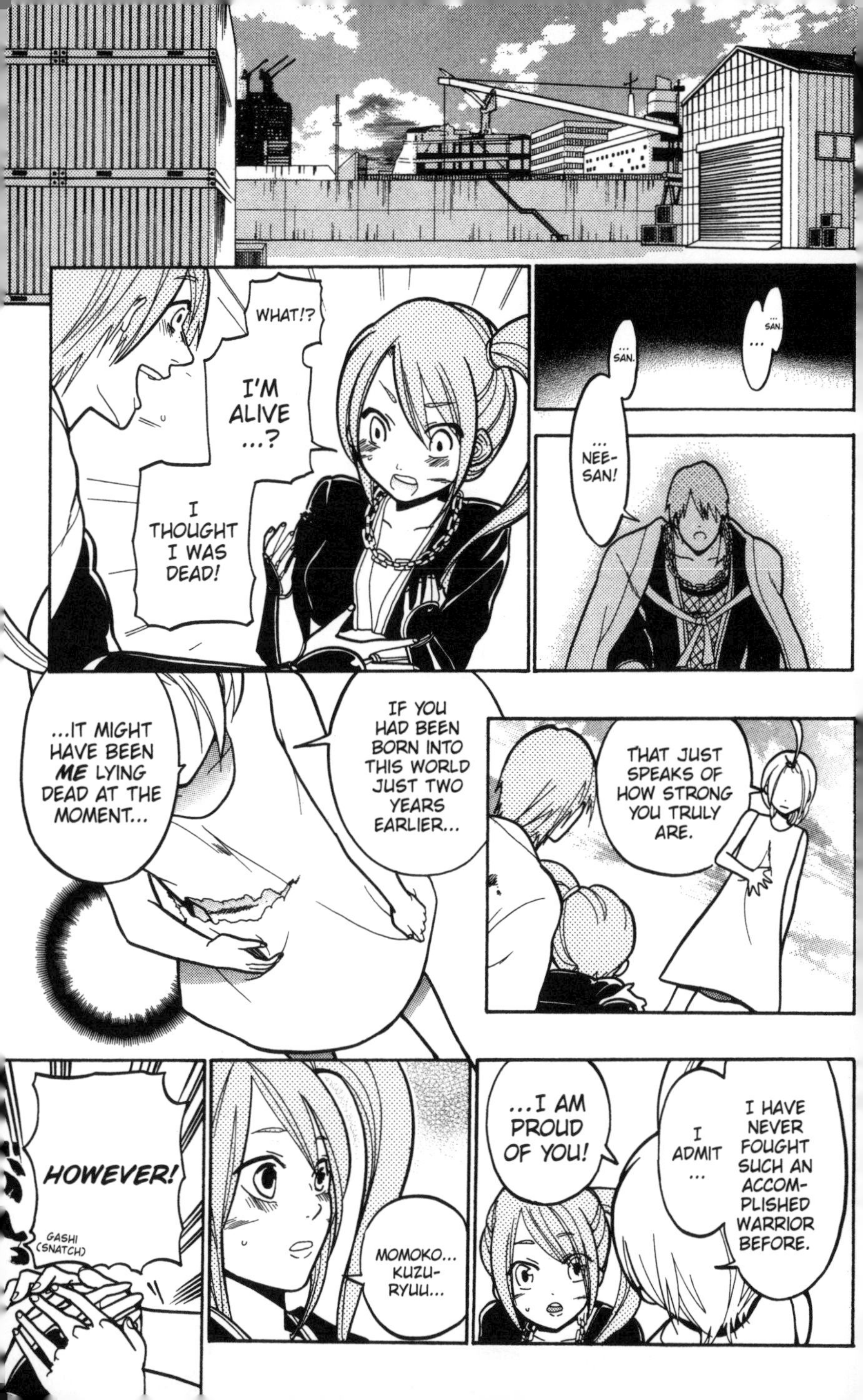

... SAN.
...
... SAN.
... NEE-SAN!
WHAT!?
I'M ALIVE ...?
I THOUGHT I WAS DEAD!
THAT JUST SPEAKS OF HOW STRONG YOU TRULY ARE.
IF YOU HAD BEEN BORN INTO THIS WORLD JUST TWO YEARS EARLIER...
...IT MIGHT HAVE BEEN *ME* LYING DEAD AT THE MOMENT...
I ADMIT ...
I HAVE NEVER FOUGHT SUCH AN ACCOMPLISHED WARRIOR BEFORE.
...I AM PROUD OF YOU!
MOMOKO... KUZURYUU...
HOWEVER!
GASHI (SNATCH)

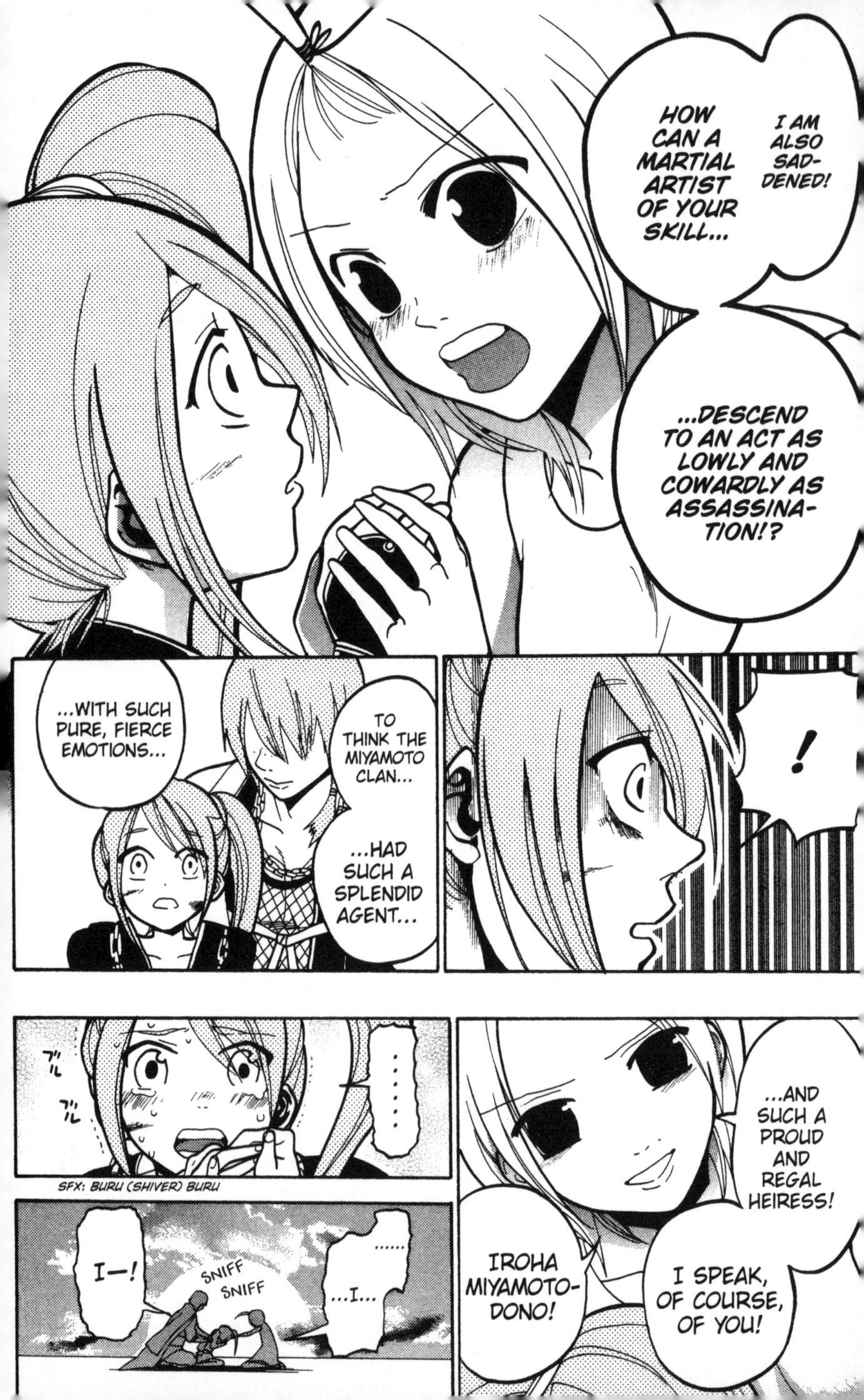
I AM ALSO SAD-DENED!
HOW CAN A MARTIAL ARTIST OF YOUR SKILL...
...DESCEND TO AN ACT AS LOWLY AND COWARDLY AS ASSASSINA-TION!?
!
TO THINK THE MIYAMOTO CLAN...
...HAD SUCH A SPLENDID AGENT...
...WITH SUCH PURE, FIERCE EMOTIONS...
...AND SUCH A PROUD AND REGAL HEIRESS!
I SPEAK, OF COURSE, OF YOU!
IROHA MIYAMOTO-DONO!
......
ブル
ブル
SFX: BURU (SHIVER) BURU
......
...I...
SNIFF SNIFF
I—!

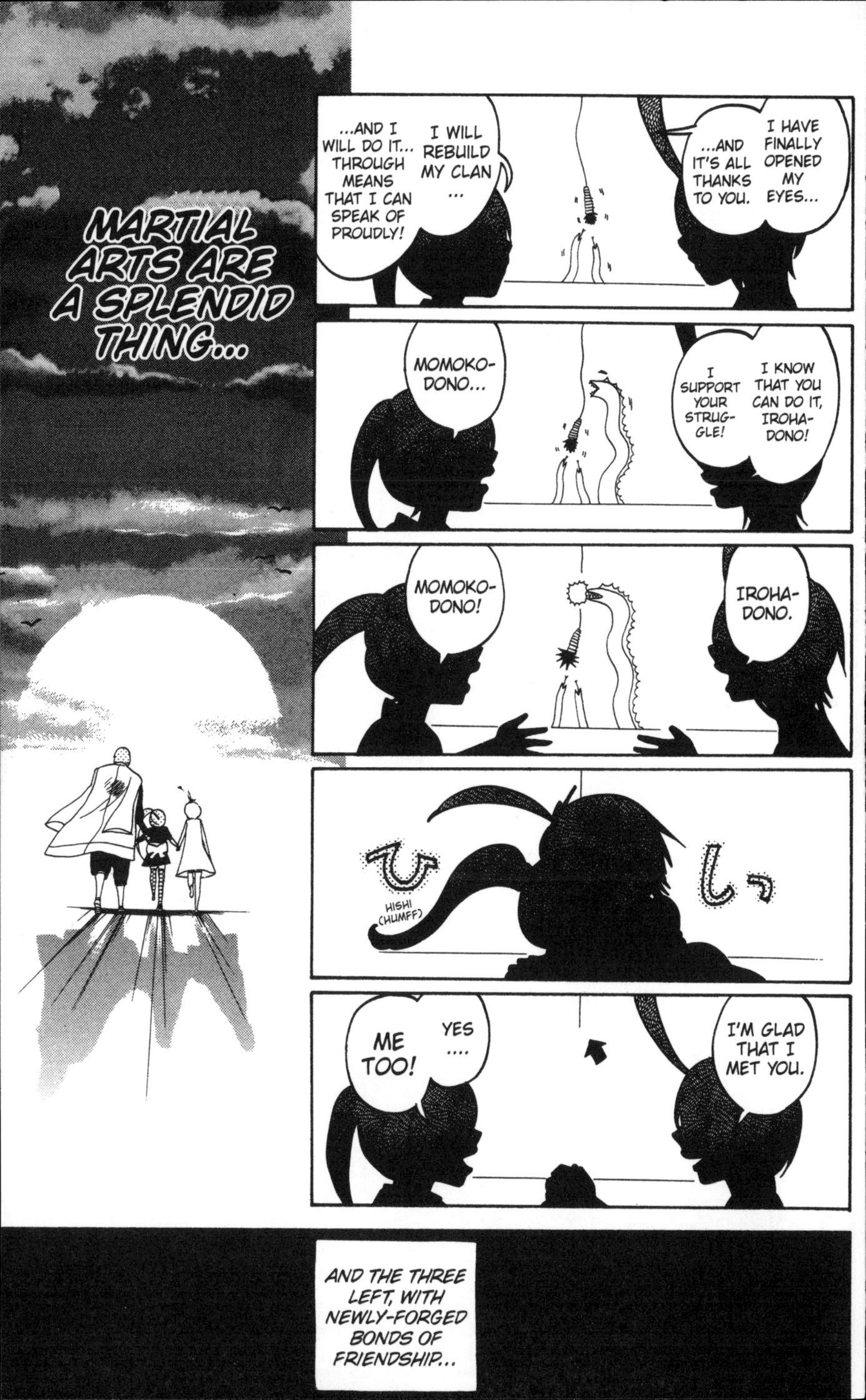
I HAVE FINALLY OPENED MY EYES...
...AND IT'S ALL THANKS TO YOU.
I WILL REBUILD MY CLAN ...
...AND I WILL DO IT... THROUGH MEANS THAT I CAN SPEAK OF PROUDLY!
I KNOW THAT YOU CAN DO IT, IROHA-DONO!
I SUPPORT YOUR STRUG-GLE!
MOMOKO-DONO...
IROHA-DONO.
MOMOKO-DONO!
HISHI (HUMFF)
I'M GLAD THAT I MET YOU.
YES ....
ME TOO!
MARTIAL ARTS ARE A SPLENDID THING...
AND THE THREE LEFT, WITH NEWLY-FORGED BONDS OF FRIENDSHIP...

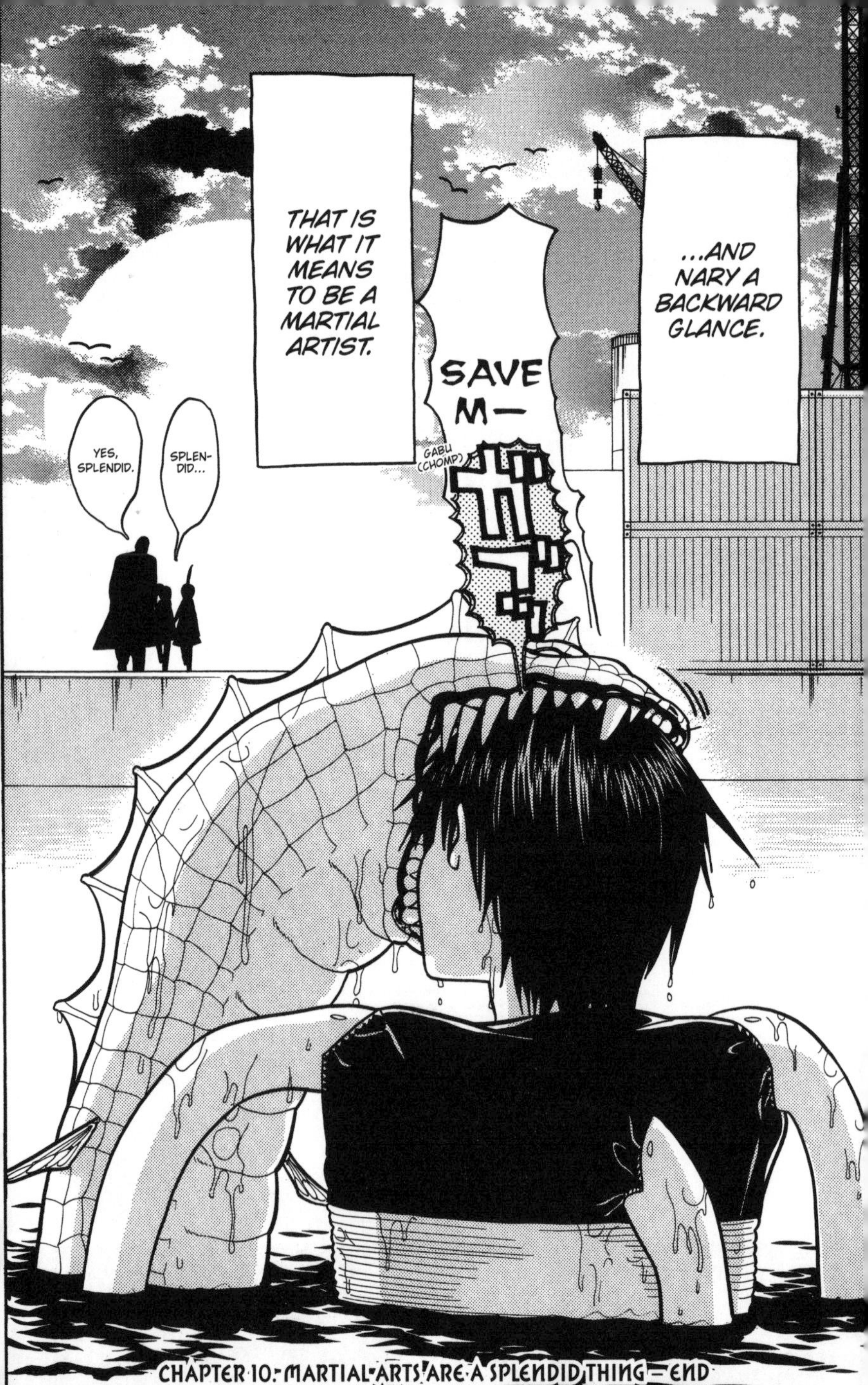
...AND NARY A BACKWARD GLANCE.
SAVE M—
ガブッ
GABU (CHOMP)
THAT IS WHAT IT MEANS TO BE A MARTIAL ARTIST.
SPLEN-DID...
YES, SPLENDID.

CHAPTER 10: MARTIAL ARTS ARE A SPLENDID THING — END

11. PUT YOUR ALL INTO LOVE

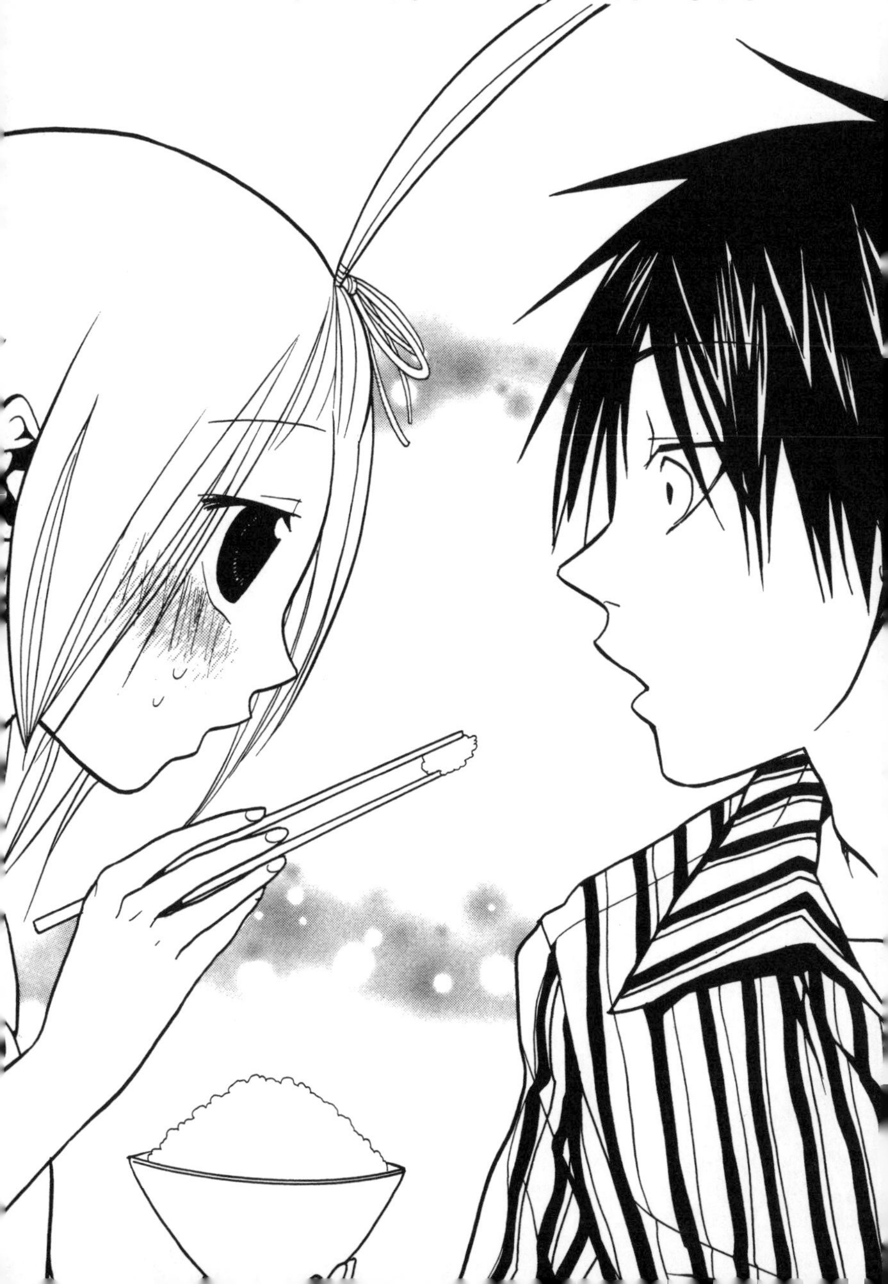

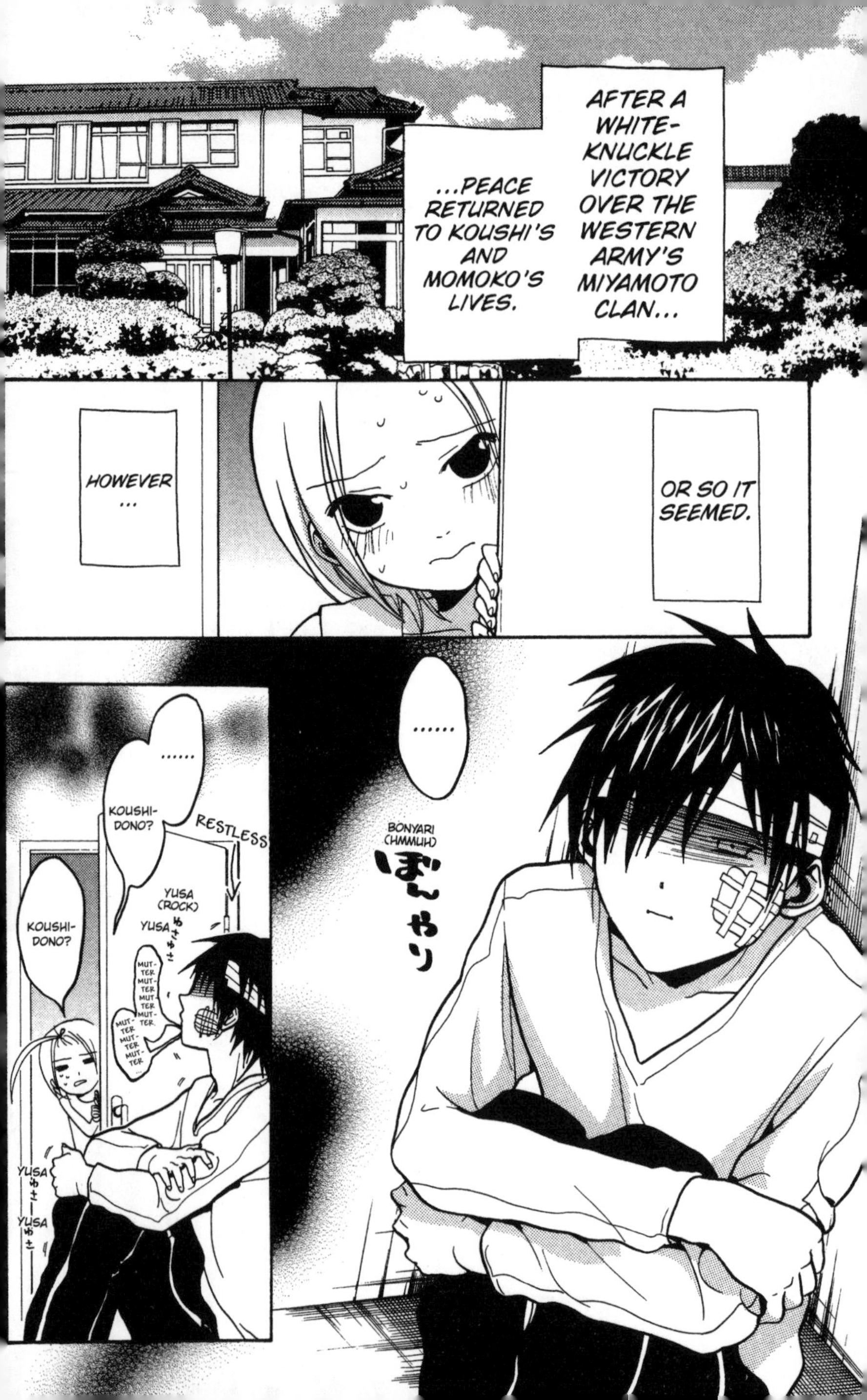
AFTER A WHITE-KNUCKLE VICTORY OVER THE WESTERN ARMY'S MIYAMOTO CLAN...
...PEACE RETURNED TO KOUSHI'S AND MOMOKO'S LIVES.
OR SO IT SEEMED.
HOWEVER...
......
BONYARI (HMMUH)
ぼんやり
......
KOUSHI-DONO?
RESTLESS
YUSA (ROCK)
YUSA ゆさゆさ
MUTTER MUTTER MUTTER MUTTER MUTTER MUTTER.
MUTTER MUTTER MUTTER MUTTER
KOUSHI-DONO?
YUSA ゆさー
YUSA ゆさー

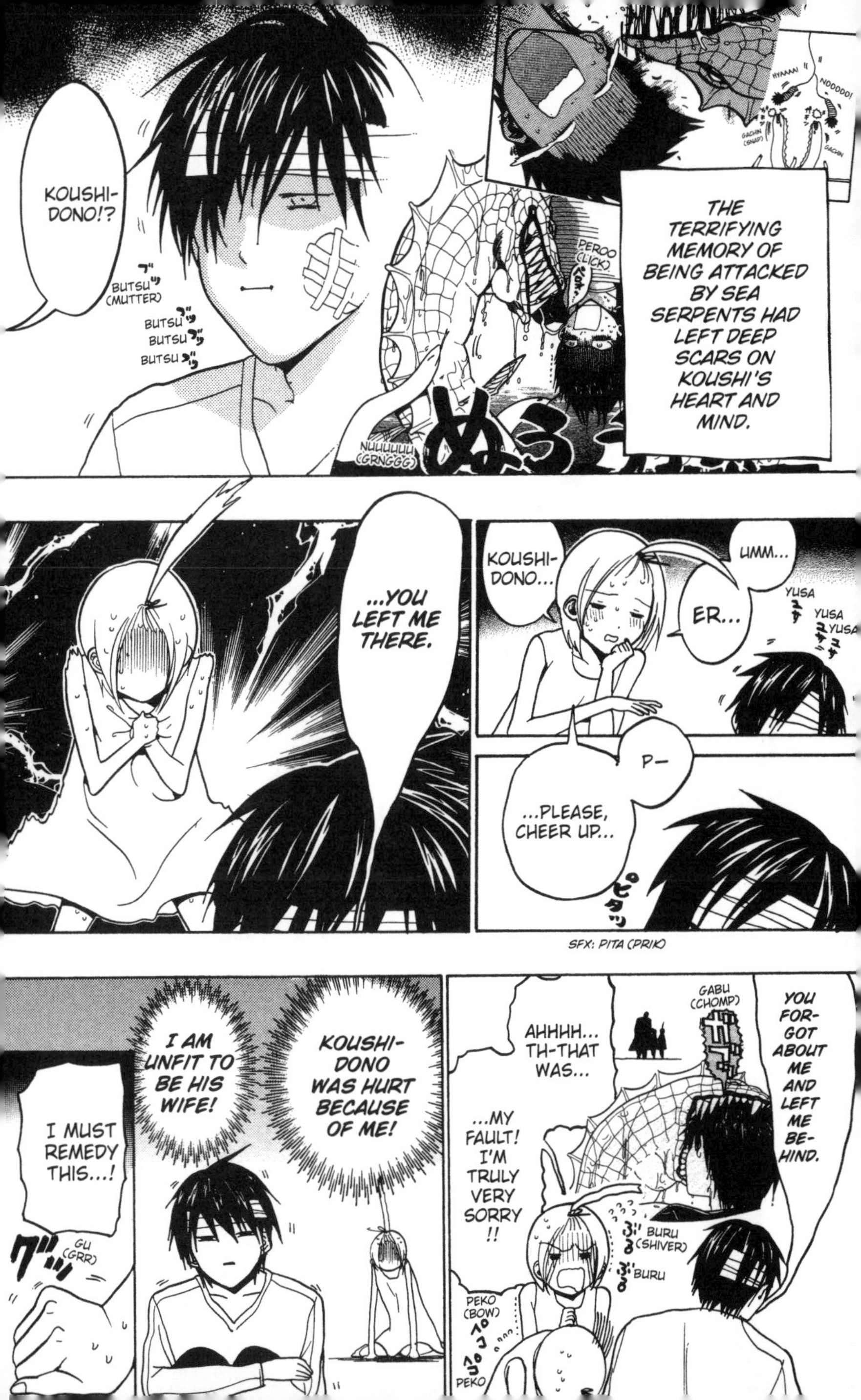
HYAAAA
NOOOOO!
GACHIN (SNAP)
GACHIN
THE TERRIFYING MEMORY OF BEING ATTACKED BY SEA SERPENTS HAD LEFT DEEP SCARS ON KOUSHI'S HEART AND MIND.
PEROO (LICK)
NUUUUUU (GRNGGG)
KOUSHI-DONO!?
BUTSU (MUTTER)
BUTSU
BUTSU
BUTSU
UMM...
KOUSHI-DONO...
ER...
YUSA
YUSA
YUSA
P—
...PLEASE, CHEER UP...
...YOU LEFT ME THERE.
SFX: PITA (PRIK)
YOU FOR-GOT ABOUT ME AND LEFT ME BE-HIND.
GABU (CHOMP)
AHHHH... TH-THAT WAS...
...MY FAULT! I'M TRULY VERY SORRY!!
BURU (SHIVER)
BURU
PEKO (BOW)
PEKO
KOUSHI-DONO WAS HURT BECAUSE OF ME!
I AM UNFIT TO BE HIS WIFE!
I MUST REMEDY THIS...!
GU (GRR)

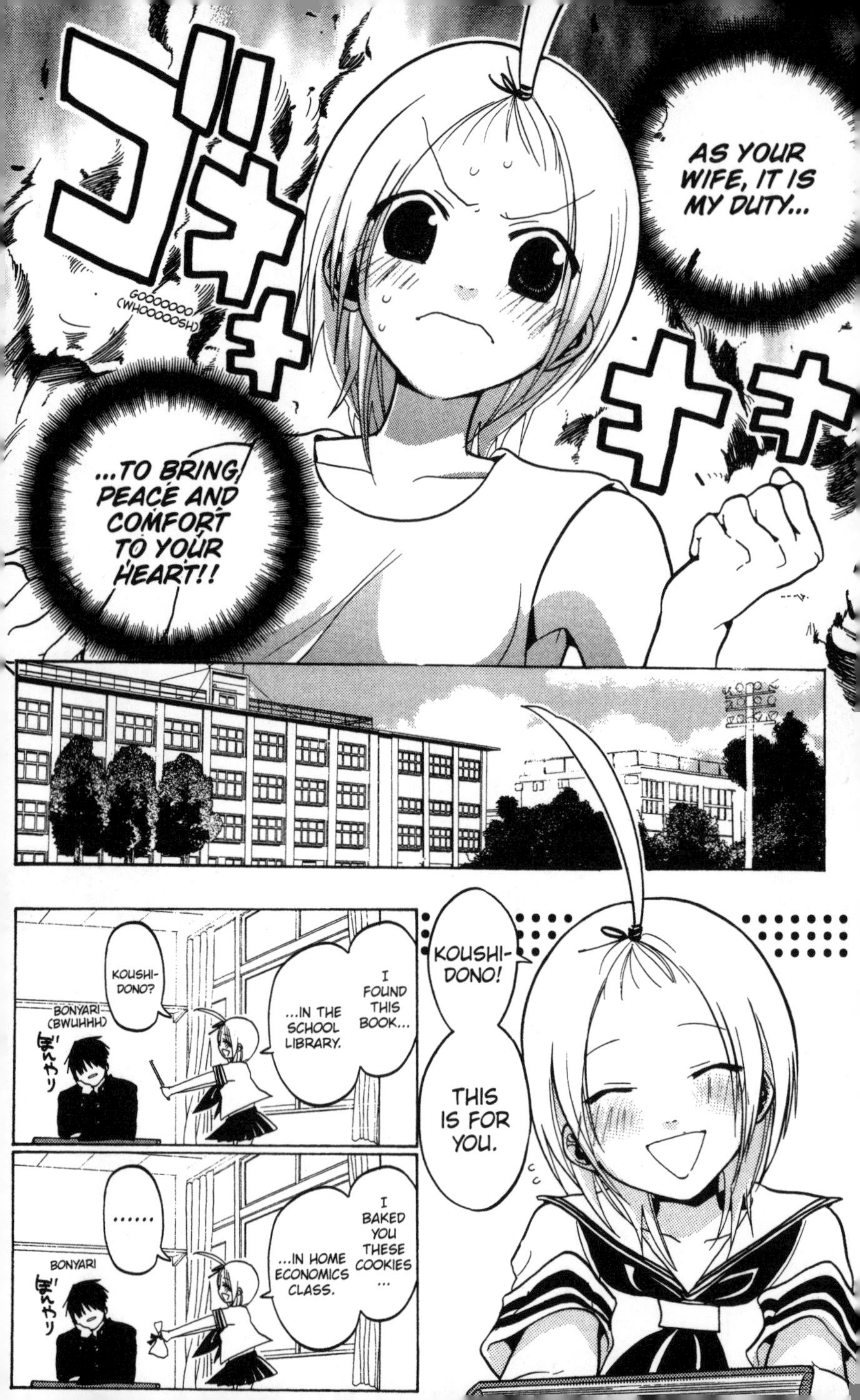
AS YOUR WIFE, IT IS MY DUTY...
GOOOOOOO (WHOOOOOSH)
...TO BRING PEACE AND COMFORT TO YOUR HEART!!
KOUSHI-DONO!
THIS IS FOR YOU.
I FOUND THIS BOOK...
...IN THE SCHOOL LIBRARY.
KOUSHI-DONO?
BONYARI (BWUHHH)
ぼんやり
I BAKED YOU THESE COOKIES...
...IN HOME ECONOMICS CLASS.
......
BONYARI
ぼんやり

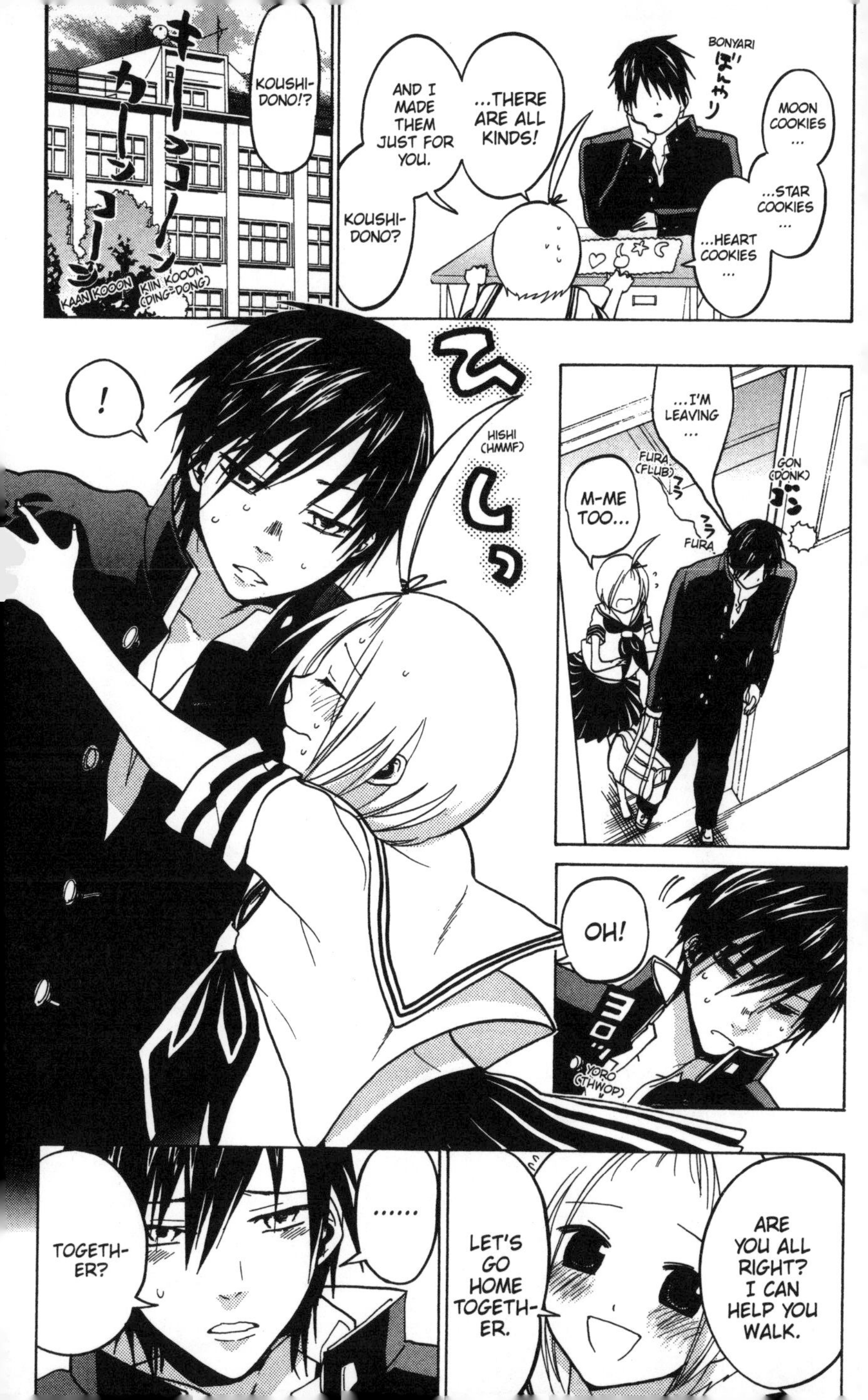
BONYARI
ぼんやり
MOON COOKIES ...
...STAR COOKIES ...
...HEART COOKIES ...
...THERE ARE ALL KINDS!
AND I MADE THEM JUST FOR YOU.
KOUSHI-DONO?
KOUSHI-DONO!?
KIIN KOOON (DING-DONG)
KAAN KOOON
...I'M LEAVING ...
GON (DONK)
FURA (FLUB)
FURA
M-ME TOO...
OH!
YORO (THWOP)
HISHI (HMMF)
!
ARE YOU ALL RIGHT? I CAN HELP YOU WALK.
LET'S GO HOME TOGETH-ER.
......
TOGETH-ER?

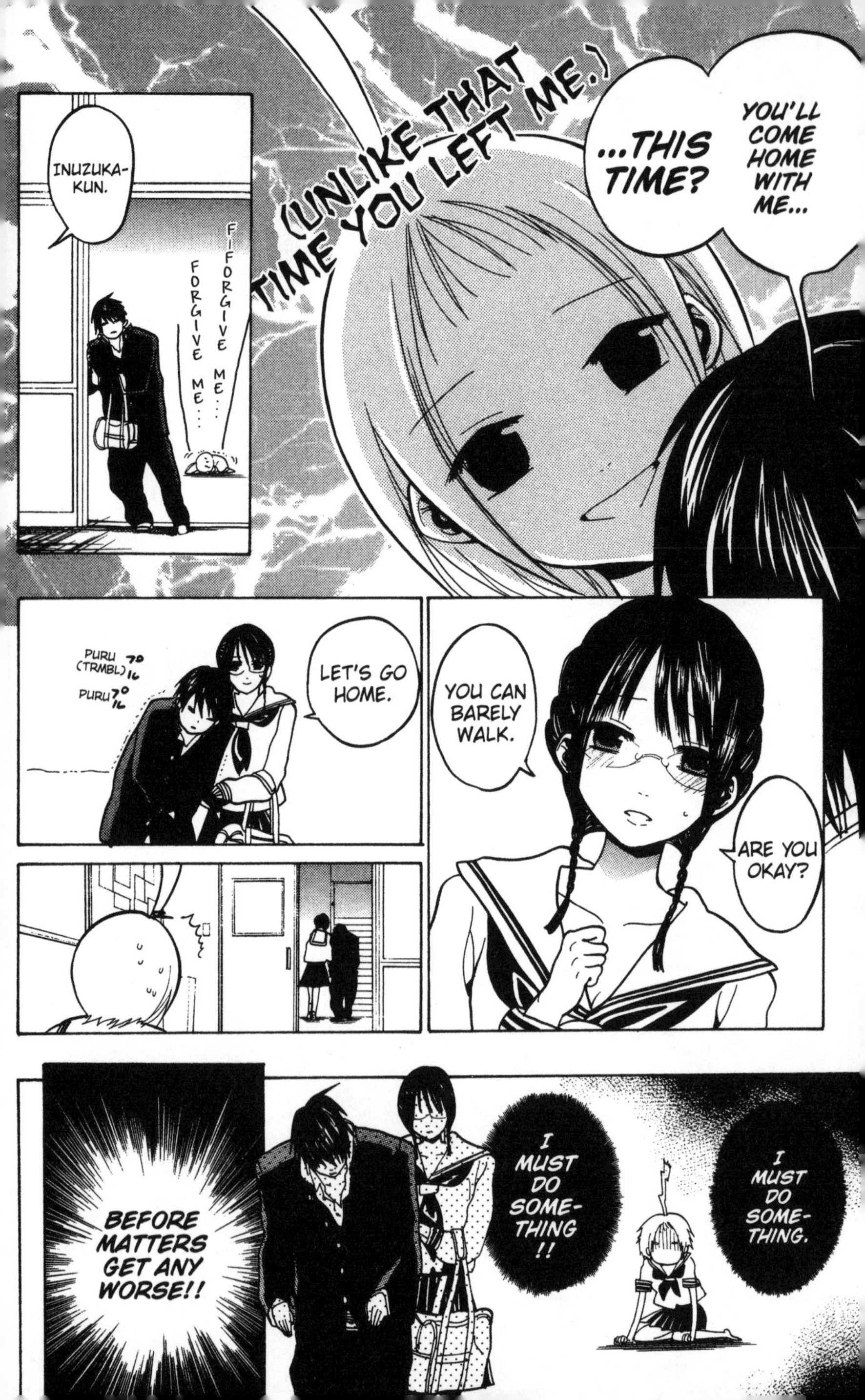
YOU'LL COME HOME WITH ME...
...THIS TIME?
(UNLIKE THAT TIME YOU LEFT ME.)
INUZUKA-KUN.
FIFORGIVE ME...
FORGIVE ME...
ARE YOU OKAY?
YOU CAN BARELY WALK.
LET'S GO HOME.
PURU (TRMBL)
PURU
I MUST DO SOME-THING.
I MUST DO SOME-THING!!
BEFORE MATTERS GET ANY WORSE!!

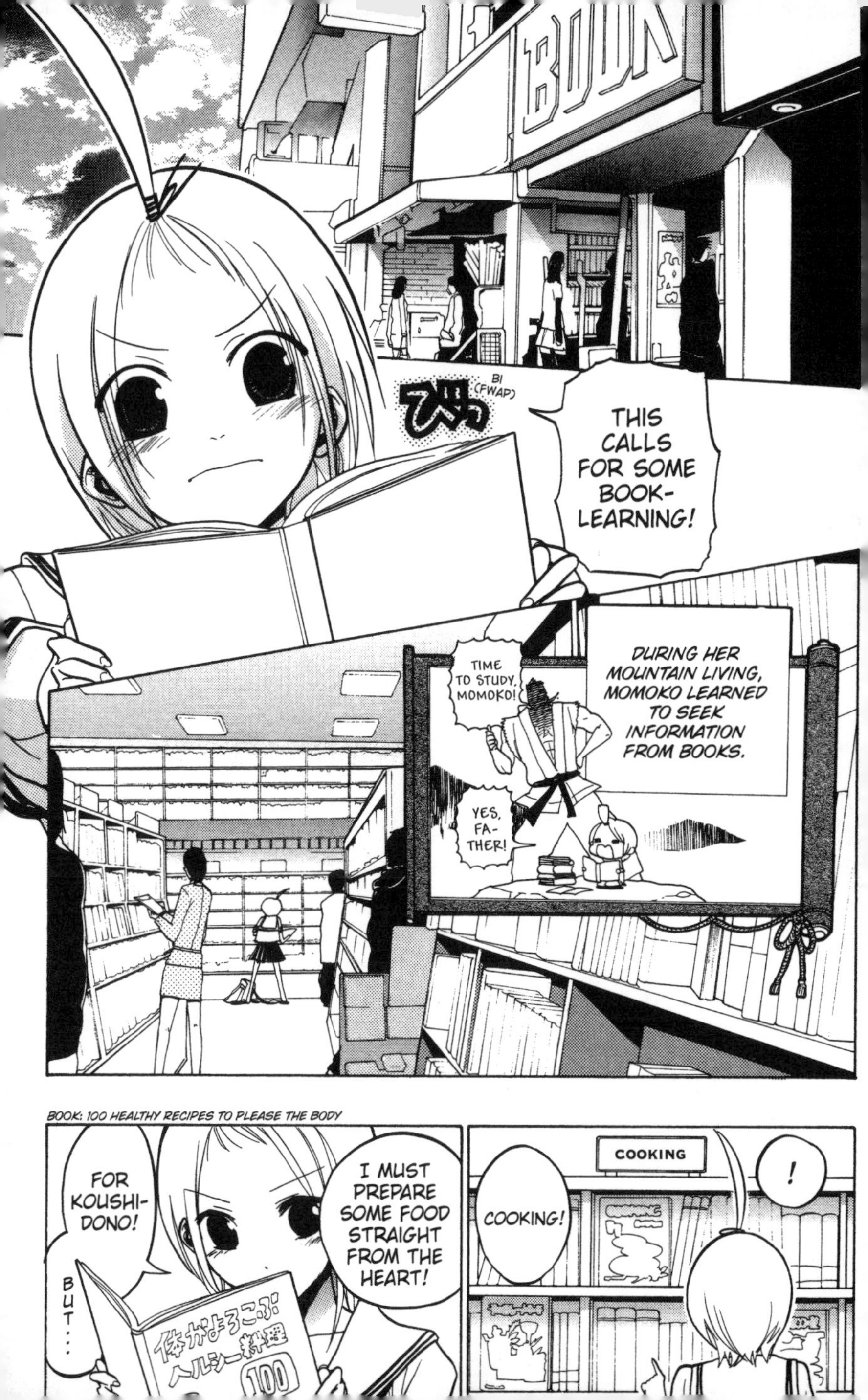
BI (FWAP)
THIS CALLS FOR SOME BOOK-LEARNING!
DURING HER MOUNTAIN LIVING, MOMOKO LEARNED TO SEEK INFORMATION FROM BOOKS.
TIME TO STUDY, MOMOKO!
YES, FATHER!
BOOK: 100 HEALTHY RECIPES TO PLEASE THE BODY
COOKING
!
COOKING!
I MUST PREPARE SOME FOOD STRAIGHT FROM THE HEART!
FOR KOUSHI-DONO!
BUT...
体がよろこぶ! ヘルシー料理 100

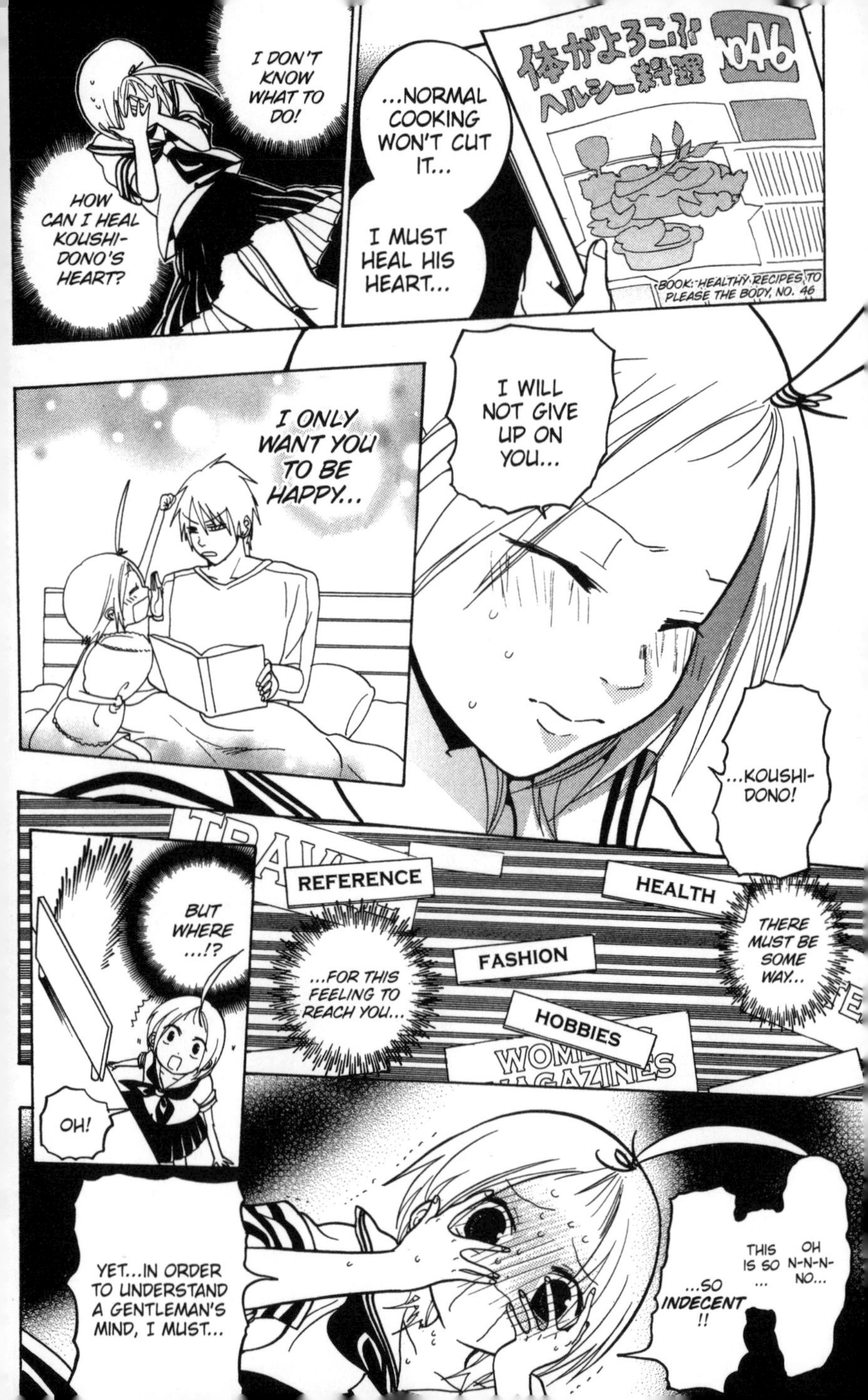
体がよろこぶ ヘルシー料理 No46
...NORMAL COOKING WON'T CUT IT...
I MUST HEAL HIS HEART...
BOOK: HEALTHY RECIPES TO PLEASE THE BODY, NO. 46
I DON'T KNOW WHAT TO DO!
HOW CAN I HEAL KOUSHI-DONO'S HEART?
I WILL NOT GIVE UP ON YOU...
...KOUSHI-DONO!
I ONLY WANT YOU TO BE HAPPY...
THERE MUST BE SOME WAY...
HEALTH
REFERENCE
FASHION
HOBBIES
WOMEN'S MAGAZINES
...FOR THIS FEELING TO REACH YOU...
BUT WHERE ...!?
OH!
OH N-N-N-NO...
THIS IS SO ...
...SO INDECENT!!
YET...IN ORDER TO UNDERSTAND A GENTLEMAN'S MIND, I MUST...

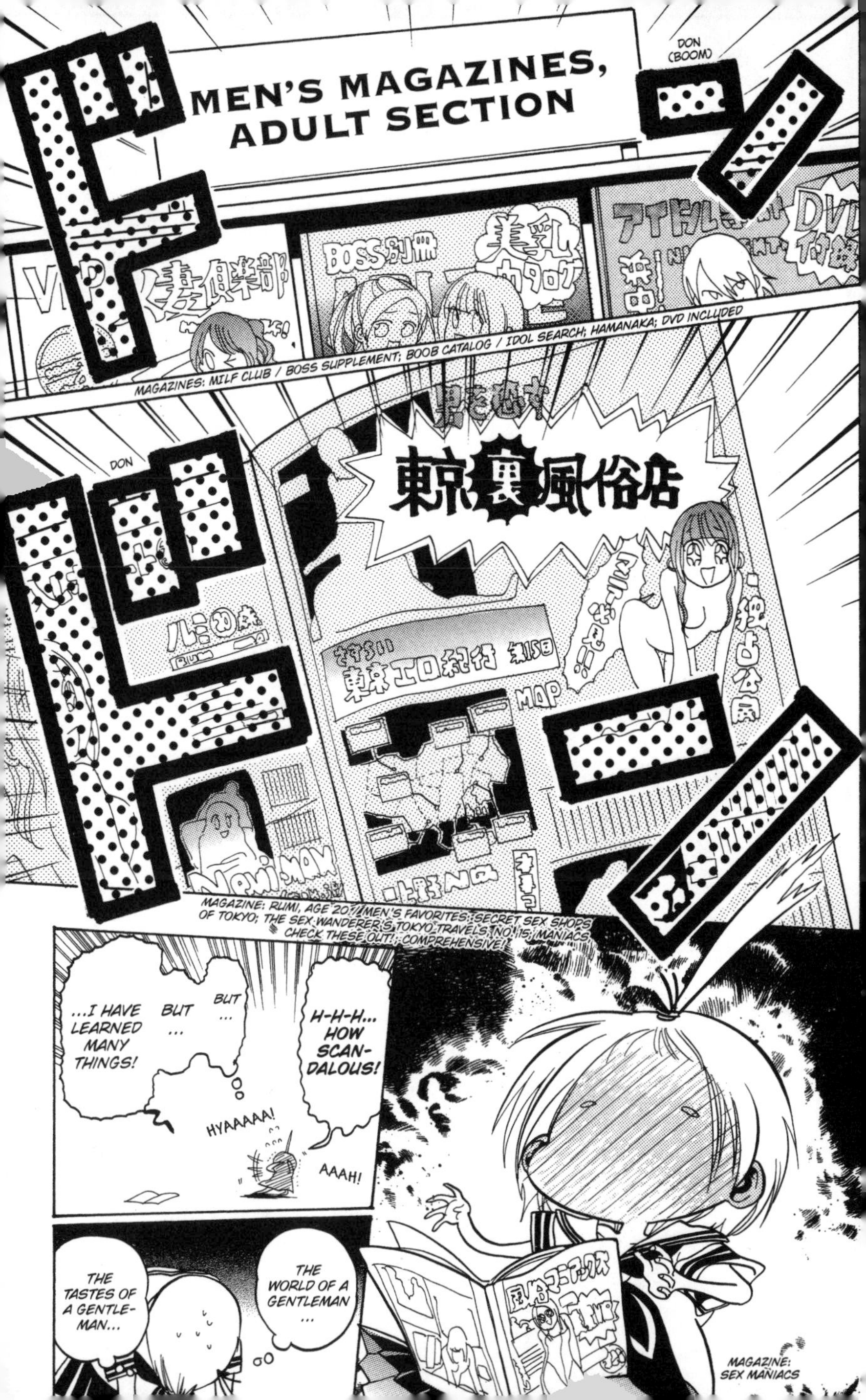

MEN'S MAGAZINES, ADULT SECTION
DON (BOOM)
MAGAZINES: MILF CLUB / BOSS SUPPLEMENT: BOOB CATALOG / IDOL SEARCH: HAMANAKA; DVD INCLUDED
DON
東京裏風俗店
MAGAZINE: RUMI, AGE 20 / MEN'S FAVORITES: SECRET SEX SHOPS OF TOKYO; THE SEX WANDERER'S TOKYO TRAVELS NO. 15; MANIACS CHECK THESE OUT!; COMPREHENSIVE!
MAGAZINE: SEX MANIACS
H-H-H... HOW SCANDALOUS!
AAAH!
HYAAAAA!
BUT...
BUT...
...I HAVE LEARNED MANY THINGS!
THE WORLD OF A GENTLEMAN...
THE TASTES OF A GENTLEMAN...

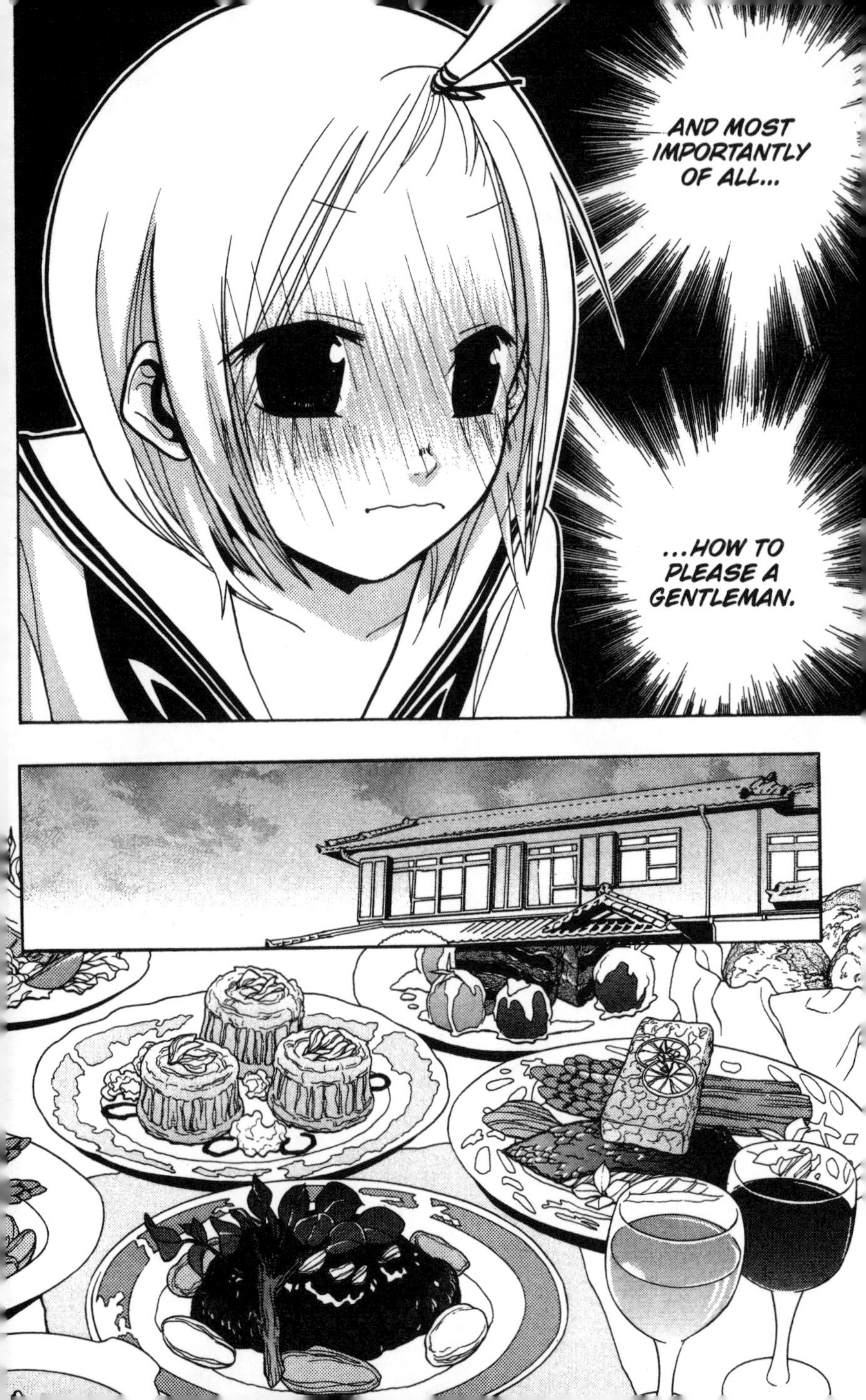
AND MOST IMPORTANTLY OF ALL...
...HOW TO PLEASE A GENTLEMAN.

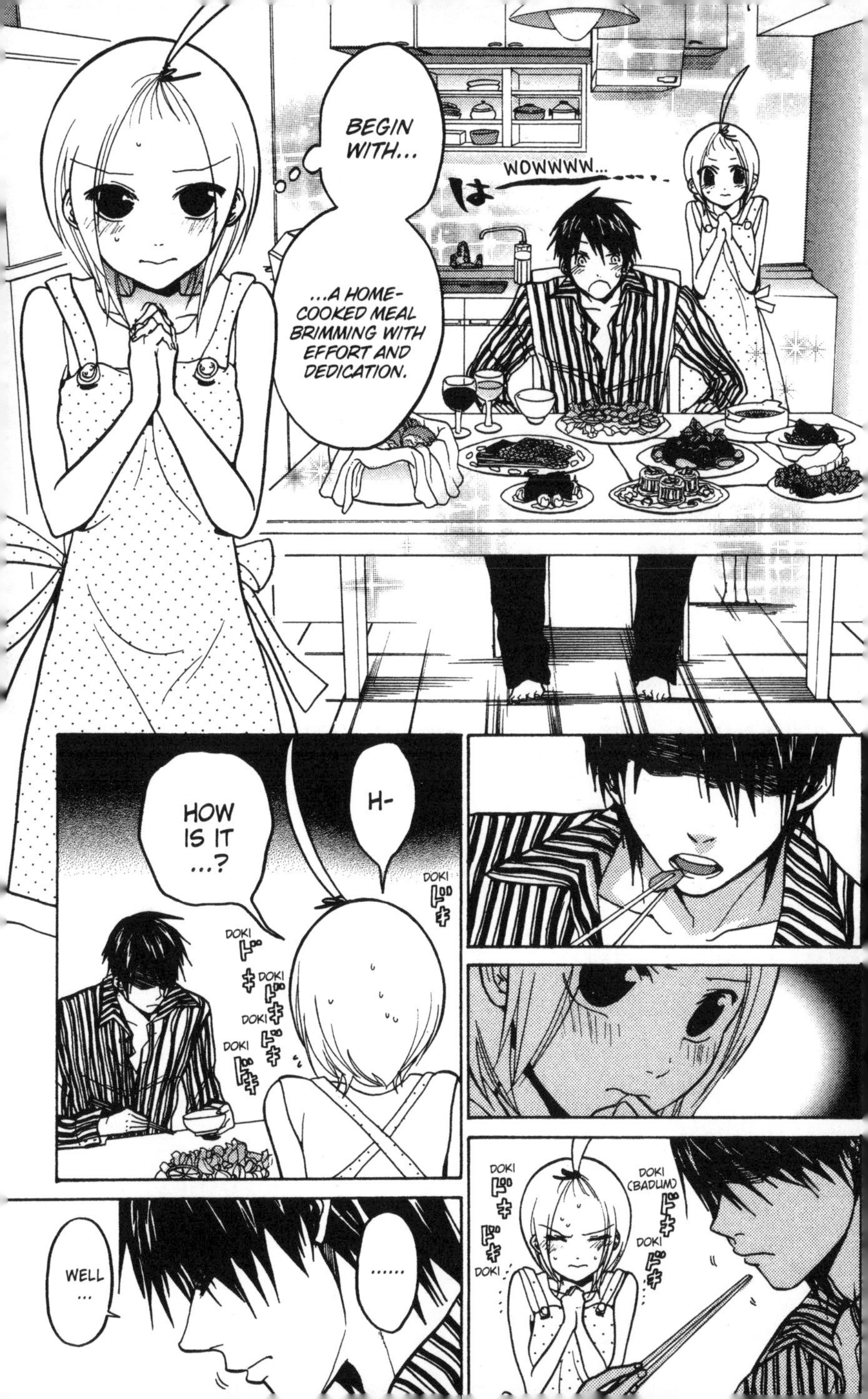
BEGIN WITH...
...A HOME-COOKED MEAL BRIMMING WITH EFFORT AND DEDICATION.
は WOWWWW...
H-
HOW IS IT ...?
DOKI ドキ
DOKI ドキ
DOKI ドキ
DOKI ドキ
DOKI ドキ
DOKI (BADUM) ドキ
DOKI ドキ
DOKI ドキ
DOKI ドキ
......
WELL ...

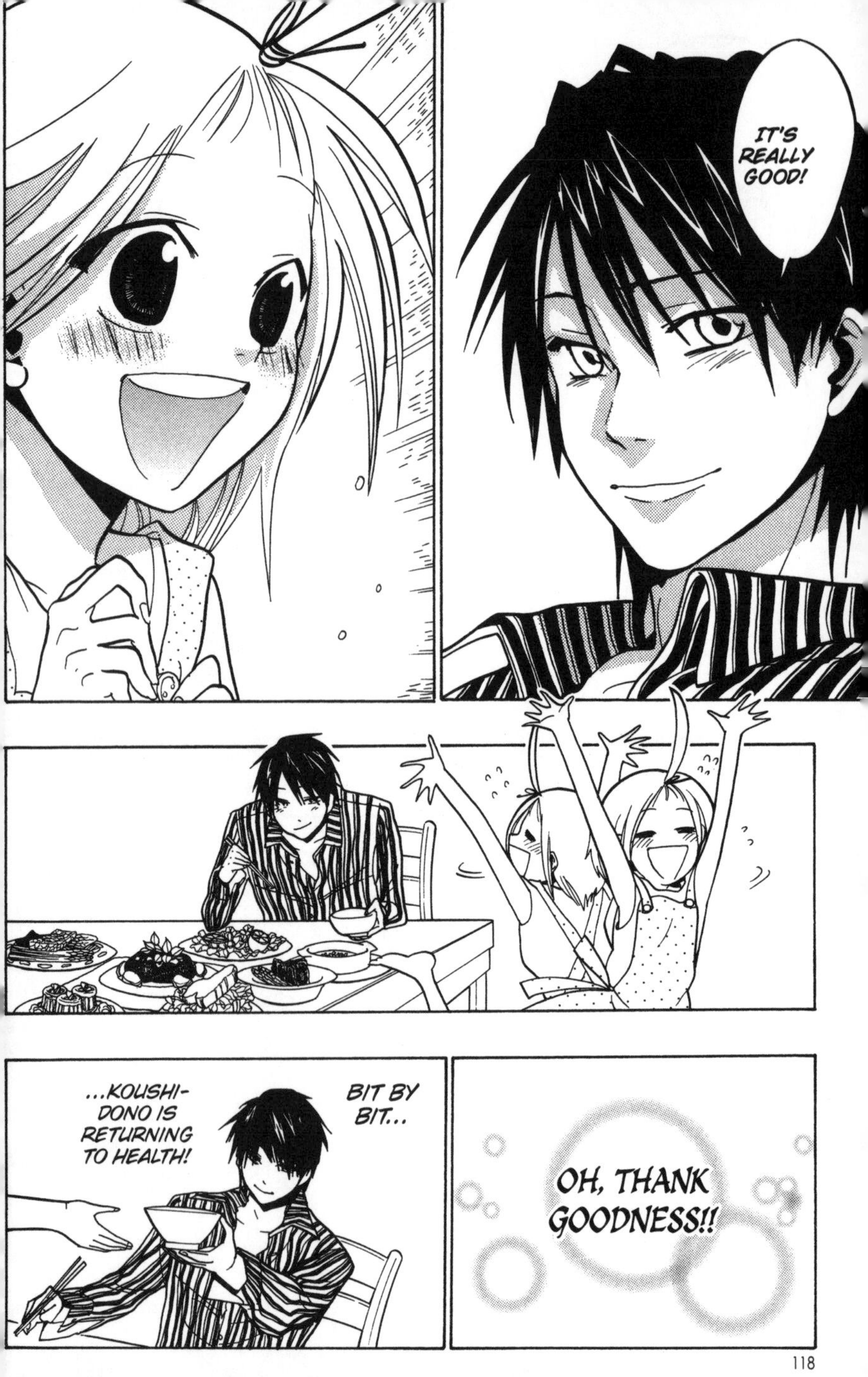
IT'S REALLY GOOD!
BIT BY BIT...
...KOUSHI-DONO IS RETURNING TO HEALTH!
OH, THANK GOODNESS!!

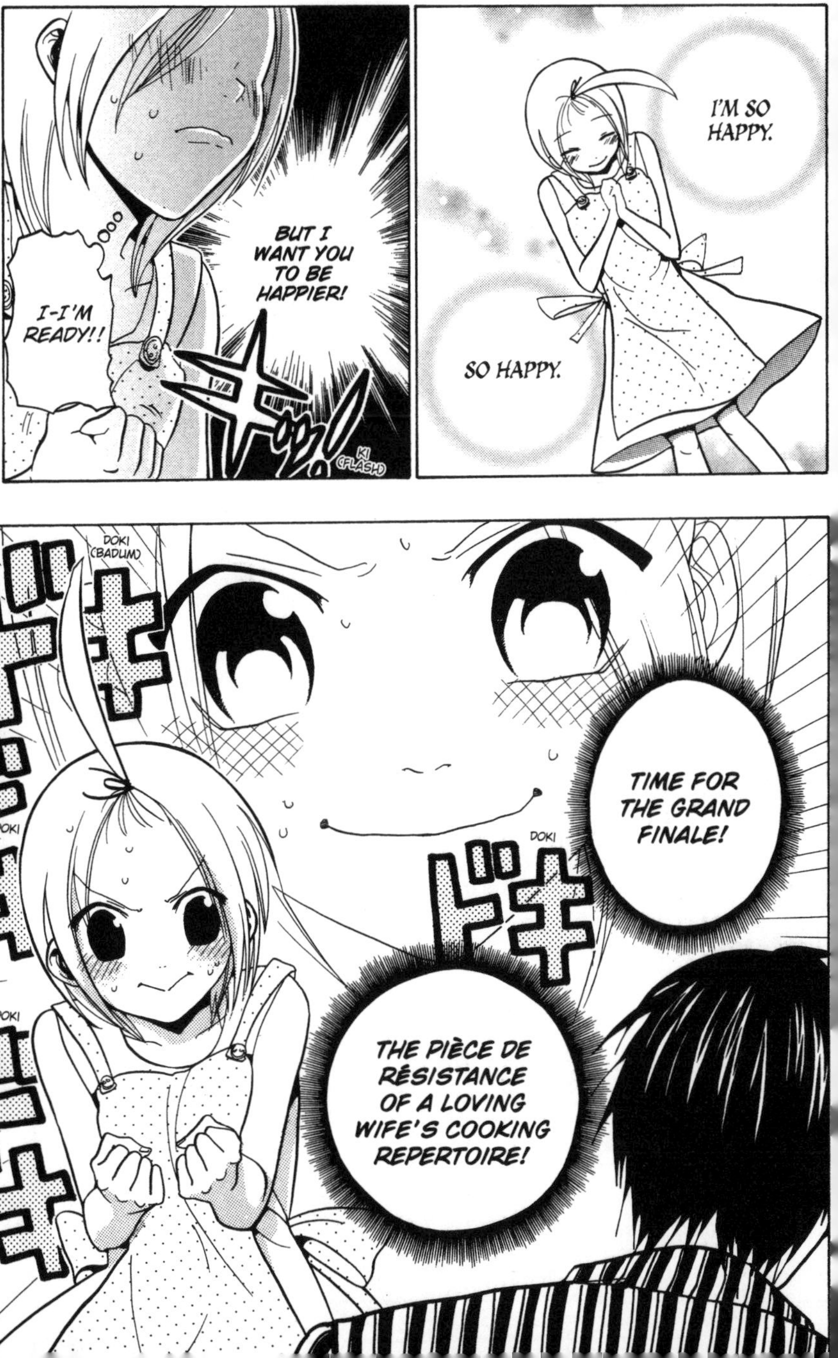
I'M SO HAPPY.
SO HAPPY.
BUT I WANT YOU TO BE HAPPIER!
I-I'M READY!!
KI (FLASH)
TIME FOR THE GRAND FINALE!
DOKI
THE PIÈCE DE RÉSISTANCE OF A LOVING WIFE'S COOKING REPERTOIRE!
DOKI (BADUM)
DOKI
DOKI

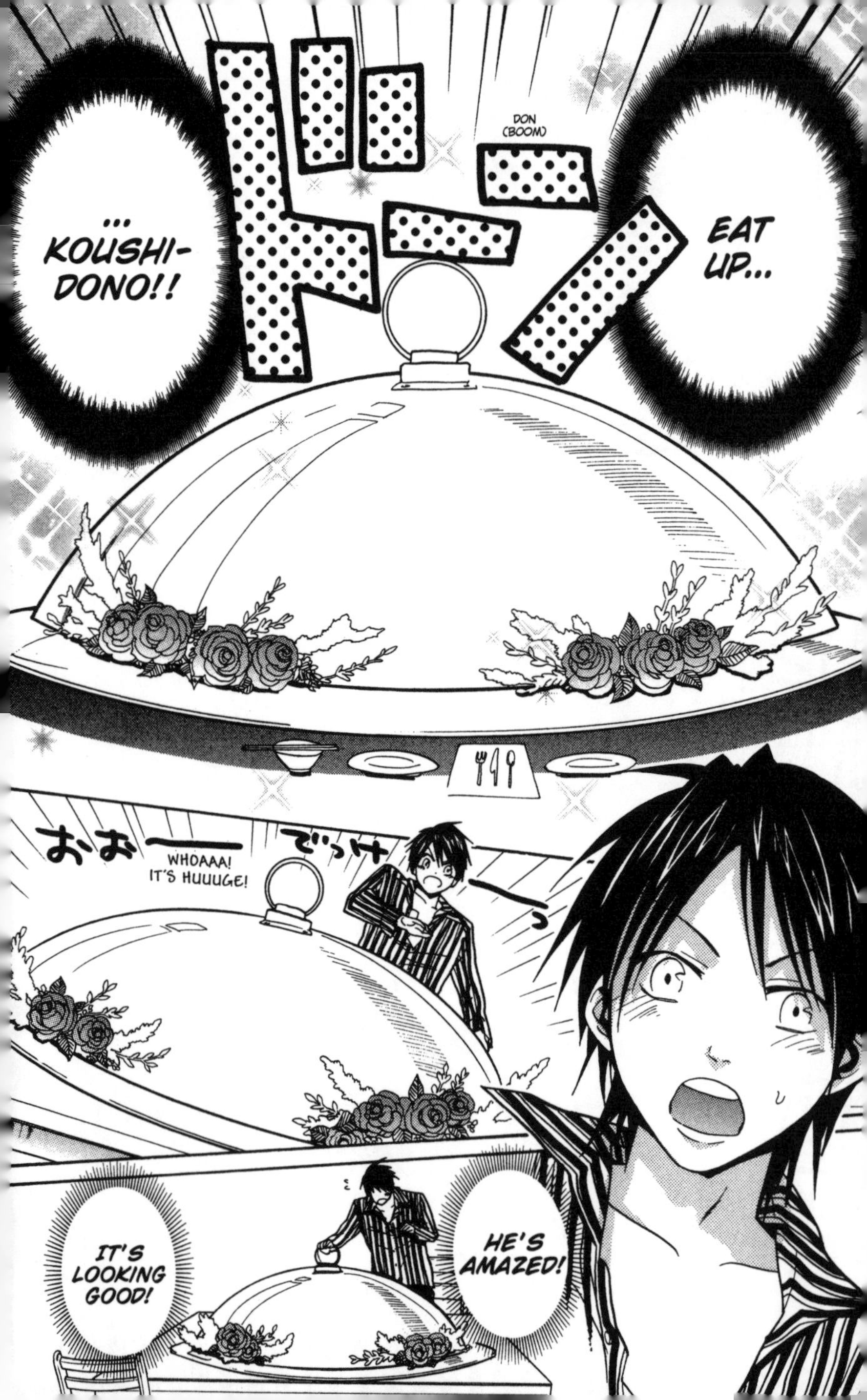
EAT UP...
DON (BOOM)
... KOUSHI-DONO!!
おおーー でっけーっ
WHOAAA! IT'S HUUUGE!
HE'S AMAZED!
IT'S LOOKING GOOD!

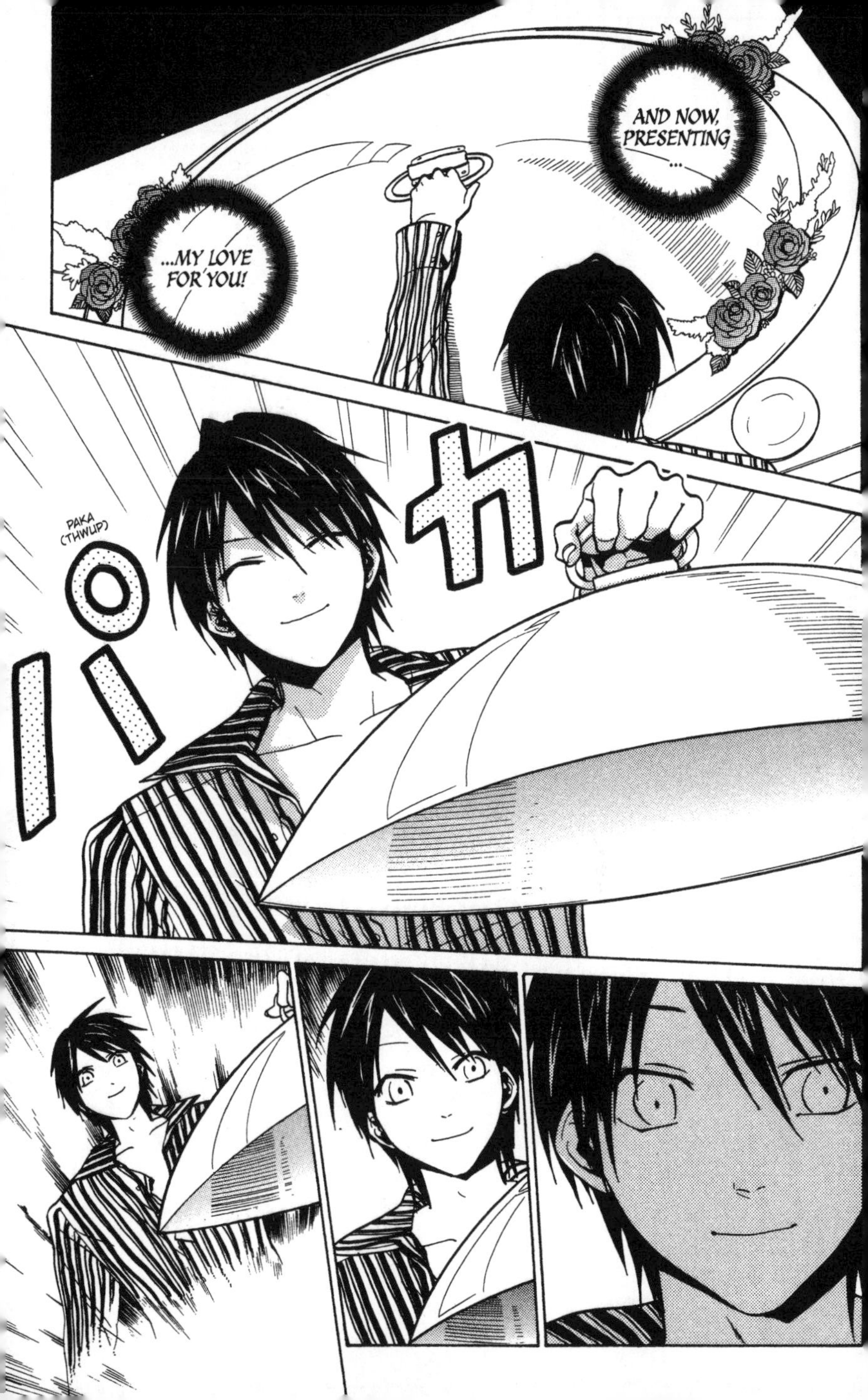
AND NOW, PRESENTING ...
...MY LOVE FOR YOU!
パカ
PAKA (THWUP)

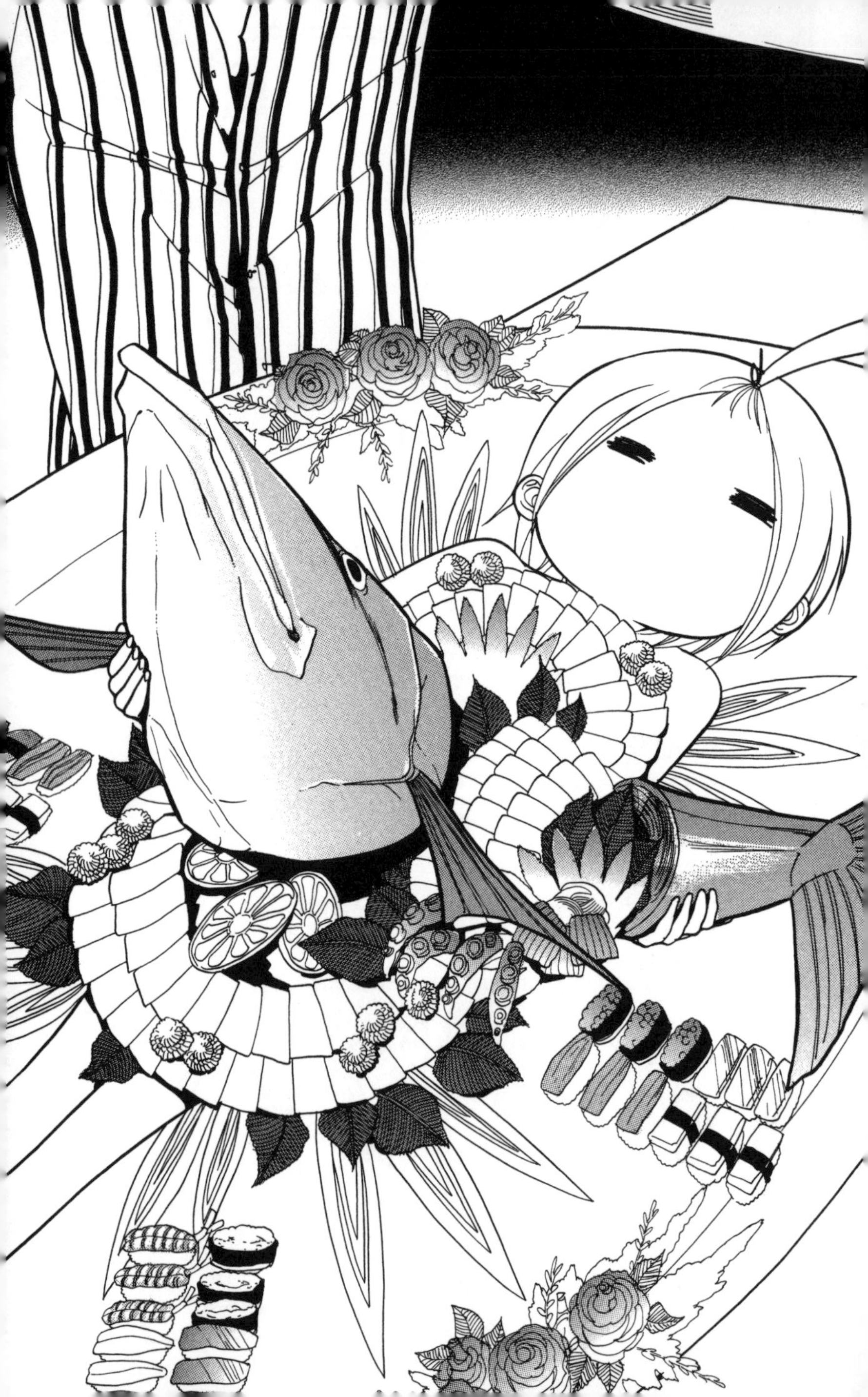

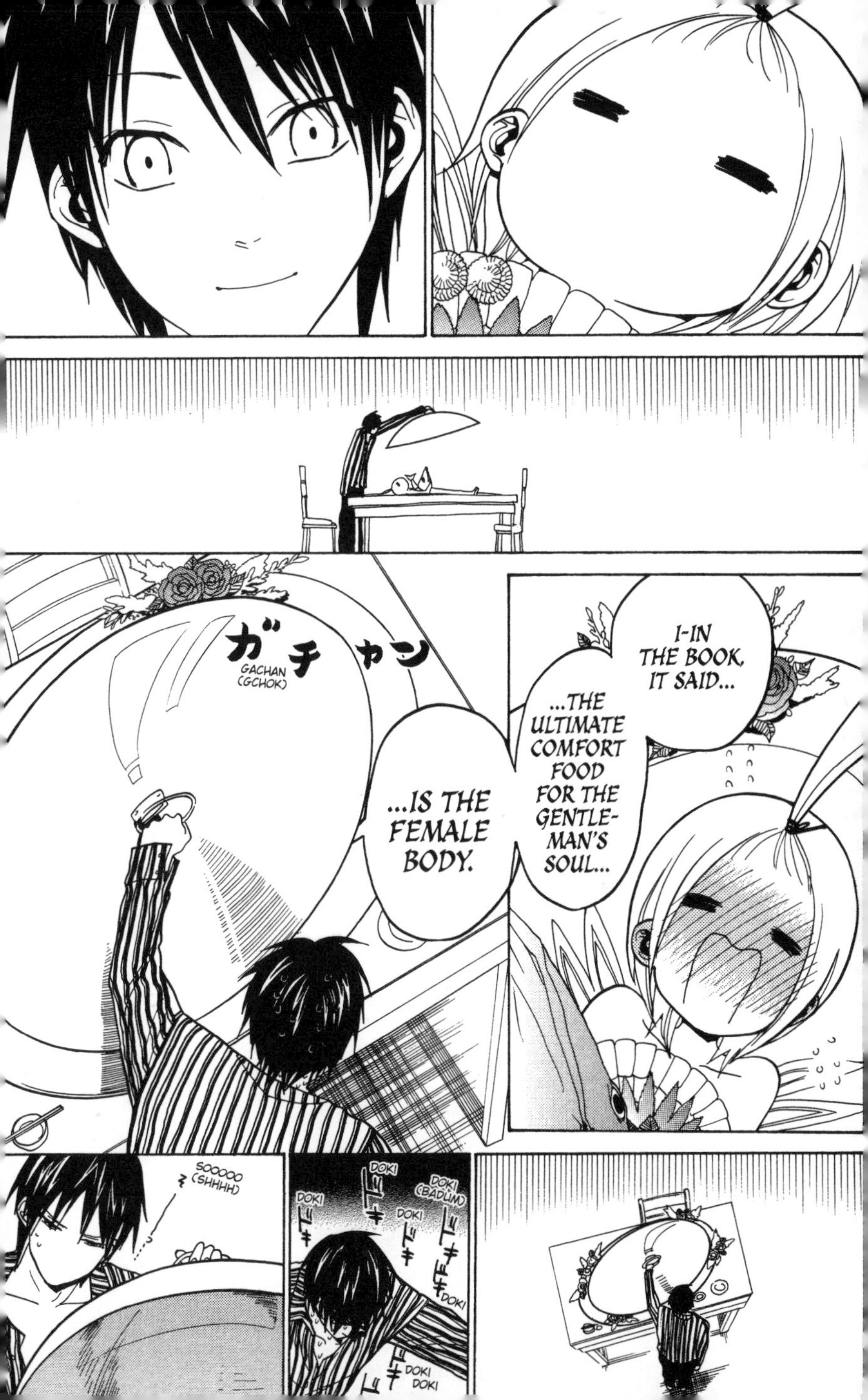
I-IN THE BOOK, IT SAID...
...THE ULTIMATE COMFORT FOOD FOR THE GENTLEMAN'S SOUL...
...IS THE FEMALE BODY.
ガチャン
GACHAN (GCHOK)
ドキ ドキ ドキ ドキ
DOKI DOKI (BADUMP) DOKI DOKI DOKI DOKI DOKI
SOOOOO (SHHHH)

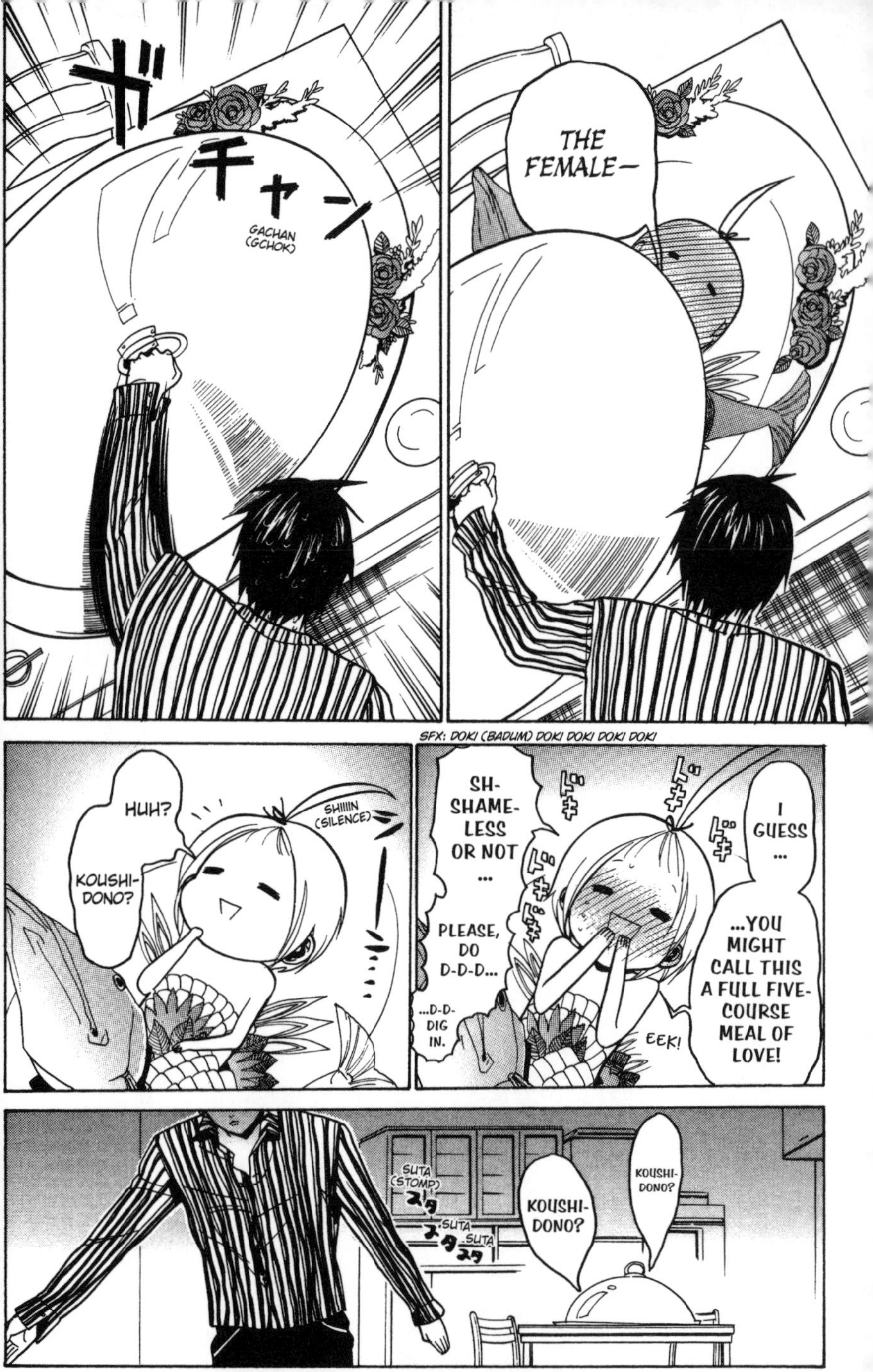
THE FEMALE—
ガチャン
GACHAN (GCHOK)
SFX: DOKI (BADUM) DOKI DOKI DOKI DOKI
I GUESS...
...YOU MIGHT CALL THIS A FULL FIVE-COURSE MEAL OF LOVE!
SH-SHAMELESS OR NOT...
PLEASE, DO D-D-D...
...D-D-DIG IN.
EEK!
SHIIIN (SILENCE)
HUH?
KOUSHI-DONO?
KOUSHI-DONO?
KOUSHI-DONO?
SUTA (STOMP)
SUTA
SUTA

CHAPTER 11. PUT YOUR ALL INTO LOVE – END

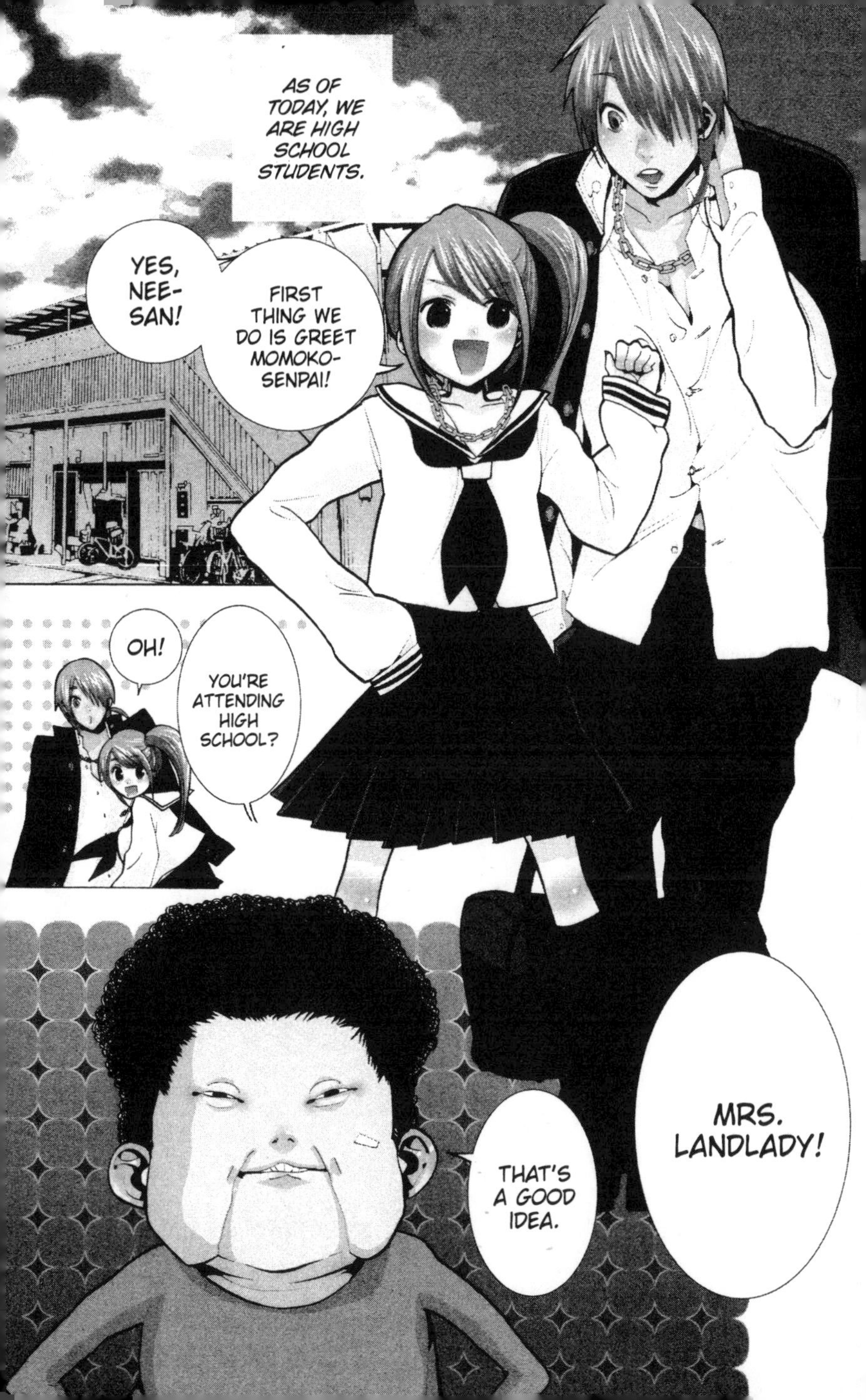
AS OF TODAY, WE ARE HIGH SCHOOL STUDENTS.
FIRST THING WE DO IS GREET MOMOKO-SENPAI!
YES, NEE-SAN!
YOU'RE ATTENDING HIGH SCHOOL?
OH!
MRS. LANDLADY!
THAT'S A GOOD IDEA.

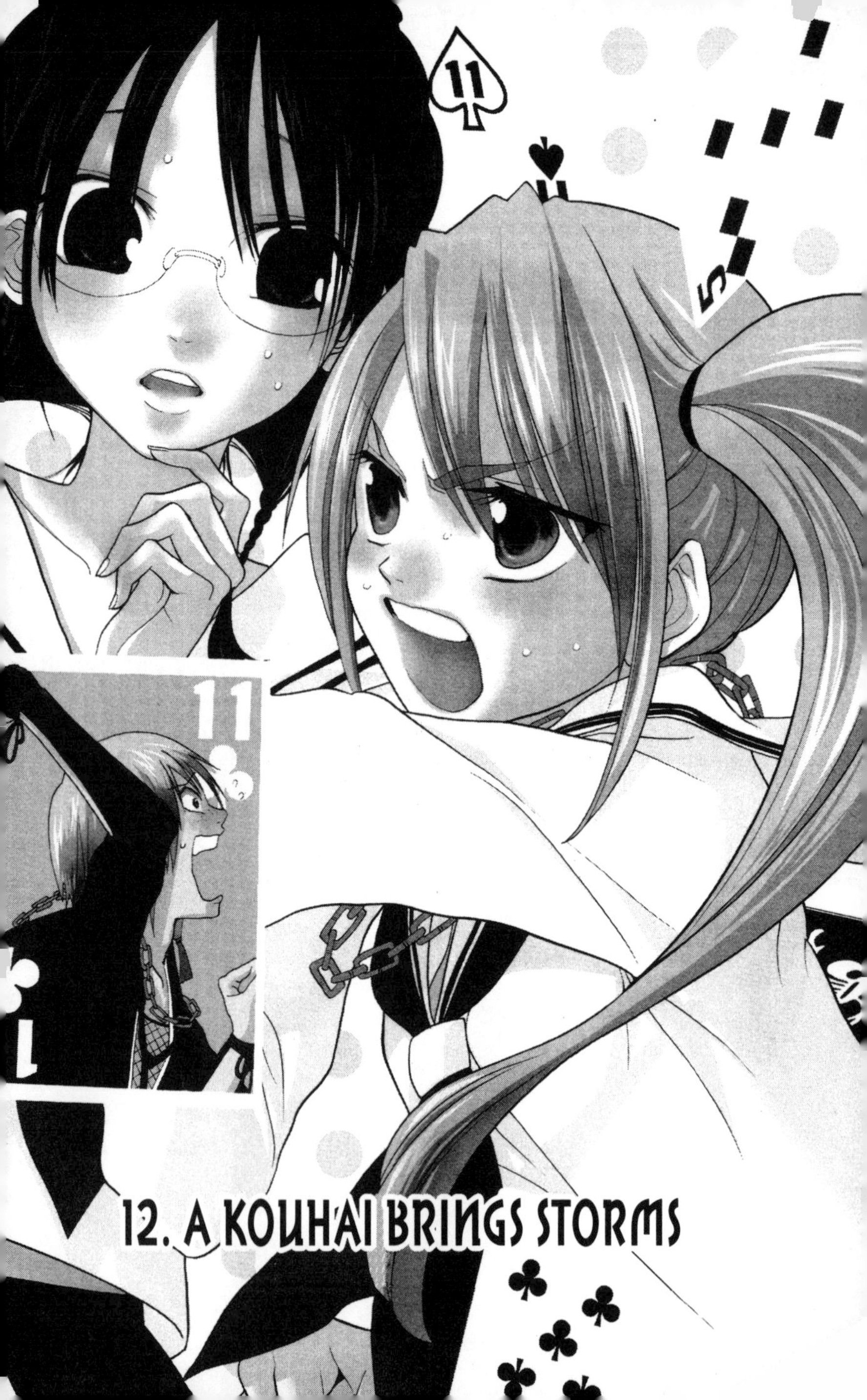
12. A KOUHAI BRINGS STORMS

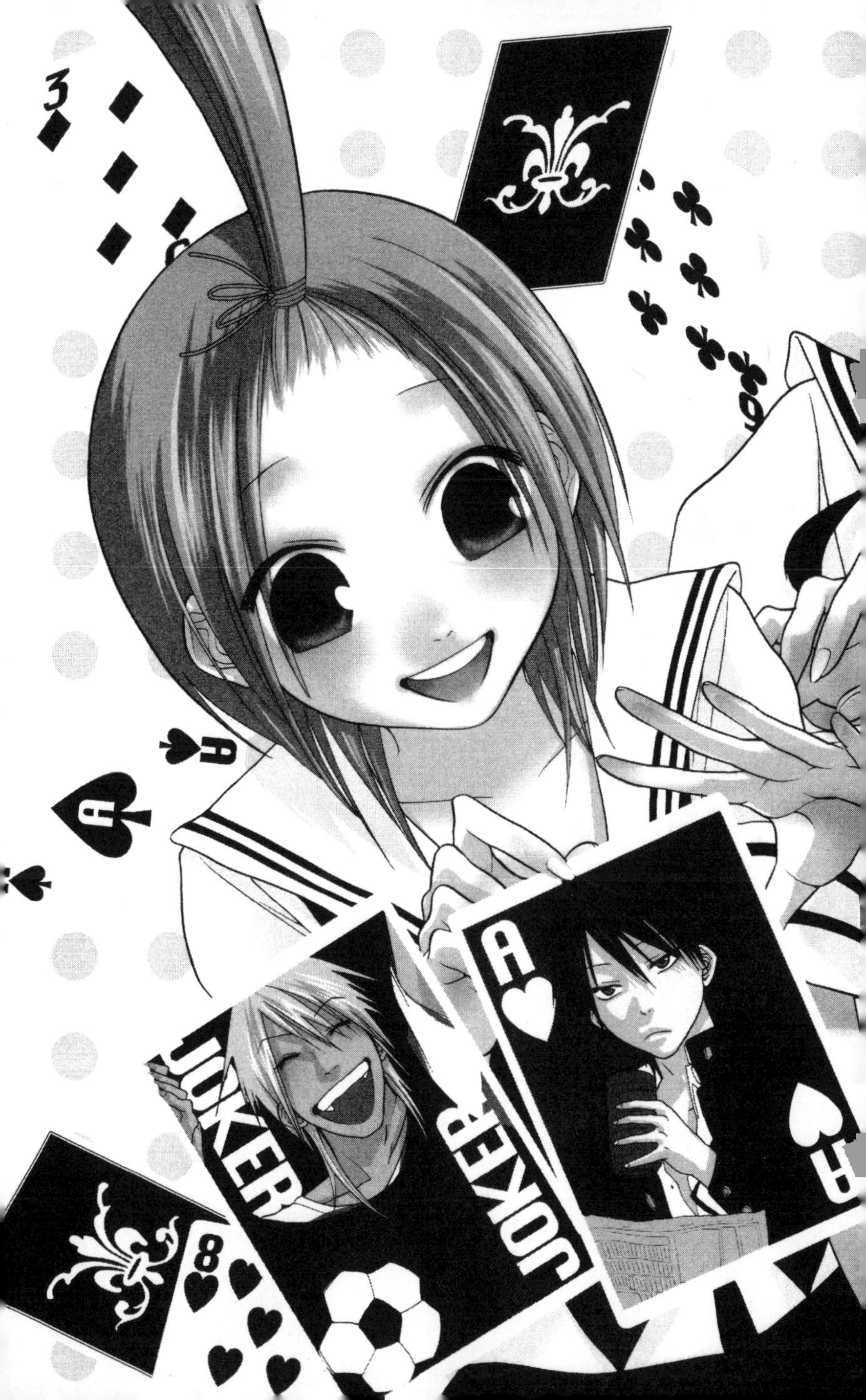
JOKER
JOKER

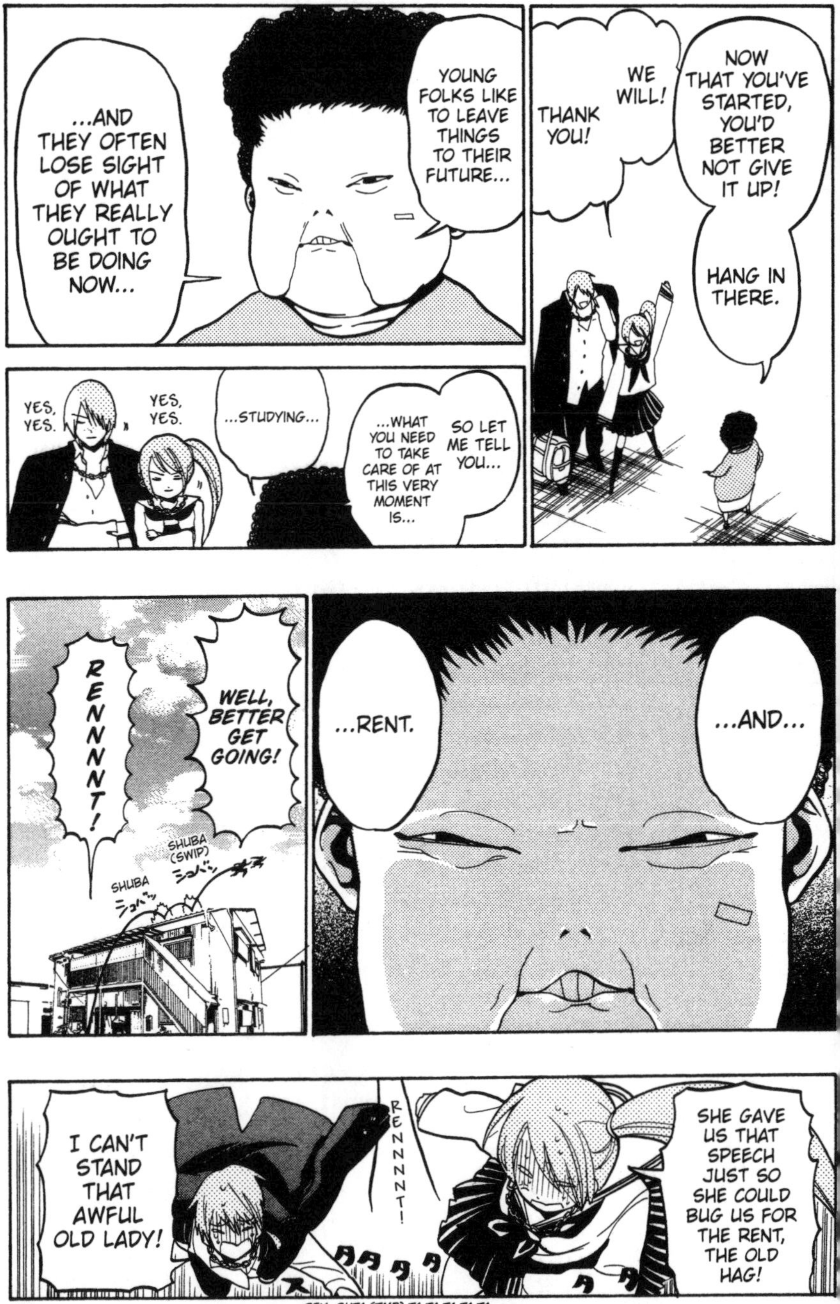
NOW THAT YOU'VE STARTED, YOU'D BETTER NOT GIVE IT UP!
HANG IN THERE.
WE WILL!
THANK YOU!
YOUNG FOLKS LIKE TO LEAVE THINGS TO THEIR FUTURE...
...AND THEY OFTEN LOSE SIGHT OF WHAT THEY REALLY OUGHT TO BE DOING NOW...
SO LET ME TELL YOU...
...WHAT YOU NEED TO TAKE CARE OF AT THIS VERY MOMENT IS...
...STUDYING...
YES, YES.
YES, YES.
...AND...
...RENT.
WELL, BETTER GET GOING!
RENNNNNT!
SHUBA (SWIP)
SHUBA
SHE GAVE US THAT SPEECH JUST SO SHE COULD BUG US FOR THE RENT, THE OLD HAG!
RENNNNT!
I CAN'T STAND THAT AWFUL OLD LADY!

SFX: SUTA (TMP) TA TA TA TA TA

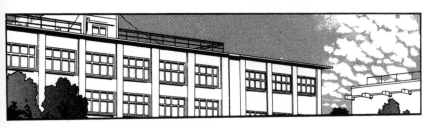

IROHA-DONO!?

MOMOKO-SENPAI?

EXCUSE ME.

HYOKO (POP)
ひょこ

SENPAI!

WHY ARE YOU HERE?

DON'T YOU REMEMBER WHAT HAPPENED BY THE SEA?

I WAS VERY MOVED BY YOUR STIRRING SPEECH ABOUT MARTIAL ARTS!

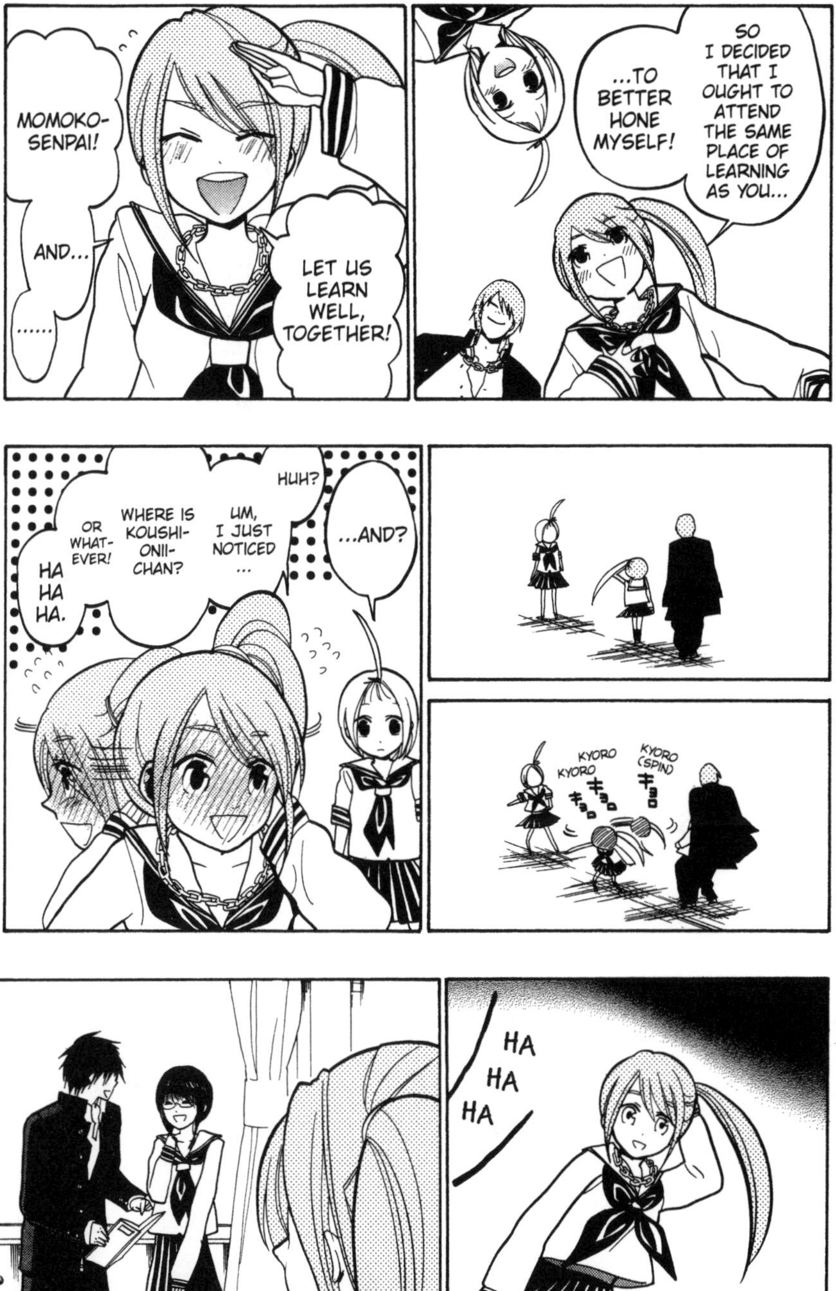
SO I DECIDED THAT I OUGHT TO ATTEND THE SAME PLACE OF LEARNING AS YOU...
...TO BETTER HONE MYSELF!
MOMOKO-SENPAI!
LET US LEARN WELL, TOGETHER!
AND...
......
KYORO (SPIN)
キョロ
KYORO
キョロ
KYORO
キョロ
...AND?
HUH?
UM, I JUST NOTICED...
WHERE IS KOUSHI-ONII-CHAN?
OR WHAT-EVER!
HA HA HA.
HA HA HA

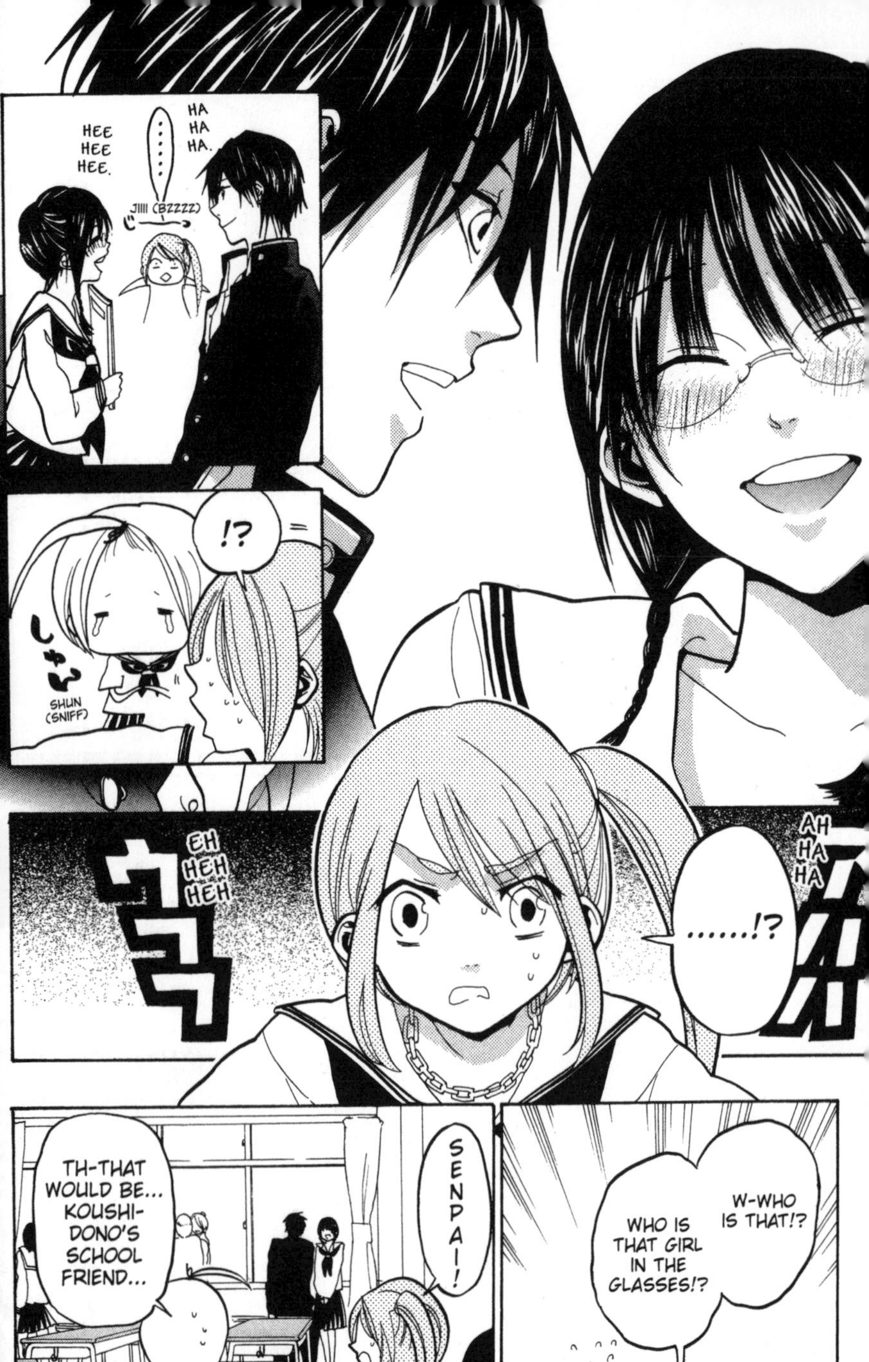
HA HA HA.
......!
HEE HEE HEE.
JIIII (BZZZZ)
!?
SHUN (SNIFF)
AH HA HA
......!?
EH HEH HEH
W-WHO IS THAT!?
WHO IS THAT GIRL IN THE GLASSES!?
SENPAI!
TH-THAT WOULD BE... KOUSHI-DONO'S SCHOOL FRIEND...

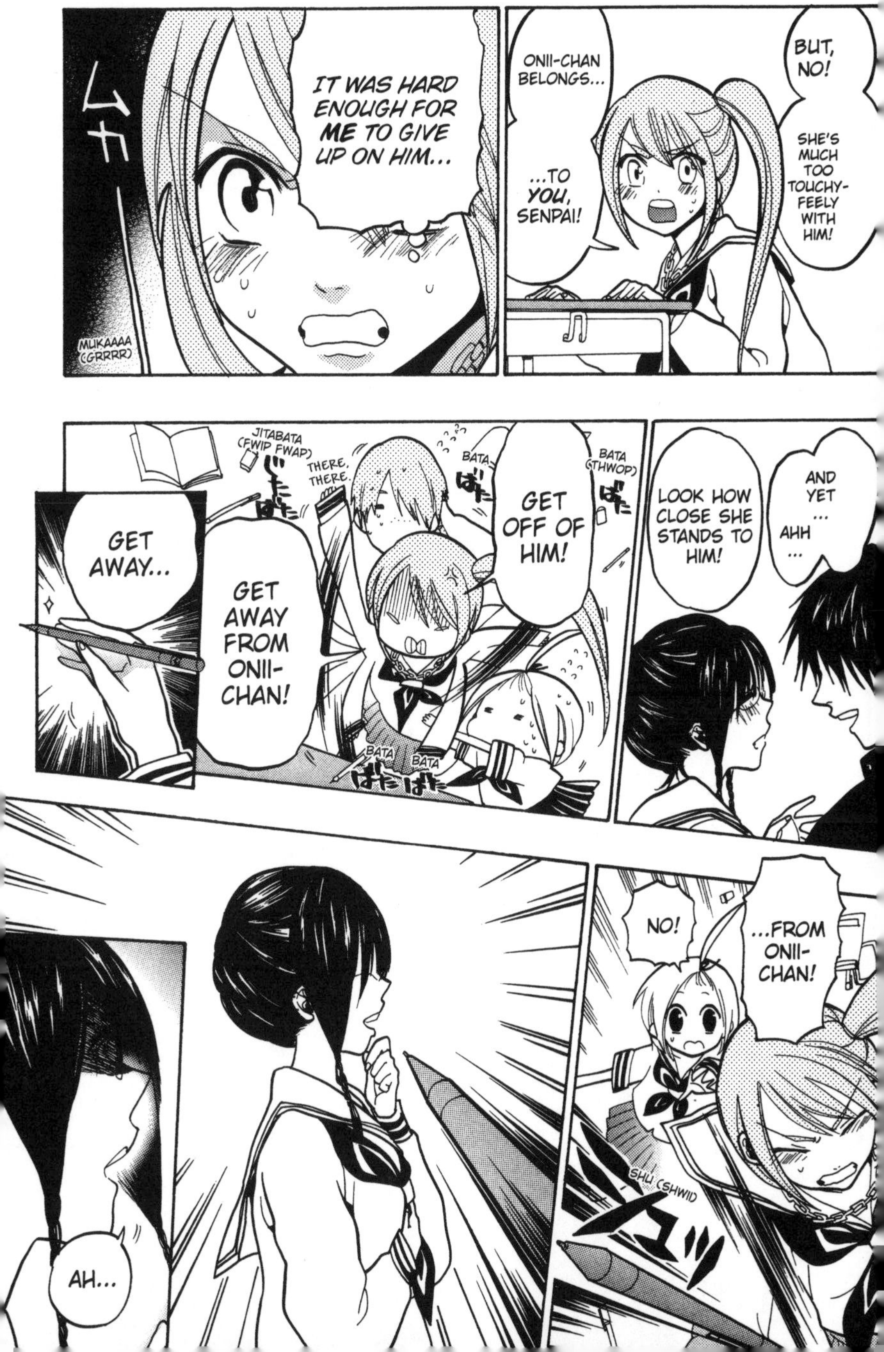
BUT, NO!
SHE'S MUCH TOO TOUCHY-FEELY WITH HIM!
ONII-CHAN BELONGS...
...TO YOU, SENPAI!
IT WAS HARD ENOUGH FOR ME TO GIVE UP ON HIM...
MUKAAAA (GRRRR)
AND YET... AHH...
LOOK HOW CLOSE SHE STANDS TO HIM!
BATA (THWOP)
GET OFF OF HIM!
BATA
THERE, THERE.
JITABATA (FWIP FWAP)
GET AWAY FROM ONII-CHAN!
BATA BATA
GET AWAY...
...FROM ONII-CHAN!
NO!
SHU (SHWID)
AH...

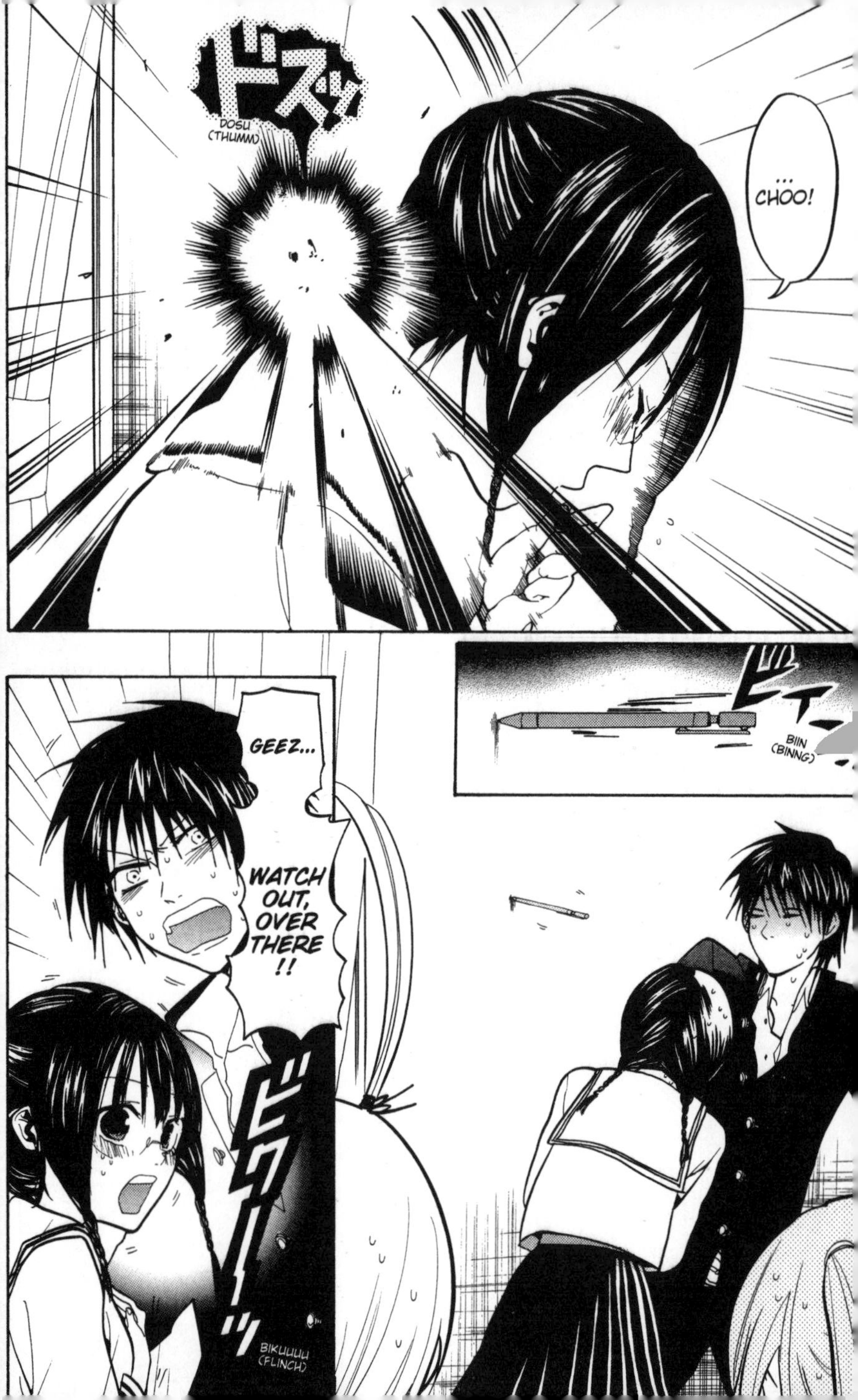
...CHOO!
DOSU (THUMM)
BIIN (BINNG)
GEEZ...
WATCH OUT, OVER THERE!!
BIKUUUU (FLINCH)

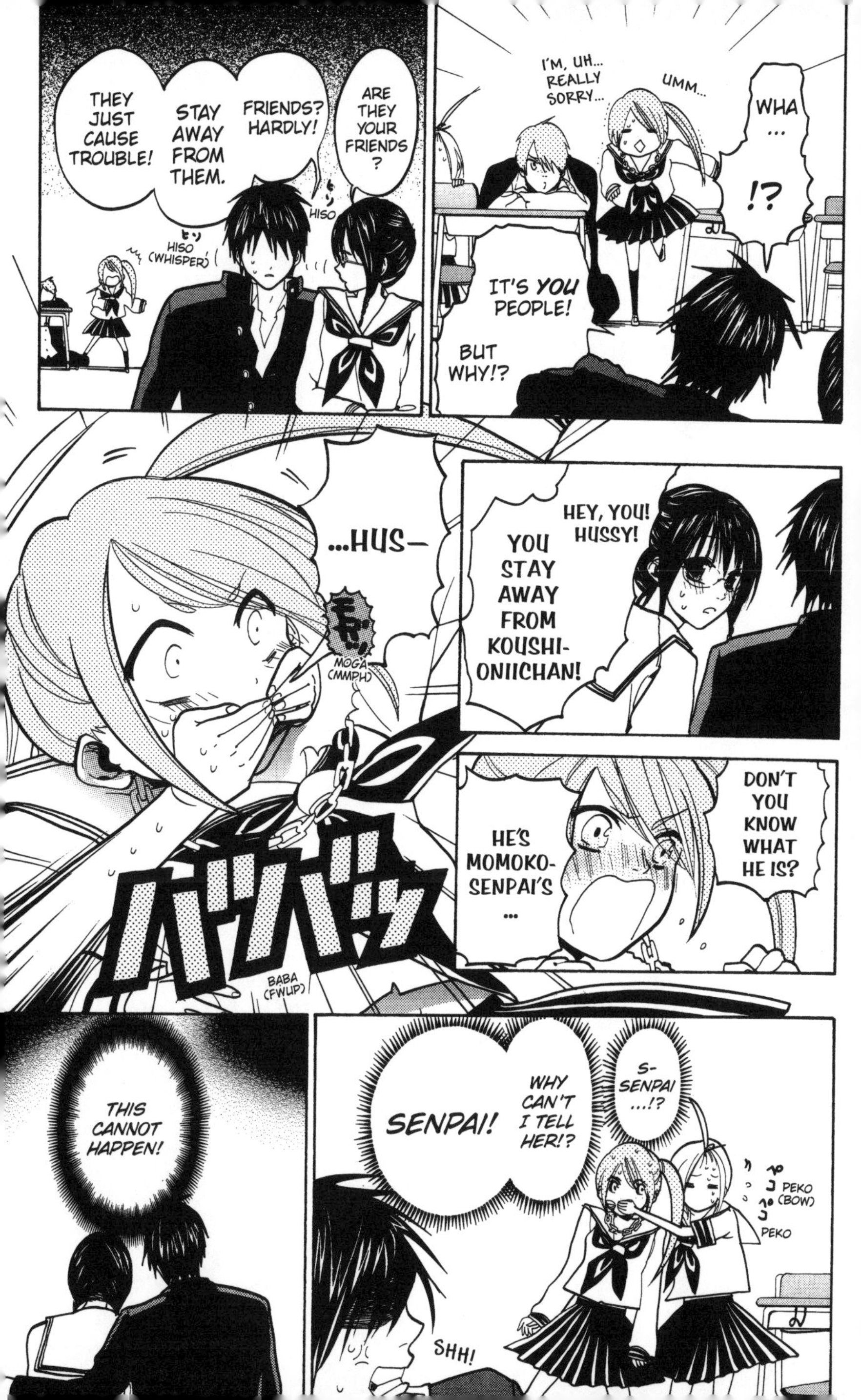
WHA ... !?
UMM...
I'M, UH... REALLY SORRY...
IT'S YOU PEOPLE!
BUT WHY!?
ARE THEY YOUR FRIENDS?
HISO
FRIENDS? HARDLY!
STAY AWAY FROM THEM.
THEY JUST CAUSE TROUBLE!
HISO (WHISPER)
HEY, YOU! HUSSY!
YOU STAY AWAY FROM KOUSHI-ONIICHAN!
DON'T YOU KNOW WHAT HE IS?
HE'S MOMOKO-SENPAI'S ...
...HUS—
MOGA (MMPH)
BABA (FWUP)
S-SENPAI ...!?
PEKO (BOW)
PEKO
WHY CAN'T I TELL HER!?
SENPAI!
SHH!
THIS CANNOT HAPPEN!

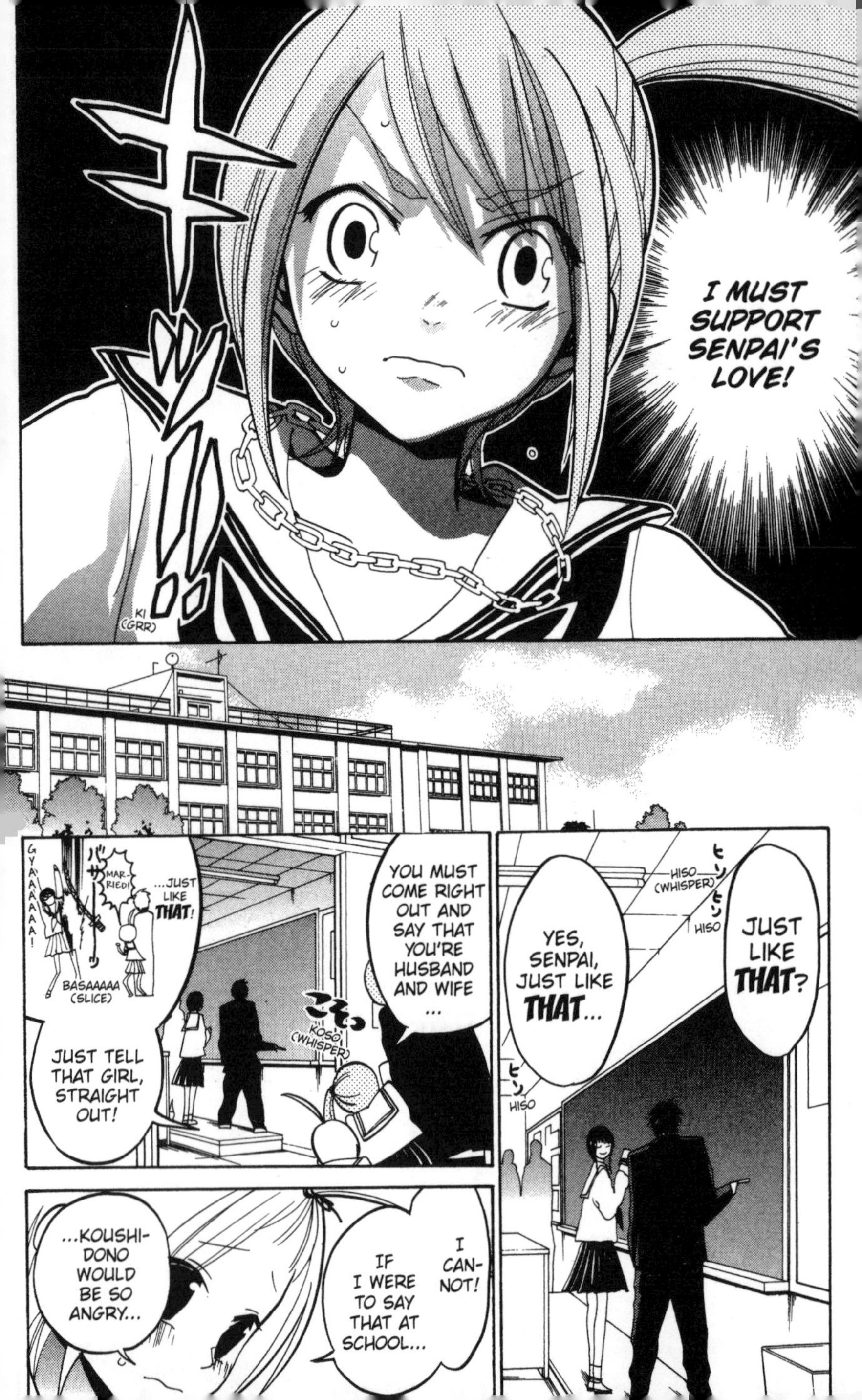
I MUST SUPPORT SENPAI'S LOVE!
KI (GRR)
JUST LIKE THAT?
HISO (WHISPER)
HISO
YES, SENPAI, JUST LIKE THAT...
HISO
YOU MUST COME RIGHT OUT AND SAY THAT YOU'RE HUSBAND AND WIFE ...
KOSO (WHISPER)
...JUST LIKE THAT!
MARRIED!
GYAAAAAA!
BASAAAAA (SLICE)
JUST TELL THAT GIRL, STRAIGHT OUT!
I CANNOT!
IF I WERE TO SAY THAT AT SCHOOL...
...KOUSHI-DONO WOULD BE SO ANGRY...

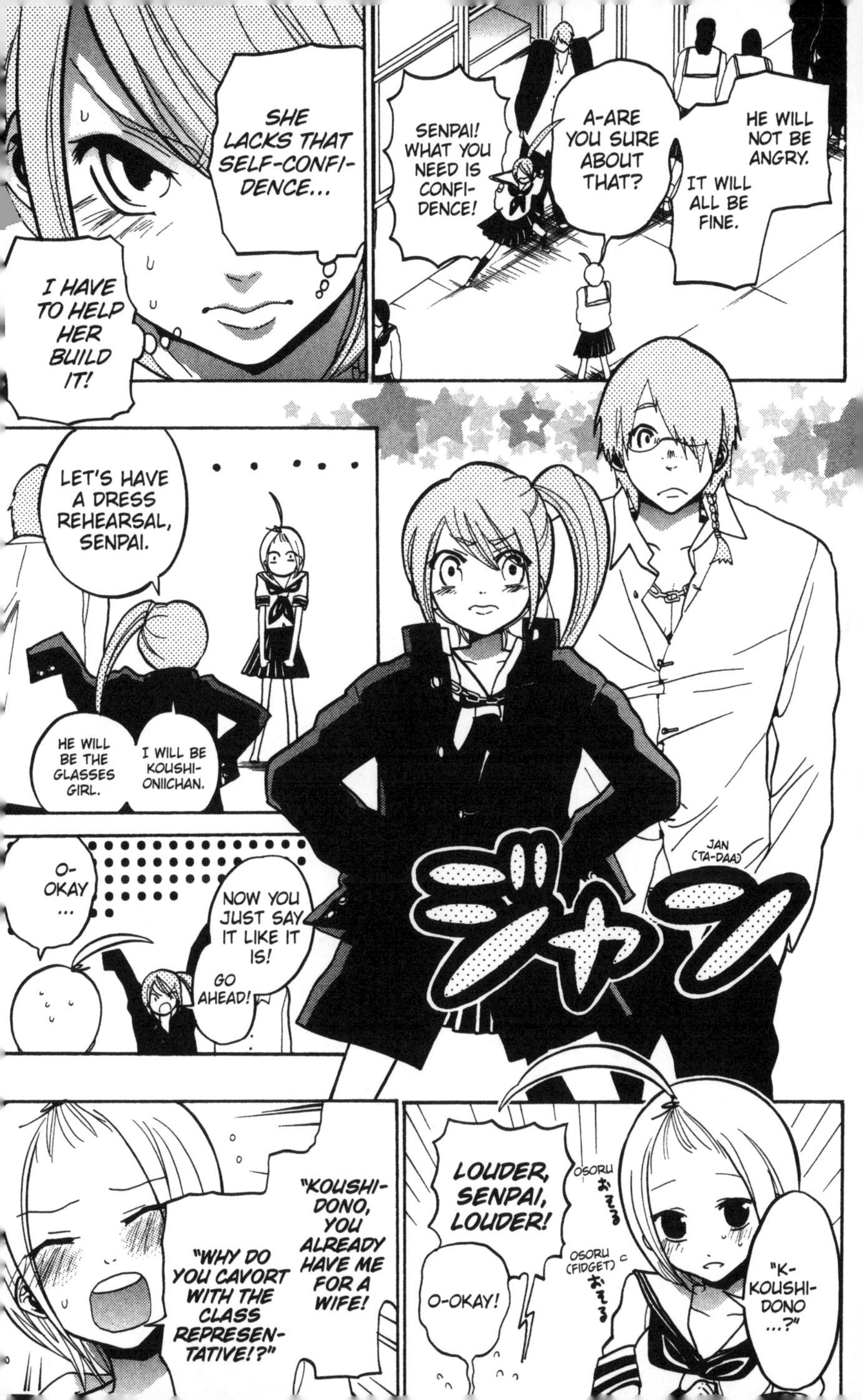
HE WILL NOT BE ANGRY.
IT WILL ALL BE FINE.
A-ARE YOU SURE ABOUT THAT?
SENPAI! WHAT YOU NEED IS CONFIDENCE!
SHE LACKS THAT SELF-CONFIDENCE...
I HAVE TO HELP HER BUILD IT!
JAN (TA-DAA)
ジャン
LET'S HAVE A DRESS REHEARSAL, SENPAI.
• • • • •
I WILL BE KOUSHI-ONIICHAN.
HE WILL BE THE GLASSES GIRL.
NOW YOU JUST SAY IT LIKE IT IS!
GO AHEAD!
O-OKAY...
"K-KOUSHI-DONO...?"
OSORU (FIDGET)
おそる
OSORU
おそる
LOUDER, SENPAI, LOUDER!
O-OKAY!
"KOUSHI-DONO, YOU ALREADY HAVE ME FOR A WIFE!
"WHY DO YOU CAVORT WITH THE CLASS REPRESENTATIVE!?"

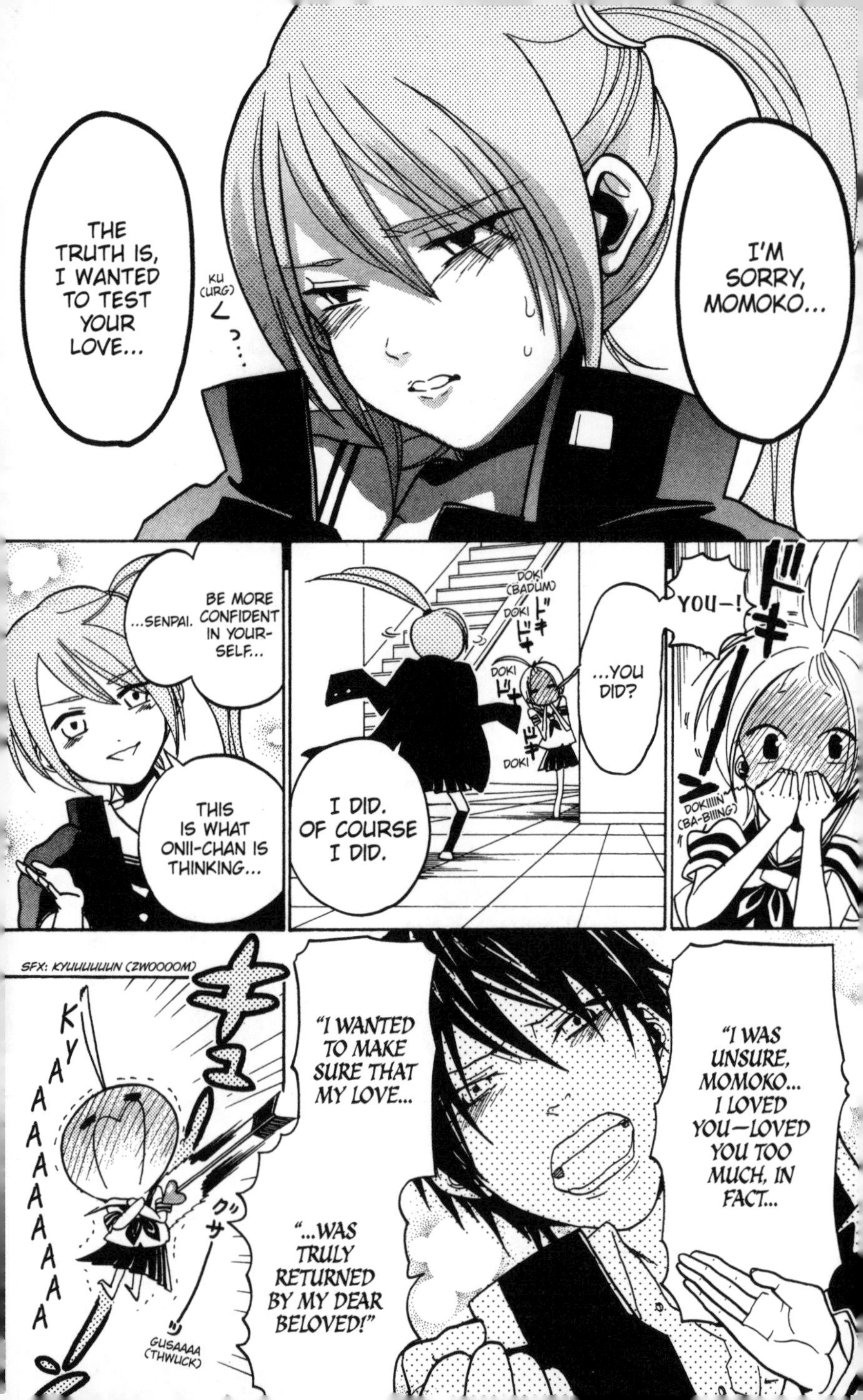
I'M SORRY, MOMOKO...
KU (URG)
THE TRUTH IS, I WANTED TO TEST YOUR LOVE...
YOU—!
DOKIIIIN (BA-BIIING)
...YOU DID?
DOKI (BADUM)
DOKI
DOKI
DOKI
I DID. OF COURSE I DID.
BE MORE CONFIDENT IN YOUR-SELF...
...SENPAI.
THIS IS WHAT ONII-CHAN IS THINKING...
"I WAS UNSURE, MOMOKO... I LOVED YOU—LOVED YOU TOO MUCH, IN FACT...
"I WANTED TO MAKE SURE THAT MY LOVE...
"...WAS TRULY RETURNED BY MY DEAR BELOVED!"
SFX: KYUUUUUUN (ZWOOOOM)
KYAAAAAAAAAAAA
GUSAAAA (THWUCK)

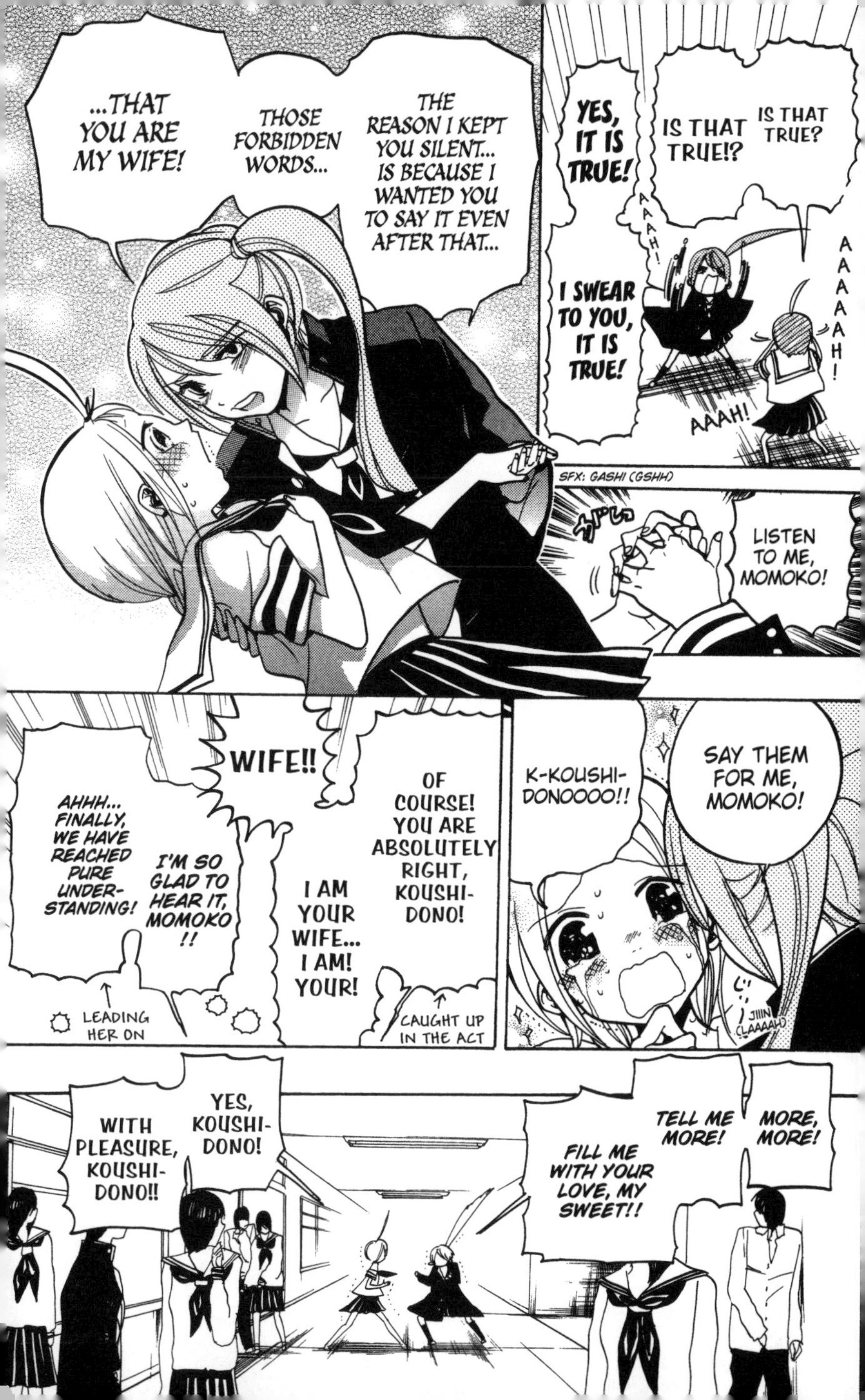
IS THAT TRUE?
IS THAT TRUE!?
YES, IT IS TRUE!
AAAAAAH!
AAAH!
I SWEAR TO YOU, IT IS TRUE!
AAAH!
SFX: GASHI (GSHH)
LISTEN TO ME, MOMOKO!
THE REASON I KEPT YOU SILENT... IS BECAUSE I WANTED YOU TO SAY IT EVEN AFTER THAT...
THOSE FORBIDDEN WORDS...
...THAT YOU ARE MY WIFE!
SAY THEM FOR ME, MOMOKO!
K-KOUSHI-DONOOOO!!
JIIIN (LAAAAH)
OF COURSE! YOU ARE ABSOLUTELY RIGHT, KOUSHI-DONO!
WIFE!!
I AM YOUR WIFE... I AM! YOUR!
CAUGHT UP IN THE ACT
I'M SO GLAD TO HEAR IT, MOMOKO!!
AHHH... FINALLY, WE HAVE REACHED PURE UNDER-STANDING!
LEADING HER ON
MORE, MORE!
TELL ME MORE!
FILL ME WITH YOUR LOVE, MY SWEET!!
YES, KOUSHI-DONO!
WITH PLEASURE, KOUSHI-DONO!!

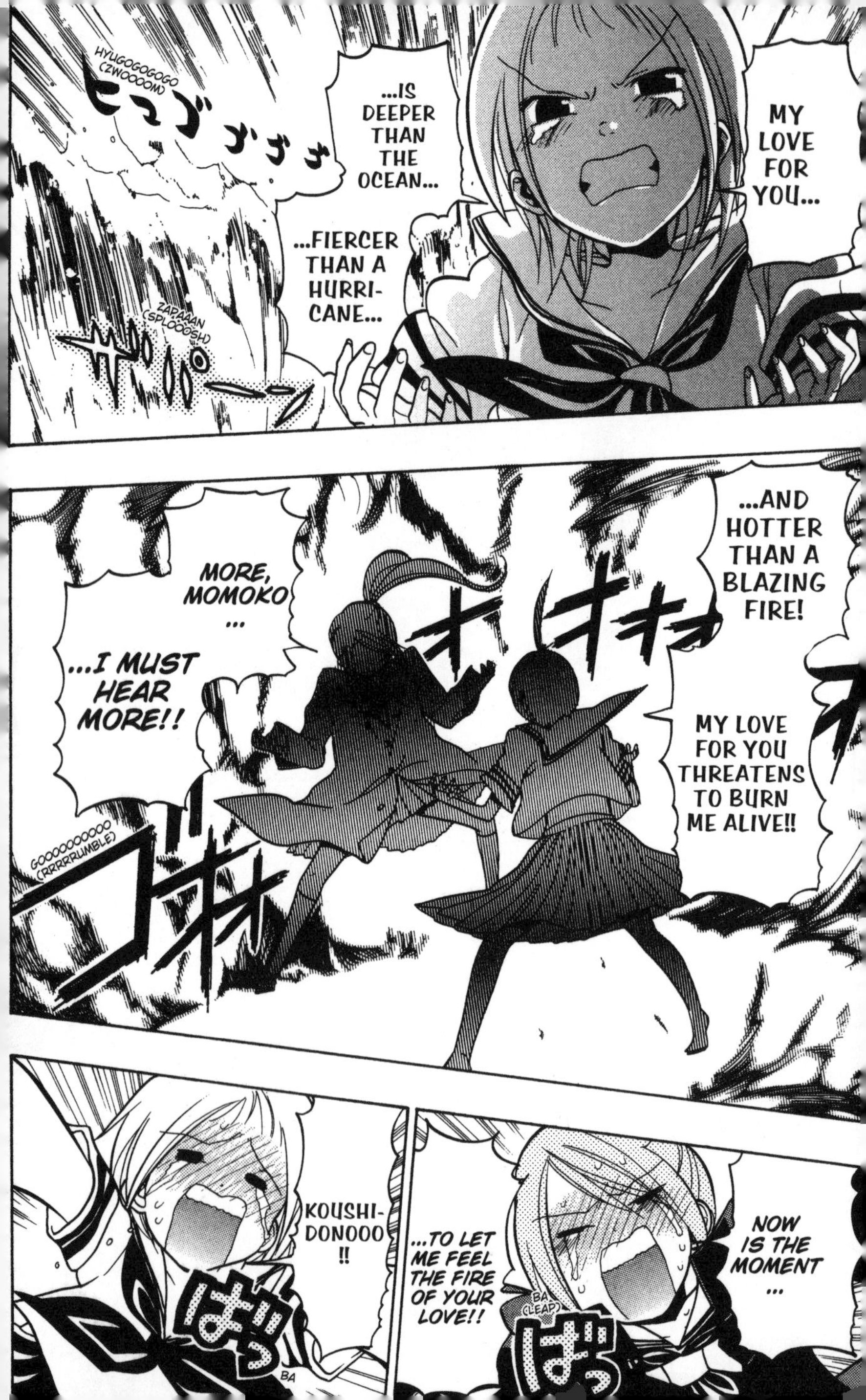
MY LOVE FOR YOU...
...IS DEEPER THAN THE OCEAN...
HYUGOGOGOGO (ZWOOOOOM)
...FIERCER THAN A HURRI-CANE...
ZAPAAAN (SPLOOOSH)
...AND HOTTER THAN A BLAZING FIRE!
MY LOVE FOR YOU THREATENS TO BURN ME ALIVE!!
MORE, MOMOKO ...
...I MUST HEAR MORE!!
GOOOOOOOOOO (RRRRRUMBLE)
NOW IS THE MOMENT ...
...TO LET ME FEEL THE FIRE OF YOUR LOVE!!
BA (LEAP)
KOUSHI-DONOOO !!
BA

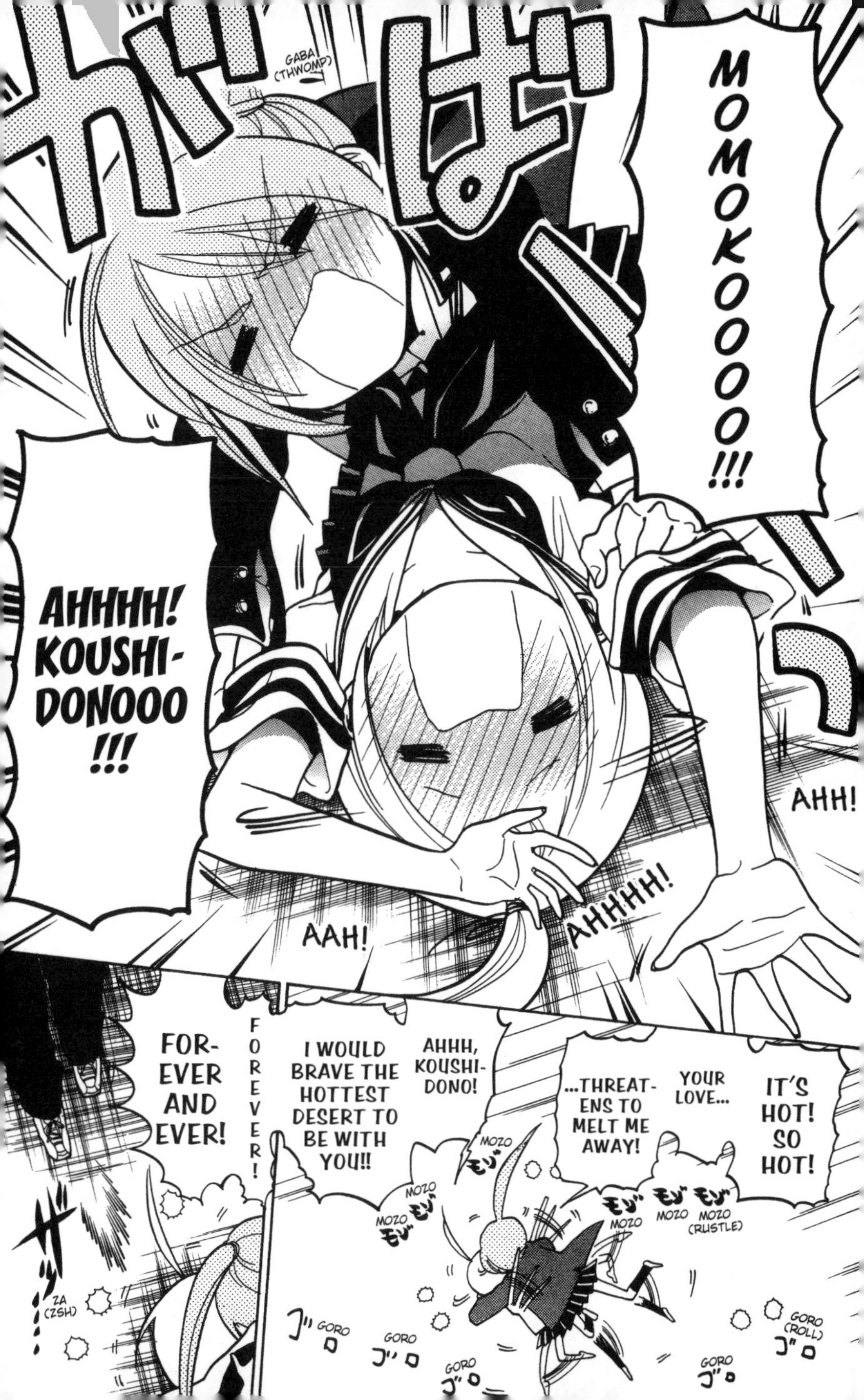
MOMOKOOOOOOO!!!
GABA (THWOMP)
AHHHH! KOUSHI-DONOOO!!!
AHH!
AHHHH!
AAH!
IT'S HOT! SO HOT!
YOUR LOVE...
...THREAT-ENS TO MELT ME AWAY!
AHHH, KOUSHI-DONO!
I WOULD BRAVE THE HOTTEST DESERT TO BE WITH YOU!!
FOREVER!
FOR-EVER AND EVER!
MOZO MOZO MOZO MOZO MOZO MOZO MOZO (RUSTLE)
GORO (ROLL) GORO GORO GORO GORO
ZA (ZSH)

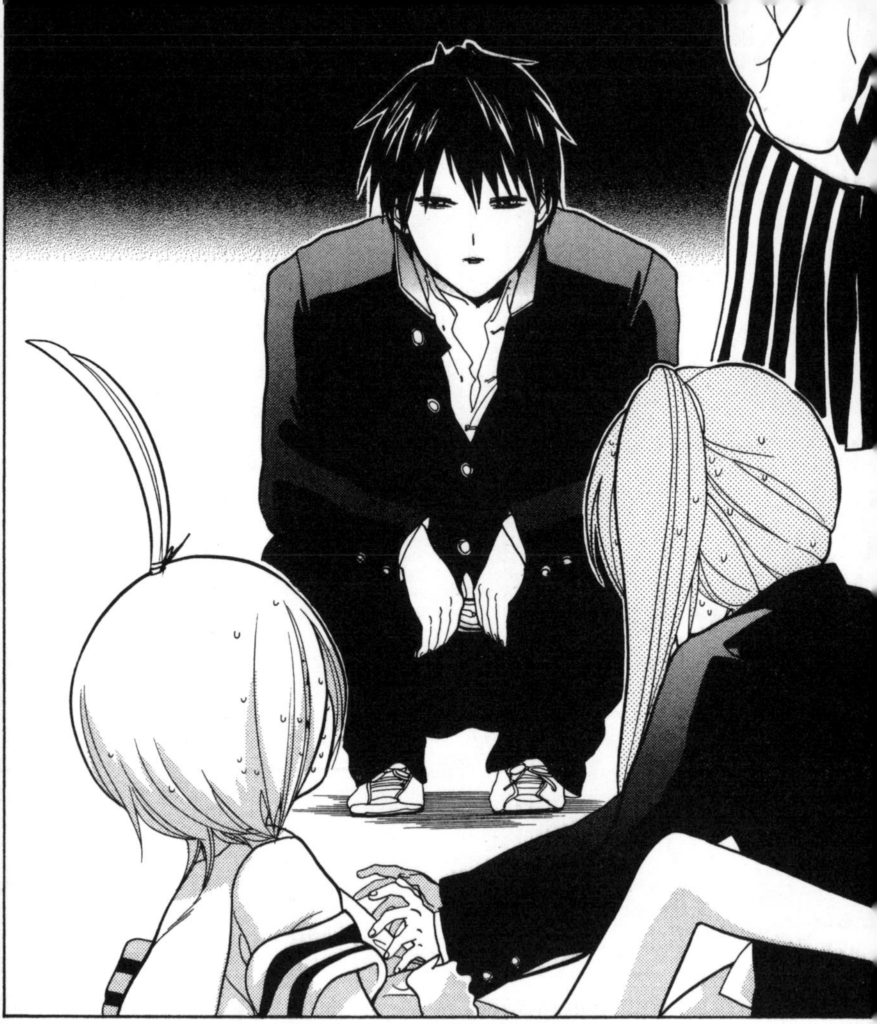

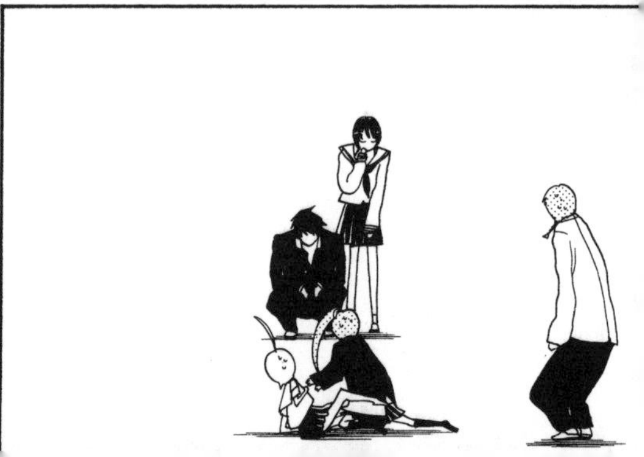

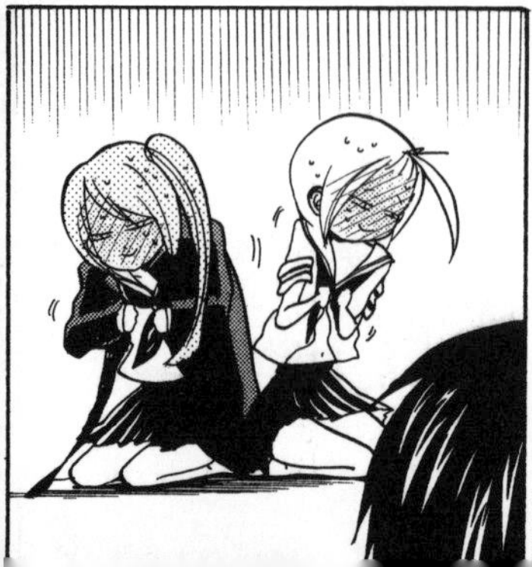

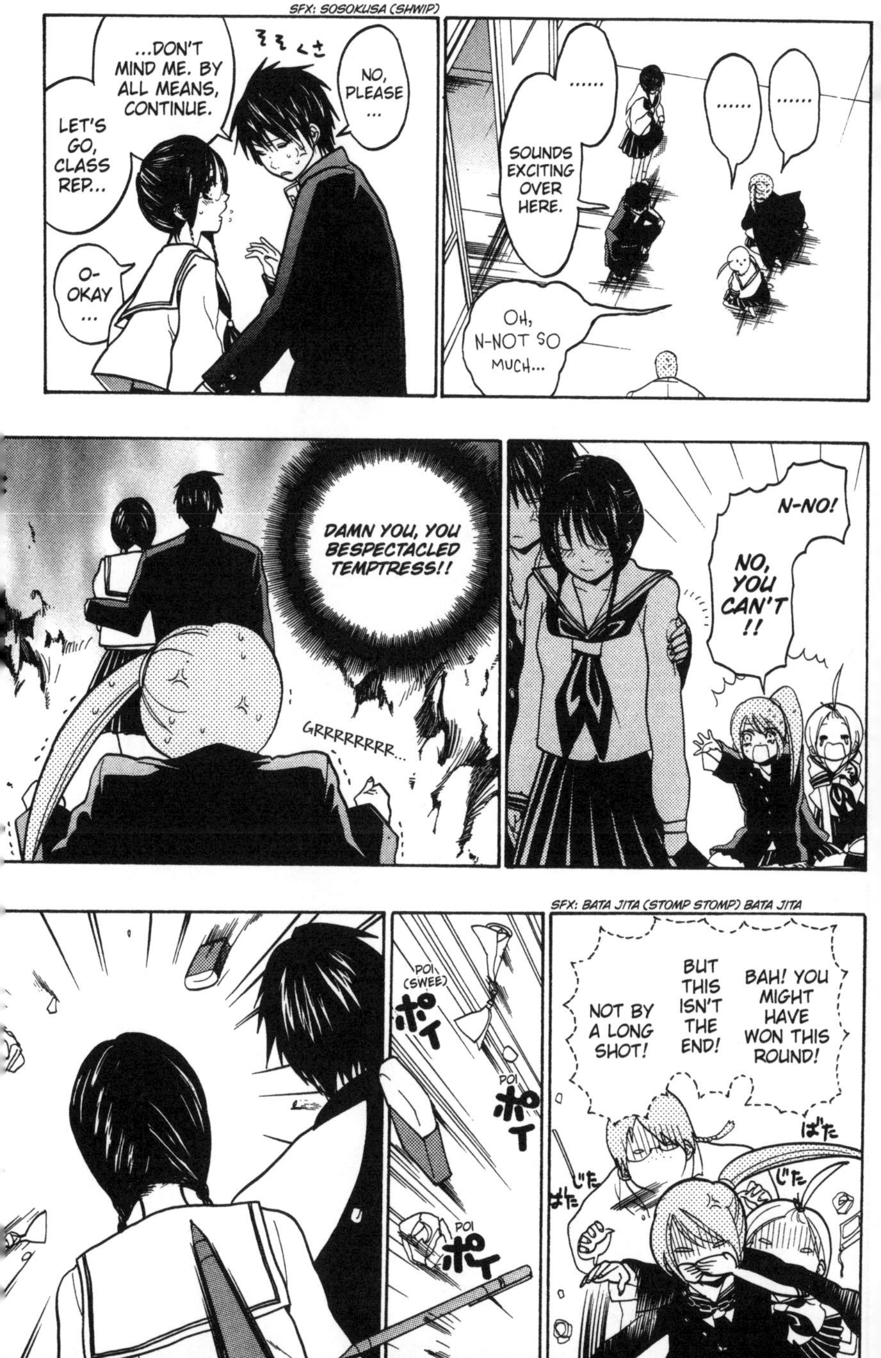
......
......
......
SOUNDS EXCITING OVER HERE.
OH, N-NOT SO MUCH...
SFX: SOSOKUSA (SHWIP)
そそくさ
NO, PLEASE ...
...DON'T MIND ME. BY ALL MEANS, CONTINUE.
LET'S GO, CLASS REP...
O-OKAY ...
N-NO!
NO, YOU CAN'T !!
DAMN YOU, YOU BESPECTACLED TEMPTRESS!!
GRRRRRRRR...
SFX: BATA JITA (STOMP STOMP) BATA JITA
BAH! YOU MIGHT HAVE WON THIS ROUND!
BUT THIS ISN'T THE END!
NOT BY A LONG SHOT!
ばた
じた
じた
ばた
POI (SWEE)
ポイ
POI
ポイ
POI
ポイ

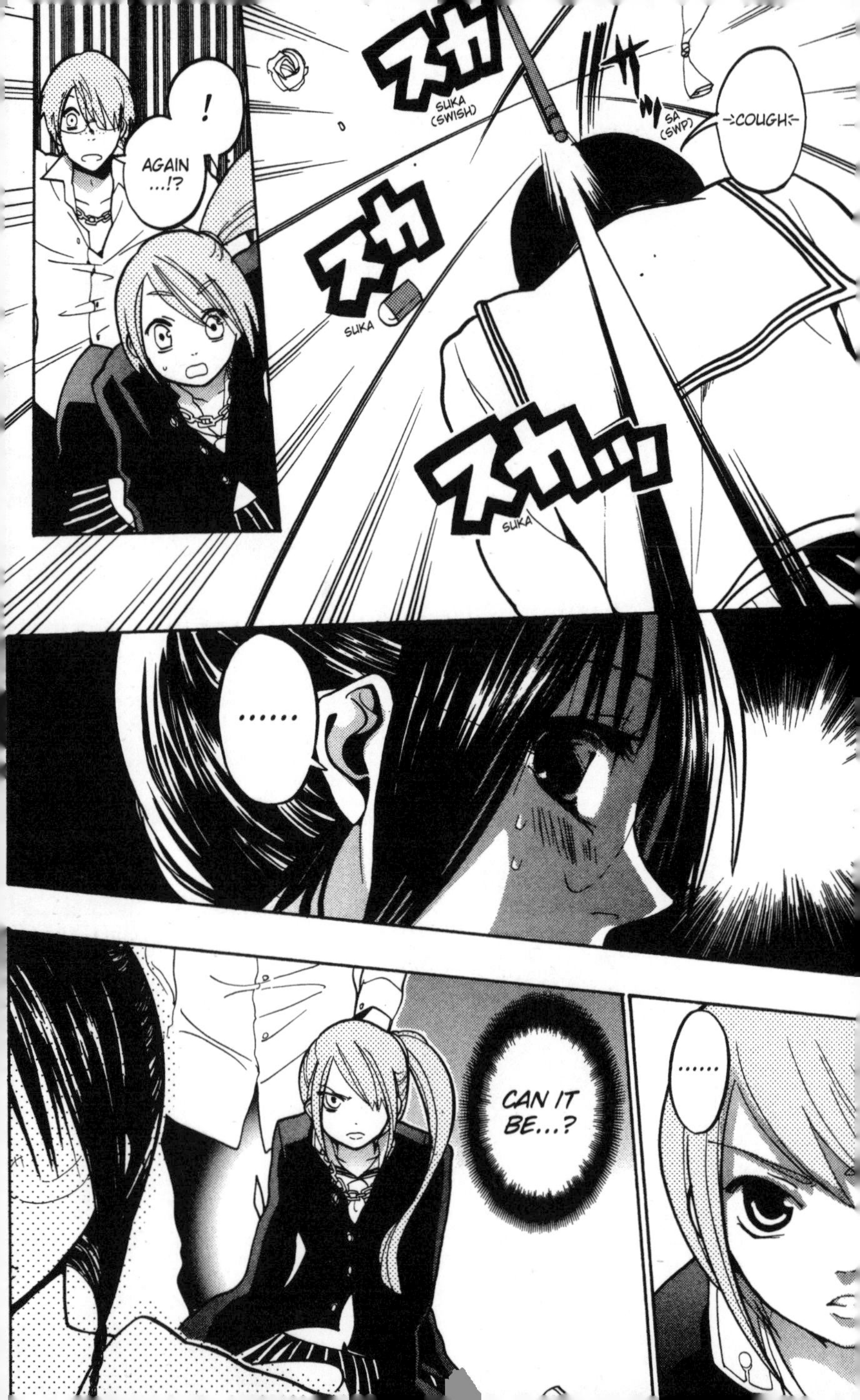

スカ
SUKA (SWISH)
SA (SWP)
-:COUGH:-
スカ
SUKA
スカ...
SUKA
!
AGAIN ...!?
......
......
CAN IT BE...?

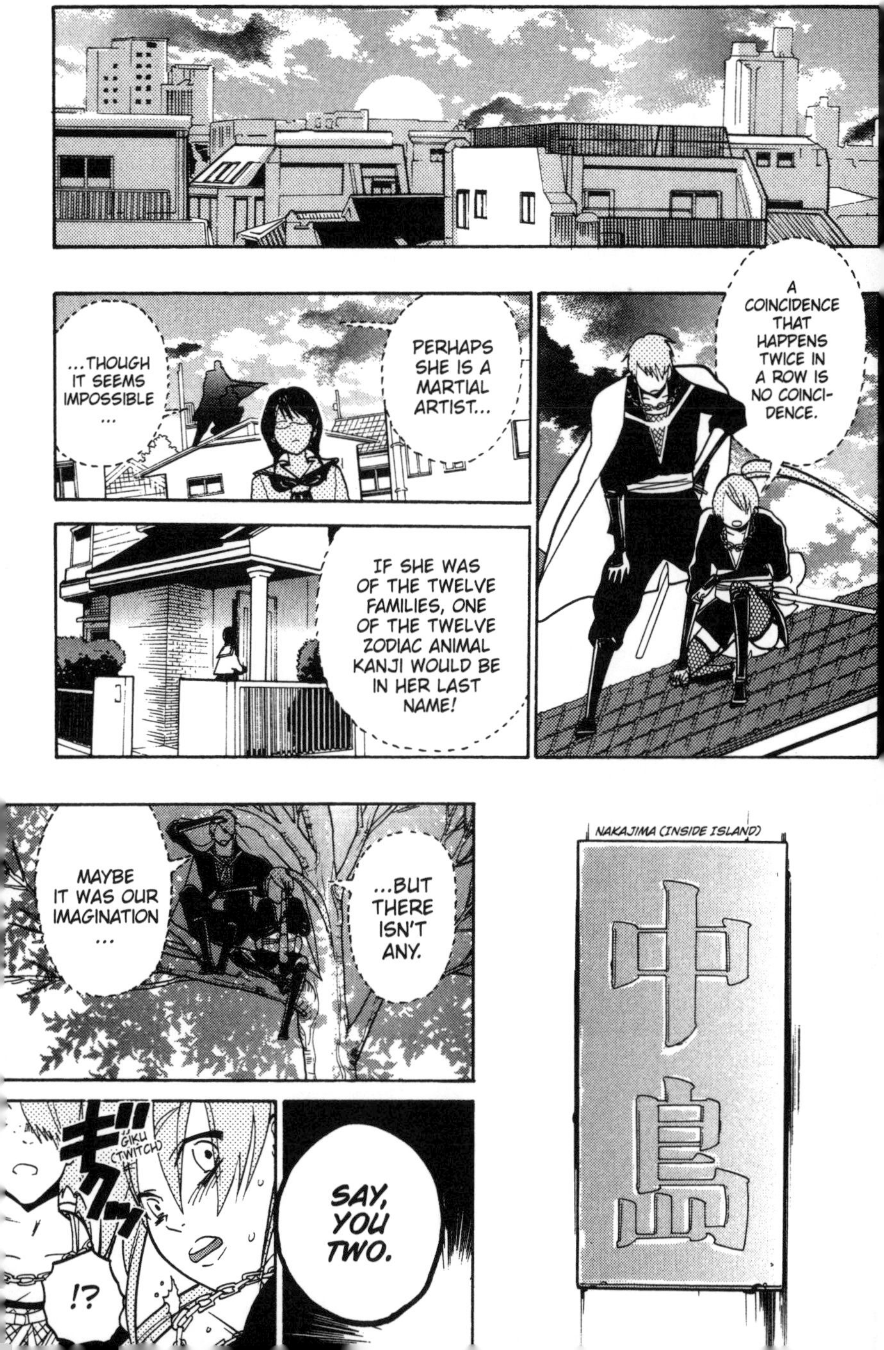
A COINCIDENCE THAT HAPPENS TWICE IN A ROW IS NO COINCIDENCE.
PERHAPS SHE IS A MARTIAL ARTIST...
...THOUGH IT SEEMS IMPOSSIBLE...
IF SHE WAS OF THE TWELVE FAMILIES, ONE OF THE TWELVE ZODIAC ANIMAL KANJI WOULD BE IN HER LAST NAME!
NAKAJIMA (INSIDE ISLAND)
中島
...BUT THERE ISN'T ANY.
MAYBE IT WAS OUR IMAGINATION...
SAY, YOU TWO.
GIKU (TWITCH)
!?

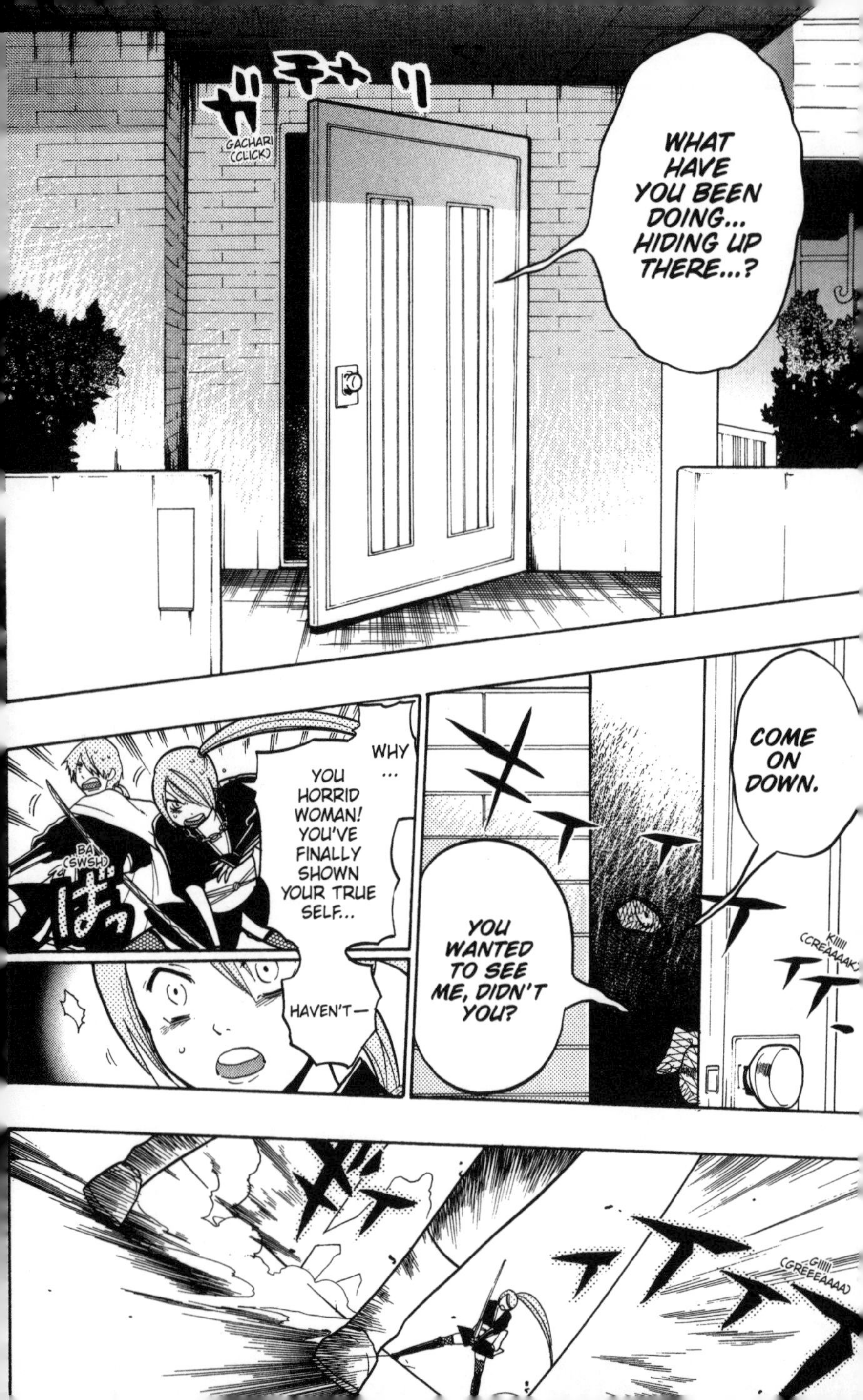
ガチャリ
GACHARI (CLICK)
WHAT HAVE YOU BEEN DOING... HIDING UP THERE...?
COME ON DOWN.
KIIII (CREAAAAK)
YOU WANTED TO SEE ME, DIDN'T YOU?
WHY ...
YOU HORRID WOMAN! YOU'VE FINALLY SHOWN YOUR TRUE SELF...
BA (SWSH)
HAVEN'T—
GIIII (GREEEAAAA)

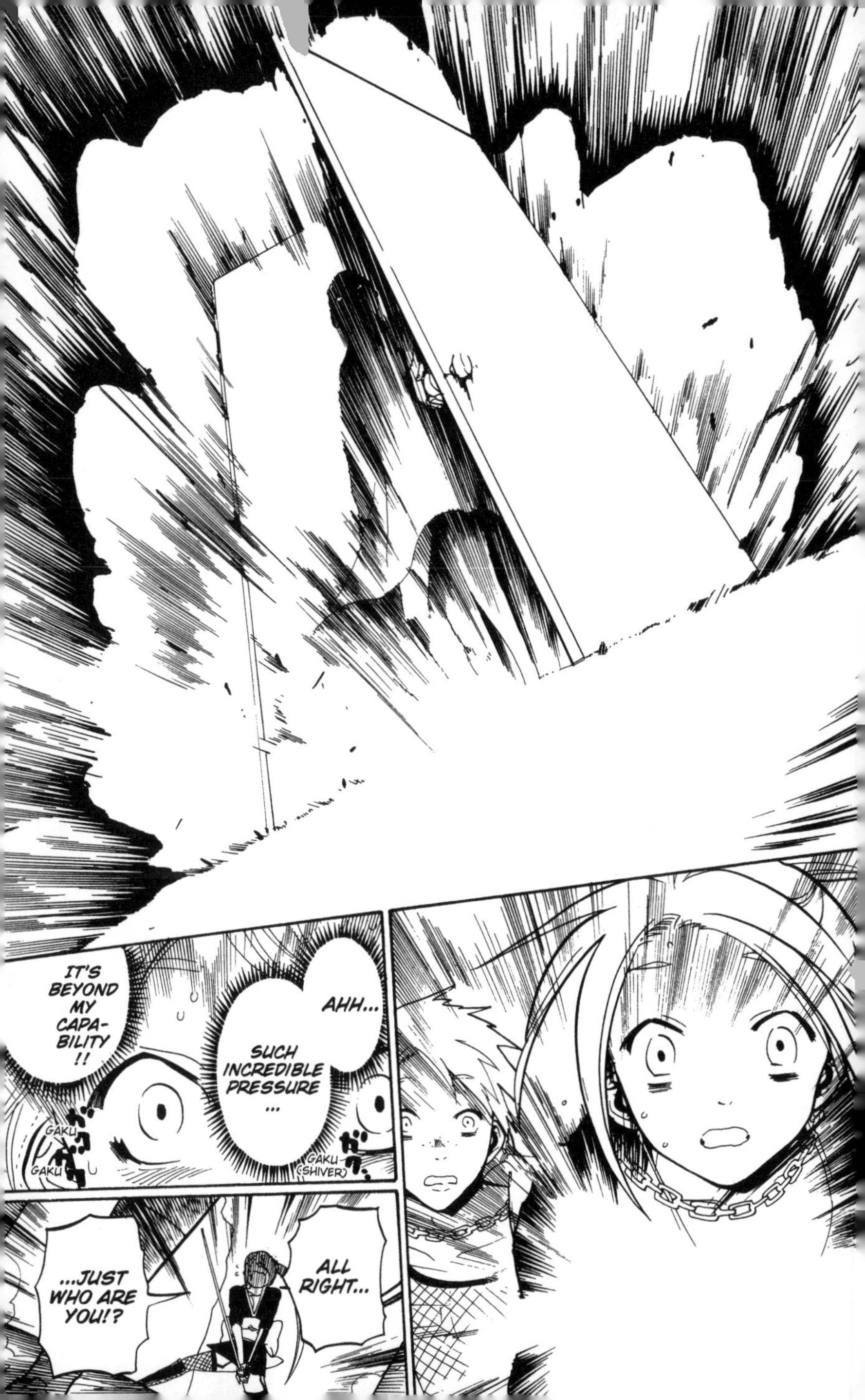
AHH...
SUCH INCREDIBLE PRESSURE...
GAKU (SHIVER)
IT'S BEYOND MY CAPABILITY!!
GAKU
GAKU
ALL RIGHT...
...JUST WHO ARE YOU!?

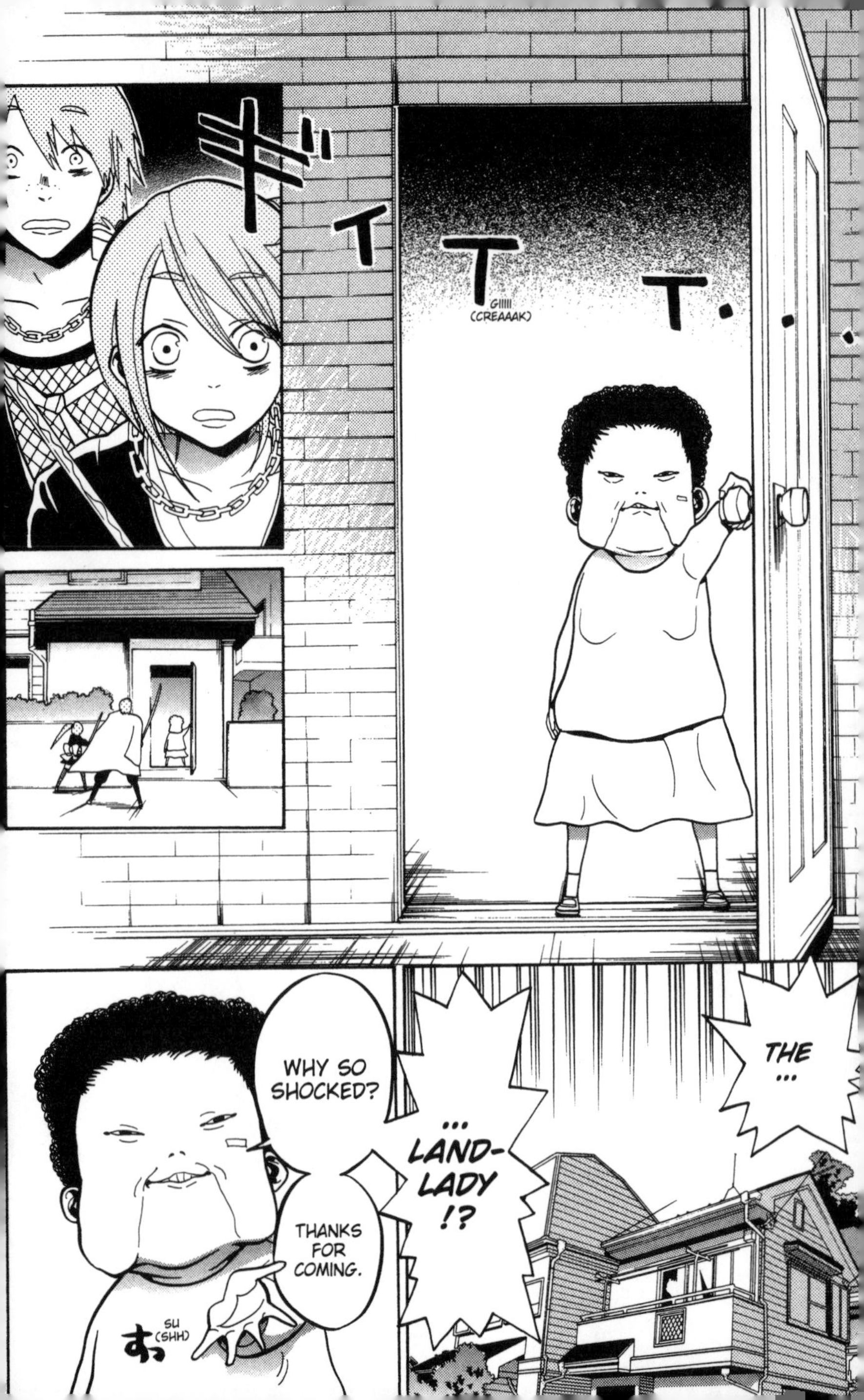
GIIII
(CREAAAK)
THE ...
... LAND-LADY !?
WHY SO SHOCKED?
THANKS FOR COMING.
すっ
SU
(SHH)

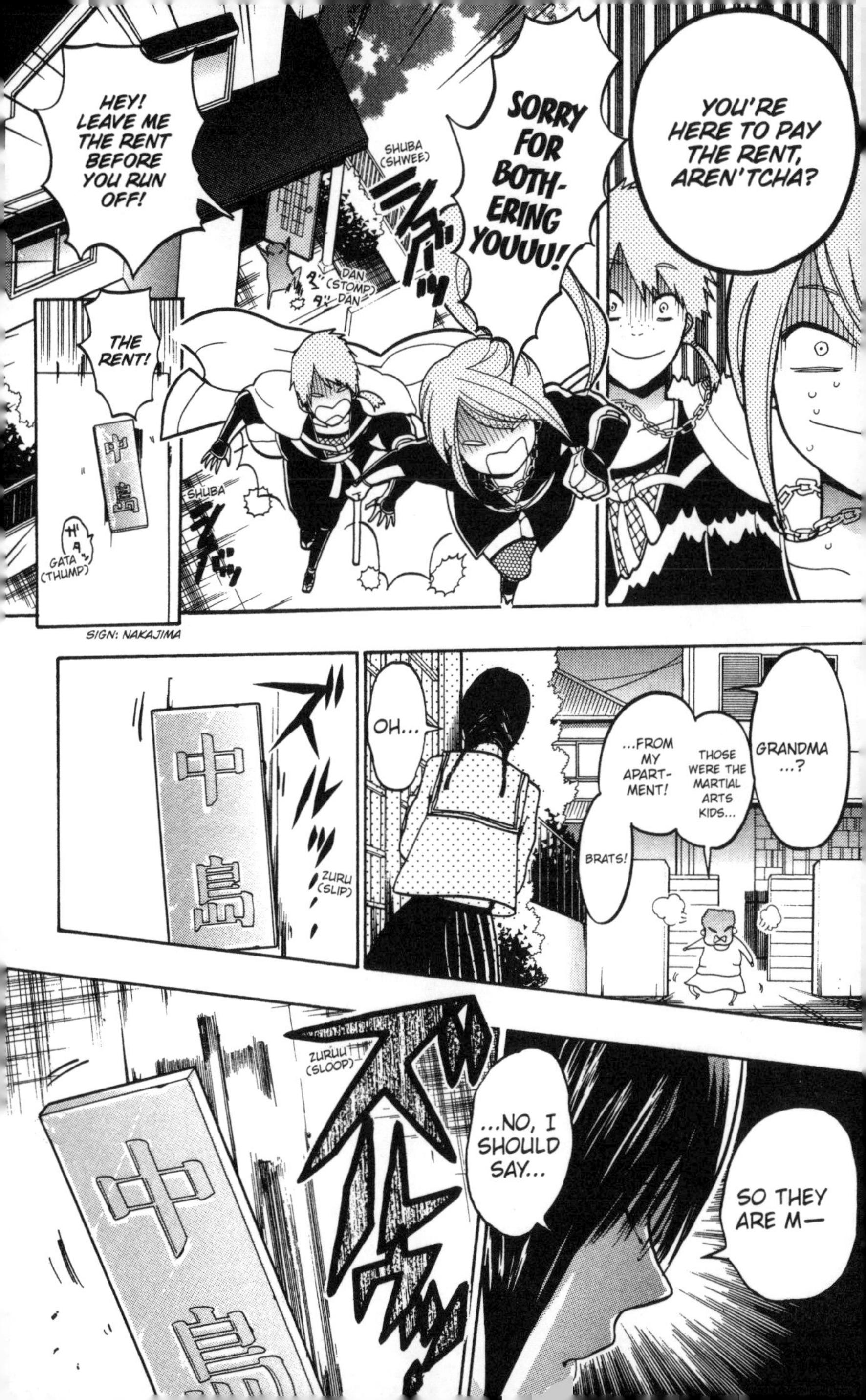
YOU'RE HERE TO PAY THE RENT, AREN'TCHA?
SORRY FOR BOTHERING YOUUU!
SHUBA (SHWEE)
DAN (STOMP) DAN
HEY! LEAVE ME THE RENT BEFORE YOU RUN OFF!
THE RENT!
SHUBA
GATA (THUMP)
SIGN: NAKAJIMA
GRANDMA ...?
THOSE WERE THE MARTIAL ARTS KIDS...
...FROM MY APARTMENT!
BRATS!
OH...
ZURU (SLIP)
SO THEY ARE M—
...NO, I SHOULD SAY...
ZURUU (SLOOP)

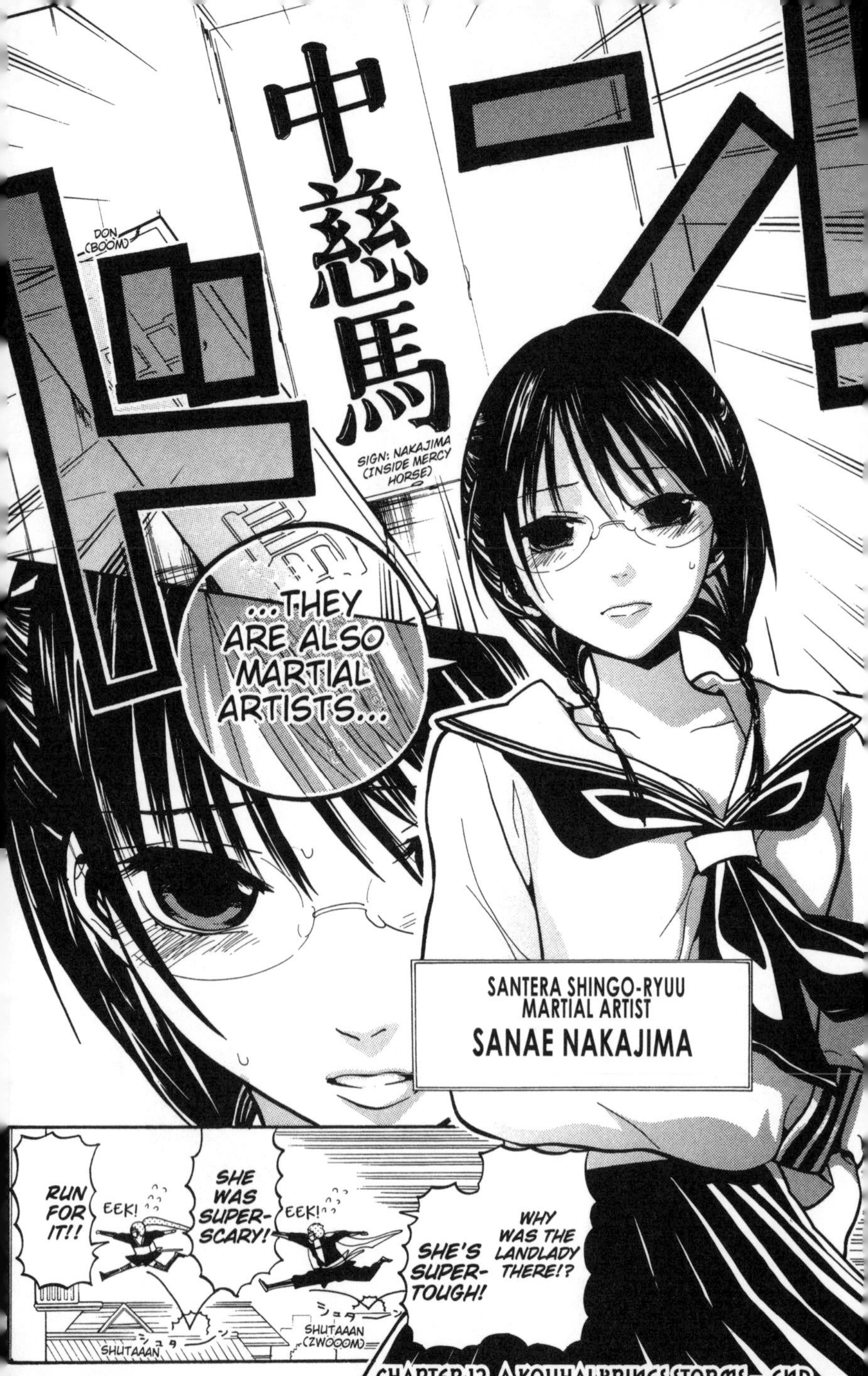
中慈馬
DON (BOOM)
SIGN: NAKAJIMA (INSIDE MERCY HORSE)
...THEY ARE ALSO MARTIAL ARTISTS...
SANTERA SHINGO-RYUU MARTIAL ARTIST
SANAE NAKAJIMA
WHY WAS THE LANDLADY THERE!?
SHE'S SUPER-TOUGH!
EEK!
SHE WAS SUPER-SCARY!
EEK!
RUN FOR IT!!
SHUTAAAN (ZWOOOM)
SHUTAAAN

CHAPTER 12. A KOUHAI BRINGS STORMS – END

13. HEAVENLY WARRIOR HORSE MASK (1)

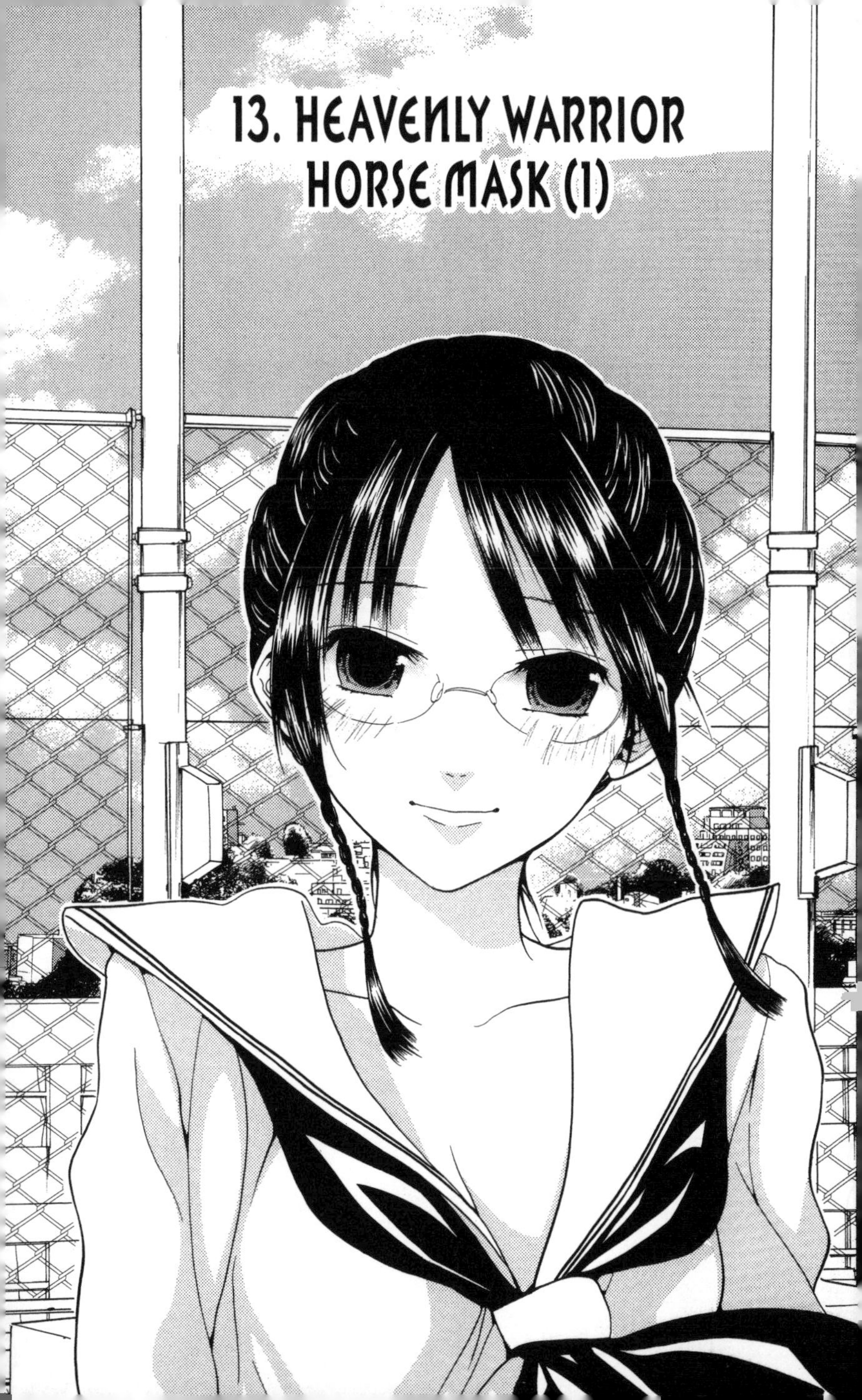

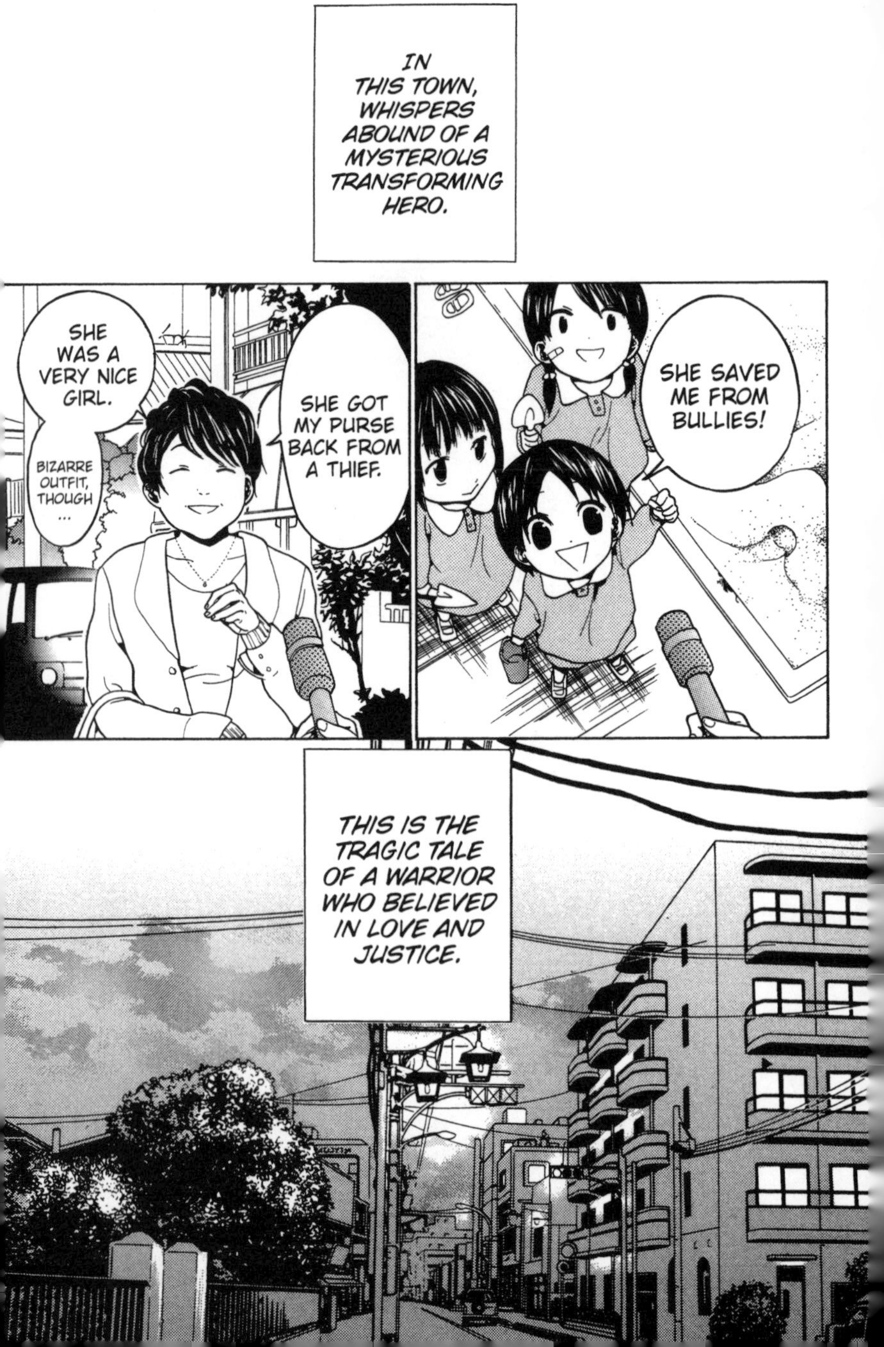
IN THIS TOWN, WHISPERS ABOUND OF A MYSTERIOUS TRANSFORMING HERO.
SHE SAVED ME FROM BULLIES!
SHE GOT MY PURSE BACK FROM A THIEF.
SHE WAS A VERY NICE GIRL.
BIZARRE OUTFIT, THOUGH ...
THIS IS THE TRAGIC TALE OF A WARRIOR WHO BELIEVED IN LOVE AND JUSTICE.

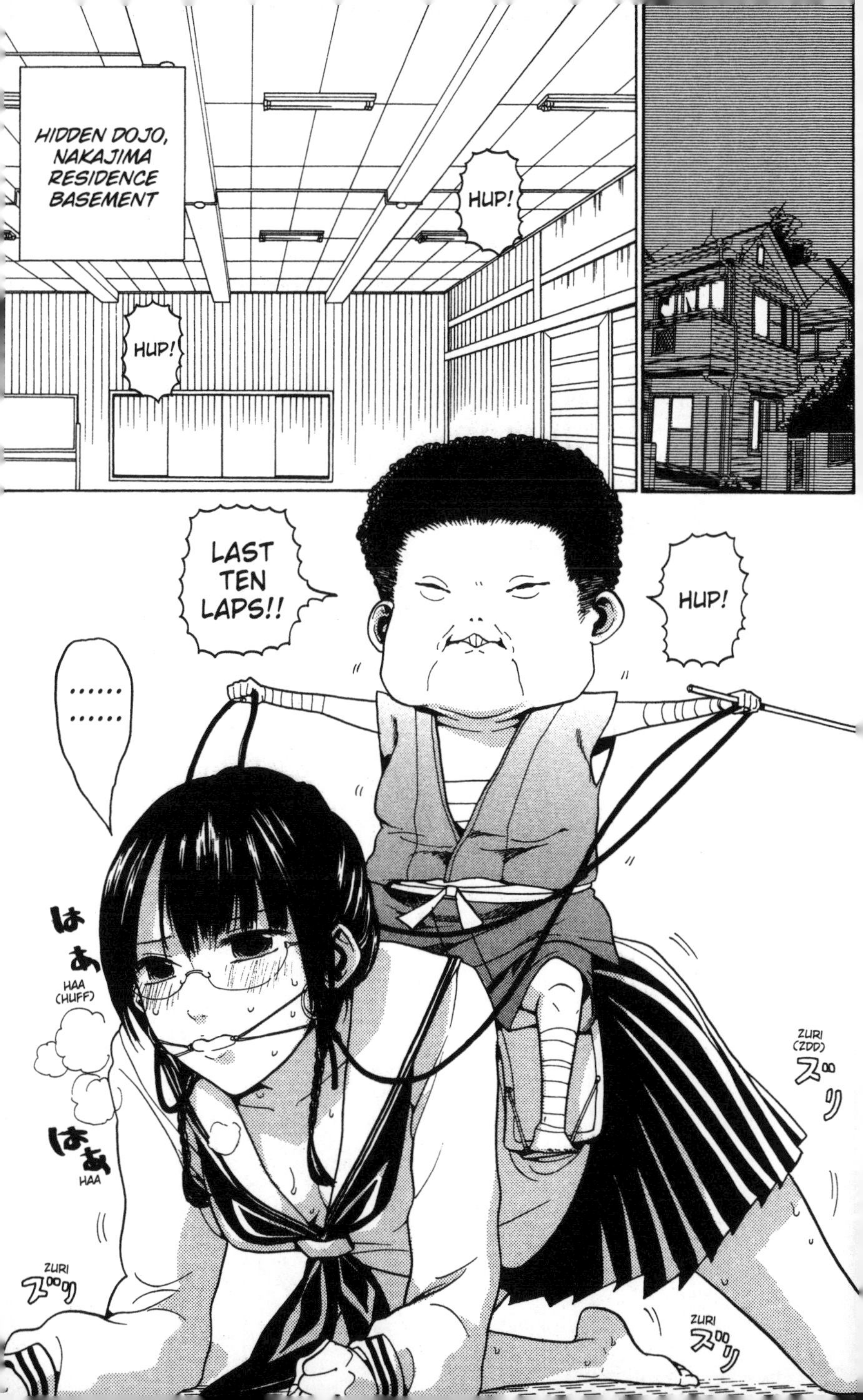
HIDDEN DOJO, NAKAJIMA RESIDENCE BASEMENT
HUP!
HUP!
HUP!
LAST TEN LAPS!!
......
......
ZURI (ZDD) ズリ
はぁ HAA (HUFF)
はぁ HAA
ZURI ズリ
ZURI ズリ

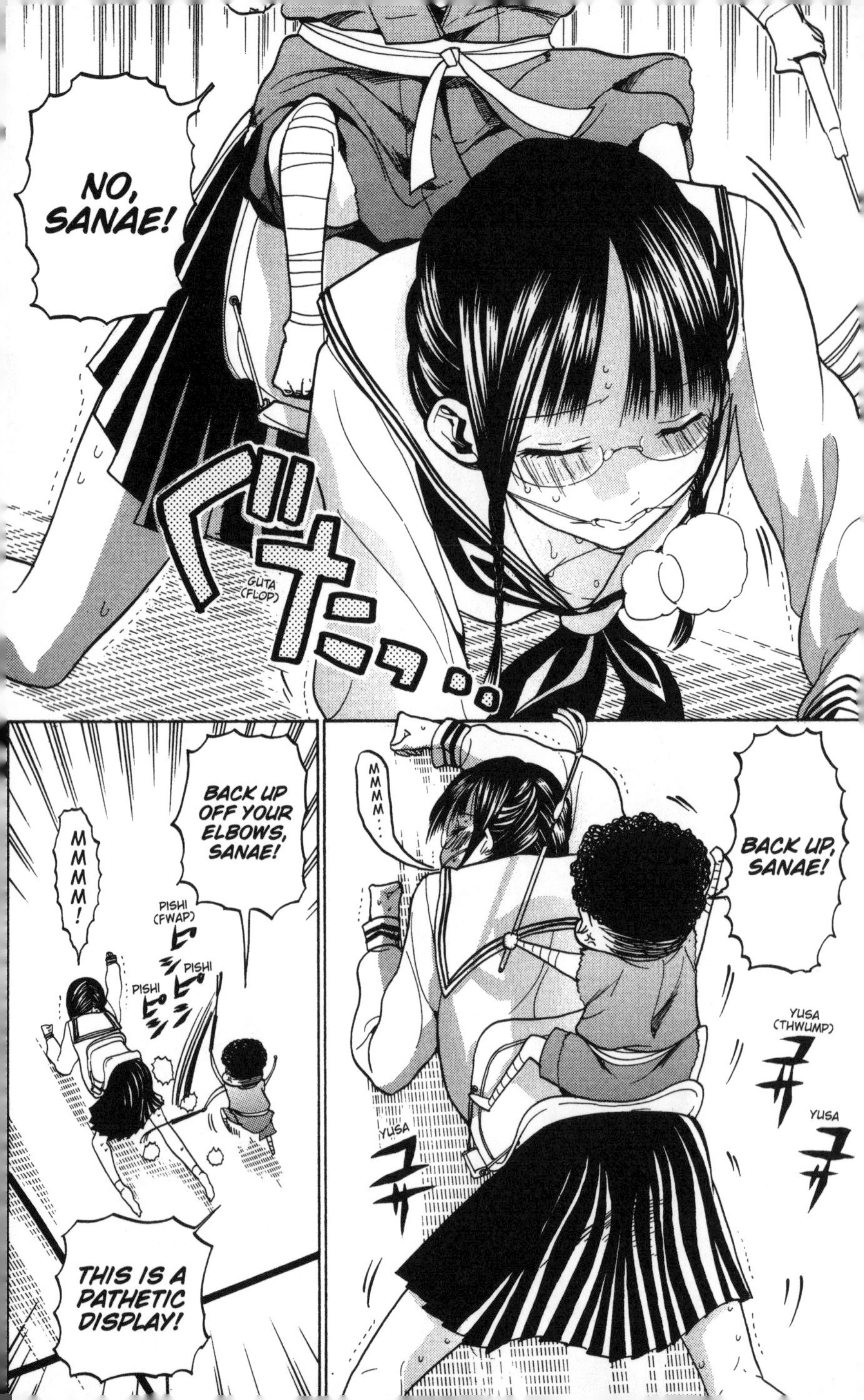
NO, SANAE!
GUTA (FLOP)
BACK UP, SANAE!
MMMM...
YUSA (THWUMP)
YUSA
YUSA
BACK UP OFF YOUR ELBOWS, SANAE!
MMMMM!
PISHI (FWAP)
PISHI
PISHI
THIS IS A PATHETIC DISPLAY!

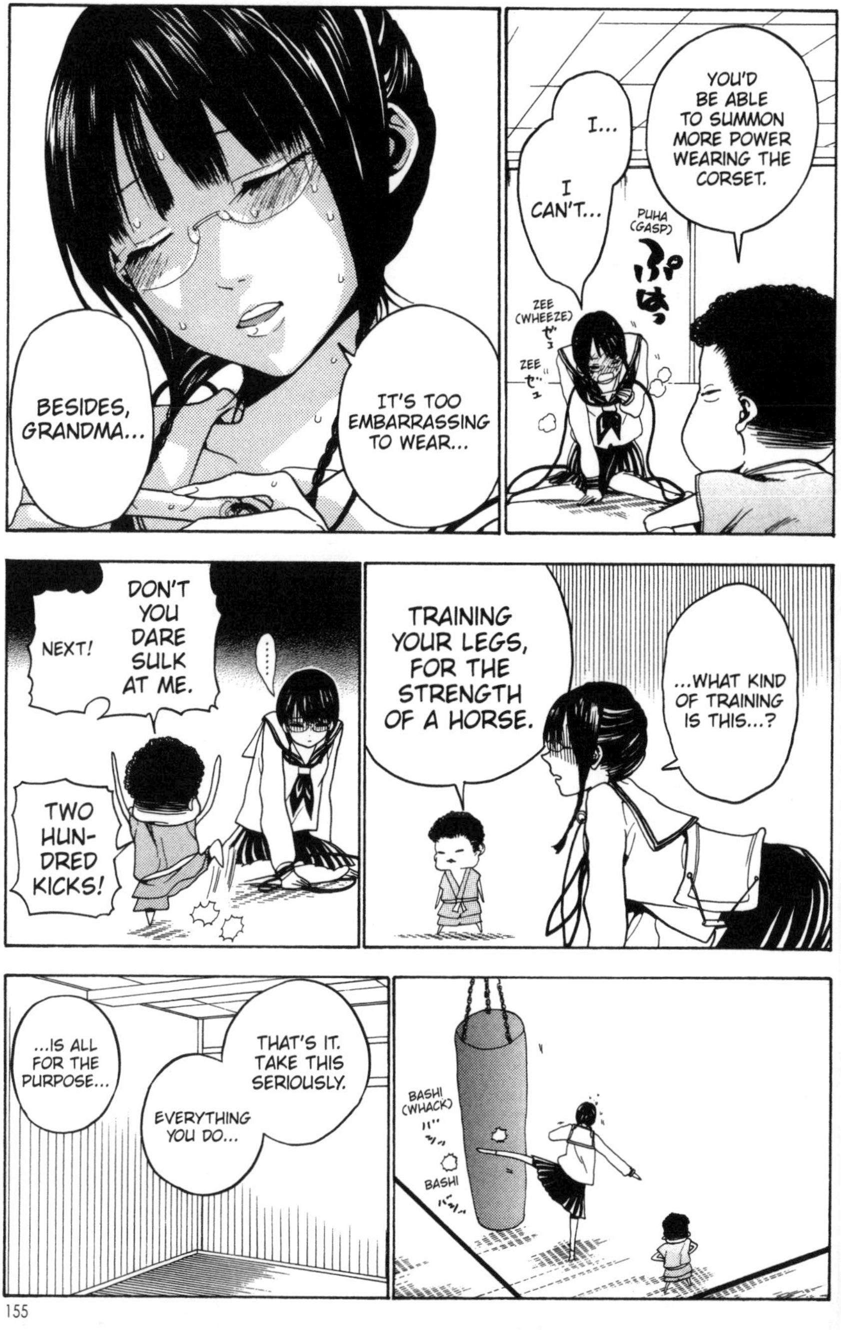
YOU'D BE ABLE TO SUMMON MORE POWER WEARING THE CORSET.
I...
I CAN'T...
PUHA (GASP)
ぷはっ
ZEE (WHEEZE)
ZEE
IT'S TOO EMBARRASSING TO WEAR...
BESIDES, GRANDMA...
...WHAT KIND OF TRAINING IS THIS...?
TRAINING YOUR LEGS, FOR THE STRENGTH OF A HORSE.
......
DON'T YOU DARE SULK AT ME.
NEXT!
TWO HUN-DRED KICKS!
BASHI (WHACK)
BASHI
THAT'S IT. TAKE THIS SERIOUSLY.
EVERYTHING YOU DO...
...IS ALL FOR THE PURPOSE...

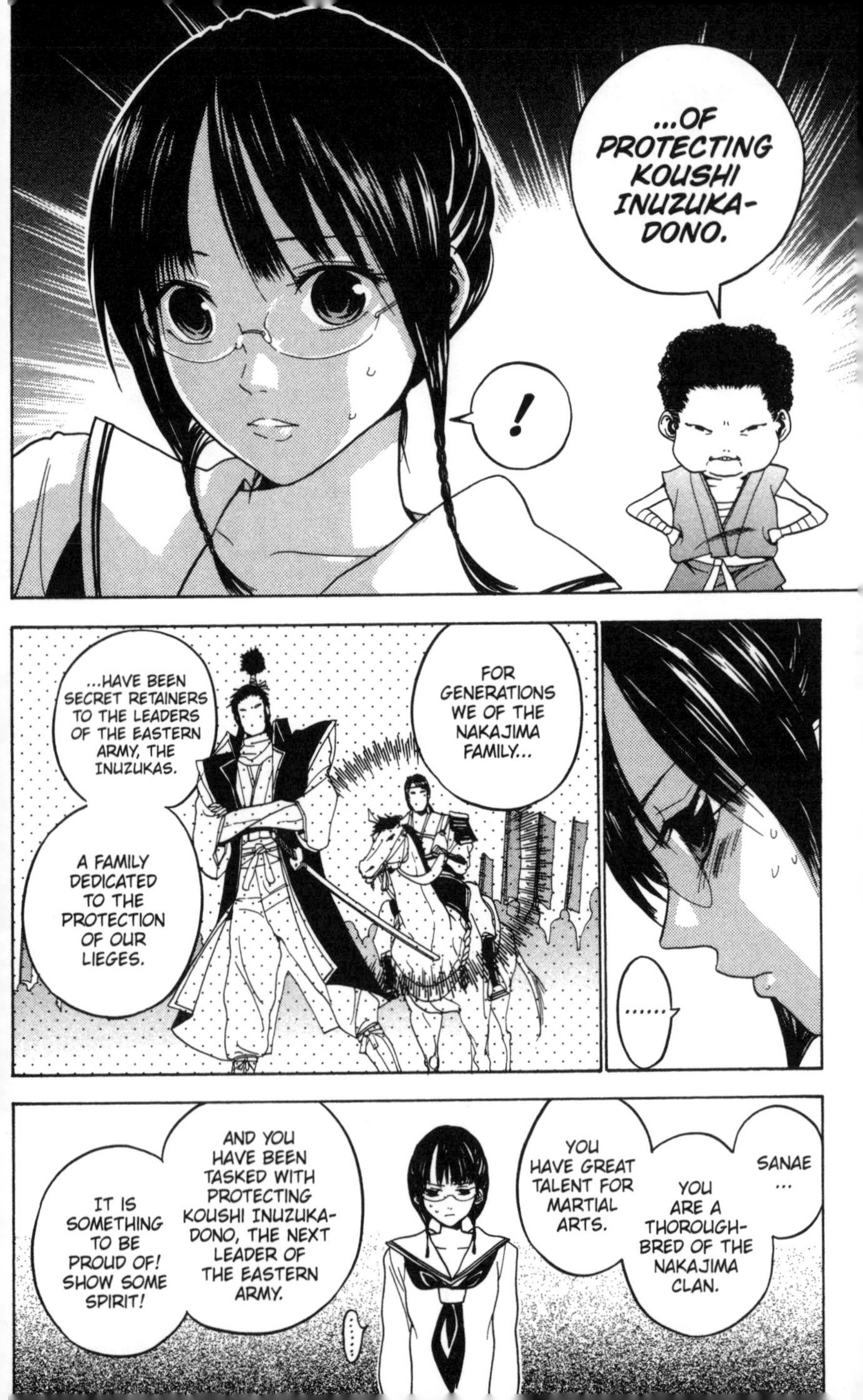

...OF PROTECTING KOUSHI INUZUKA-DONO.
!
......
FOR GENERATIONS WE OF THE NAKAJIMA FAMILY...
...HAVE BEEN SECRET RETAINERS TO THE LEADERS OF THE EASTERN ARMY, THE INUZUKAS.
A FAMILY DEDICATED TO THE PROTECTION OF OUR LIEGES.
SANAE ...
YOU ARE A THOROUGHBRED OF THE NAKAJIMA CLAN.
YOU HAVE GREAT TALENT FOR MARTIAL ARTS.
AND YOU HAVE BEEN TASKED WITH PROTECTING KOUSHI INUZUKA-DONO, THE NEXT LEADER OF THE EASTERN ARMY.
IT IS SOMETHING TO BE PROUD OF! SHOW SOME SPIRIT!
......

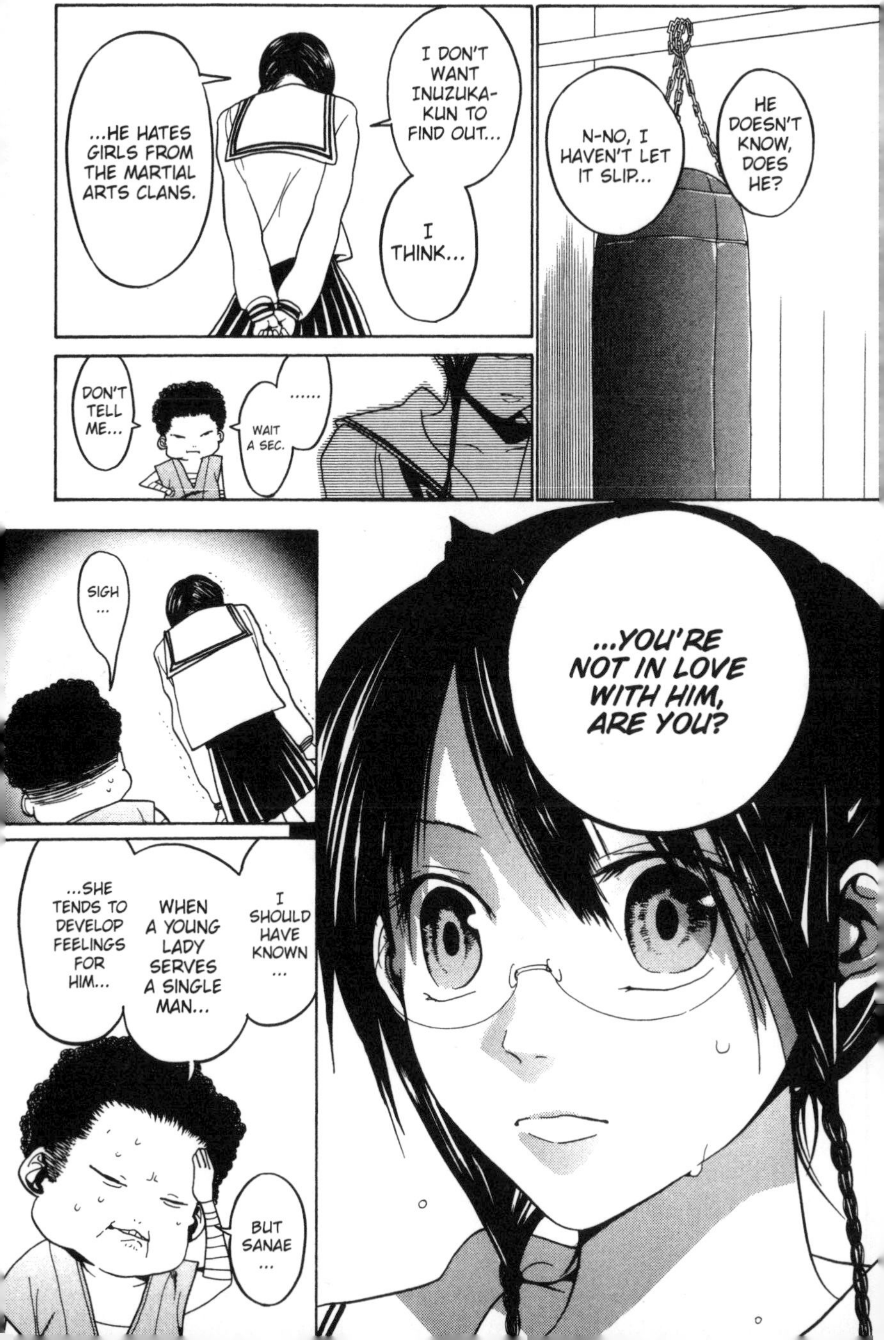
HE DOESN'T KNOW, DOES HE?
N-NO, I HAVEN'T LET IT SLIP...
I DON'T WANT INUZUKA-KUN TO FIND OUT...
I THINK...
...HE HATES GIRLS FROM THE MARTIAL ARTS CLANS.
......
WAIT A SEC.
DON'T TELL ME...
...YOU'RE NOT IN LOVE WITH HIM, ARE YOU?
SIGH...
I SHOULD HAVE KNOWN...
WHEN A YOUNG LADY SERVES A SINGLE MAN...
...SHE TENDS TO DEVELOP FEELINGS FOR HIM...
BUT SANAE...

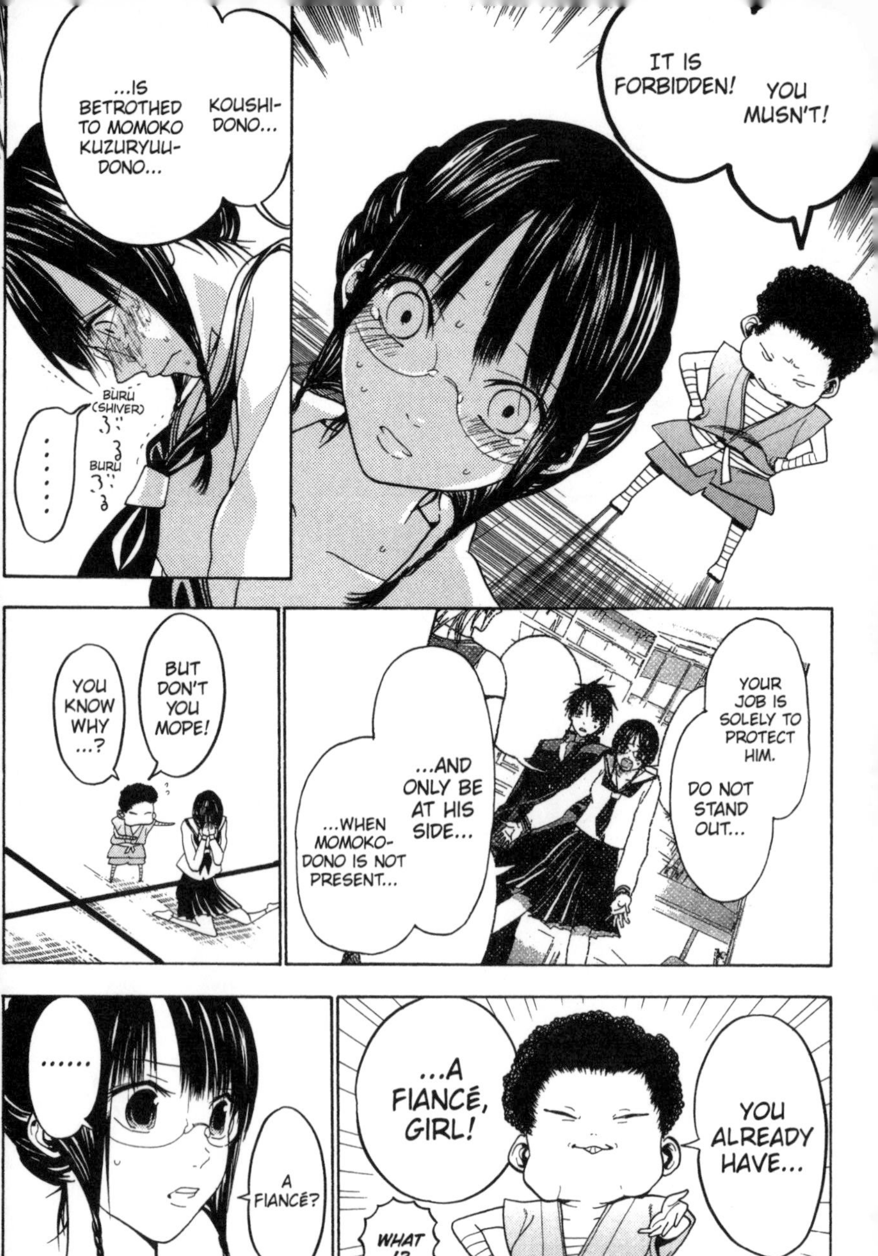
IT IS FORBIDDEN! YOU MUSN'T!
KOUSHI-DONO...
...IS BETROTHED TO MOMOKO KUZURYUU-DONO...
BURU (SHIVER)
BURU
....
YOUR JOB IS SOLELY TO PROTECT HIM.
DO NOT STAND OUT...
...AND ONLY BE AT HIS SIDE...
...WHEN MOMOKO-DONO IS NOT PRESENT...
BUT DON'T YOU MOPE!
YOU KNOW WHY...?
YOU ALREADY HAVE...
...A FIANCÉ, GIRL!
WHAT!?
......
A FIANCÉ?

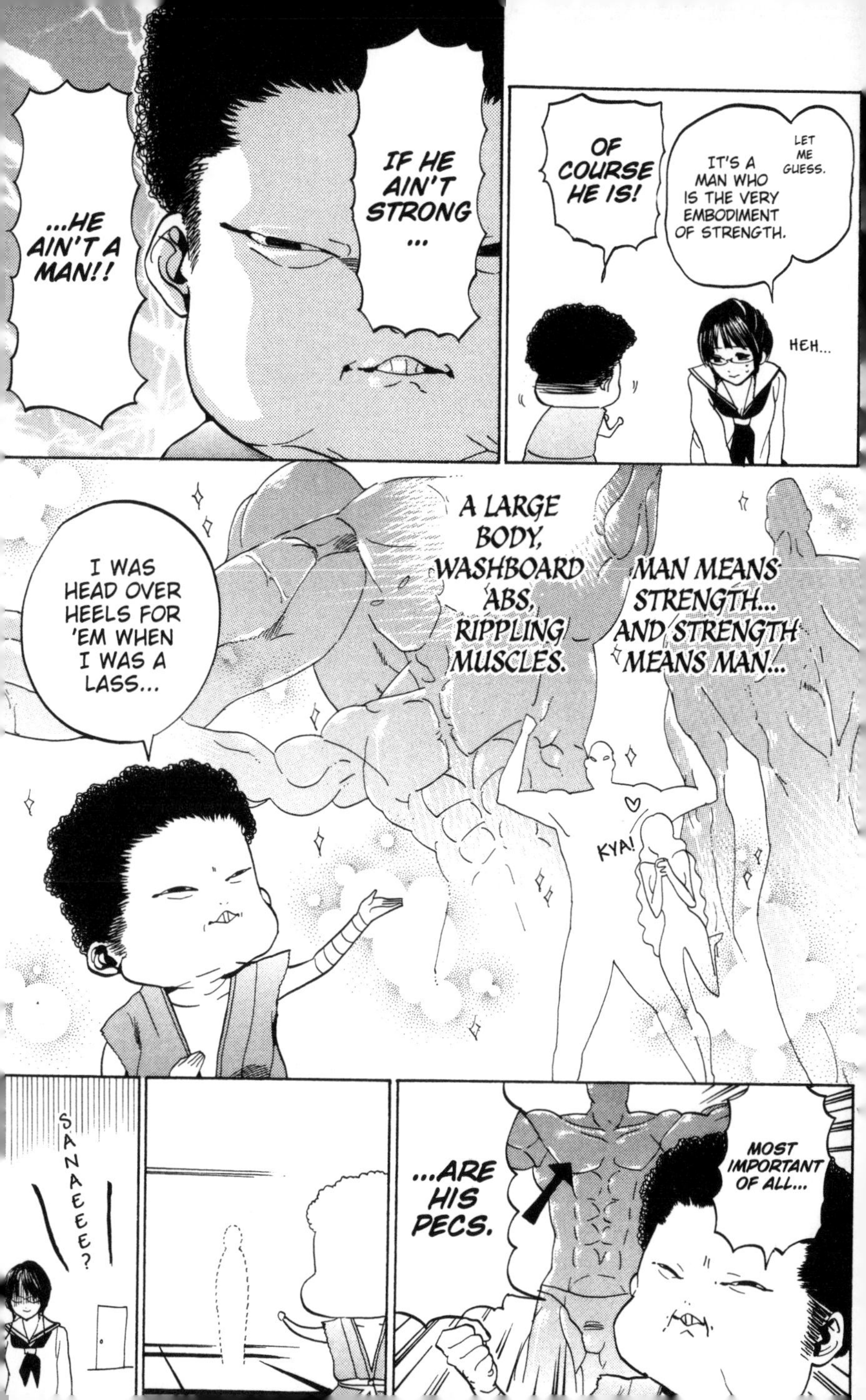
LET ME GUESS.
IT'S A MAN WHO IS THE VERY EMBODIMENT OF STRENGTH.
OF COURSE HE IS!
HEH...
IF HE AIN'T STRONG ...
...HE AIN'T A MAN!!
MAN MEANS STRENGTH... AND STRENGTH MEANS MAN...
A LARGE BODY, WASHBOARD ABS, RIPPLING MUSCLES.
I WAS HEAD OVER HEELS FOR 'EM WHEN I WAS A LASS...
KYA!
MOST IMPORTANT OF ALL...
...ARE HIS PECS.
SANAEEE?

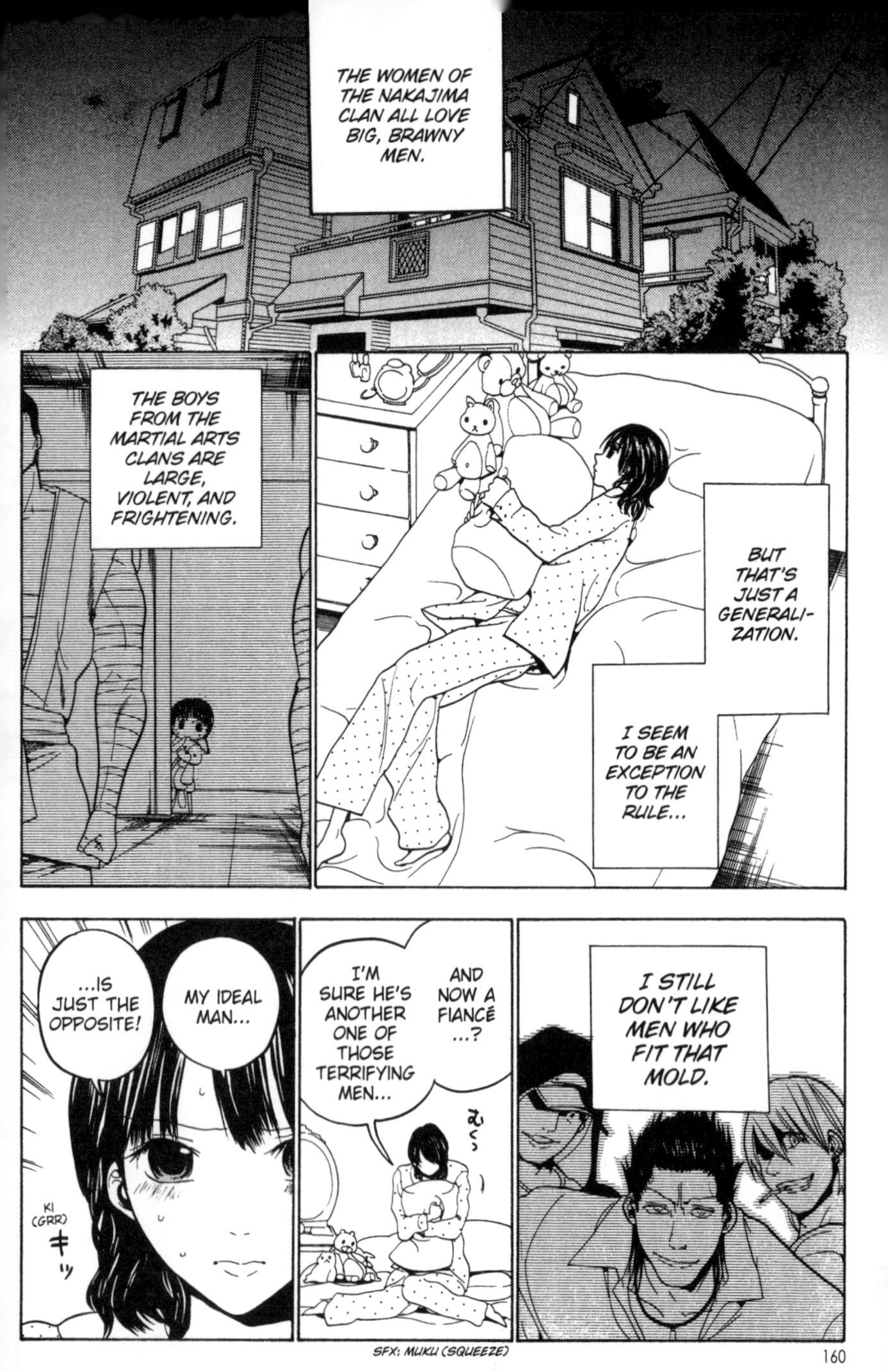
THE WOMEN OF THE NAKAJIMA CLAN ALL LOVE BIG, BRAWNY MEN.
BUT THAT'S JUST A GENERALI-ZATION.
I SEEM TO BE AN EXCEPTION TO THE RULE...
THE BOYS FROM THE MARTIAL ARTS CLANS ARE LARGE, VIOLENT, AND FRIGHTENING.
I STILL DON'T LIKE MEN WHO FIT THAT MOLD.
AND NOW A FIANCÉ ...?
I'M SURE HE'S ANOTHER ONE OF THOSE TERRIFYING MEN...
むくっ
MY IDEAL MAN...
...IS JUST THE OPPOSITE!
KI (GRR)
キッ

SFX: MUKU (SQUEEZE)

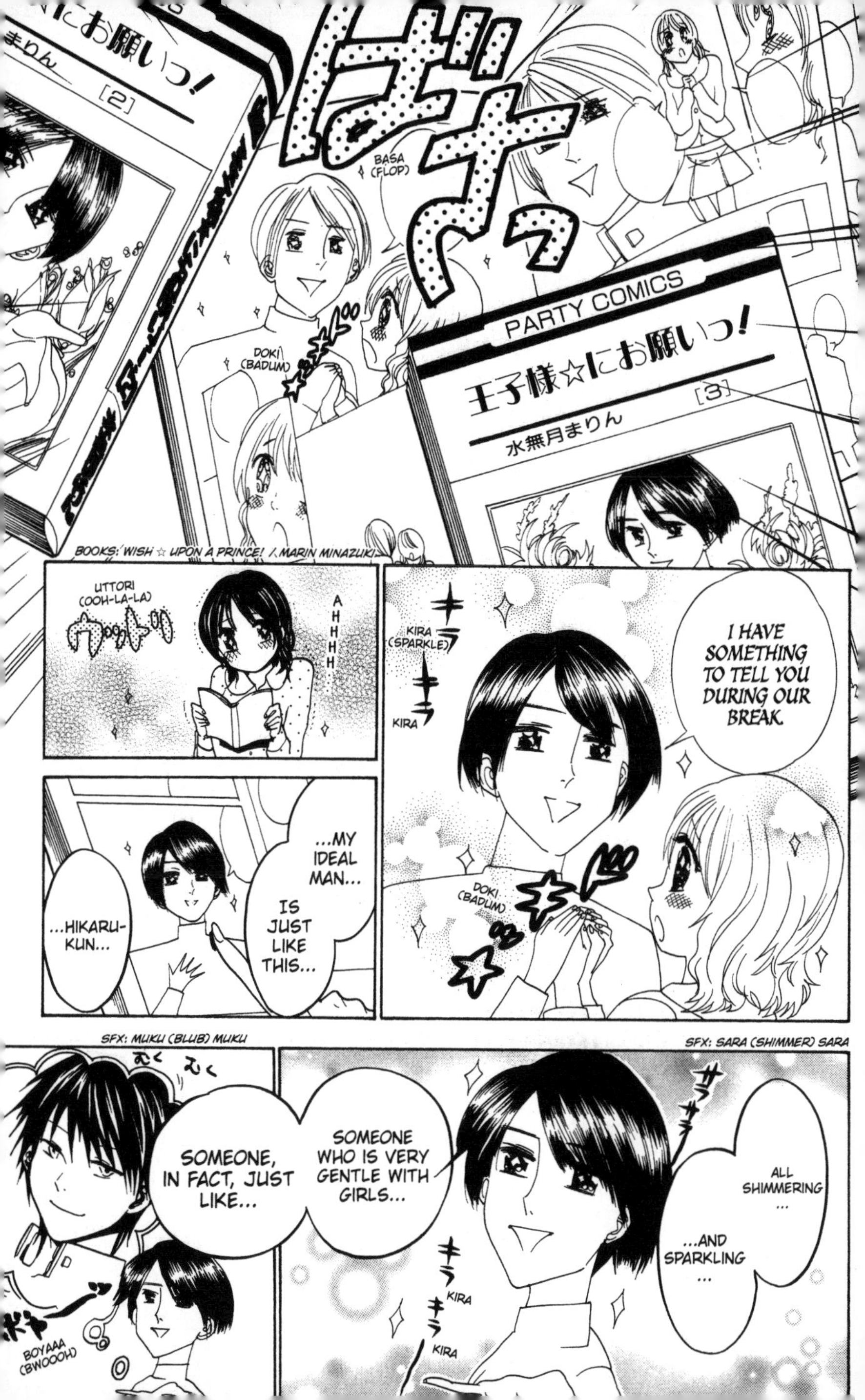
PARTY COMICS
王子様☆にお願いっ!
[3]
水無月まりん
にお願いっ!
[2]
まりん
BASA (FLOP)
DOKI (BADUM)
BOOKS: WISH ☆ UPON A PRINCE! / MARIN MINAZUKI
KIRA (SPARKLE)
KIRA
I HAVE SOMETHING TO TELL YOU DURING OUR BREAK.
DOKI (BADUM)
UTTORI (OOH-LA-LA)
AHHHH...
...MY IDEAL MAN...
IS JUST LIKE THIS...
...HIKARU-KUN...
SFX: SARA (SHIMMER) SARA
ALL SHIMMERING ...
...AND SPARKLING ...
KIRA
KIRA
SOMEONE WHO IS VERY GENTLE WITH GIRLS...
SFX: MUKU (BLUB) MUKU
SOMEONE, IN FACT, JUST LIKE...
BOYAAA (BWOOOH)

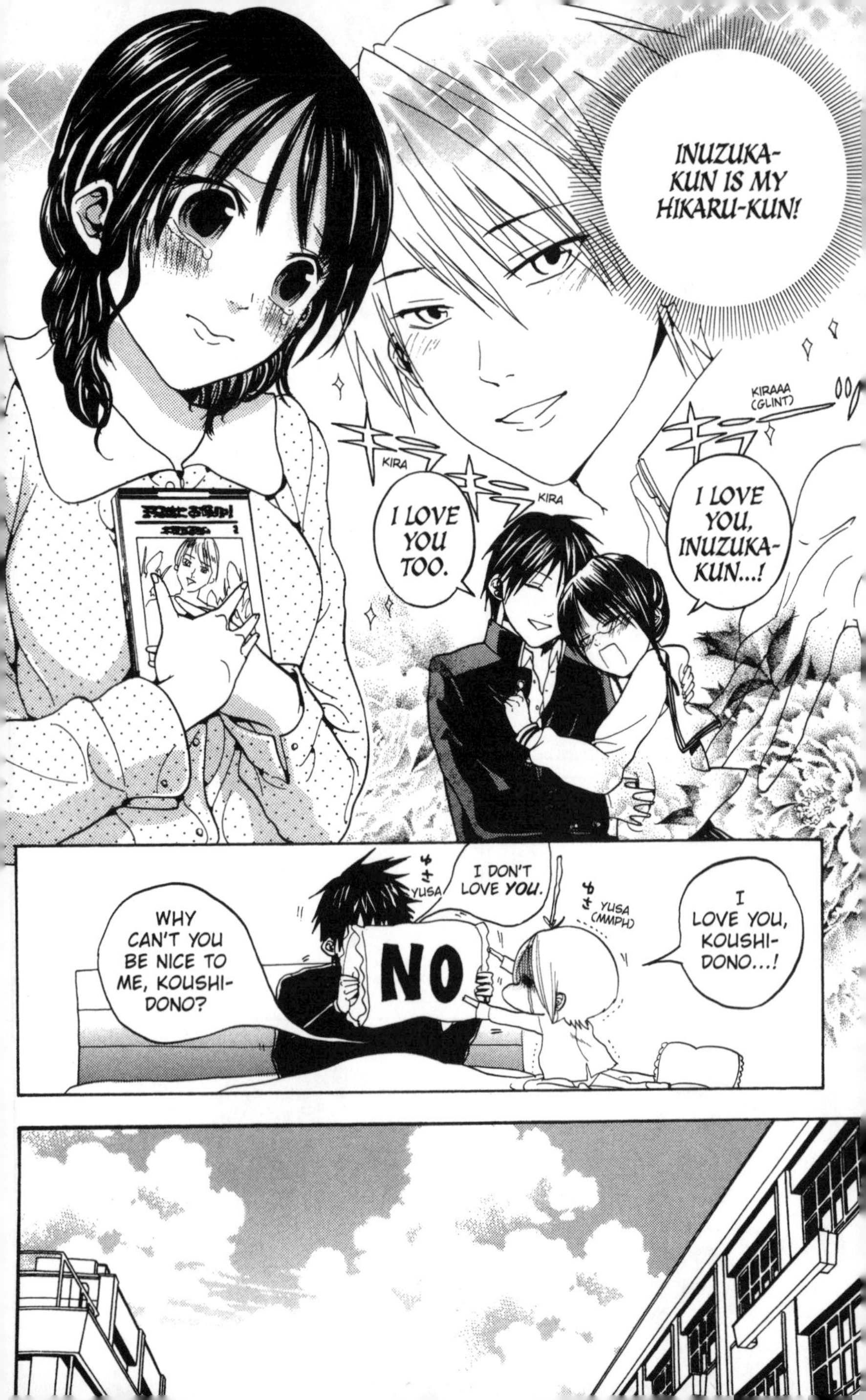
INUZUKA-KUN IS MY HIKARU-KUN!
KIRAAA (GLINT)
KIRA
KIRA
I LOVE YOU, INUZUKA-KUN...!
I LOVE YOU TOO.
I LOVE YOU, KOUSHI-DONO...!
ゆさ YUSA (MMPH)
I DON'T LOVE ***YOU***.
ゆさ YUSA
NO
WHY CAN'T YOU BE NICE TO ME, KOUSHI-DONO?

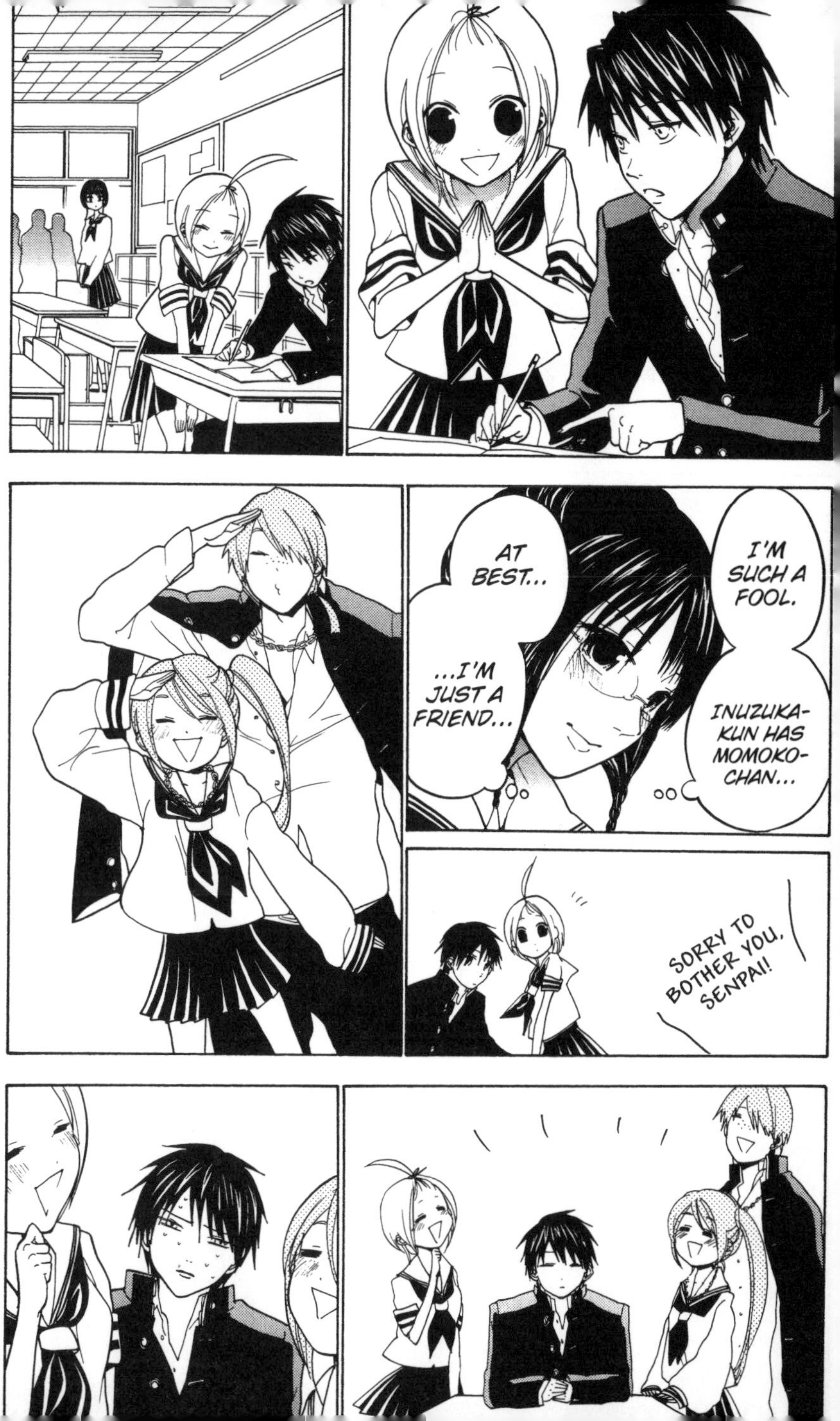
I'M SUCH A FOOL.
INUZUKA-KUN HAS MOMOKO-CHAN...
AT BEST...
...I'M JUST A FRIEND...
SORRY TO BOTHER YOU, SENPAI!

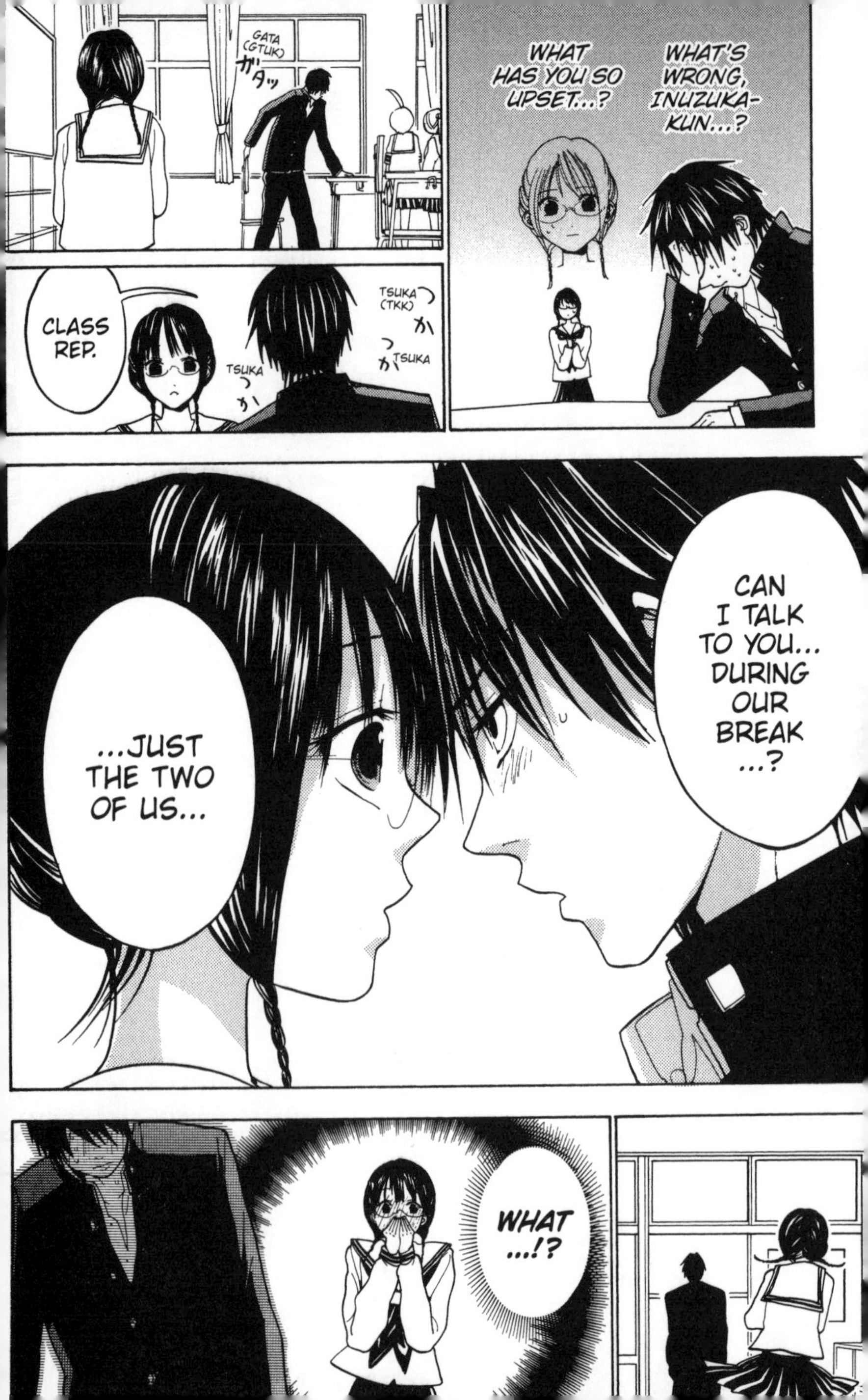
WHAT'S WRONG, INUZUKA-KUN...?
WHAT HAS YOU SO UPSET...?
GATA (GTUK)
ガタッ
TSUKA (TKK)
つか
TSUKA
つか
TSUKA
つか
CLASS REP.
CAN I TALK TO YOU... DURING OUR BREAK ...?
...JUST THE TWO OF US...
WHAT ...!?

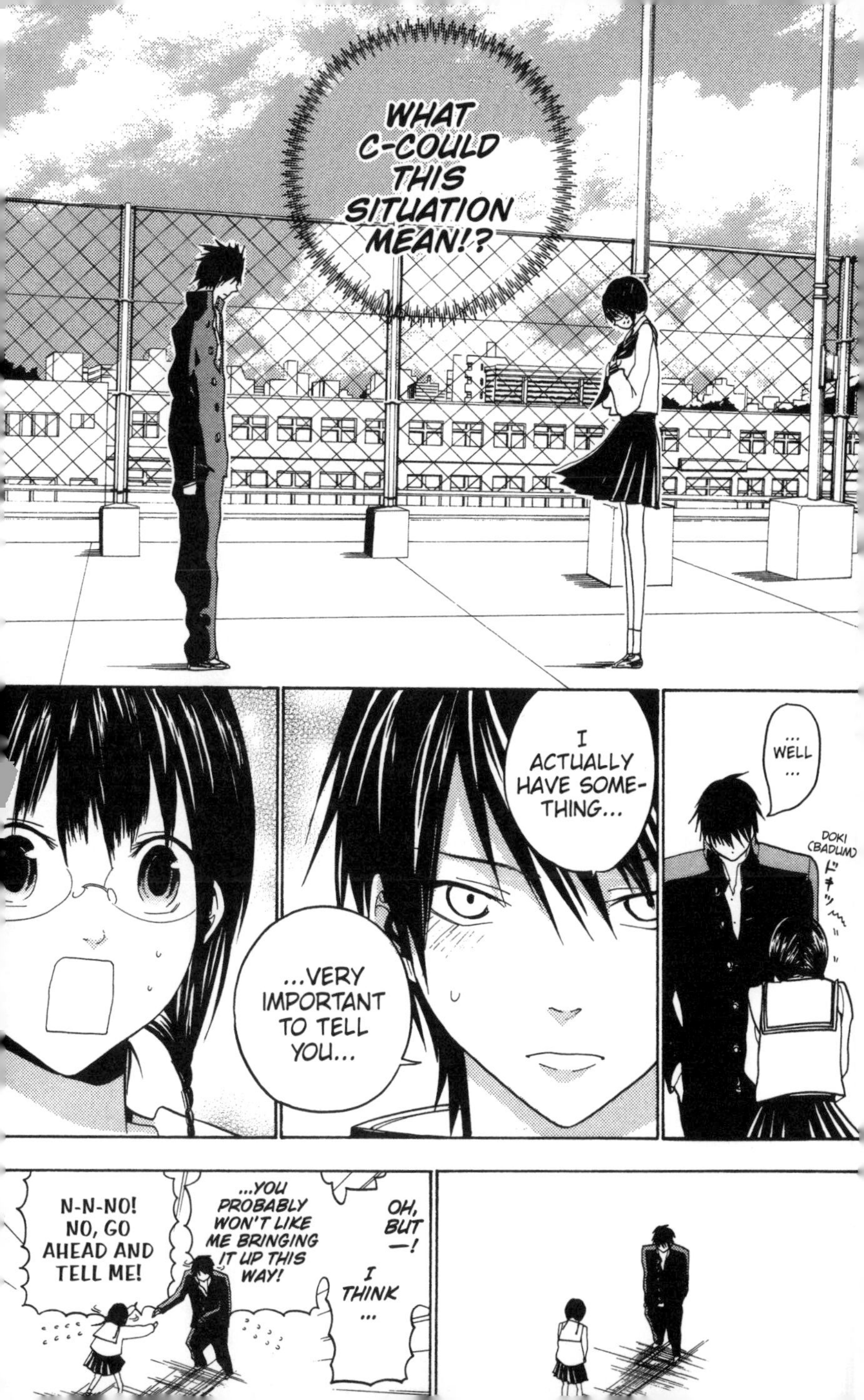
WHAT C-COULD THIS SITUATION MEAN!?
... WELL ...
DOKI (BADUM)
I ACTUALLY HAVE SOMETHING...
...VERY IMPORTANT TO TELL YOU...
I THINK ...
...YOU PROBABLY WON'T LIKE ME BRINGING IT UP THIS WAY!
OH, BUT—!
N-N-NO! NO, GO AHEAD AND TELL ME!

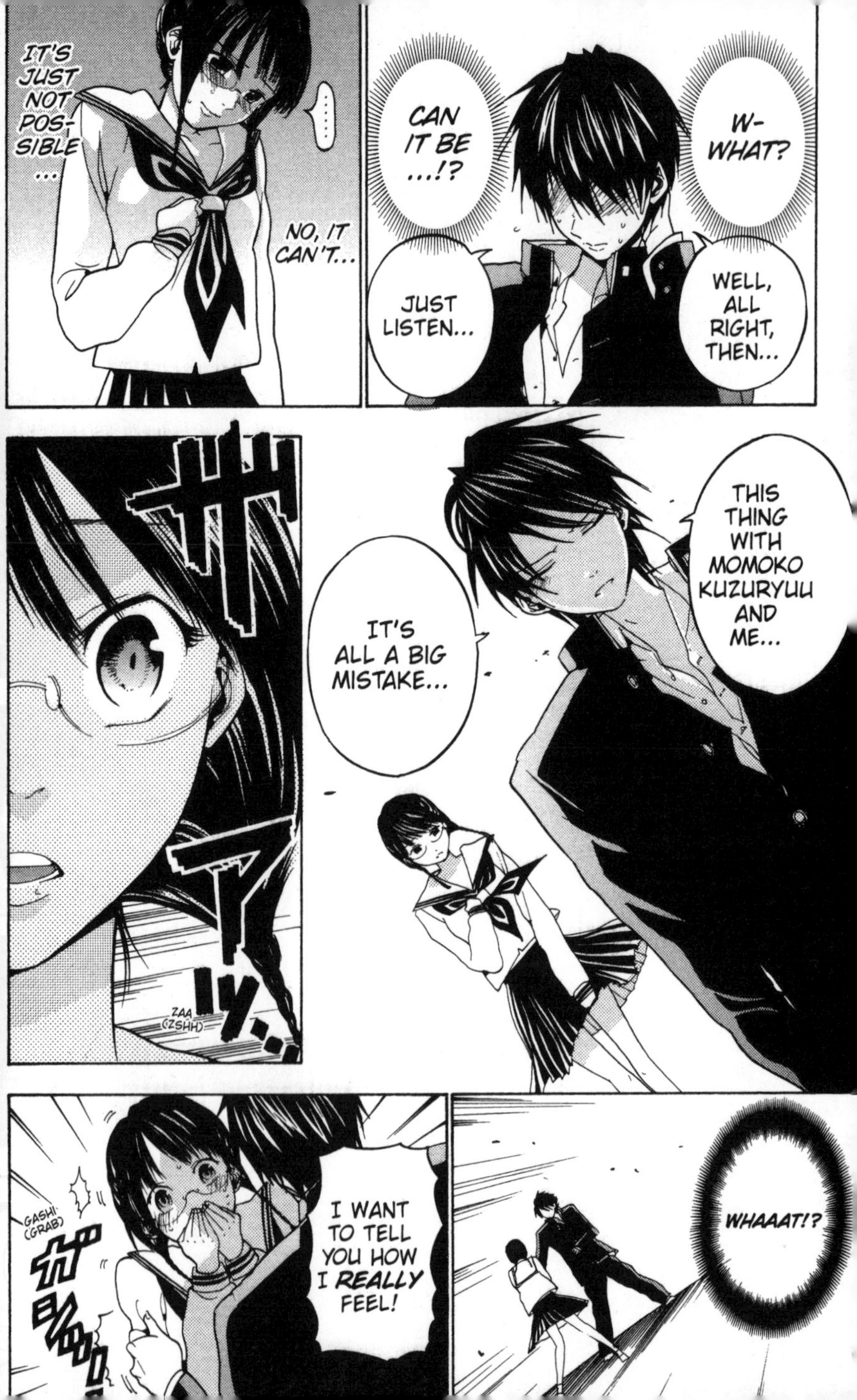
W- WHAT?
CAN IT BE ...!?
WELL, ALL RIGHT, THEN...
JUST LISTEN...
...
IT'S JUST NOT POSSIBLE ...
NO, IT CAN'T...
THIS THING WITH MOMOKO KUZURYUU AND ME...
IT'S ALL A BIG MISTAKE...
ZAA (ZSHH)
WHAAAT!?
I WANT TO TELL YOU HOW I REALLY FEEL!
GASHI (GRAB)

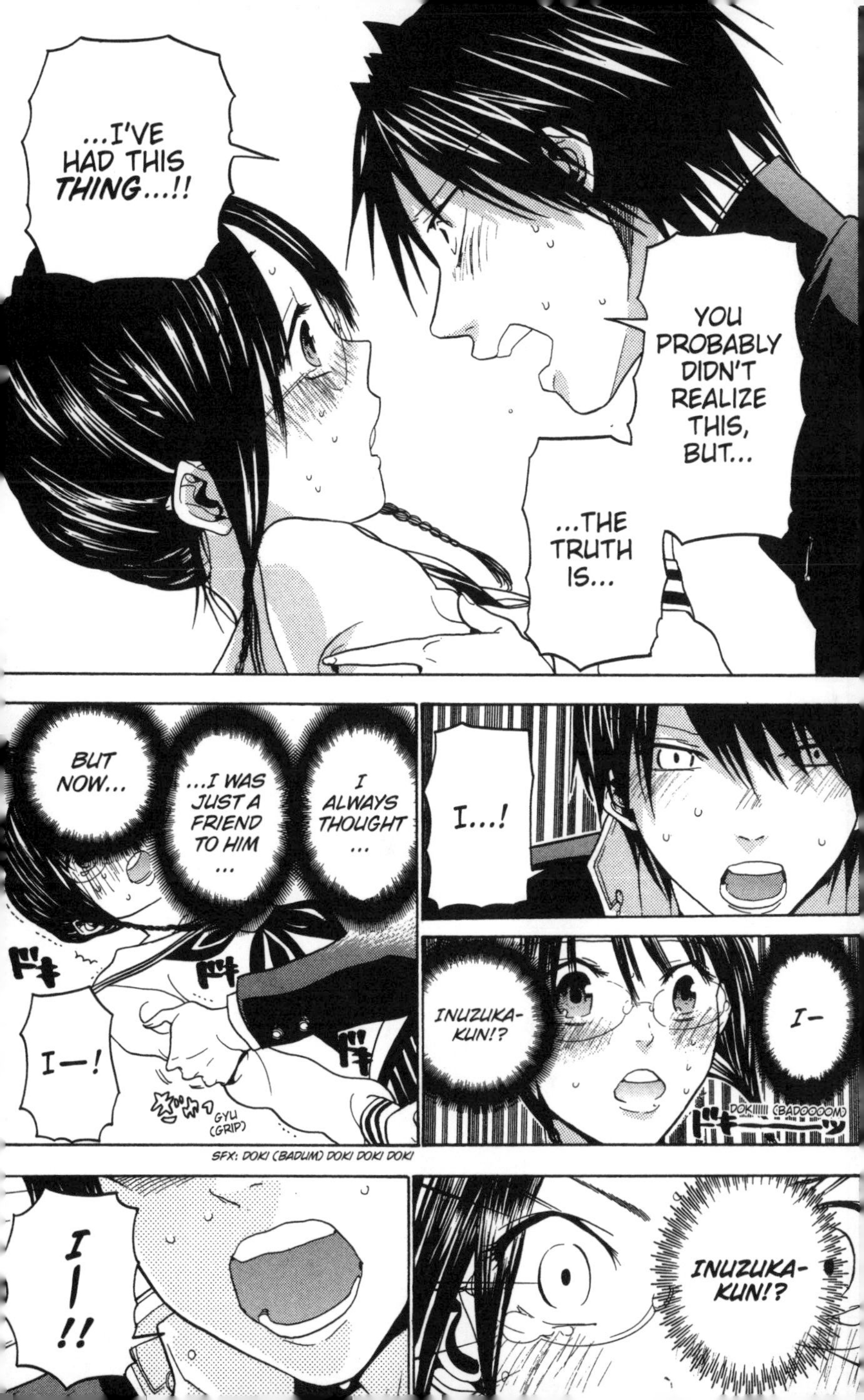
YOU PROBABLY DIDN'T REALIZE THIS, BUT...
...THE TRUTH IS...
...I'VE HAD THIS *THING*...!!
I...!
I-
INUZUKA-KUN!?
DOKI!!!!! (BADOOOOM)
I ALWAYS THOUGHT...
...I WAS JUST A FRIEND TO HIM...
BUT NOW...
I-!
GYU (GRIP)
SFX: DOKI (BADUM) DOKI DOKI DOKI
INUZUKA-KUN!?
I-!!

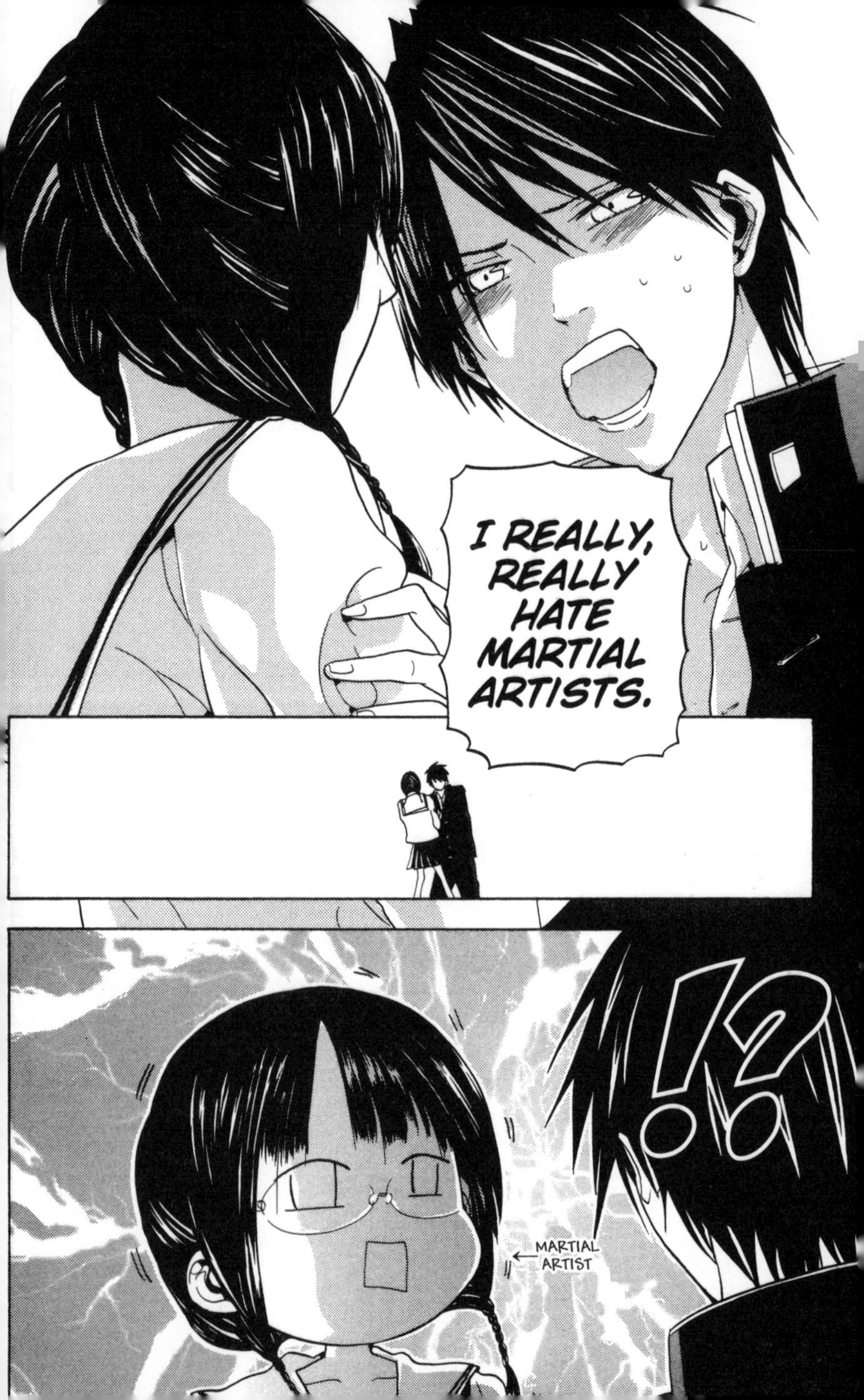
I REALLY, REALLY HATE MARTIAL ARTISTS.
!?
MARTIAL ARTIST

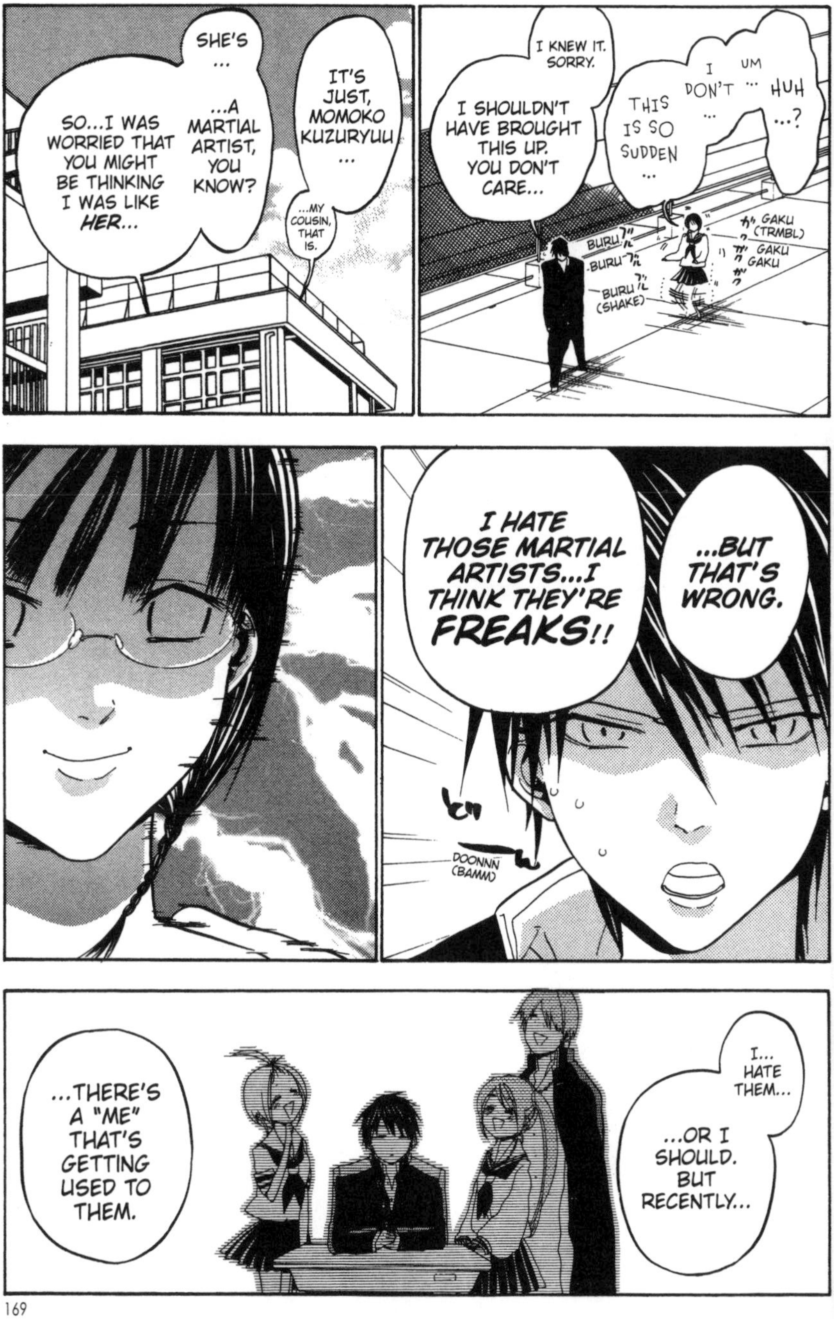
UM ... HUH ...?
I DON'T ...
THIS IS SO SUDDEN ...
I KNEW IT. SORRY.
I SHOULDN'T HAVE BROUGHT THIS UP. YOU DON'T CARE...
GAKU (TRMBL) GAKU GAKU
BURU BURU BURU (SHAKE)
IT'S JUST, MOMOKO KUZURYUU ...
...MY COUSIN, THAT IS.
SHE'S ...
...A MARTIAL ARTIST, YOU KNOW?
SO...I WAS WORRIED THAT YOU MIGHT BE THINKING I WAS LIKE *HER*...
I HATE THOSE MARTIAL ARTISTS...I THINK THEY'RE ***FREAKS!!***
...BUT THAT'S WRONG.
DOONNN (BAMM)
I... HATE THEM...
...OR I SHOULD. BUT RECENTLY...
...THERE'S A "ME" THAT'S GETTING USED TO THEM.

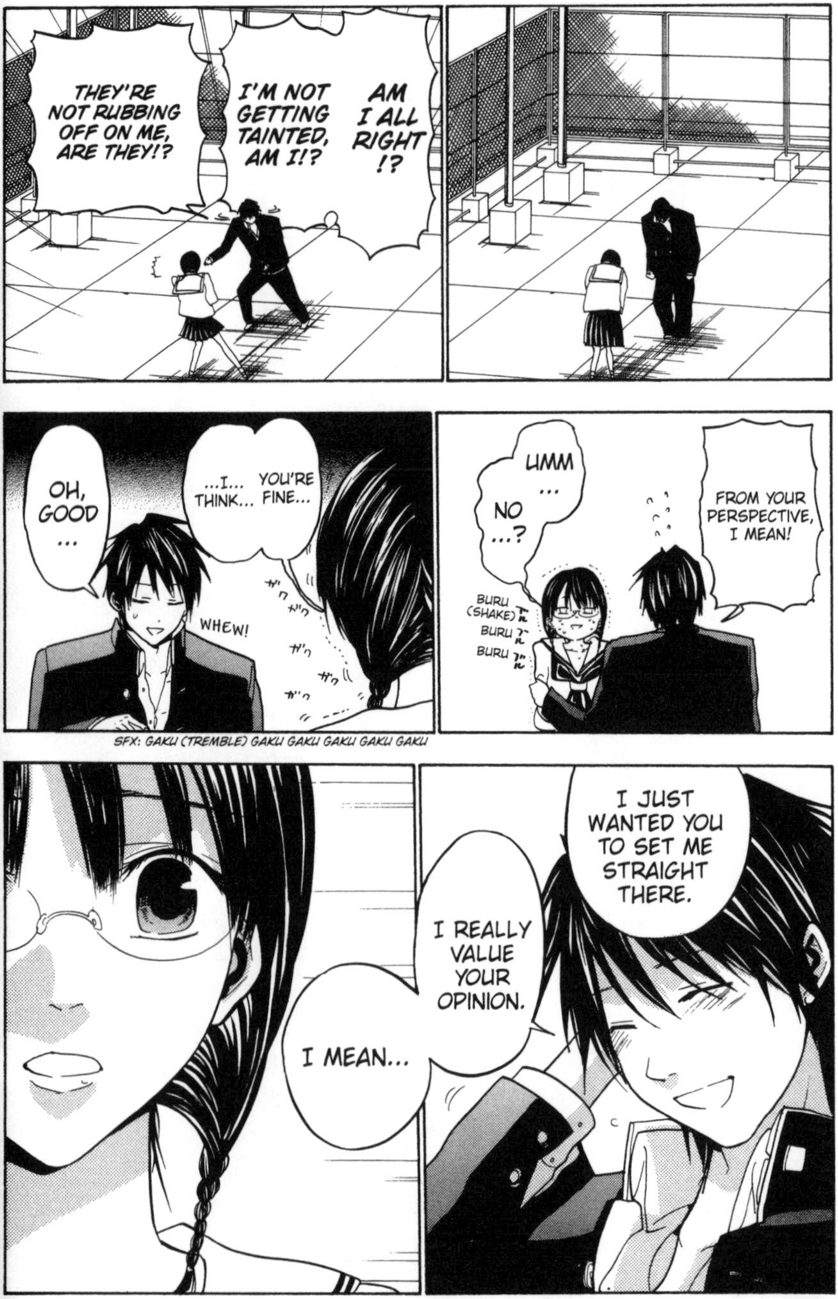
AM I ALL RIGHT!?
I'M NOT GETTING TAINTED, AM I!?
THEY'RE NOT RUBBING OFF ON ME, ARE THEY!?
FROM YOUR PERSPECTIVE, I MEAN!
UMM... NO...?
BURU (SHAKE) BURU BURU
YOU'RE FINE...
...I... THINK...
WHEW!
OH, GOOD...
SFX: GAKU (TREMBLE) GAKU GAKU GAKU GAKU GAKU
I JUST WANTED YOU TO SET ME STRAIGHT THERE.
I REALLY VALUE YOUR OPINION.
I MEAN...

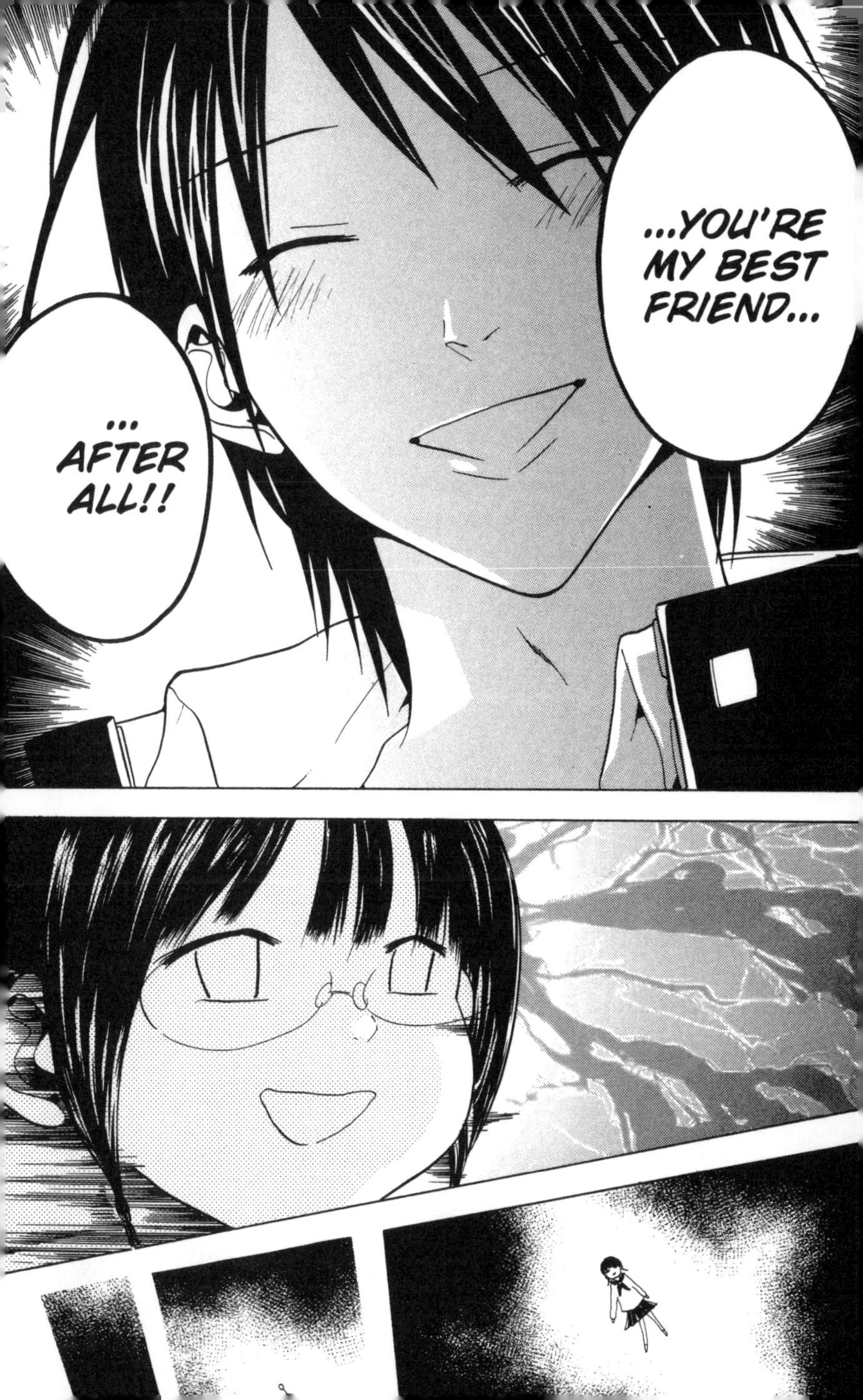
...YOU'RE MY BEST FRIEND...
... AFTER ALL!!

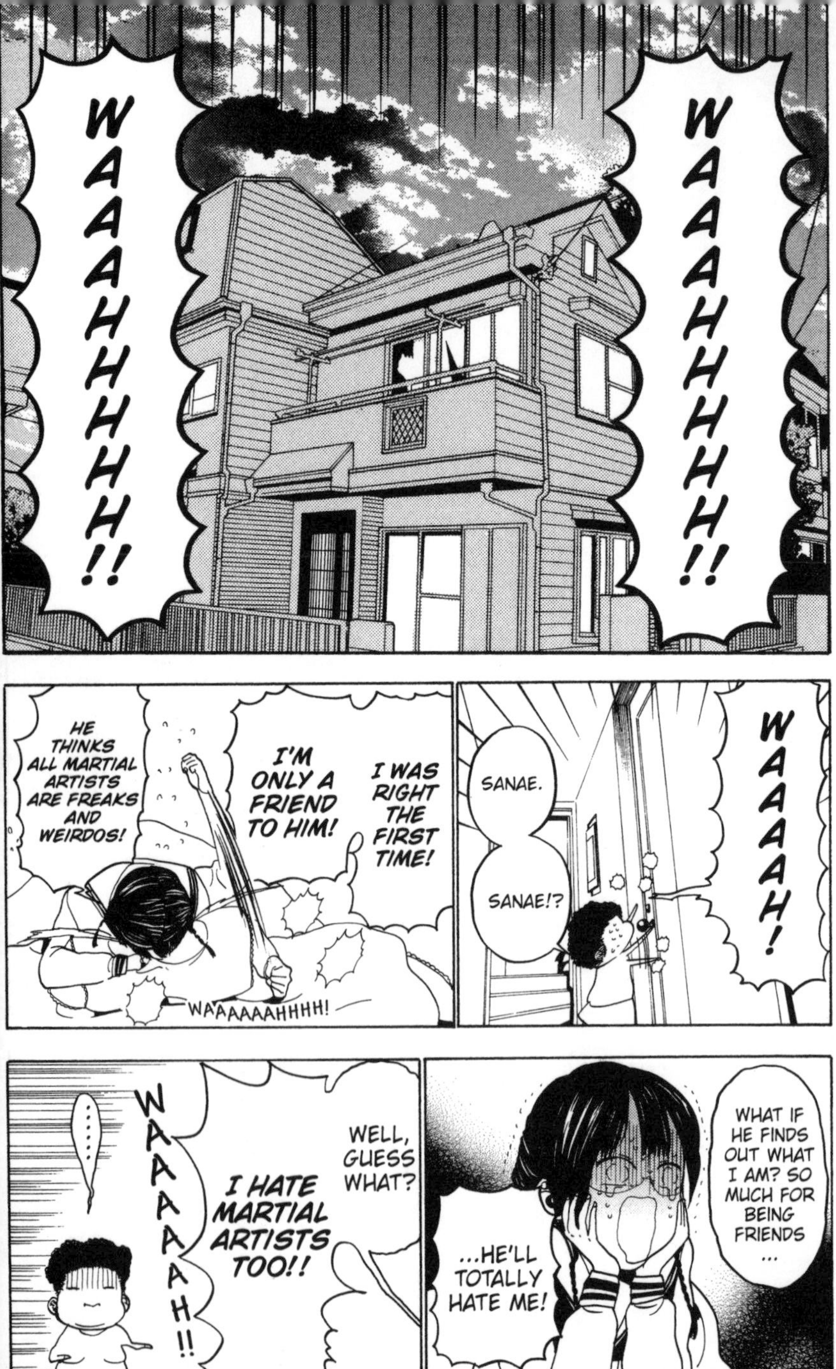

WAAAAHHHHHHH!!
WAAAHHHHHHH!!
WAAAAAH!
SANAE.
SANAE!?
I WAS RIGHT THE FIRST TIME!
I'M ONLY A FRIEND TO HIM!
HE THINKS ALL MARTIAL ARTISTS ARE FREAKS AND WEIRDOS!
WAAAAAAHHHH!
WHAT IF HE FINDS OUT WHAT I AM? SO MUCH FOR BEING FRIENDS ...
...HE'LL TOTALLY HATE ME!
WELL, GUESS WHAT?
I HATE MARTIAL ARTISTS TOO!!
WAAAAAH!!
......

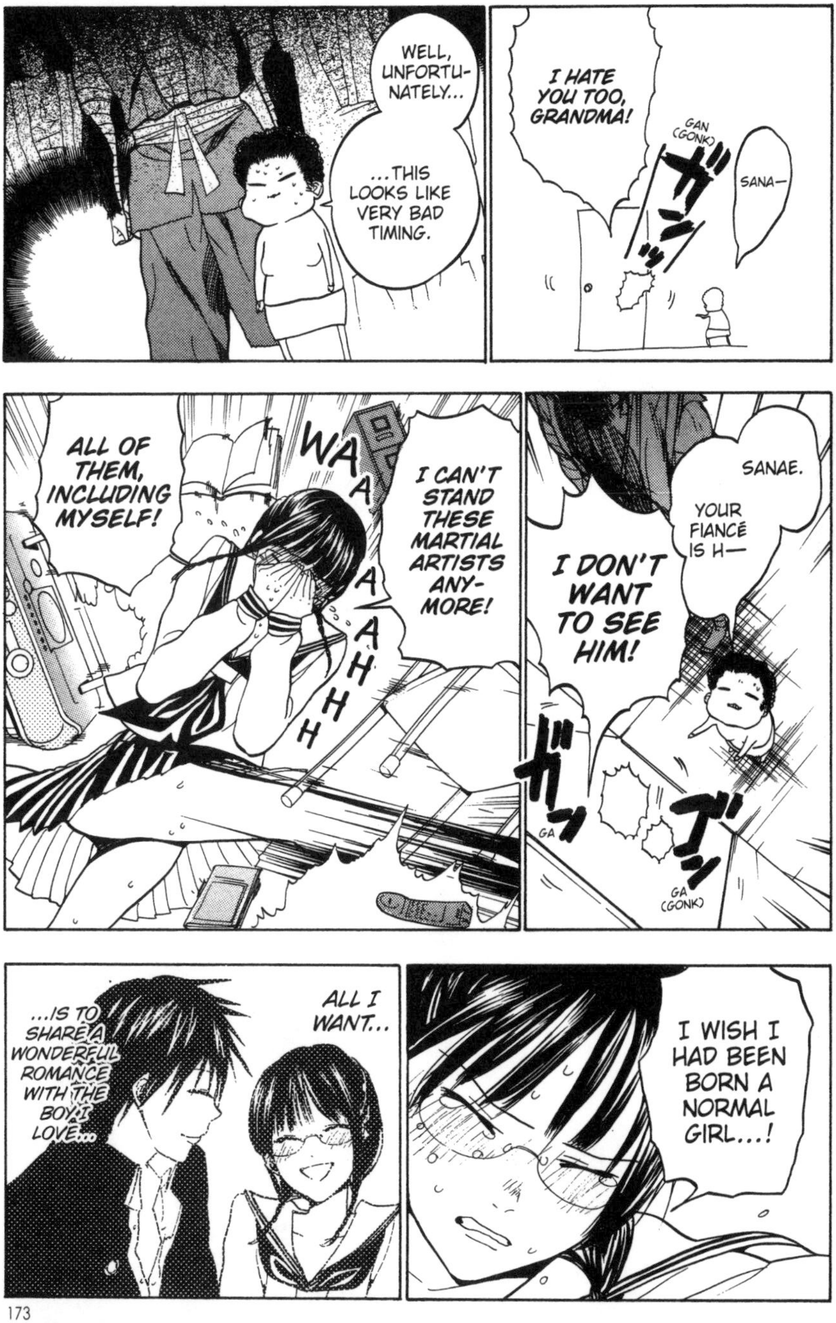
I HATE YOU TOO, GRANDMA!
GAN (GONK)
SANA—
WELL, UNFORTU-NATELY...
...THIS LOOKS LIKE VERY BAD TIMING.
SANAE.
YOUR FIANCÉ IS H—
I DON'T WANT TO SEE HIM!
GA
GA (GONK)
I CAN'T STAND THESE MARTIAL ARTISTS ANY-MORE!
WAAAAAHHHH
ALL OF THEM, INCLUDING MYSELF!
I WISH I HAD BEEN BORN A NORMAL GIRL...!
ALL I WANT...
...IS TO SHARE A WONDERFUL ROMANCE WITH THE BOY I LOVE...

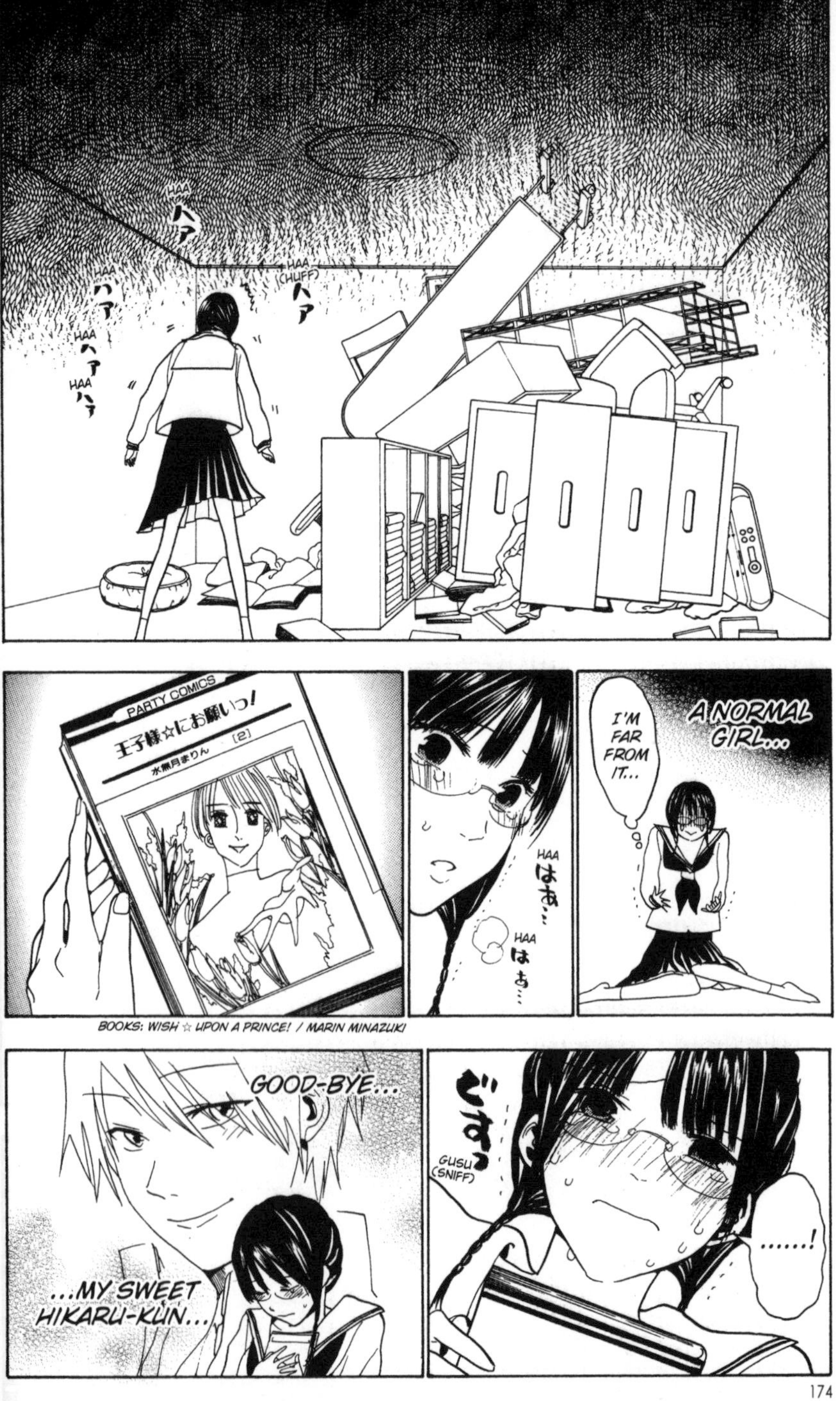
HAA ハァ
HAA ハァ
HAA (CHUFF) ハァ
HAA ハァ
HAA ハァ
A NORMAL GIRL...
I'M FAR FROM IT...
HAA はぁ
HAA はぁ
PARTY COMICS
王子様☆にお願いっ!
水無月まりん (2)
ぐすっ
GUSU (SNIFF)
......!
GOOD-BYE...
...MY SWEET HIKARU-KUN...
BOOKS: WISH ☆ UPON A PRINCE! / MARIN MINAZUKI

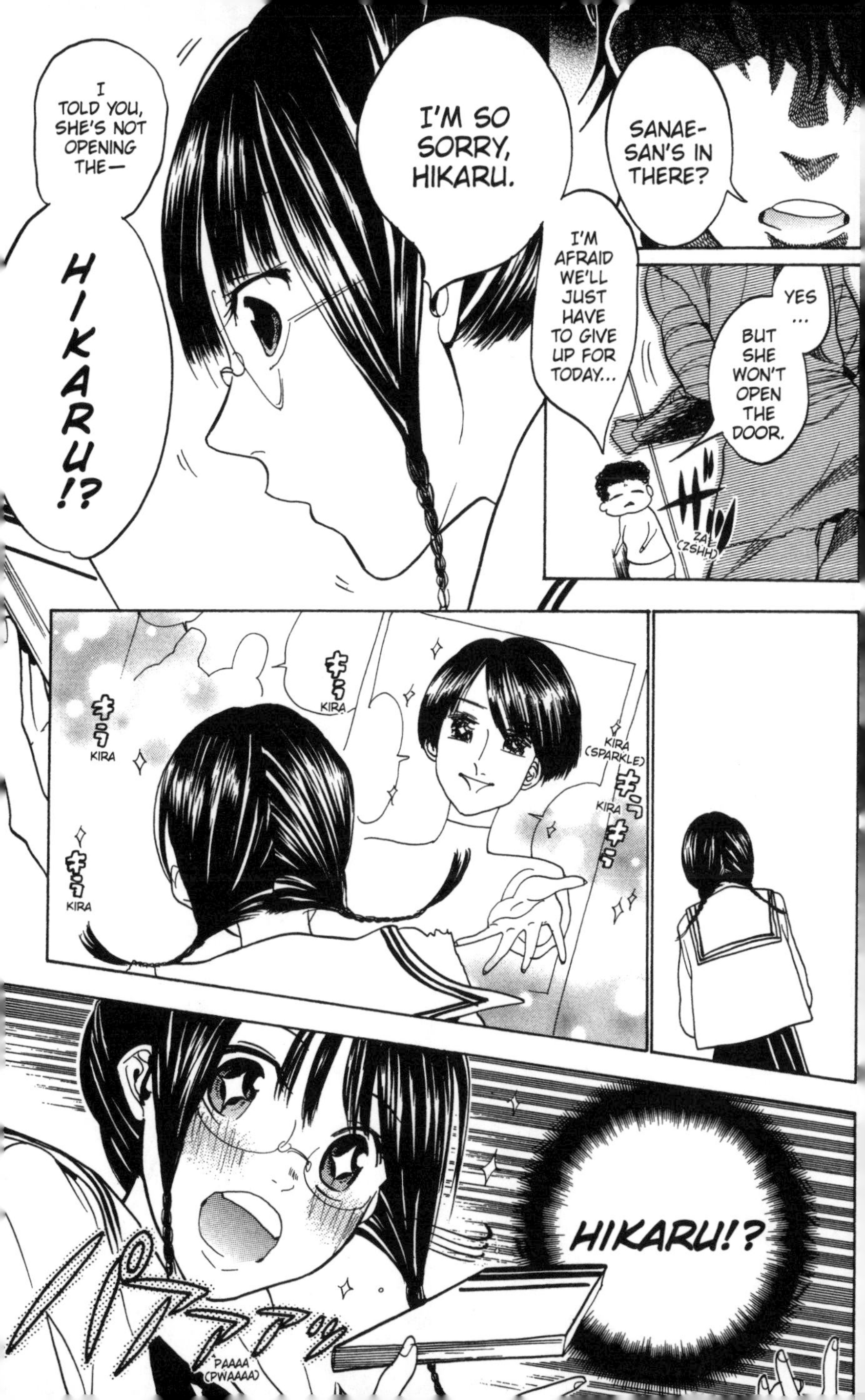
SANAE-SAN'S IN THERE?
YES ... BUT SHE WON'T OPEN THE DOOR.
I'M AFRAID WE'LL JUST HAVE TO GIVE UP FOR TODAY...
ZA (ZSHH)
I'M SO SORRY, HIKARU.
I TOLD YOU, SHE'S NOT OPENING THE—
HIKARU!?
KIRA (SPARKLE)
KIRA
KIRA
KIRA
KIRA
HIKARU!?
PAAAA (PWAAAA)

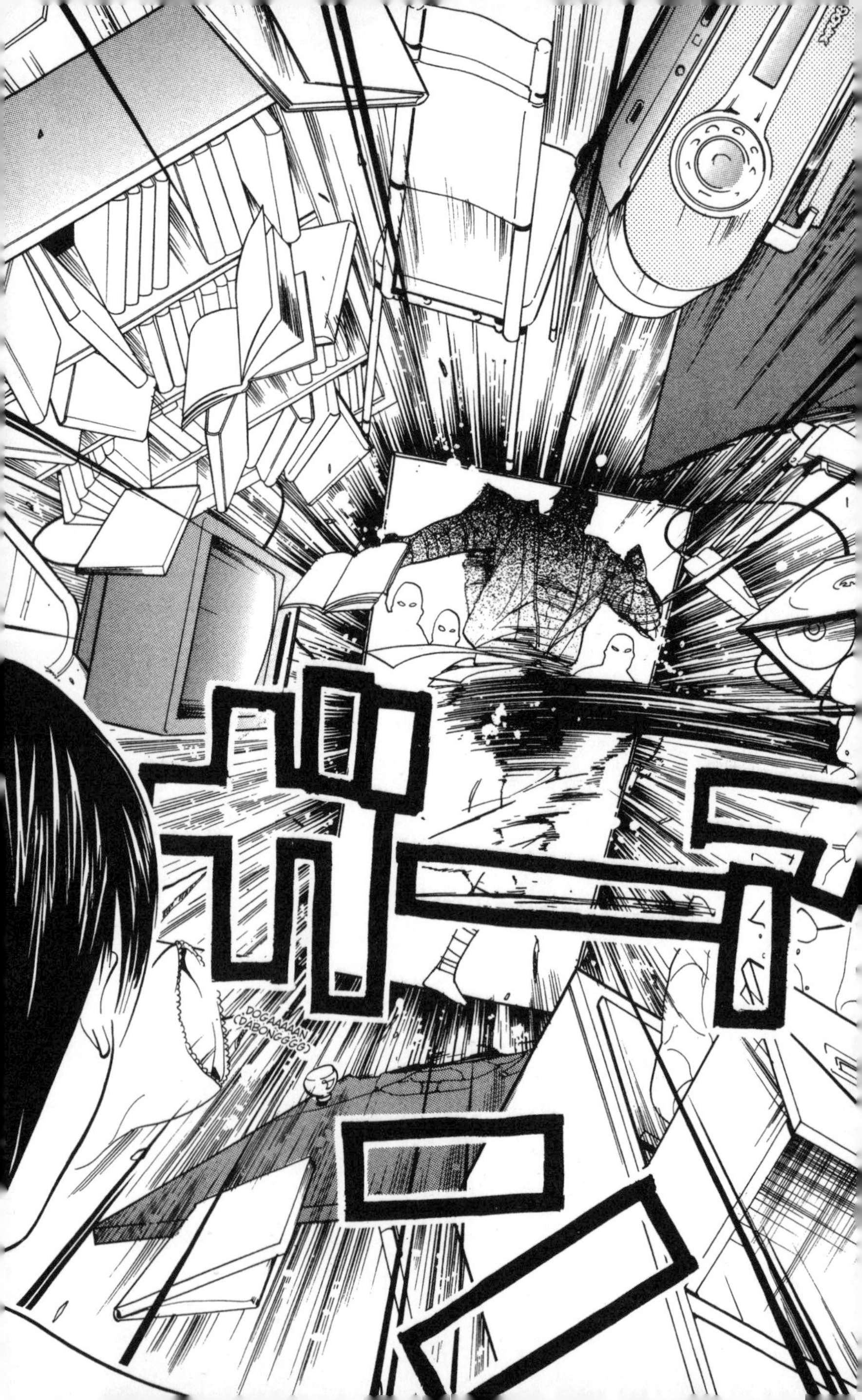
DOGAAAAAN
(DABONGGGG)

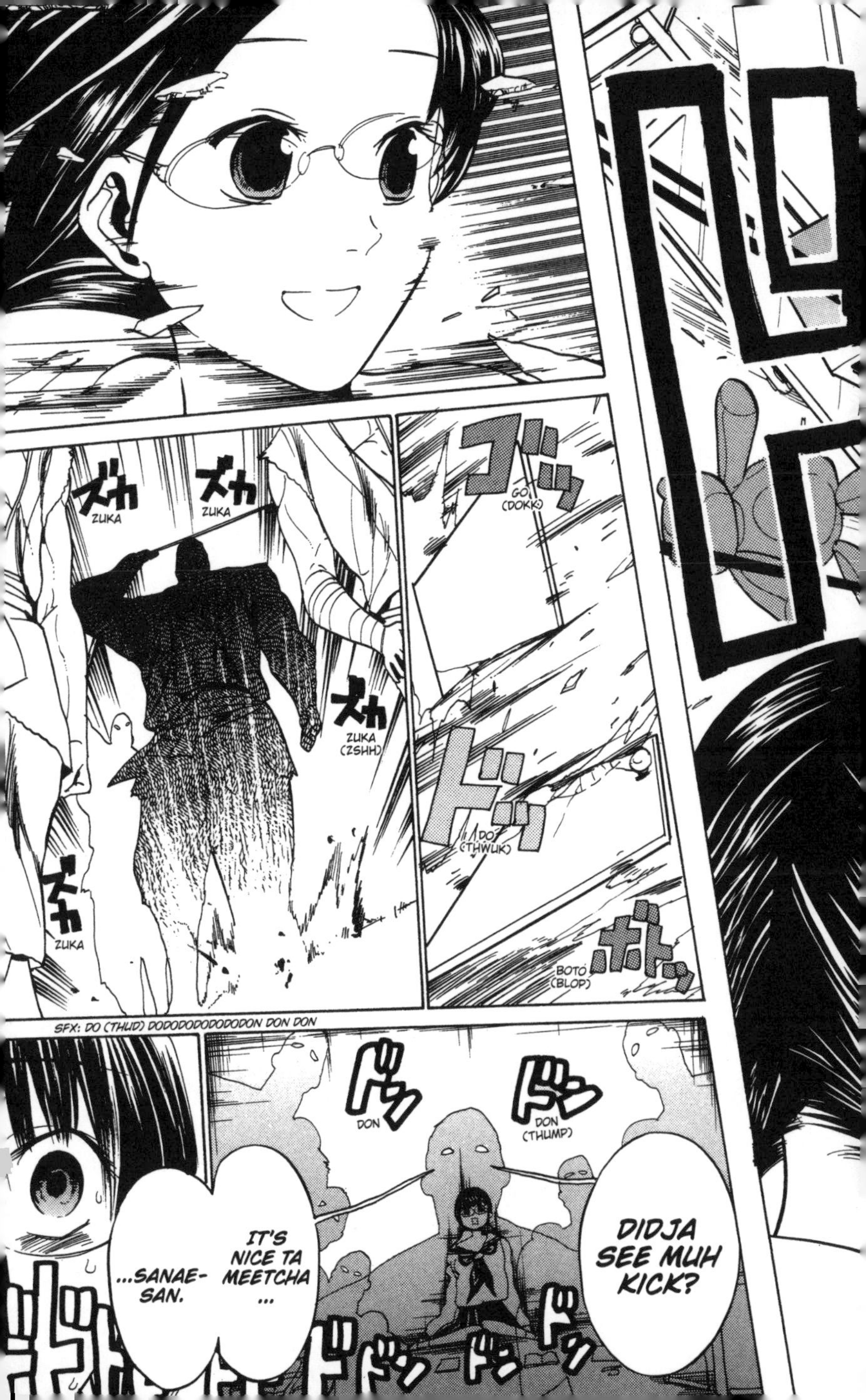
GO (DOKK)
DO (THWUK)
BOTO (BLOP)
ZUKA
ZUKA
ZUKA (ZSHH)
ZUKA
SFX: DO (THUD) DODODODODODODON DON DON
DON (THUMP)
DON
DIDJA SEE MUH KICK?
IT'S NICE TA MEETCHA ...
...SANAE-SAN.

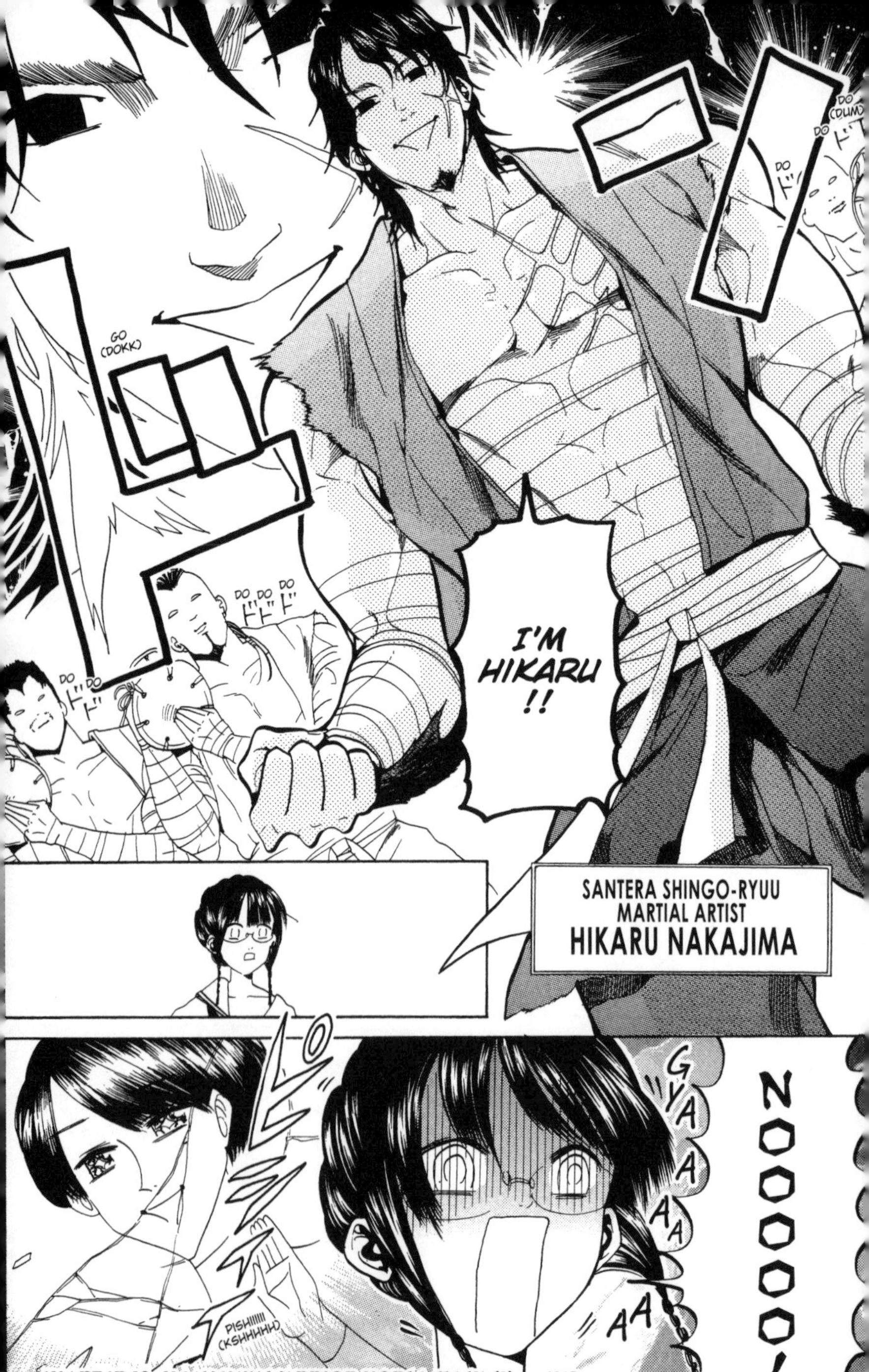
DO (DUM)
DO
DO
GO (DOKK)
DO DO DO
DO DO
I'M HIKARU!!
SANTERA SHINGO-RYUU
MARTIAL ARTIST
HIKARU NAKAJIMA
GYAAAAAA
NOOOOOO!
PISHIIIII (KSHHHHH)

CHAPTER 13: HEAVENLY WARRIOR HORSE MASK (1) – END

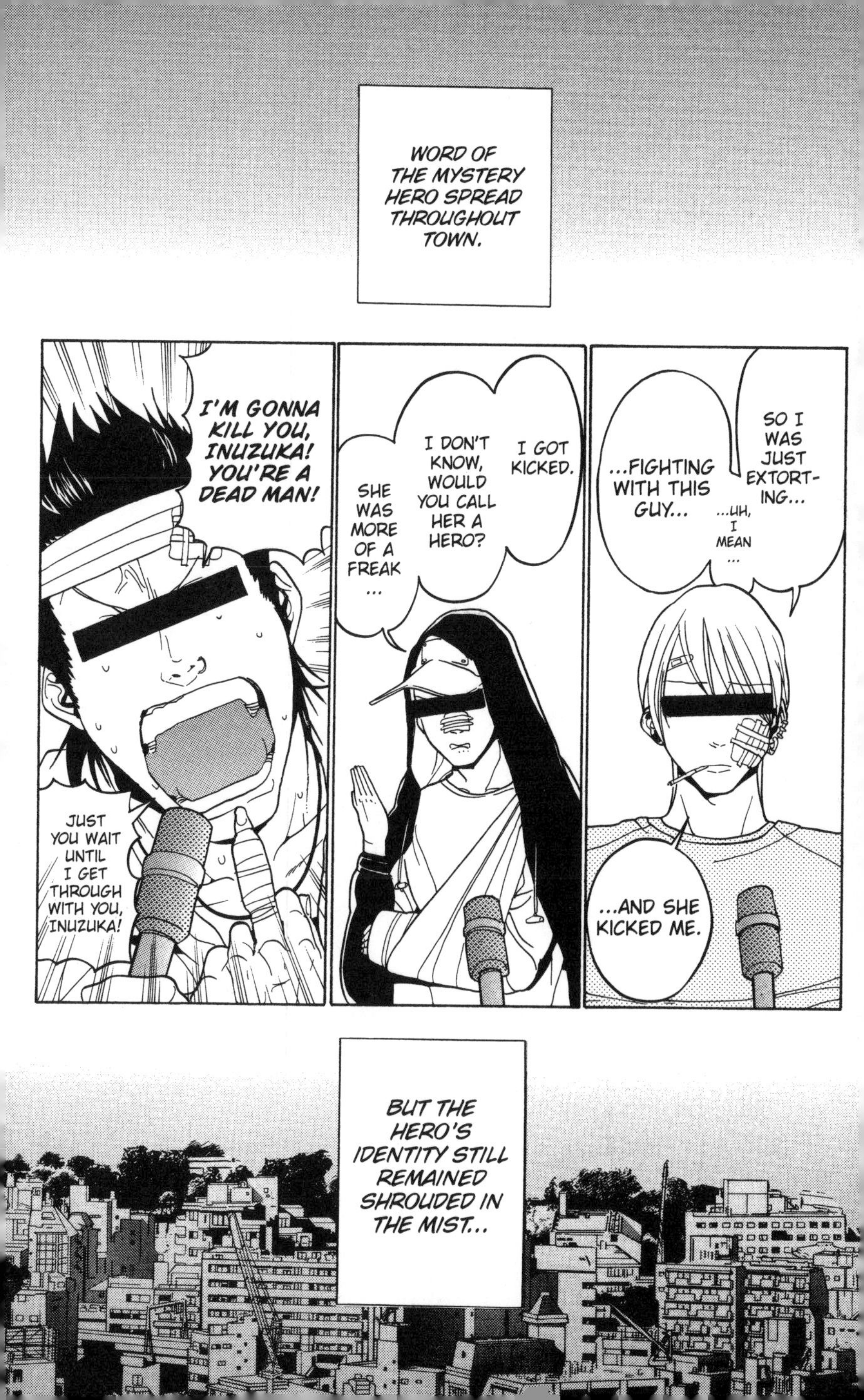
WORD OF THE MYSTERY HERO SPREAD THROUGHOUT TOWN.
SO I WAS JUST EXTORTING...
...UH, I MEAN...
...FIGHTING WITH THIS GUY...
...AND SHE KICKED ME.
I GOT KICKED.
I DON'T KNOW, WOULD YOU CALL HER A HERO?
SHE WAS MORE OF A FREAK...
I'M GONNA KILL YOU, INUZUKA! YOU'RE A DEAD MAN!
JUST YOU WAIT UNTIL I GET THROUGH WITH YOU, INUZUKA!
BUT THE HERO'S IDENTITY STILL REMAINED SHROUDED IN THE MIST...

14. HEAVENLY WARRIOR HORSE MASK (2)

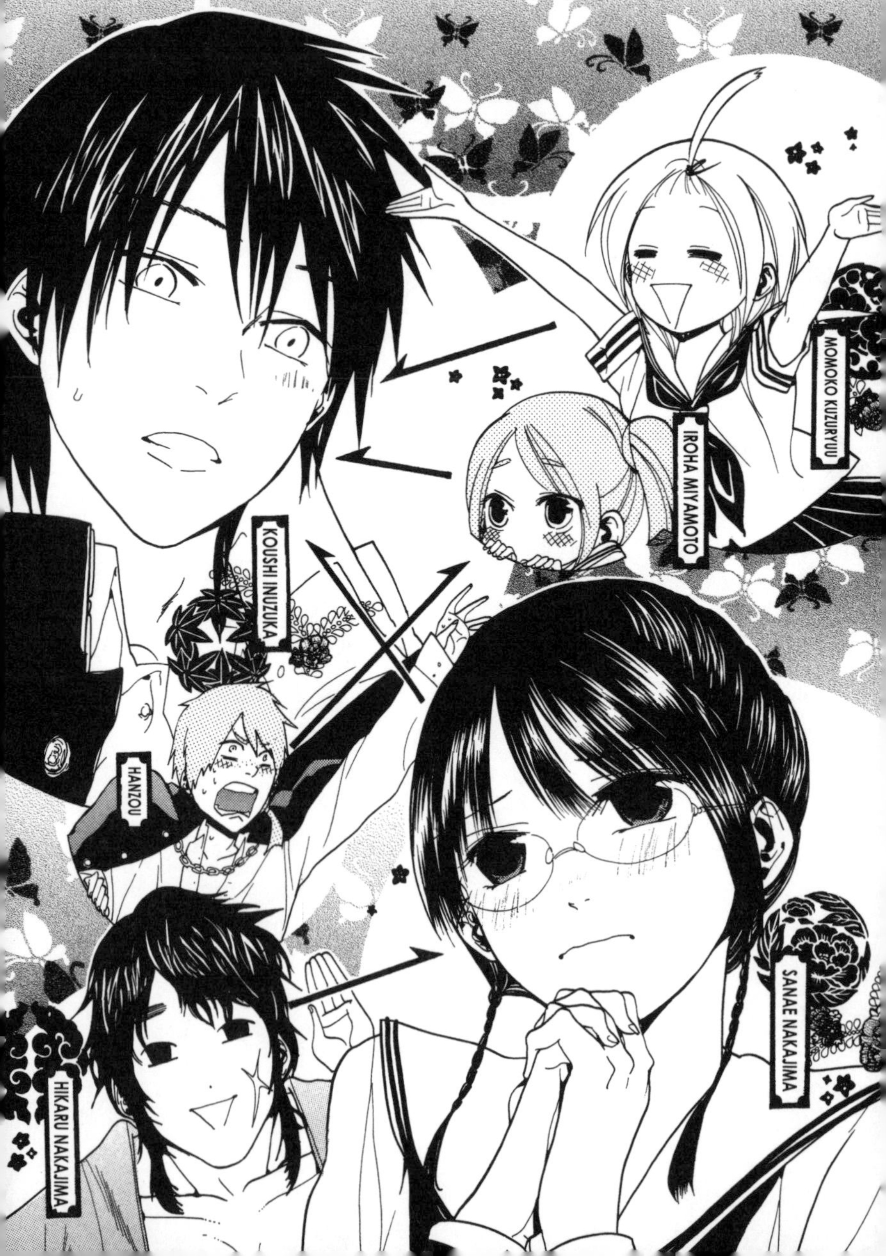
MOMOKO KUZURYUU
IROHA MIYAMOTO
KOUSHI INUZUKA
SANAE NAKAJIMA
HANZOU
HIKARU NAKAJIMA

SANAE'S FIANCÉ SHOWED UP.

I'M HIKARU...

...HIKARU NAKAJIMA!

NOOOOOOO!

HER IDEAL HIKARU-KUN

SFX: ZUGOGOGOGOGOGO (ZWOOOOOMMM)

SANAE-SAN!

KYAAAAAA!

むさ——っ
MUSAAAAAA
(MMMMBUFF)

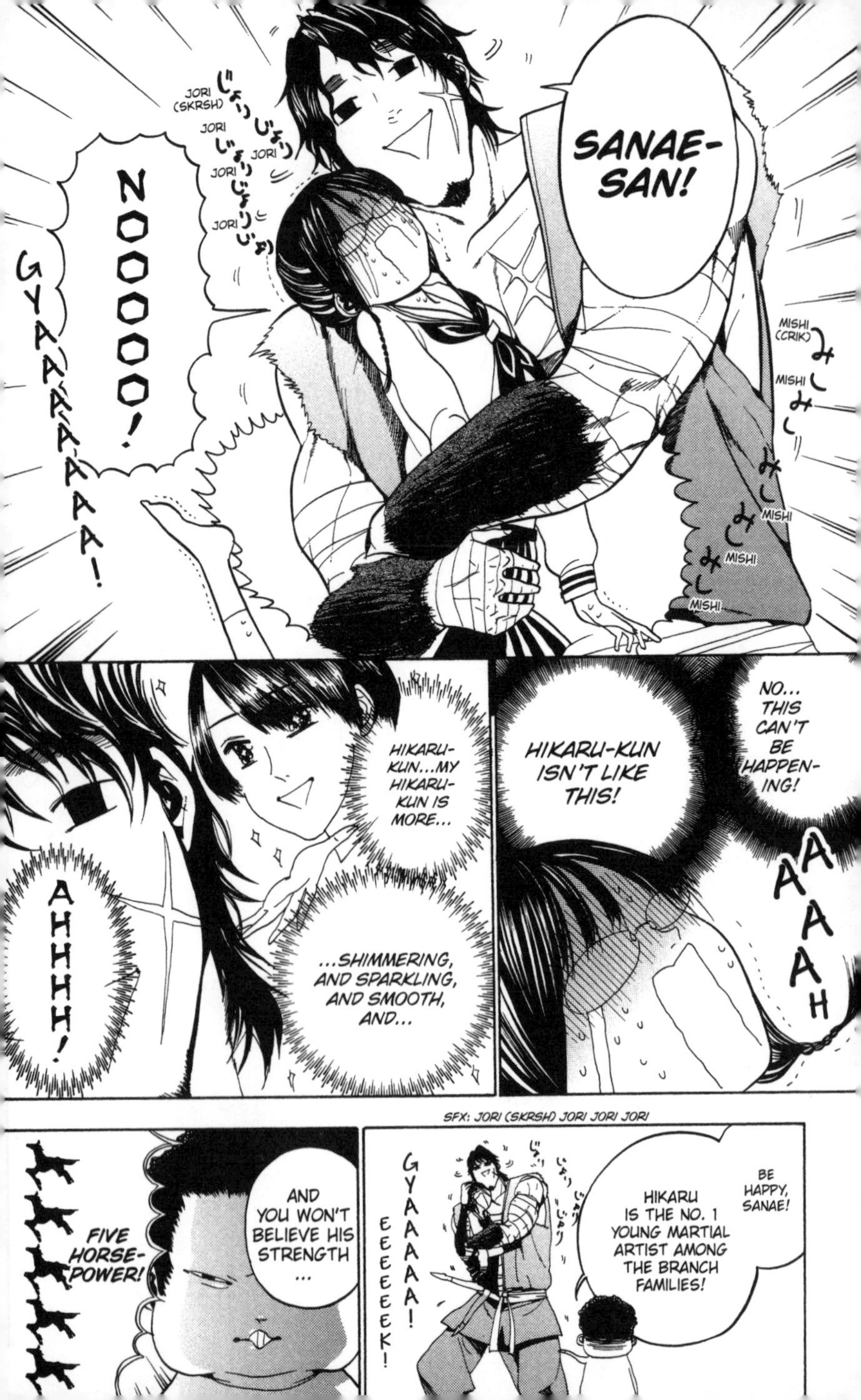
SANAE-SAN!
MISHI (CRIK) MISHI MISHI MISHI MISHI
JORI (SKRSH) JORI JORI JORI JORI
NOOOOO!
GYAAAAAAAAA!
NO... THIS CAN'T BE HAPPENING!
HIKARU-KUN ISN'T LIKE THIS!
AAAAAH
HIKARU-KUN...MY HIKARU-KUN IS MORE...
...SHIMMERING, AND SPARKLING, AND SMOOTH, AND...
AHHHH!
SFX: JORI (SKRSH) JORI JORI JORI
BE HAPPY, SANAE!
HIKARU IS THE NO. 1 YOUNG MARTIAL ARTIST AMONG THE BRANCH FAMILIES!
GYAAAAA EEEEEEK!
AND YOU WON'T BELIEVE HIS STRENGTH...
FIVE HORSE-POWER!

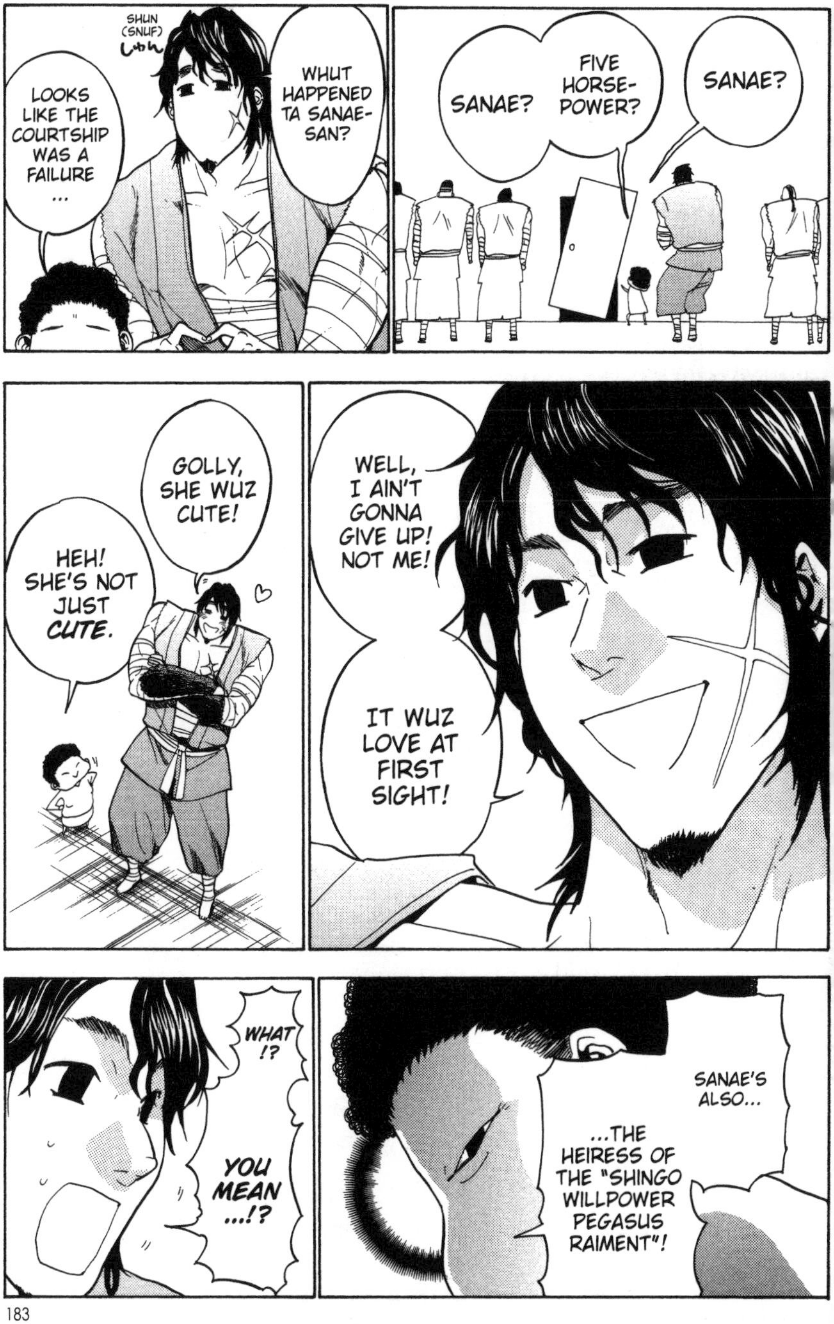
SANAE?
FIVE HORSE-POWER?
SANAE?
WHUT HAPPENED TA SANAE-SAN?
SHUN (SNUF)
しゅん
LOOKS LIKE THE COURTSHIP WAS A FAILURE ...
WELL, I AIN'T GONNA GIVE UP! NOT ME!
IT WUZ LOVE AT FIRST SIGHT!
GOLLY, SHE WUZ CUTE!
HEH! SHE'S NOT JUST CUTE.
SANAE'S ALSO...
...THE HEIRESS OF THE "SHINGO WILLPOWER PEGASUS RAIMENT"!
WHAT!?
YOU MEAN ...!?

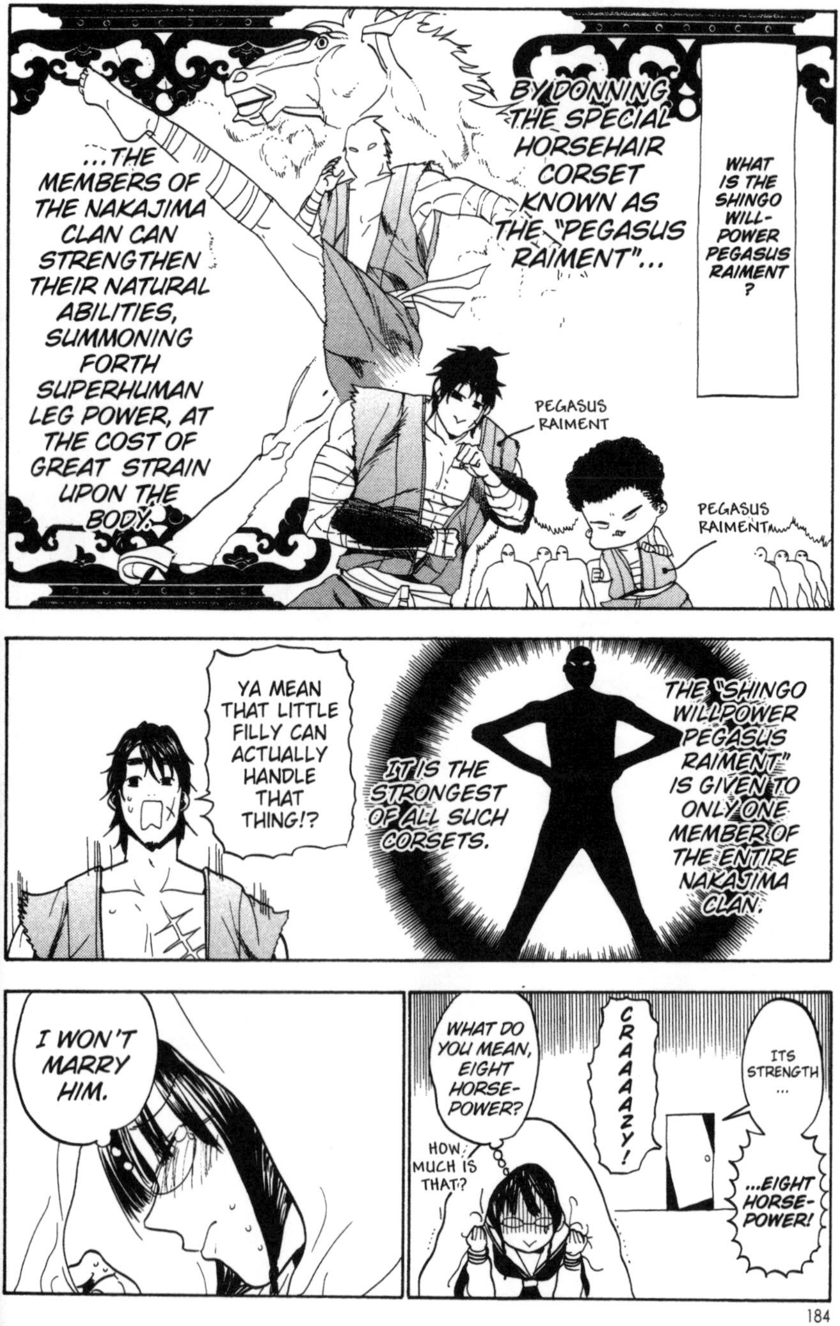
WHAT IS THE SHINGO WILL-POWER PEGASUS RAIMENT?
BY DONNING THE SPECIAL HORSEHAIR CORSET KNOWN AS THE "PEGASUS RAIMENT"...
...THE MEMBERS OF THE NAKAJIMA CLAN CAN STRENGTHEN THEIR NATURAL ABILITIES, SUMMONING FORTH SUPERHUMAN LEG POWER, AT THE COST OF GREAT STRAIN UPON THE BODY.
PEGASUS RAIMENT
PEGASUS RAIMENT
THE "SHINGO WILLPOWER PEGASUS RAIMENT" IS GIVEN TO ONLY ONE MEMBER OF THE ENTIRE NAKAJIMA CLAN.
IT IS THE STRONGEST OF ALL SUCH CORSETS.
YA MEAN THAT LITTLE FILLY CAN ACTUALLY HANDLE THAT THING!?
ITS STRENGTH...
...EIGHT HORSE-POWER!
CRAAAAAZY!
WHAT DO YOU MEAN, EIGHT HORSE-POWER?
HOW MUCH IS THAT?
I WON'T MARRY HIM.

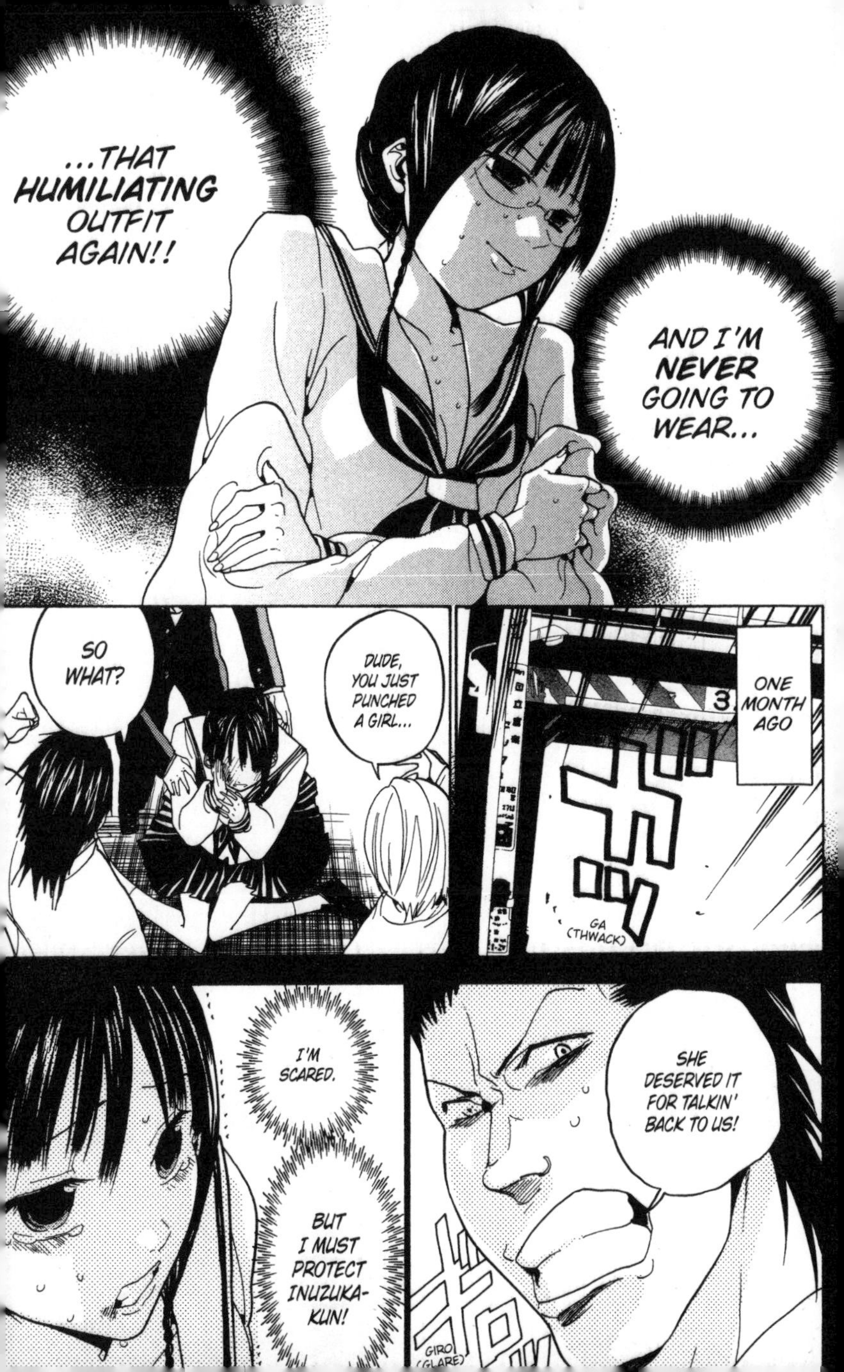
AND I'M NEVER GOING TO WEAR...
...THAT HUMILIATING OUTFIT AGAIN!!
ONE MONTH AGO
GA (THWACK)
DUDE, YOU JUST PUNCHED A GIRL...
SO WHAT?
SHE DESERVED IT FOR TALKIN' BACK TO US!
GIRO (GLARE)
I'M SCARED.
BUT I MUST PROTECT INUZUKA-KUN!

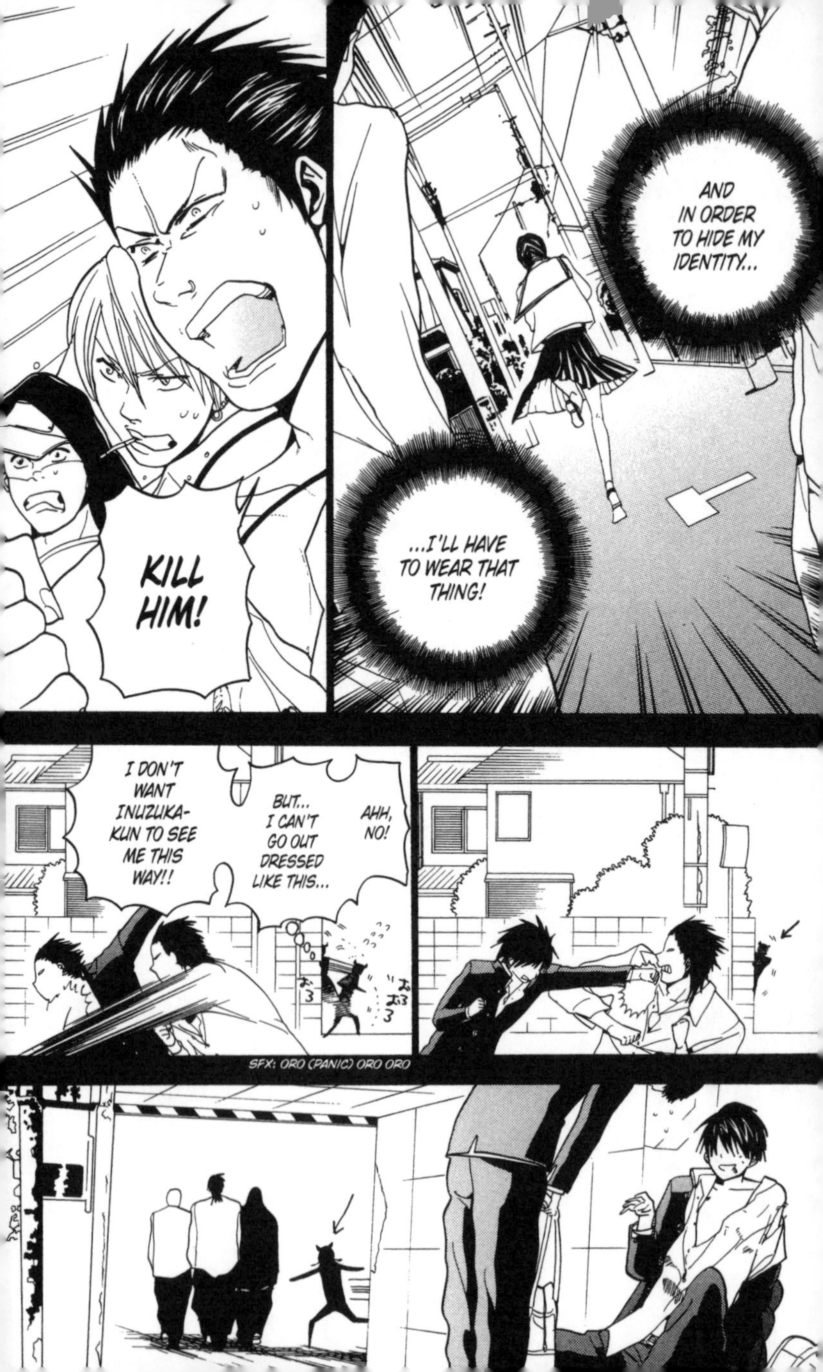
AND IN ORDER TO HIDE MY IDENTITY...
...I'LL HAVE TO WEAR THAT THING!
KILL HIM!
AHH, NO!
BUT... I CAN'T GO OUT DRESSED LIKE THIS...
I DON'T WANT INUZUKA-KUN TO SEE ME THIS WAY!!
SFX: ORO (PANIC) ORO ORO

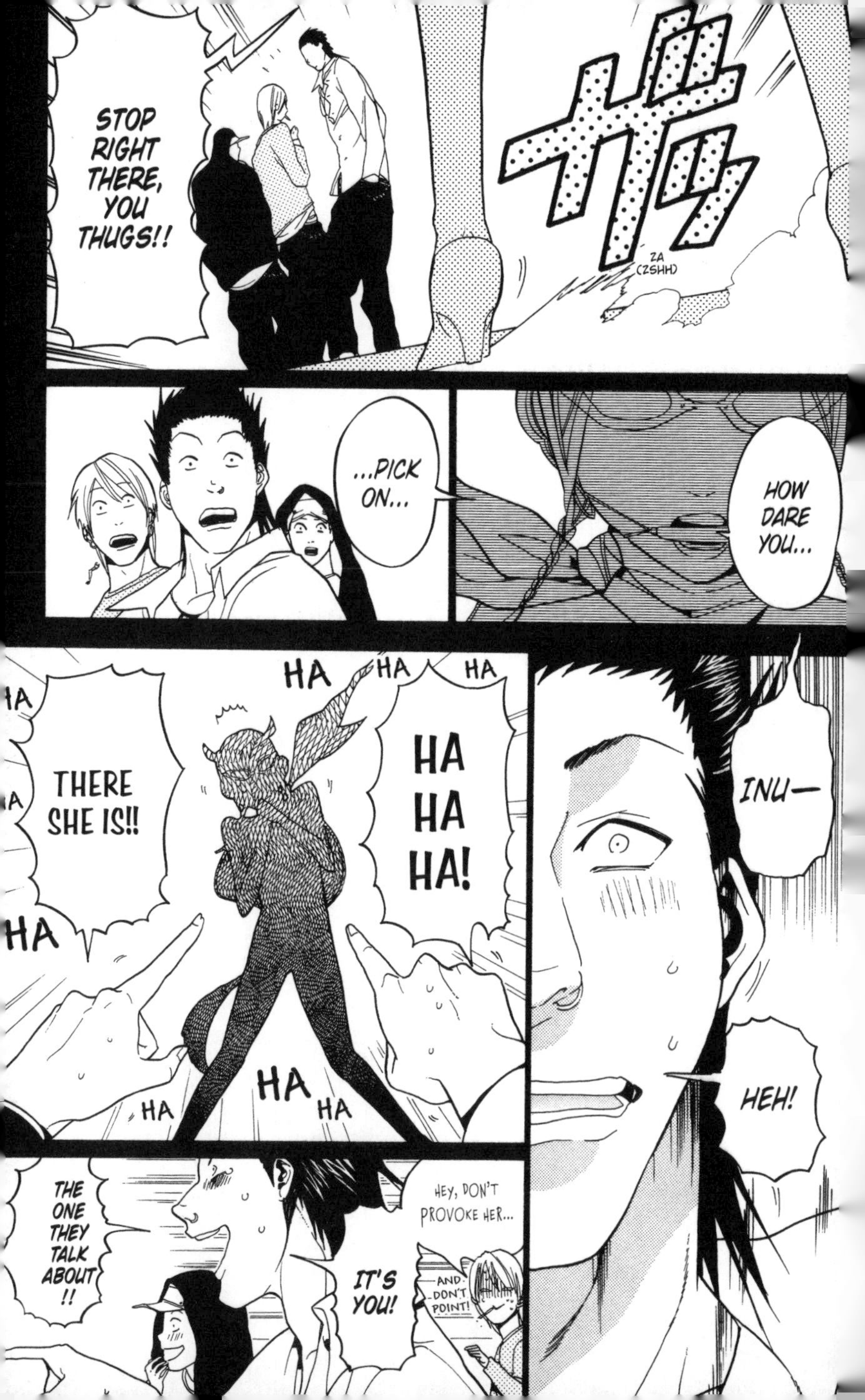
ZA (ZSHH)
STOP RIGHT THERE, YOU THUGS!!
HOW DARE YOU...
...PICK ON...
INU—
HEH!
HA HA HA HA!
HA HA HA
THERE SHE IS!!
HA
HA
HA HA HA
HEY, DON'T PROVOKE HER...
AND DON'T POINT!
IT'S YOU!
THE ONE THEY TALK ABOUT!!

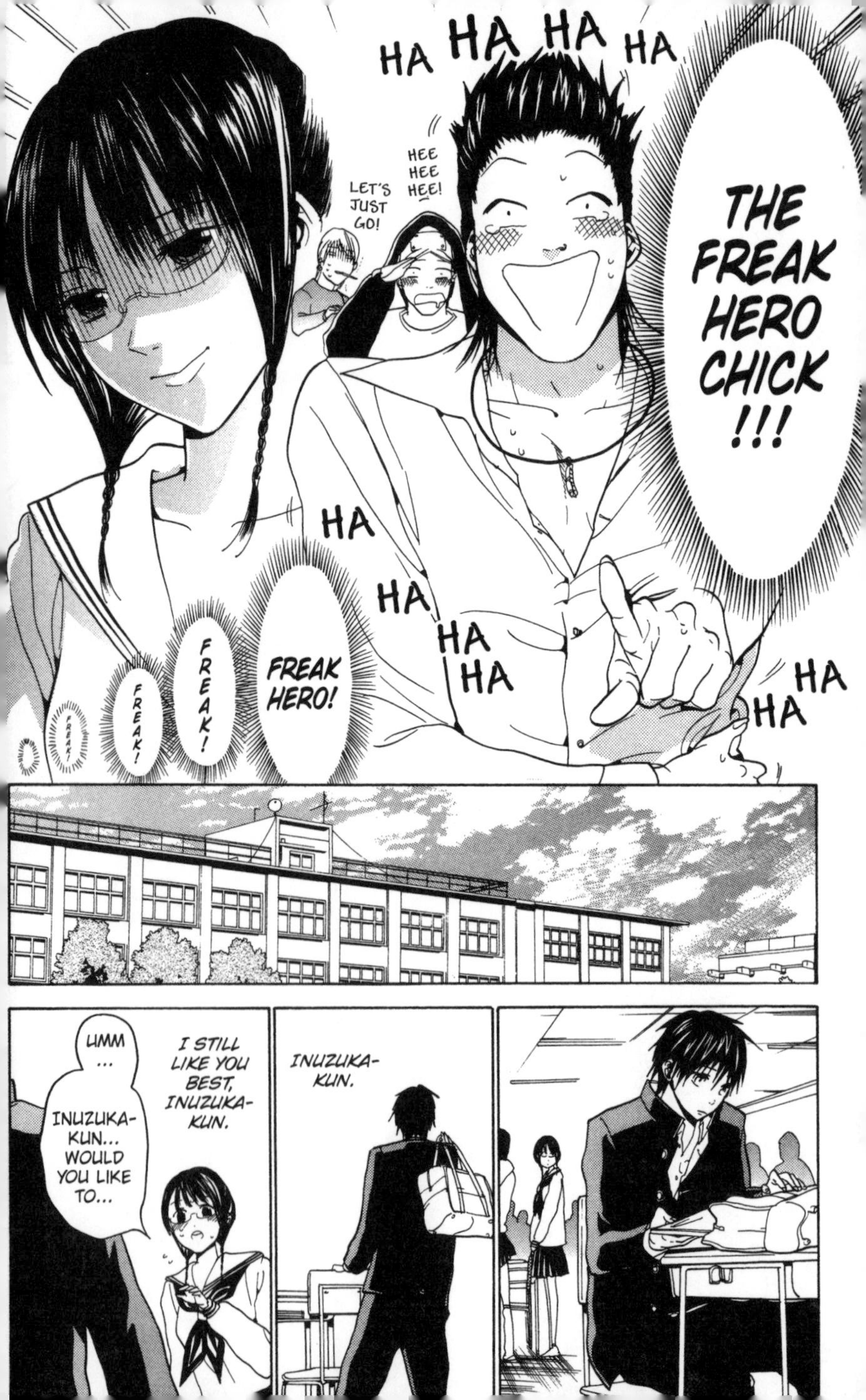
HA HA HA HA
THE FREAK HERO CHICK!!!
HEE HEE HEE!
LET'S JUST GO!
HA
HA
HA
HA
HA HA
FREAK HERO!
FREAK!
FREAK!
FREAK!
INUZUKA-KUN.
I STILL LIKE YOU BEST, INUZUKA-KUN.
UMM ...
INUZUKA-KUN... WOULD YOU LIKE TO...

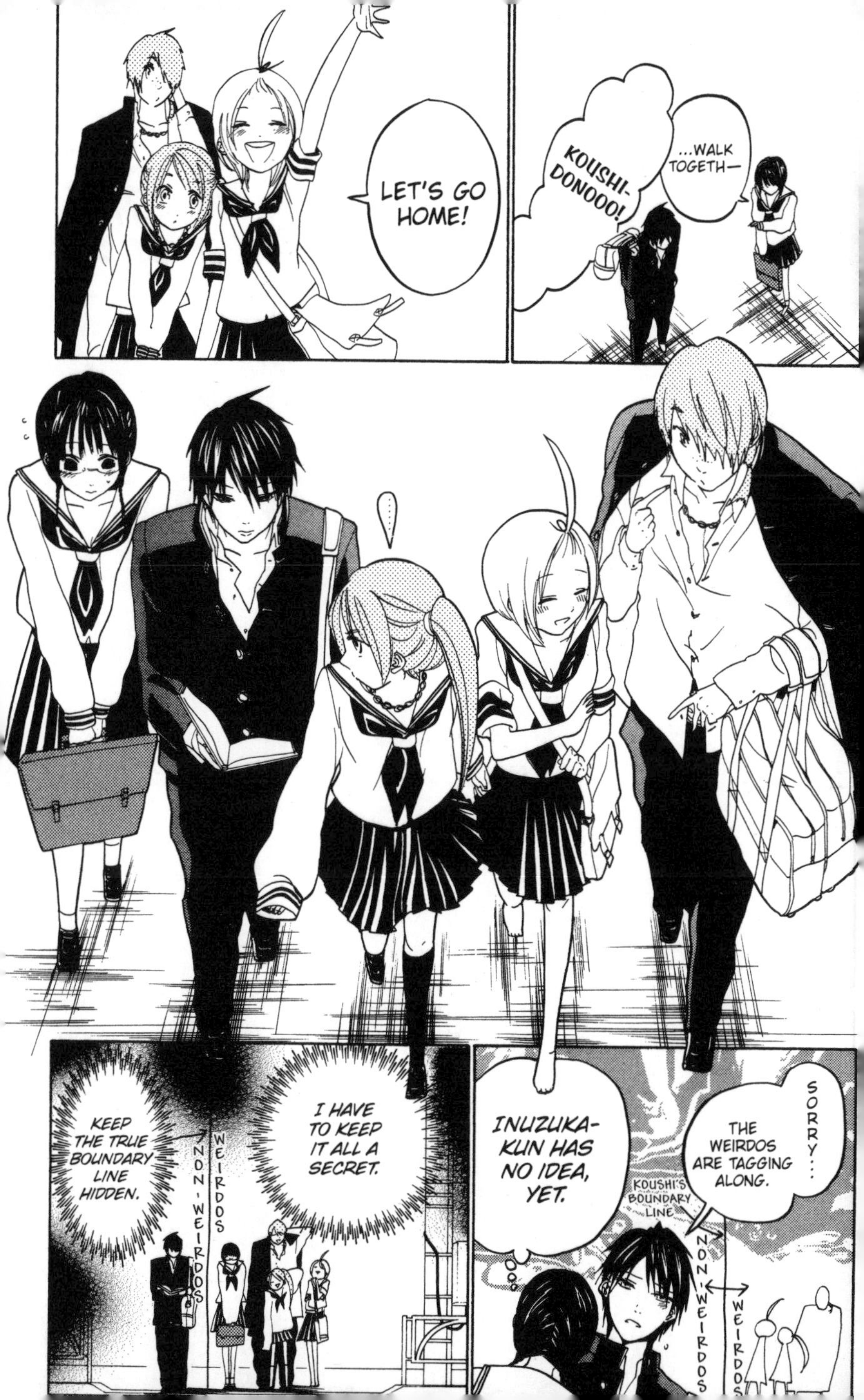
...WALK TOGETH—
KOUSHI-DONOOO!
LET'S GO HOME!
SORRY...
THE WEIRDOS ARE TAGGING ALONG.
INUZUKA-KUN HAS NO IDEA, YET.
KOUSHI'S BOUNDARY LINE
NON-WEIRDOS
WEIRDOS
I HAVE TO KEEP IT ALL A SECRET.
KEEP THE TRUE BOUNDARY LINE HIDDEN.
WEIRDOS
NON-WEIRDOS

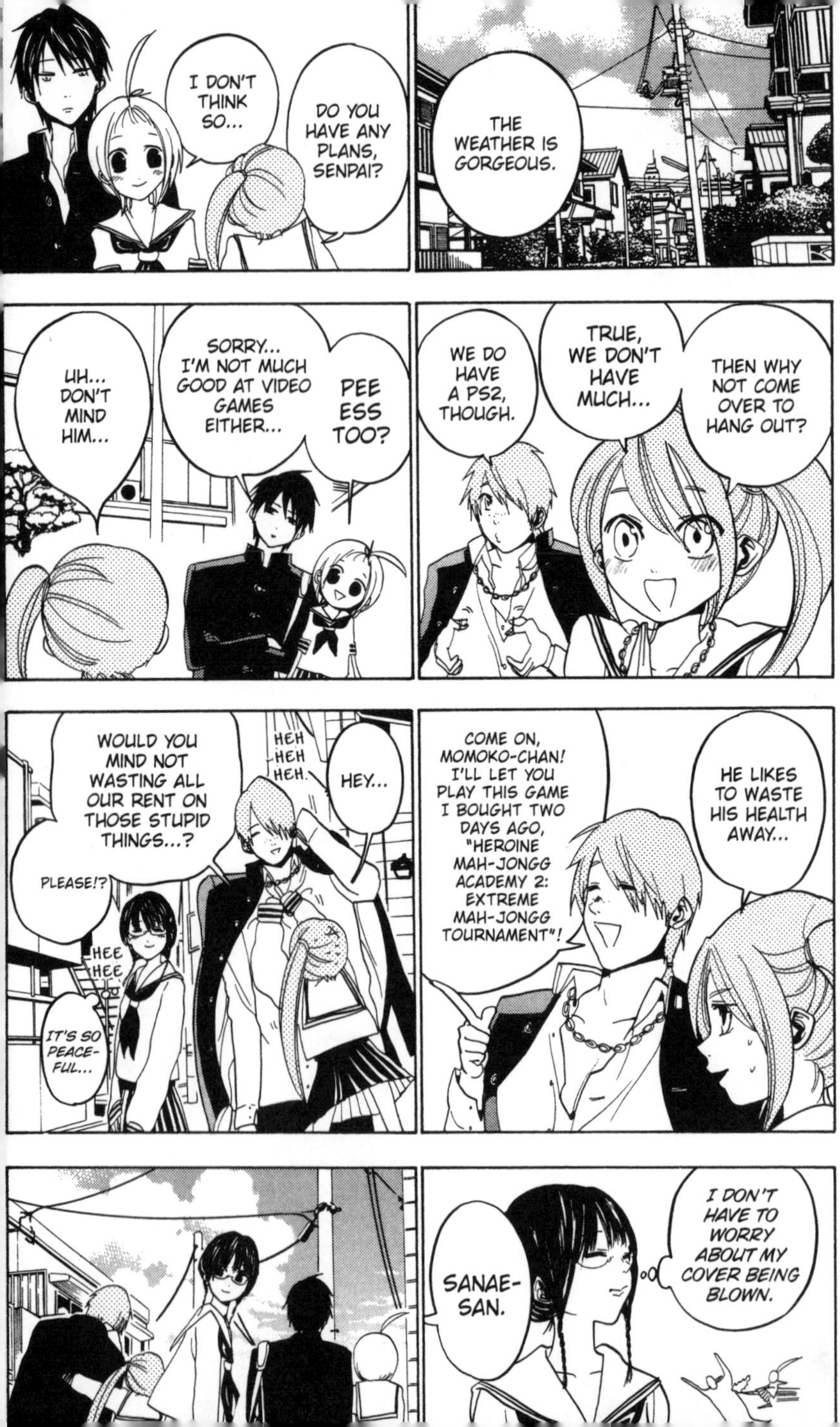
THE WEATHER IS GORGEOUS.
DO YOU HAVE ANY PLANS, SENPAI?
I DON'T THINK SO...
THEN WHY NOT COME OVER TO HANG OUT?
TRUE, WE DON'T HAVE MUCH...
WE DO HAVE A PS2, THOUGH.
PEE ESS TOO?
SORRY... I'M NOT MUCH GOOD AT VIDEO GAMES EITHER...
UH... DON'T MIND HIM...
HE LIKES TO WASTE HIS HEALTH AWAY...
COME ON, MOMOKO-CHAN! I'LL LET YOU PLAY THIS GAME I BOUGHT TWO DAYS AGO, "HEROINE MAH-JONGG ACADEMY 2: EXTREME MAH-JONGG TOURNAMENT"!
HEY...
HEH HEH HEH
WOULD YOU MIND NOT WASTING ALL OUR RENT ON THOSE STUPID THINGS...?
PLEASE!?
HEE HEE
IT'S SO PEACEFUL...
I DON'T HAVE TO WORRY ABOUT MY COVER BEING BLOWN.
SANAE-SAN.

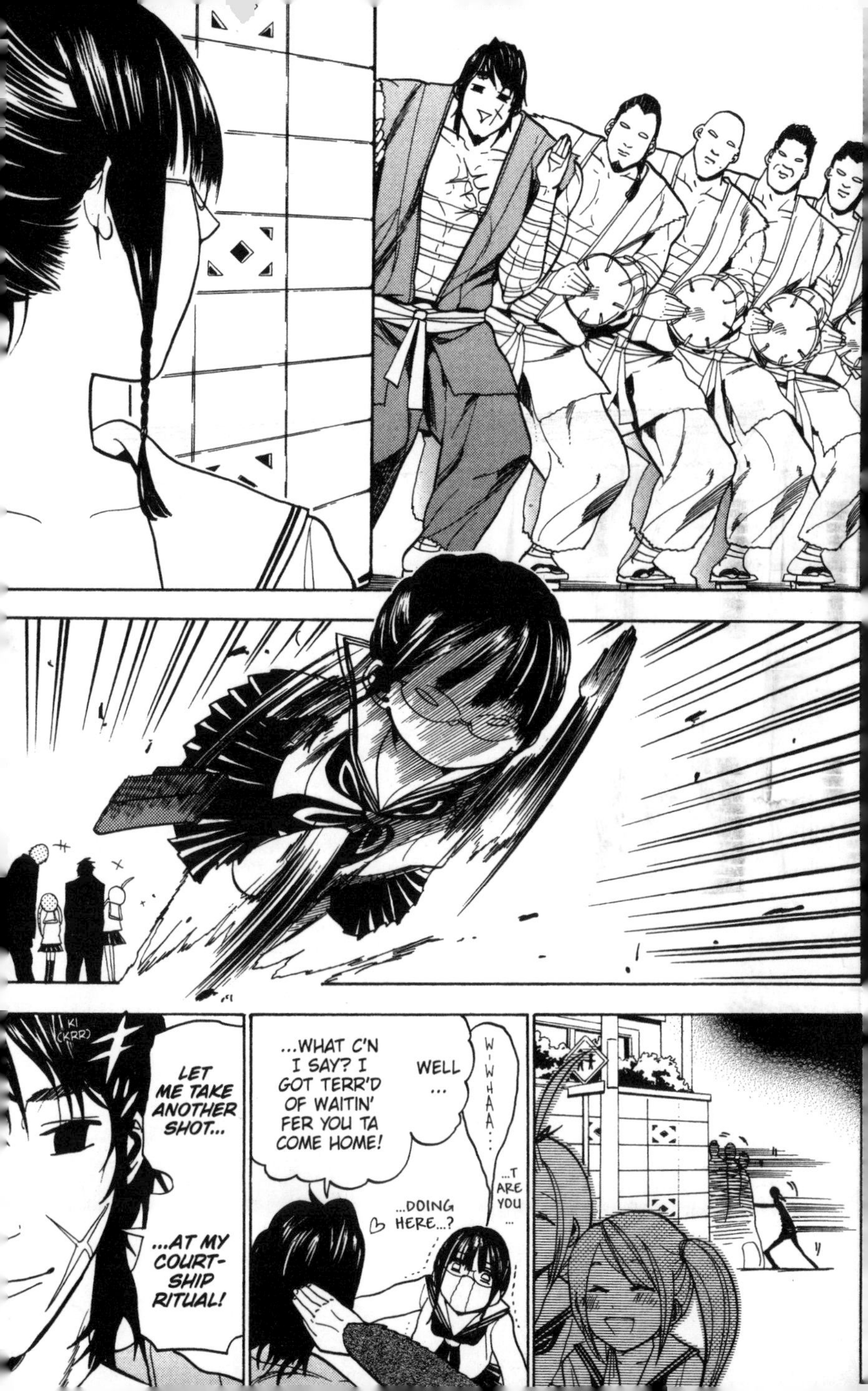
W-WHAA...
...T ARE YOU ...
...DOING HERE...?
WELL ...
...WHAT C'N I SAY? I GOT TERR'D OF WAITIN' FER YOU TA COME HOME!
KI (KRR)
LET ME TAKE ANOTHER SHOT...
...AT MY COURT-SHIP RITUAL!

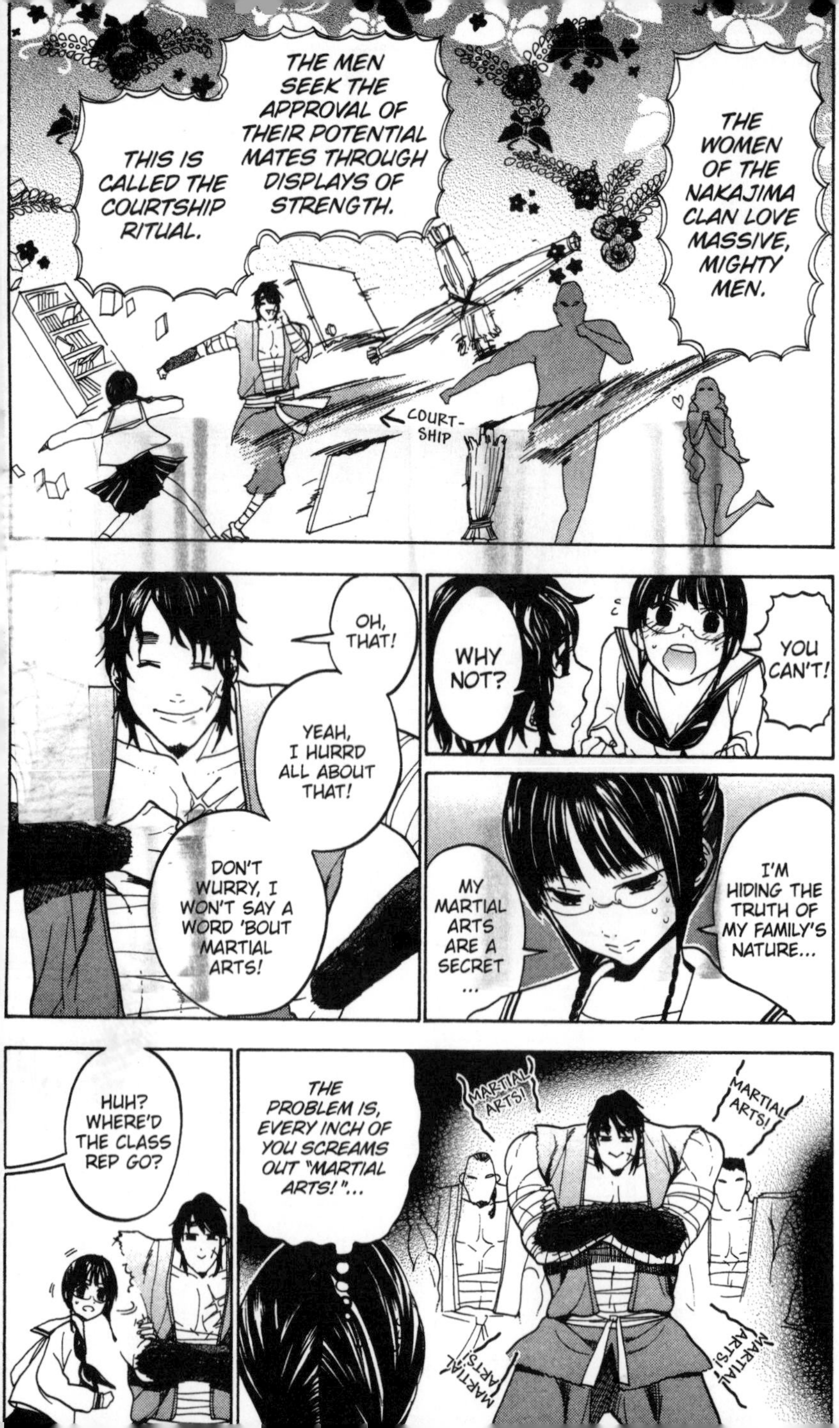
THE WOMEN OF THE NAKAJIMA CLAN LOVE MASSIVE, MIGHTY MEN.
THE MEN SEEK THE APPROVAL OF THEIR POTENTIAL MATES THROUGH DISPLAYS OF STRENGTH.
THIS IS CALLED THE COURTSHIP RITUAL.
COURT-SHIP
YOU CAN'T!
WHY NOT?
I'M HIDING THE TRUTH OF MY FAMILY'S NATURE...
MY MARTIAL ARTS ARE A SECRET ...
OH, THAT!
YEAH, I HURRD ALL ABOUT THAT!
DON'T WURRY, I WON'T SAY A WORD 'BOUT MARTIAL ARTS!
MARTIAL ARTS!
MARTIAL ARTS!
THE PROBLEM IS, EVERY INCH OF YOU SCREAMS OUT "MARTIAL ARTS!"...
MARTIAL ARTS!
MARTIAL ARTS!
HUH? WHERE'D THE CLASS REP GO?

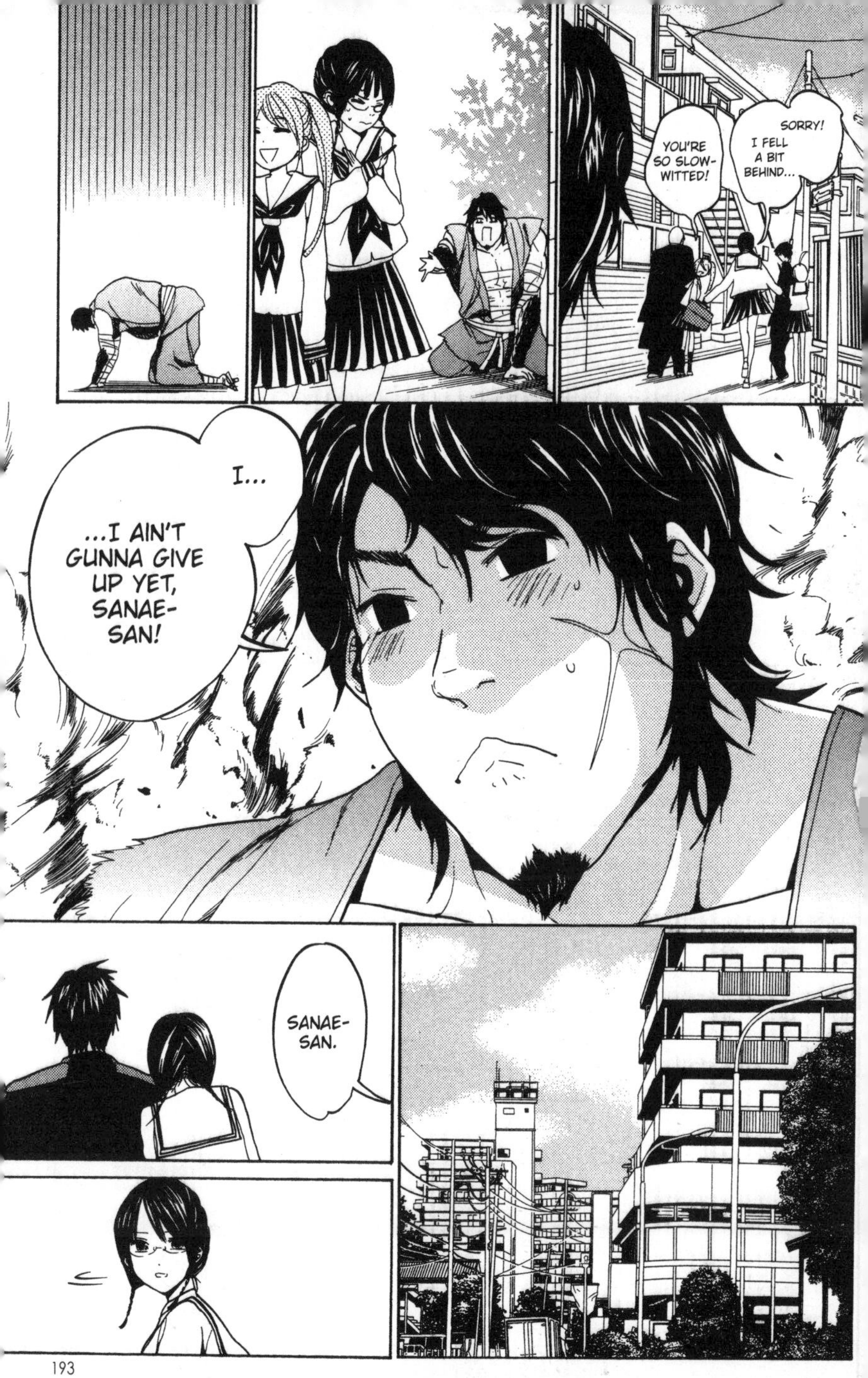
SORRY! I FELL A BIT BEHIND...
YOU'RE SO SLOW-WITTED!
I...
...I AIN'T GUNNA GIVE UP YET, SANAE-SAN!
SANAE-SAN.

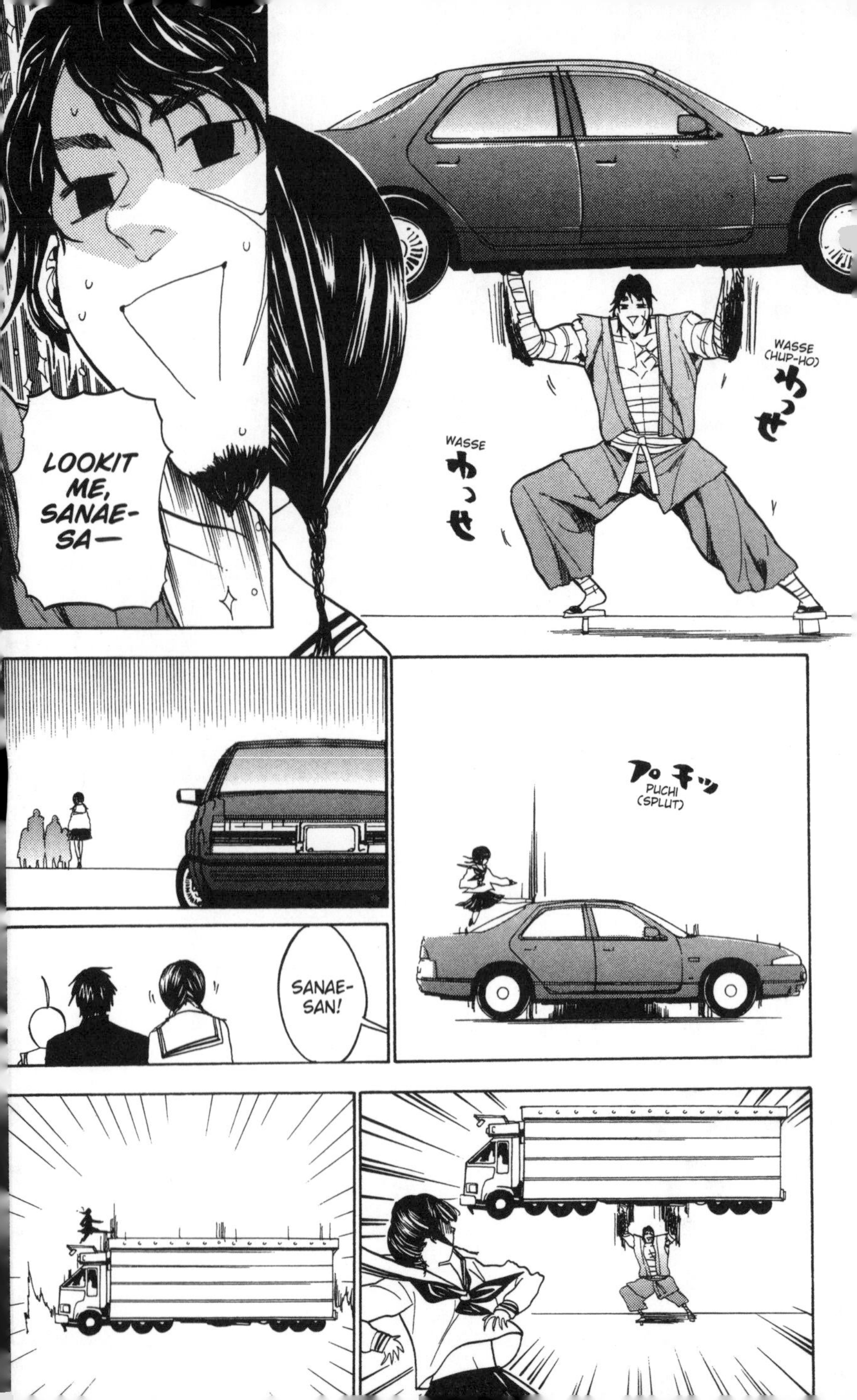

WASSE (HUP-HO)
わっせ
WASSE
わっせ
LOOKIT ME, SANAE-SA—
プチッ
PUCHI (SPLUT)
SANAE-SAN!

SANAE-
SAAAN!

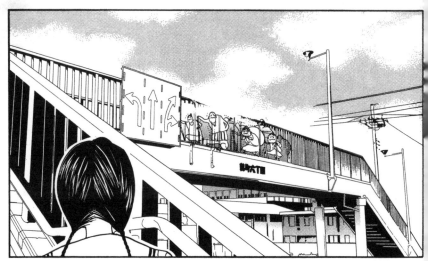

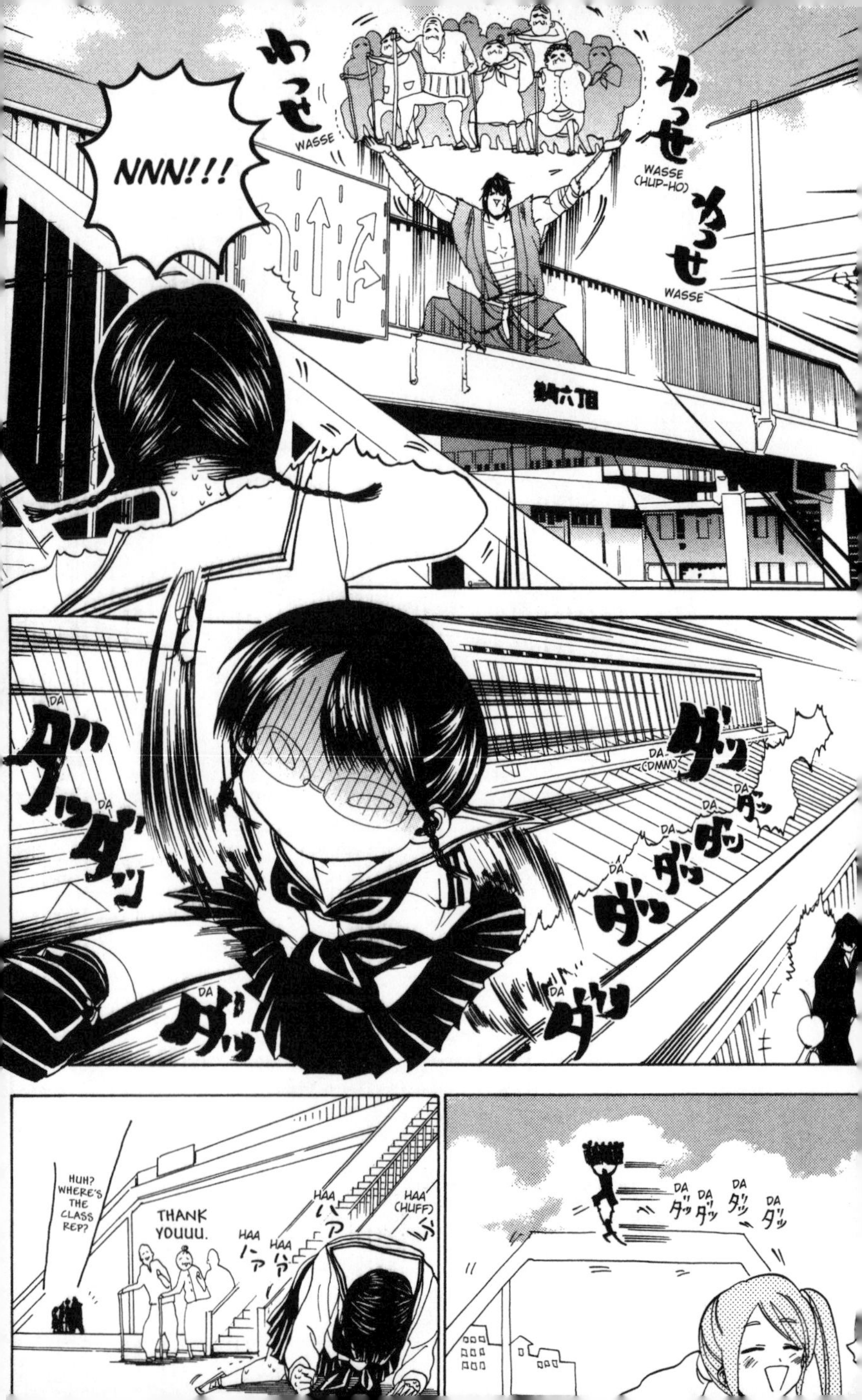

ワッセ
WASSE (HUP-HO)
ワッセ
WASSE
ワッセ
WASSE
NNN!!!
ダッ
DA (DMM)
DA
DA
DA
DA
DA
DA
DA
DA
DA
DA
DA
HAA (HUFF)
HAA
HAA
HAA
THANK YOUUU.
HUH? WHERE'S THE CLASS REP?

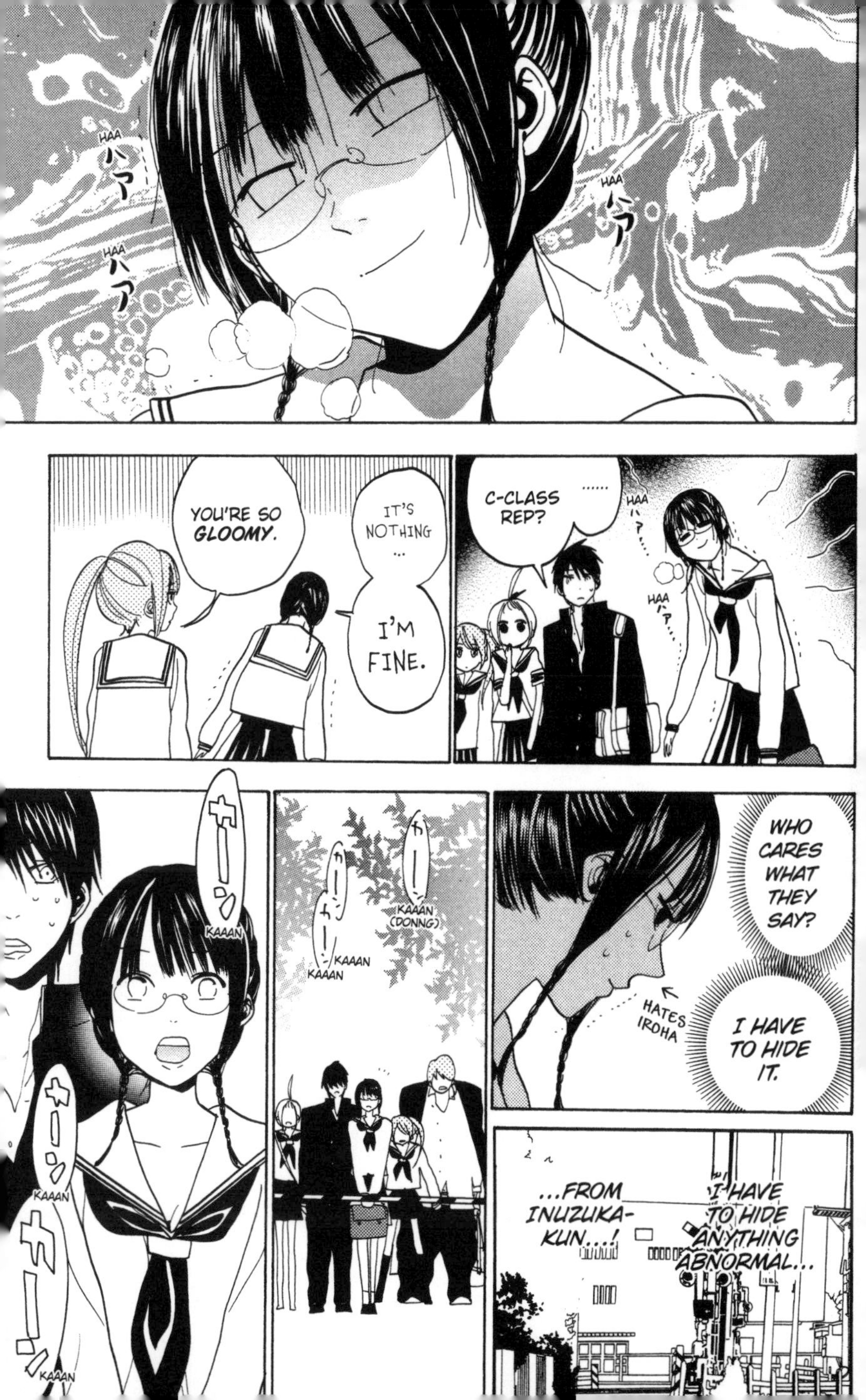
HAA ハア
HAA ハア
HAA ハア
HAA ハ ア
......
C-CLASS REP?
HAA ハ ア
YOU'RE SO GLOOMY.
IT'S NOTHING ... I'M FINE.
WHO CARES WHAT THEY SAY?
I HAVE TO HIDE IT.
HATES IROHA
I HAVE TO HIDE ANYTHING ABNORMAL...
...FROM INUZUKA-KUN...!
カーン KAAAN (DONNG)
カーン KAAAN
カーン KAAAN
カーン KAAAN
カーン KAAAN
カーン KAAAN

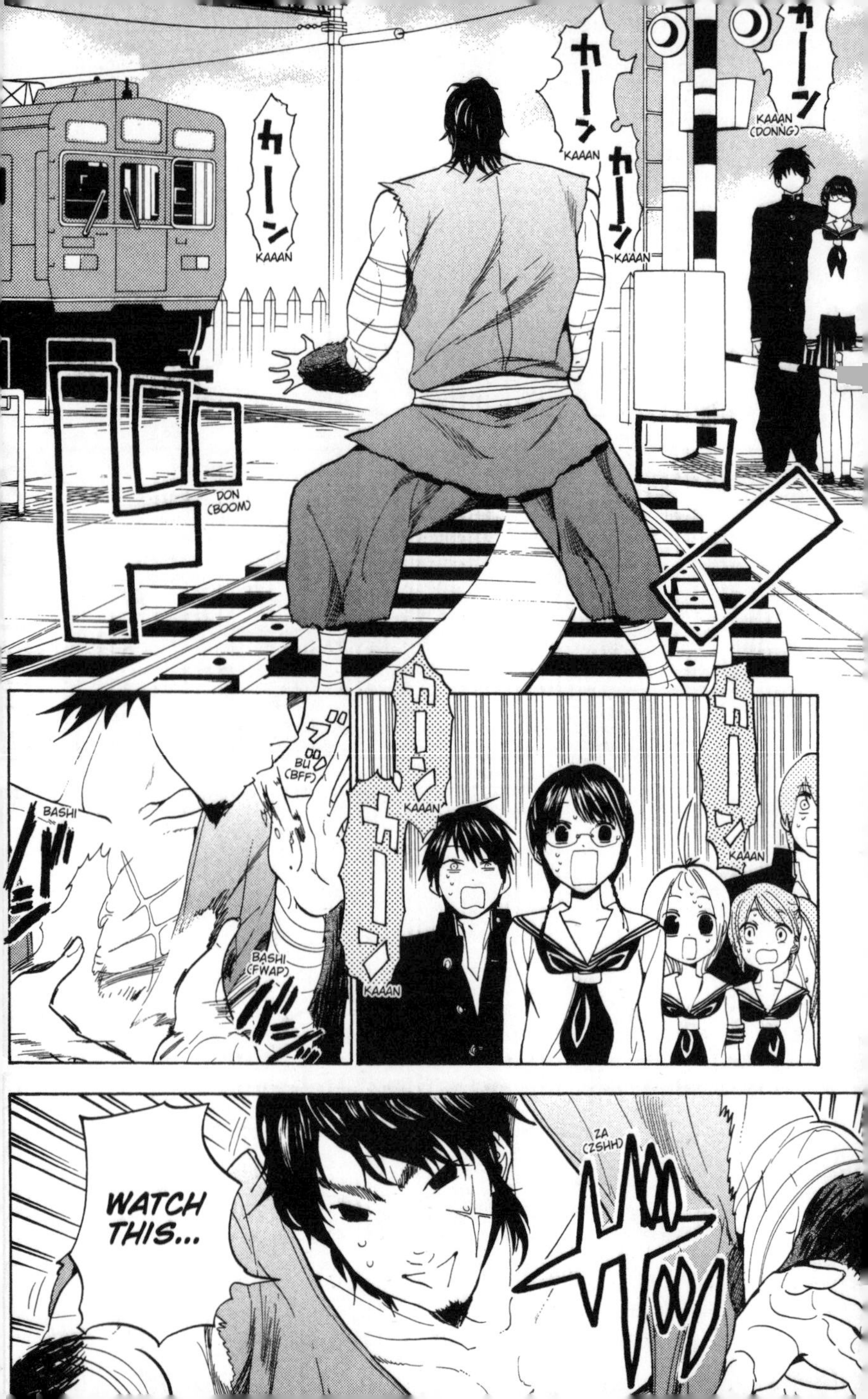

カーン
KAAAN (DONNG)
カーン
KAAAN
カーン
KAAAN
カーン
KAAAN
DON (BOOM)
カーン
KAAAN
カーン
KAAAN
カーン
KAAAN
ブッ
BU (BFF)
BASHI
BASHI (FWAP)
ZA (ZSHH)
WATCH THIS...

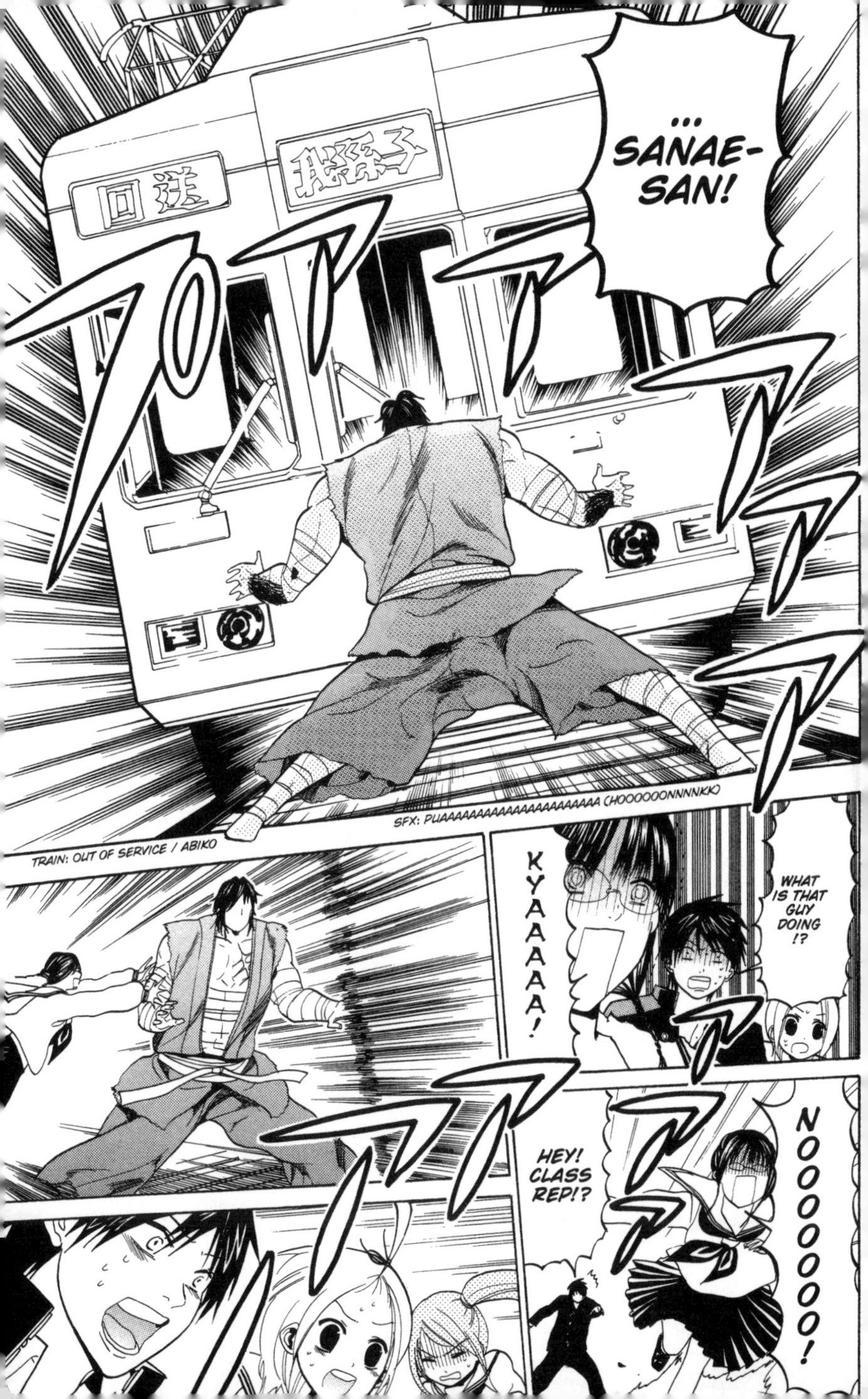

... SANAE-SAN!
SFX: PUAAAAAAAAAAAAAAAAAAAAAA (HOOOOOONNNNKK)
TRAIN: OUT OF SERVICE / ABIKO
KYAAAAAA!
WHAT IS THAT GUY DOING!?
NOOOOOOOOO!
HEY! CLASS REP!?

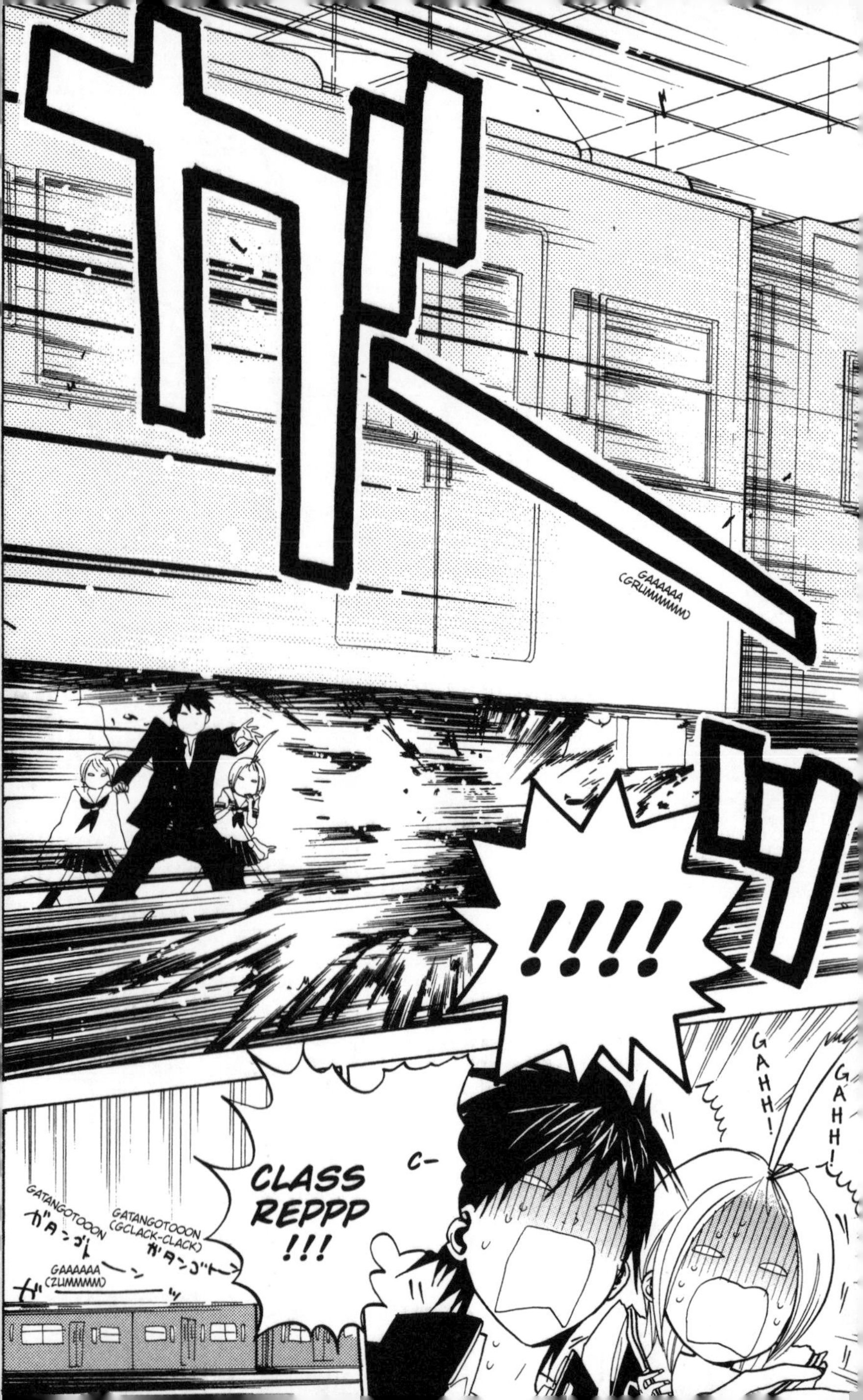
GAAAAAA (GRUMMMMMM)
!!!!
GAHH!
GAHH!
C–
CLASS REPPP !!!
GATANGOTOOON (GCLACK-CLACK)
GATANGOTOOON
GAAAAAA (ZUMMMMM)

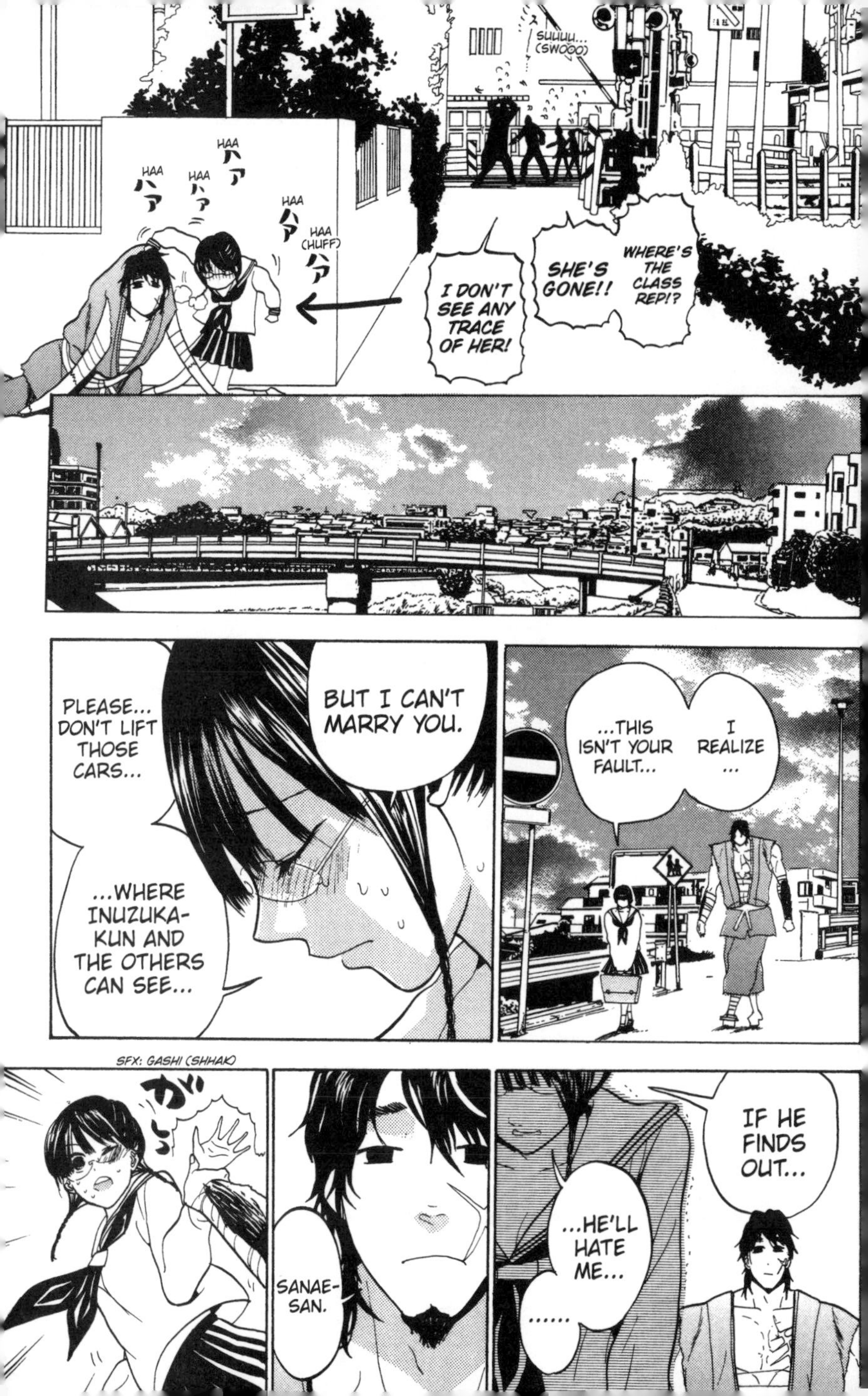
SUUUU... (SWOOO)
WHERE'S THE CLASS REP!?
SHE'S GONE!!
I DON'T SEE ANY TRACE OF HER!
HAA (HUFF) ハア
HAA ハア
HAA ハア
HAA ハア
HAA ハア
I REALIZE...
...THIS ISN'T YOUR FAULT...
BUT I CAN'T MARRY YOU.
PLEASE... DON'T LIFT THOSE CARS...
...WHERE INUZUKA-KUN AND THE OTHERS CAN SEE...
IF HE FINDS OUT...
...HE'LL HATE ME...
......
SANAE-SAN.
SFX: GASHI (SHHAK)

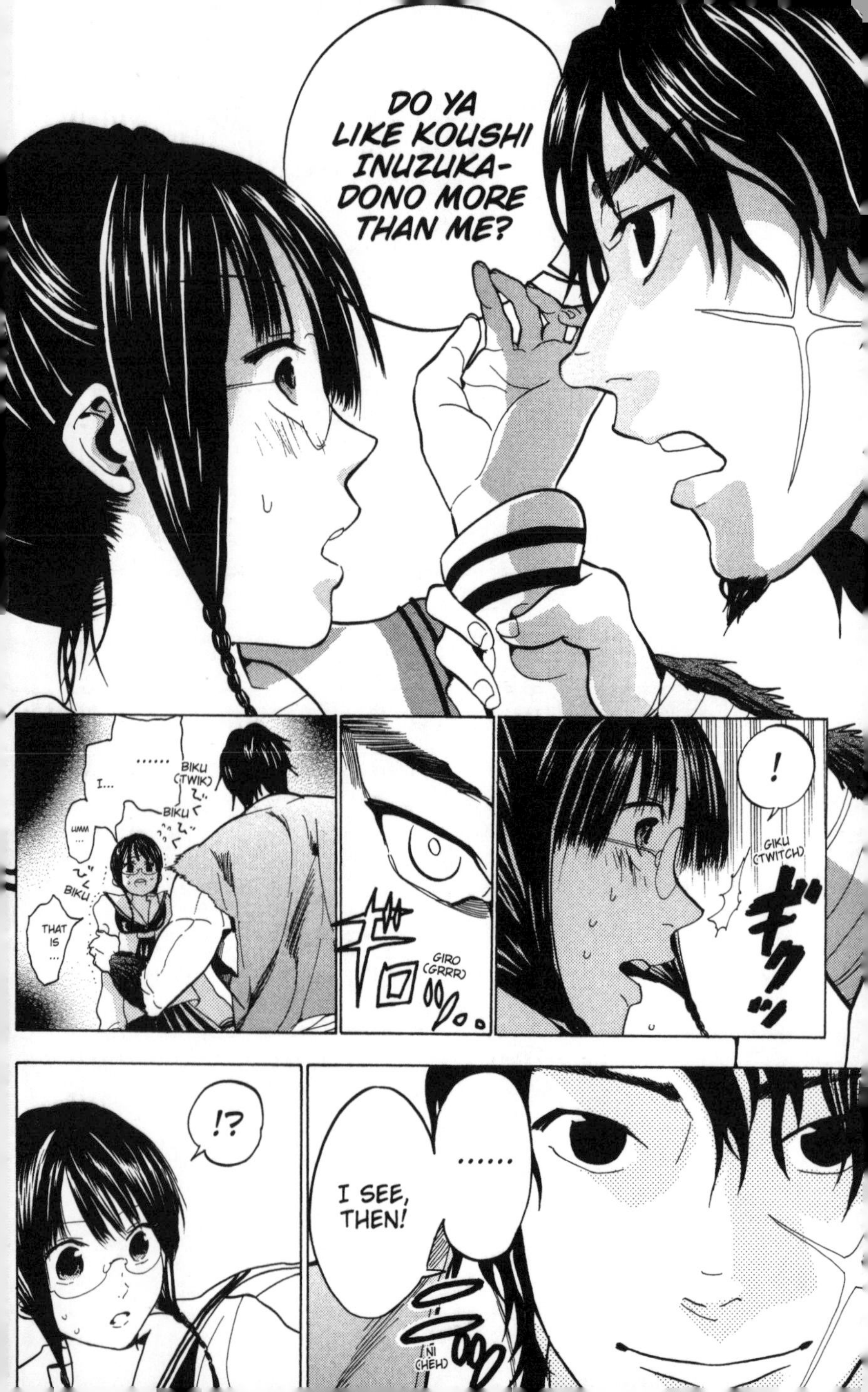
DO YA LIKE KOUSHI INUZUKA-DONO MORE THAN ME?
!
GIKU (TWITCH)
ギクッ
ギロ
GIRO (GRRR)
......
BIKU (TWIK)
I...
BIKU
UMM ...
BIKU
THAT IS ...
......
I SEE, THEN!
NI (HEH)
!?

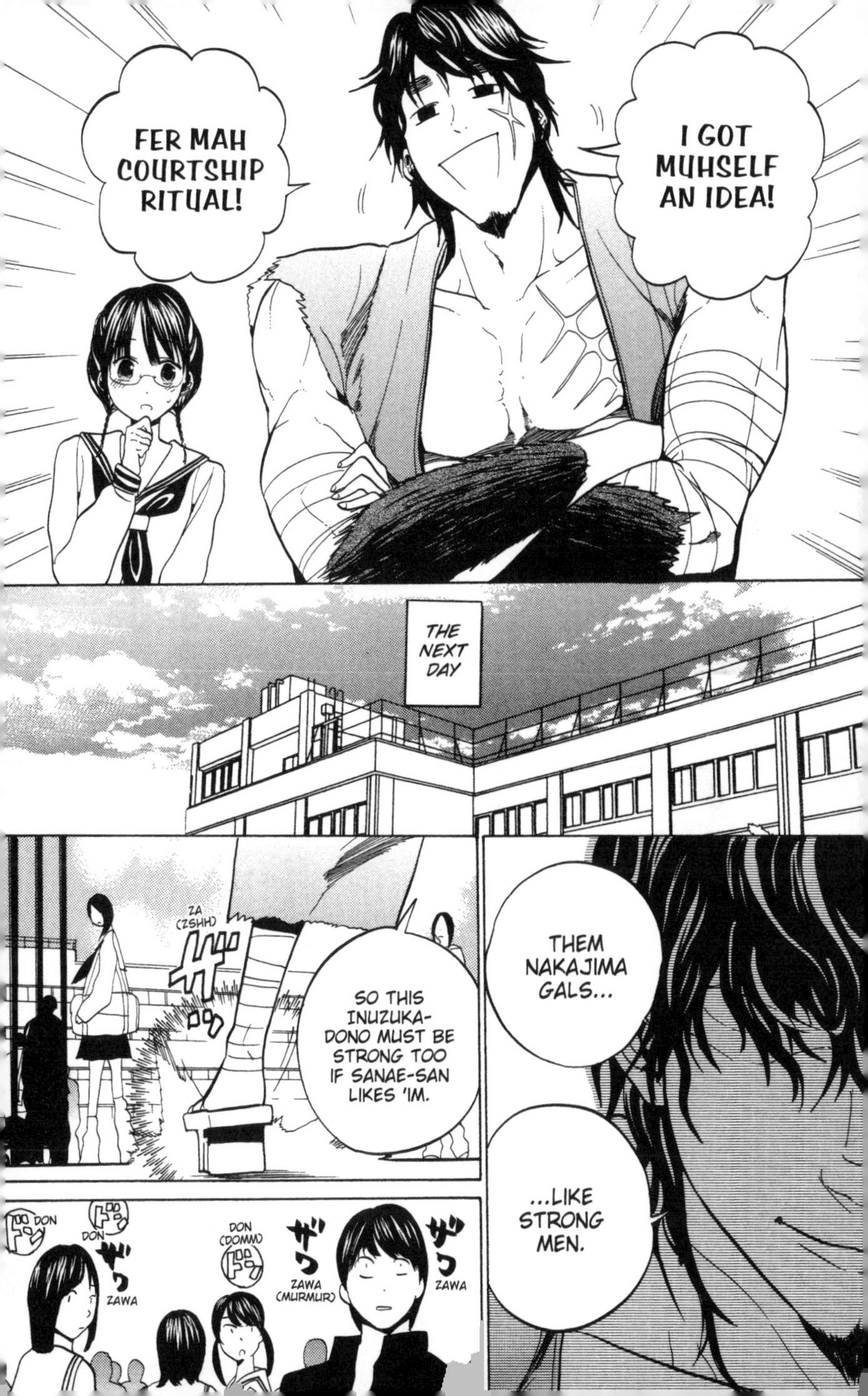
I GOT MUHSELF AN IDEA!
FER MAH COURTSHIP RITUAL!
THE NEXT DAY
THEM NAKAJIMA GALS...
...LIKE STRONG MEN.
SO THIS INUZUKA-DONO MUST BE STRONG TOO IF SANAE-SAN LIKES 'IM.
ZA (ZSHH)
ZAWA
ZAWA (MURMUR)
DON (DOMM)
ZAWA
DON
DON

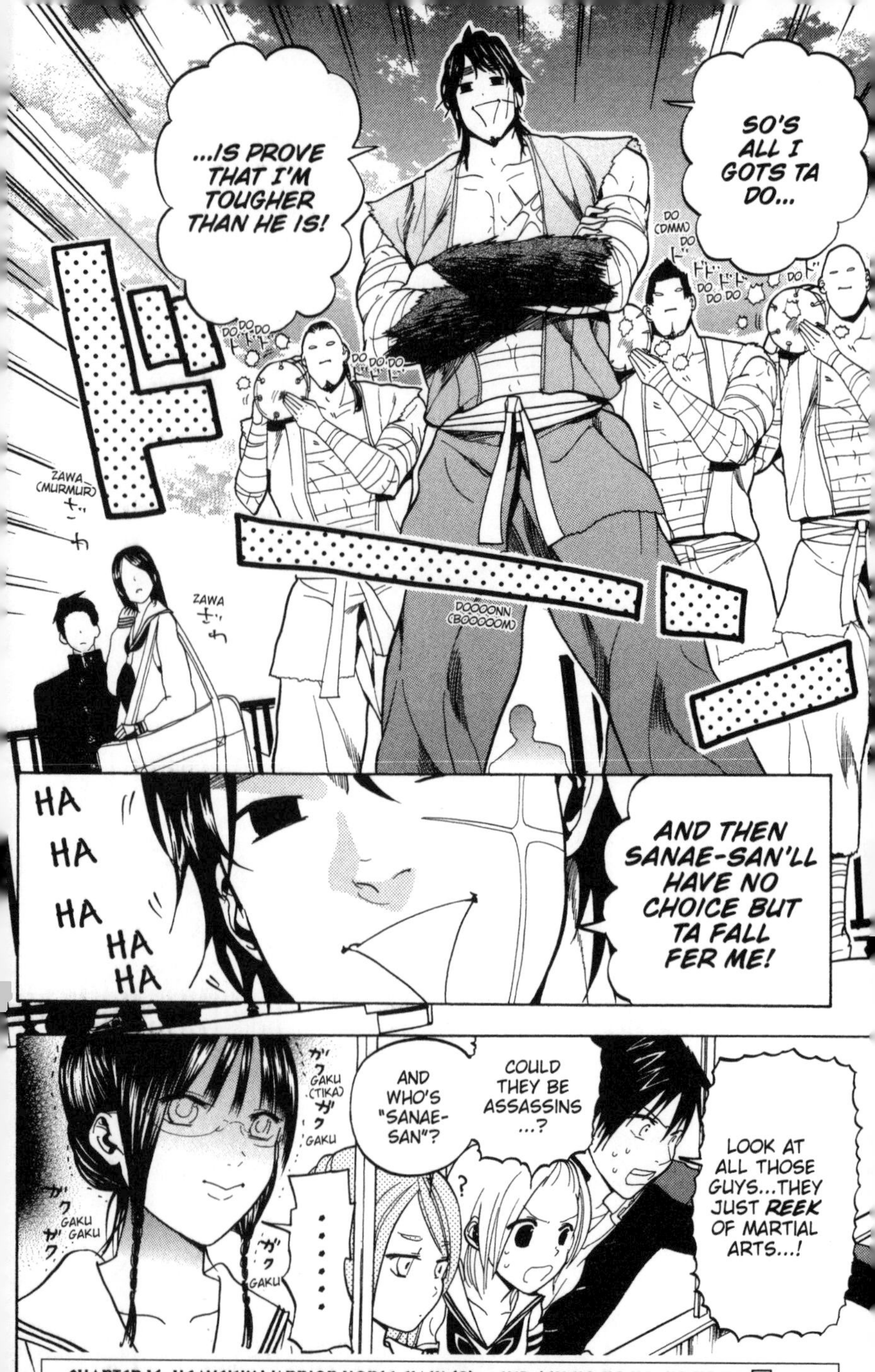
SO'S ALL I GOTS TA DO...
...IS PROVE THAT I'M TOUGHER THAN HE IS!
DO (DMM) DO
DO DO DO
DO DO DO
DO DO DO
DO DO DO
DOOOONN (BOOOOOM)
ZAWA (MURMUR)
ZAWA
AND THEN SANAE-SAN'LL HAVE NO CHOICE BUT TA FALL FER ME!
HA HA HA HA HA
LOOK AT ALL THOSE GUYS...THEY JUST REEK OF MARTIAL ARTS...!
COULD THEY BE ASSASSINS ...?
AND WHO'S "SANAE-SAN"?
?
......
GAKU (TIKA) GAKU
GAKU GAKU
GAKU

CHAPTER 14. HEAVENLY WARRIOR HORSE MASK (2) – END / SUMOMOMO MOMOMO 2 END

TRANSLATION NOTES

Sumomomo Momomo is part of a well-known Japanese tongue twister which reads, *"Sumomo mo momo mo momo no uchi,"* and roughly means, "Plums and peaches are part of the peach family."

Page 11

Nittai-Dai: While it is a combination of the name Daigoro Nittai (Nittai Daigoro in the Japnese order), it also means Japanese Sports University, which is a fitting nickname for the P.E. teacher.

Page 17

Miyamoto: In keeping with the Chinese zodiac pattern, the name "Miyamoto" contains the kanji for "snake."

Page 32

Nee-san: Normally meaning "older sister," this term is being used here in the yakuza sense. In yakuza culture, close, affectionate "sibling" titles are commonly used for other yakuza that do not hold actual office, i.e. the clan head or next-in-line. For example, when an older man is paired up with a younger guy to "show him the ropes," it is quite common for the younger man to call his superior *aniki* (older brother), while the "aniki" might call his younger protégé *otouto-bun* (younger brother in spirit). When women are present and in a position of superiority, as in this case, they might be referred to as *aneki* or *nee-san*, meaning "older sister."

Page 64

Onii-chan: Another term of endearment, meaning "older brother." It can be widely used on basically any young man from teenager to twenty-something, regardless of whether he is actually the speaker's brother or not. As we will see, the cute, reverent younger sister who refers to her brother by "Onii-chan" is a highly prized and fetishized concept among many Japanese men, particularly in the otaku demographic.

Page 85

Indara Jaei Genma-ryuu: As with the other styles of martial arts, this one contains the name of the Twelve Heavenly Generals of Buddhism. Indara pertains to the snake of the Chinese zodiac, like the snake in the name "Miyamoto." The full title translates roughly to: "Indara Snake Shadows, Illusions and Evil Style."

Page 98

Madara: A vaguely "Buddhist-sounding" name much like Haira, Indara, etc.; however, it does not have any actual historical or theological basis. It's also the title of an old early '90s manga and video game series, so perhaps Shinobu Oh-taka is paying tribute.

Page 126-127

Kouhai: The counterpart of *senpai* (upperclass-man). Whereas one's senpai is an elder within the group, a kouhai is a younger, newer person. Iroha is Momoko's kouhai in this instance because she is younger and in a lower grade.

Page 150

Nakajima: As seen by the nameplate on the front of her house, Sanae's family hides its true name by using different combinations of Chinese characters. They are both pronounced "Naka-jima," but the façade name is a very common and mundane combination while the true spelling of their name includes a dead giveaway for those who know what to look for: the character for "horse"!

Santera Shingo-ryuu: As I'm sure you can guess already, Santera is the name of the heavenly general aligned with the horse. Shingo-ryuu translates to "God's Protection Style."

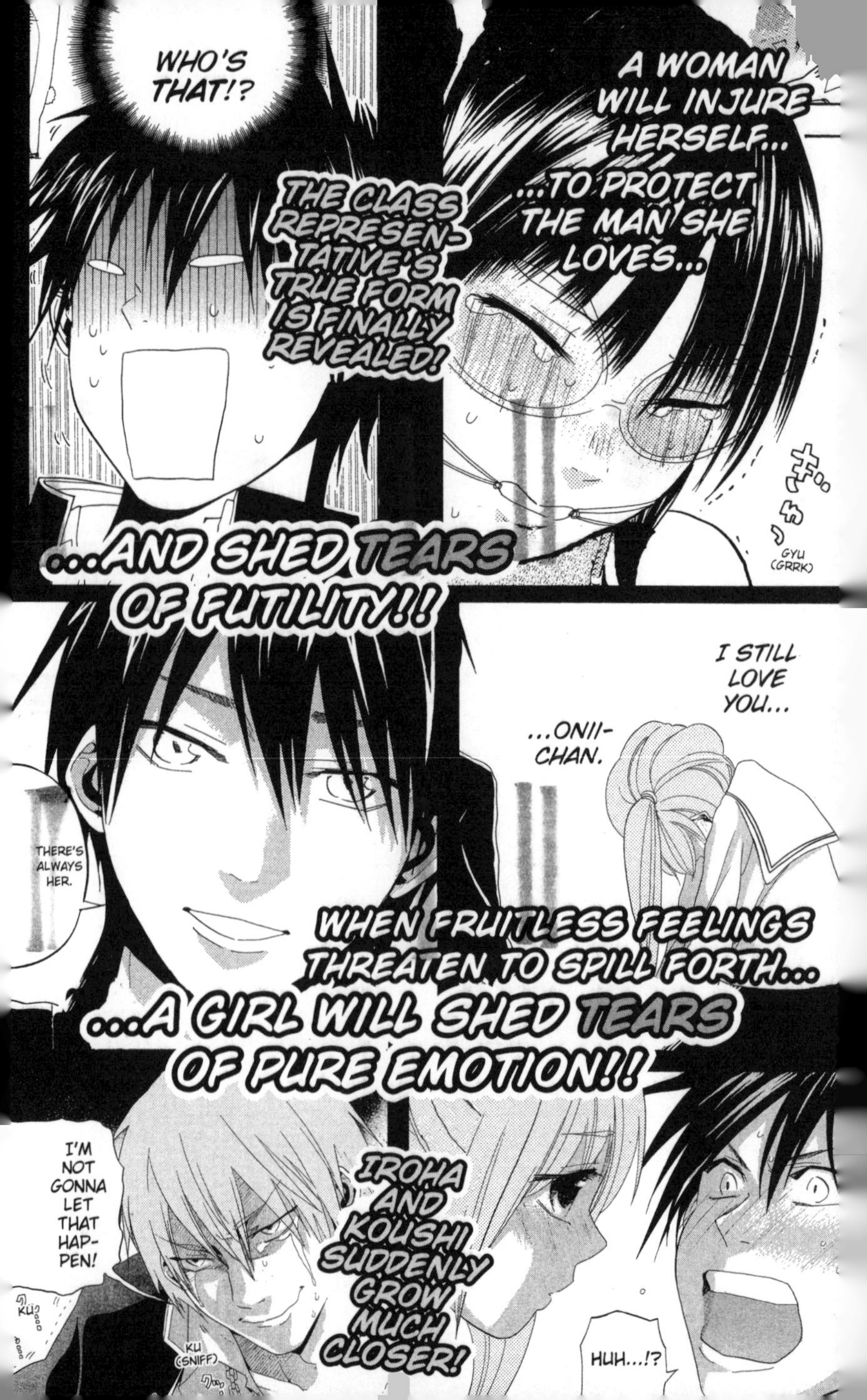
A WOMAN WILL INJURE HERSELF...
...TO PROTECT THE MAN SHE LOVES...
...AND SHED TEARS OF FUTILITY!!
GYU (GRRK)
WHO'S THAT!?
THE CLASS REPRESEN-TATIVE'S TRUE FORM IS FINALLY REVEALED!
I STILL LOVE YOU...
...ONII-CHAN.
WHEN FRUITLESS FEELINGS THREATEN TO SPILL FORTH...
...A GIRL WILL SHED TEARS OF PURE EMOTION!!
THERE'S ALWAYS HER.
HUH...!?
IROHA AND KOUSHI SUDDENLY GROW MUCH CLOSER!
I'M NOT GONNA LET THAT HAP-PEN!
KU (SNIFF)
KU

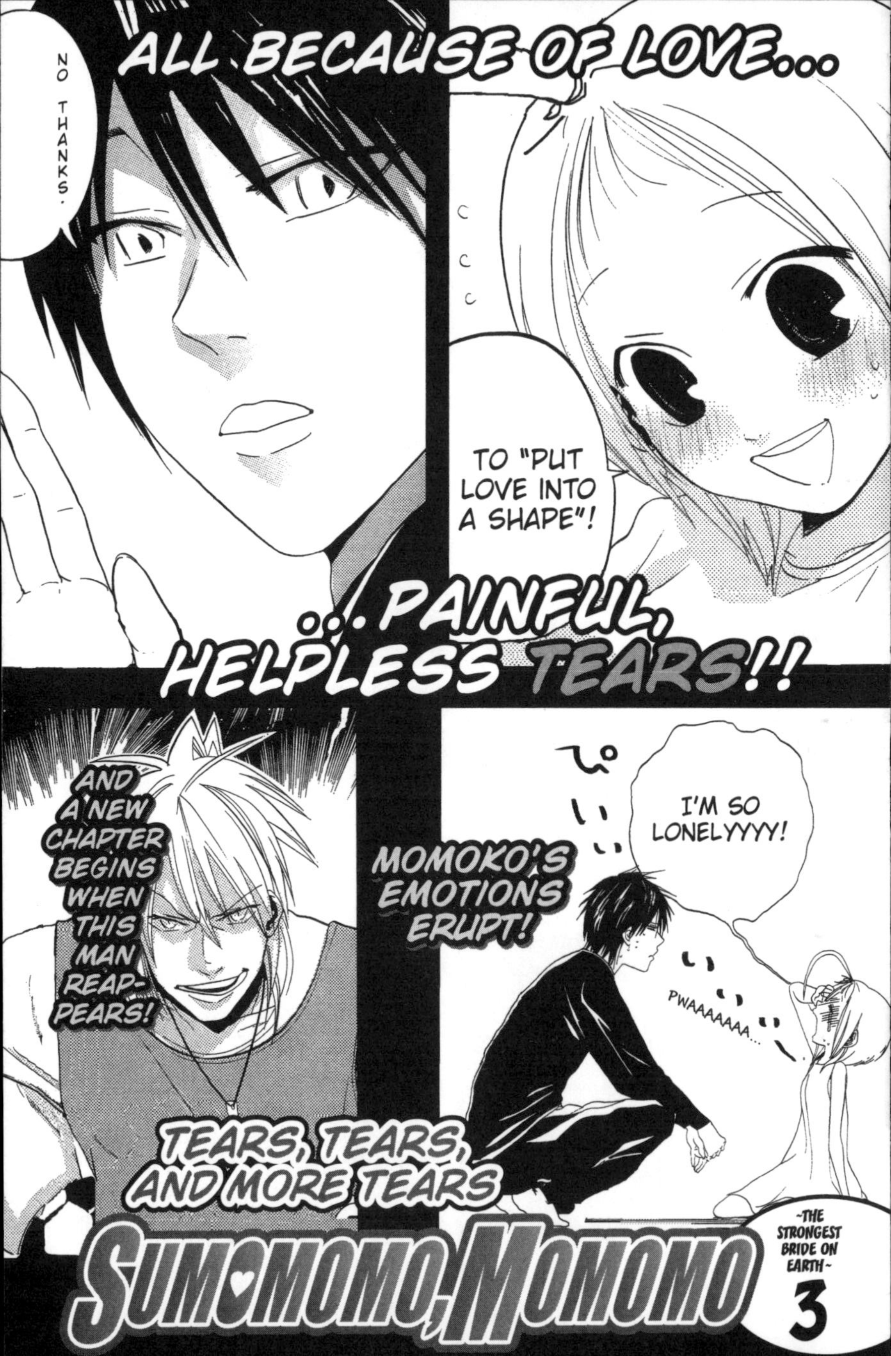
ALL BECAUSE OF LOVE...
TO "PUT LOVE INTO A SHAPE"!
NO THANKS.
...PAINFUL, HELPLESS TEARS!!
I'M SO LONELYYYY!
PWAAAAAAA...
MOMOKO'S EMOTIONS ERUPT!
AND A NEW CHAPTER BEGINS WHEN THIS MAN REAP-PEARS!
TEARS, TEARS, AND MORE TEARS
SUMOMOMO, MOMOMO
~THE STRONGEST BRIDE ON EARTH~
3

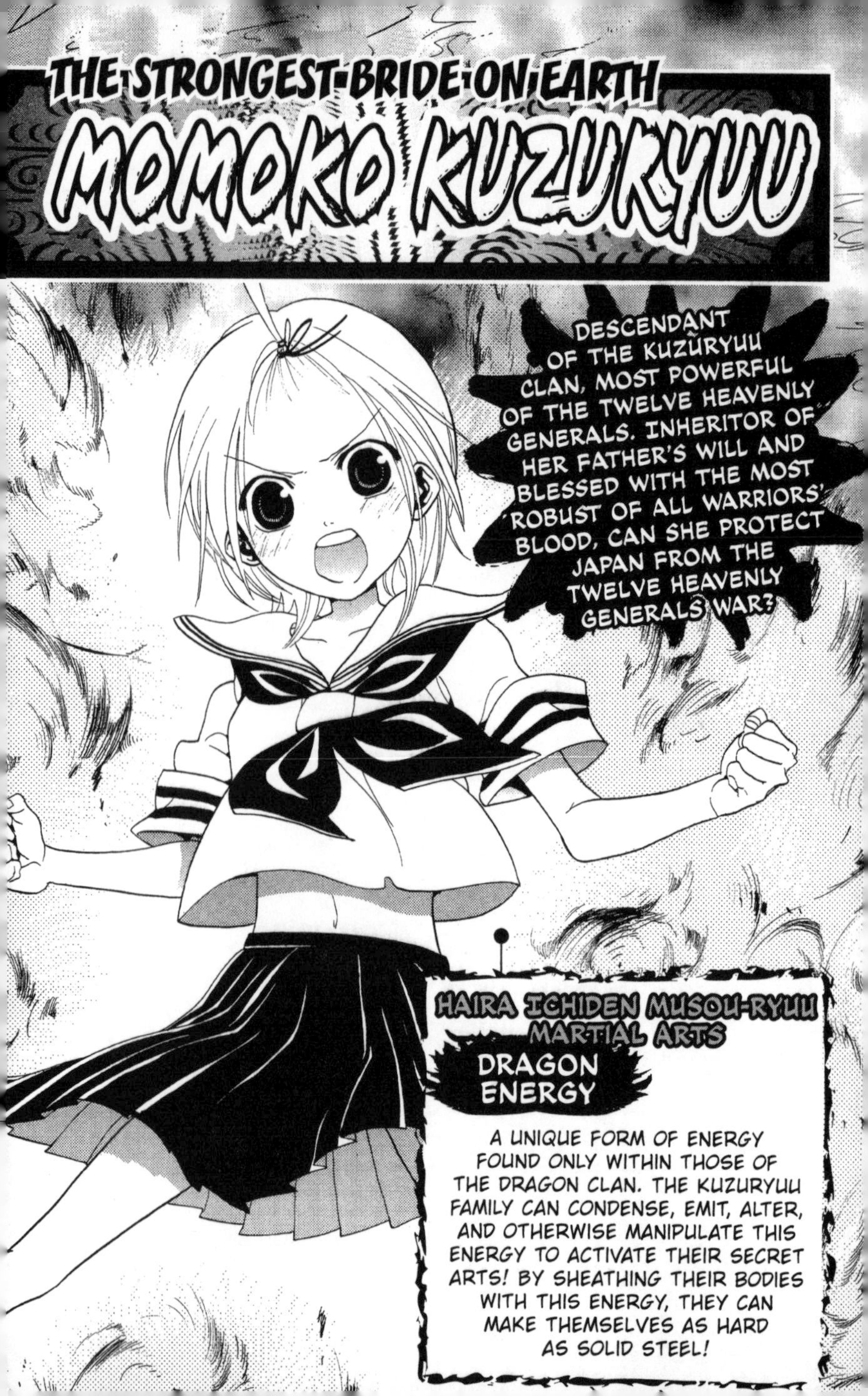
THE STRONGEST BRIDE ON EARTH
MOMOKO KUZURYUU
DESCENDANT OF THE KUZURYUU CLAN, MOST POWERFUL OF THE TWELVE HEAVENLY GENERALS. INHERITOR OF HER FATHER'S WILL AND BLESSED WITH THE MOST ROBUST OF ALL WARRIORS' BLOOD, CAN SHE PROTECT JAPAN FROM THE TWELVE HEAVENLY GENERALS WAR?
HAIRA ICHIDEN MUSOU-RYUU MARTIAL ARTS
DRAGON ENERGY
A UNIQUE FORM OF ENERGY FOUND ONLY WITHIN THOSE OF THE DRAGON CLAN. THE KUZURYUU FAMILY CAN CONDENSE, EMIT, ALTER, AND OTHERWISE MANIPULATE THIS ENERGY TO ACTIVATE THEIR SECRET ARTS! BY SHEATHING THEIR BODIES WITH THIS ENERGY, THEY CAN MAKE THEMSELVES AS HARD AS SOLID STEEL!

HAIRA ICHIDEN MUSOU-RYUU SECRET ART COMPENDIUM

● RISING DRAGON SPLITTING HEAVEN SHOCK

RELEASE

ACHIEVED BY JUTTING THE FIST UPWARD AND EMITTING A POWERFUL BLAST OF ENERGY AT THE SAME TIME. THE RISING STREAM OF FORCE CAN SPLIT WATERFALLS, PENETRATE CLOUDS AND DEVASTATE ENEMIES.

● BLACK DRAGON MORNING DESTROYER

RELEASE

THIS MOVE SHOOTS FIERCELY HONED ENERGY FORWARD FROM THE PALM. THE RESULTING BLACK DRAGON OF FLAMES PRODUCES UNTOLD DESTRUCTION.

● SHOUT BAZOOKA STRIKE

CONDENSE

CONDENSED ENERGY IS WRAPPED AROUND THE FIST AND SLAMMED INTO THE TARGET. PULVERISES OPPONENTS WHILE EMITTING A CANNON ROAR.

● FLYING DRAGON ONE-FLASH BLADE

ALTER

ENERGY IS COLLECTED AND ALIGNED INTO THE FORM OF A BLADE, WHICH IS THEN THRUST THROUGH THE TARGET. THE SWORD SHINES BRIGHTLY, BUT MOVES TO SPLIT THE FOE SO QUICKLY, THE EYE CAN BARELY FOLLOW IT.

SUMOMOMO MOMOMO②

SHINOBU OHTAKA

Translation: Stephen Paul

Lettering: Terri Delgado

SUMOMOMO MOMOMO Vol. 2 © 2005 Shinobu Ohtaka / SQUARE ENIX.
All rights reserved. First published in Japan in 2005 by SQUARE ENIX
CO., LTD. English translation rights arranged with SQUARE ENIX CO.,
LTD. and Hachette Book Group through Tuttle-Mori Agency, Inc.

Translation © 2009 by SQUARE ENIX CO., LTD.

Yen Press
Hachette Book Group
237 Park Avenue, New York, NY 10017

Visit our websites at www.HachetteBookGroup.com and
www.YenPress.com.

Yen Press is an imprint of Hachette Book Group, Inc. The Yen Press
name and logo are trademarks of Hachette Book Group, Inc.

First Yen Press Edition: October 2009

ISBN: 978-0-7595-3045-4

10 9 8 7 6 5 4 3 2 1

BVG

Printed in the United States of America